What People Are Saying about
Rendezvous with the Past

"As I paddled and portaged my way through Thurston's *Rendezvous with the Past*, my mind was refreshed with the lifelong memories of the beauty, solitude, awe, wonder, discovery, and challenges that comprised my first Sommers Wilderness canoe trip. Each person who experiences such a canoe trip becomes Louis in their own unique way. Experienced wilderness paddlers, as well as those whose dreams of adventure are still in the making, will enjoy reading this wonderful and insightful story.
   —**David M. Hyink, PhD,** Forester; Conservationist;
      Outdoorsman; Charlie Guide; Chair, Program Task Force,
      Northern Tier National High Adventure Advisory Committee,
      Boy Scouts of America

"Readers will enjoy both the characters and the adventures of the young Boy Scout, Louis, canoeing the Boundary Waters for the first time. While navigating through this pristine wilderness, Louis learns the profound lessons nature has to teach as well as valuable insights about himself.

"Though set in the 1960s, the wonder and magic of these unique wild lands is faithfully captured . . . as it was and, most importantly, as it remains today. It will surely whet the appetite of those who have not yet made the journey. It will also enfold those who have . . . with the warmth and comfort of a Hudson Bay blanket."
   —**John Van Dreese,** General Manager—Northern Tier High
      Adventure, Boy Scouts of America

"John Thurston's book, *Rendezvous with the Past*, took me back to a time of my life full of wonderful memories. I found myself reading and rereading several passages. His description of a boy's first introduction to the Boundary Waters Canoe Area and the Charles L. Sommers Wilderness Canoe Base is spot on and filled with imagery. Linking the adventure with the voyageurs who traded there and the Native Americans who called the area their home gives the story a hint of mystery which I hope he pursues in subsequent writings. Anyone who has shared this Boy Scout adventure will love this book as well as anyone who has sat and enjoyed a Boundary Waters sunset and night sky and heard the call of the loon.

—**Phillip Van Swearingen**, Author, Artist, and Charlie Guide '64

RENDEZVOUS WITH THE PAST

RENDEZVOUS WITH THE PAST

A Boy Scout Canoe Trip to the Boundary Waters Canoe Area
solves the mystery of a young boy's ancestry connecting
him with generations and cultures from his past.

JOHN THURSTON

Clovercroft Publishing

Published by Clovercroft Publishing, Franklin, Tennessee

Published in association with Shane Crabtree of Christian Book Services, LLC
www.christianbookservices.com

Edited by Gail Fallen

Interior design and cover design by Suzanne Lawing

Printed in the United States of America

978-1-954437-34-0

DEDICATION

Henry Bradlich

Sandy S. Bridges

Delbert O. Greenlee

Clifford J. Hanson

SPECIAL THANKS

To those who encouraged me and helped me to
fill in the blanks in my memory

Roy Cerny

Butch Diesslin

David Greenlee

Dave Hyink

Craig Pendergraft

Special thanks to Van Swearingen for his
fantastic patience, editing, and writing skills.

And to my dear wife, Becky, who helped me keep the dream alive.

THE CREW

Fred—The Guide

Mr. Delbert O. Greenlee—The Scoutmaster

Louis Carter

Dave

Cliff (Smitty)

Henry

Joe

Gary

Chuck

Tom

Mike

Canoe 1	Canoe 2	Canoe 3	Canoe 4
Fred	Louis	Mike	Cliff
Joe	Dave	Mr. Greenlee	Henry
	Tom	Gary	Chuck

TRIP SCHEDULE

Sunday	7/28	Travel	Sioux Falls, South Dakota to Cloquet, Minnesota
Monday	7/29	Day One	Cloquet to Charles L. Sommers Wilderness Canoe Base, Minnesota
Tuesday	7/30	Day Two	Leave on Trip—Base to Lower Lake Agnes
Wednesday	8/31	Day Three	Lower Agnes to Rose Island on Kawnipi
Thursday	8/1	Day Four	Rose Island to Kawa Bay on Kawnipi
Friday	8/2	Day Five	Kawa Bay up the Wawiag River to Mack Lake
Saturday	8/3	Day Six	Mack Lake to Joliet Lake
Sunday	8/4	Day Seven	Joliet Lake to Blackstone Lake
Monday	8/6	Day Eight	Layover day on Blackstone Lake
Tuesday	8/7	Day Nine	Blackstone Lake to Knife Lake

Wednesday	8/8	Day Ten	Knife Lake to Sommers Base
Thursday	8/9	Travel	Sommers Base to Sioux Falls, South Dakota
Friday	9/10	The Home	Grandfather

Contents

INTRODUCTION

This story is made up of both real and contrived events. Some of the characters are based on real people, and several are fictional. I made my first trip to the Boundary Waters Canoe Area as a Scout in 1960. On the first day, I decided I wanted to be a guide. Following my second trip in 1961, I met with the Base Director, Mr. Clifford J. Hanson. I applied to be a Swamper (guide in training) the following summer of 1962. The Swamper job was unpaid and involved two weeks of working on various projects around the Charles L. Sommers Wilderness Canoe Base and a 10-day trip with an experienced guide.

Several weeks later, I received joyous news. I had been accepted! I was beyond excited and immediately signed and returned the contract. My parents were as excited as I was.

In May, I received a second letter in which Mr. Hanson informed me of a recently opened full-time position for the whole summer. The job was Bull Cook and paid $30 per week. I was to arrive by June 6 and return home on August 30. It involved assisting the cook, doing dishes, and keeping the kitchen and dining hall clean. A Swamper trip with an experienced guide was also included. I was 17, and this meant I would be able to join the guide staff in 1963.

During the wondrous summer of 1962, I spent a lot of time becoming acquainted with the Base's 60-plus guides. During my free time, I polished my canoeing and portaging skills. I studied maps and read books on the history and lore of the Quetico Provincial Park and the

Superior National Forest. I made my Swamper trip with a crew guided by Jerry Cox.

During the summers of 1963 to 1966, I lived my dream as a "Charlie Guide." As guides, we were required to arrive in late May and work until the end of August.

Each summer, we took five crews out on a trip, each lasting a total of nine days. Trips varied in distance from 70- to 200-plus miles, depending on the crew's desire and fitness. At the beginning of the season, all guide staff participated in a five- or six-day guide training trip. The fictional trip described in this story is comprised of several of my favorite trips but told through an imagined crew. Some of the main character's (Louis Carter) thoughts and actions are mine as a Scout, and some of the guide's actions and behaviors are mine during the 30-plus trips I have led over the years. Mr. Greenlee was my Scoutmaster and a significant influence in my life. Most of my trips have been to Canada's Quetico Provincial Park. However, I have made Minnesota trips with family in recent years.

Scouting has always been a part of my life. I have felt its influence for as long as I can remember. My two older brothers were Scouts. David achieved Life Scout rank, and Charles was an Eagle Scout. My sister Virginia Eaton was very encouraging of my Scouting. Her husband, Louis Eaton, was also an Eagle Scout. Lou and Virginia spent their honeymoon on the Gunflint Trail in the Boundary Waters Canoe Area. The stories of their trips were the inspiration leading to my interest in the canoe trails. My father, Homer Thurston (1898–1967), often reminisced about being a Scout in South Dakota during Scouting's earliest days in this country. He served as a volunteer in numerous capacities throughout his adult life.

I started my Scouting journey in 1954. Mrs. Doolittle and Mrs. Ellis were my den mothers. Following Cub Scouts, I joined Troop 23, chartered to the First Baptist Church in Sioux Falls, South Dakota. Troop 23 provided Scouting to boys in the neighborhood around Jefferson Grade School. My family's First Methodist Church had a very active troop, and Scouters there encouraged several of us who chose to join a Scout Troop close to our homes since First Methodist was over two miles from our homes.

Following college graduation and a year working as a television announcer, the Boy Scouts of America recruited me to join its professional service. My first job was in my home council, the Sioux Council, headquartered in Sioux Falls. My first year involved serving the Ree District, a large rural area headquartered in Mitchell, South Dakota. After nine months, I was directed to provide service to a second district, including the Rosebud Reservation.

I found working with the Native American population a highlight of my 40-year career. During my first meeting with Webster Two Hawk, the Rosebud tribal chairman, I asked what I would need to do to be successful and keep my foot out of my mouth. His memorable answer was, "Be yourself! We see many who come to serve try to be 'Indian.' We tend to see through those attempts and discount their sincerity. Be yourself!"

Father Two Hawk had taken a leave of absence from his duties as an Episcopal priest to serve as chairman of the Brule Tribe. The Brule spoke Lakota and were some of the kindest, proud, and open people I have ever known. During my four years of service, I spent an entire week or more each month and enjoyed the acceptance, support, and good humor of my new friends. I learned many Lakota words and still use some of them to this day.

My next professional position took me to New Jersey for a seven-year stay at the National Headquarters in North Brunswick. My first assignment was to write and produce a filmstrip to promote the Scouting program's use by youth, parents, and tribal leaders all over the United States. I met Louis Bruce, a Mohawk, the federal commissioner of Indian Affairs, and an advocate of Indians' rights. He was already involved in Scouting at the national level and happy to help. I was also able to recruit Ben Rifle, the first Native American to serve in Congress, to help narrate the production. Ben was an easy call as his niece was one of the den mothers on the Rosebud. Several other Native American leaders helped in the audiovisual presentation.

It was determined I needed to use photographs and tape recordings of several different tribes. For the next six months, I flew all over the country. I photographed and recorded Scout leaders from Florida, New Mexico, South Dakota, North Dakota, Wyoming, and Montana. I interviewed Native American Cub Scouts, Boy Scouts, Explorers, Scout parents, and tribal and community leaders in each location. I became acutely aware of both the strengths and the challenges of Native peoples.

Two years later, I was promoted to the position of National Director of Aviation Exploring. After four years, I returned to the field as Scout Executive in western Colorado. During this time, I served nearly all of the state west of the Continental Divide, and to say I did a lot of "windshield time" would be an understatement. All this windshield time provided me with lots of time to think. It was during this time I came up with the idea of writing this book. I remember pulling over to the side of the road many times and, with a great deal of excitement, scribbling notes onto a pad as the story developed.

The rest of my career involved similar windshield time. I traveled around the National Headquarters in Irving, Texas, and traveled by plane to many week-long training locations across the US. Later, as a Scout Executive serving South Texas, I realized the story had no choice but to evolve.

With all this windshield time alone to think, I eventually decided there were several things I wanted to accomplish with the story:

- Provide an accurate description of the operation and program at the Charles L. Sommers Wilderness Canoe Base in the '60s

- Provide a description of Scouting, its programs, and its values

- Reinforce the need to be respectful when dealing with all people

- To influence the reader to become interested in learning their family's story by listening to the elders

I think it is important to note the term "Indian" is seldom used nowadays. Today, I use the words "Native American" or "First People."

However, this story is set in 1963. I use the term "Indian," which was widely used during those times with great respect. I never knew a Scout or leader to use the term in any other way.

While searching for an illustration for this story, I reached for my old 1955 edition of the *Handbook for Boys* to look up information related to the times in which this story takes place. Both the idea for the title and concept for the story was right there on the cover.

—JOHN OAKS THURSTON

Prologue

TO DO MY DUTY

As I closed our heavy front door, I turned and leaned back against its age-darkened wood. I closed my eyes and thought to myself . . . *What have I done? Where will I find the time? What possessed me to say yes? Can I really do this?*

I had the same feeling I had experienced when Betty and I had purchased a set of encyclopedias from a salesman when we were first married.

We can't afford this. Why did we do this now?

I remember wanting to chase the salesman down the street and tear up the contract.

I put my head back against the oaken door. I felt pride in being selected for such an honor and foolishness for accepting such a massive responsibility.

"Honey, you will be great! I am so proud of you."

I opened my eyes, and there Betty stood with a tray piled high with coffee cups, saucers, and dessert plates, evidence of our just-departed guests.

"Did you know they were coming?" I asked.

"Louis, like you, I assumed they were going to ask us to pledge to our church building campaign or ask us to chair a part of the drive.

I had no idea it would be this. I honestly thought our meeting would be about money and the new addition to the church, as we discussed yesterday."

"Well, I was totally unprepared for this. I just hope we didn't act too hastily."

"You can do it. I'll help you! They seem to have a terrific committee and some good assistants."

"I'll try to do my best. I just hope I can live up to the image I have in mind."

Father Milo had called the week before and asked if he and a few people from our church could come over following lunch. He said they wanted to discuss something of critical importance to our church. We were so sure it was about money we had our checkbook ready. We had already discussed how much we could pledge to the new building project.

When they left, the checkbook was still on the end table, unopened. I was now the new Scoutmaster of Troop 303 at Saint John's Episcopal Church.

What a sales job they did on us. Of course, I couldn't turn down a meeting with Father Milo, and then he shows up with four people from the troop committee. They told me they had met several times over the previous two weeks. Following the process of listing and agreeing to the qualifications they wanted in a Scoutmaster, they compared their profile against a list of possible candidates. After much deliberation, I became their selection to replace Mr. Johnson, who was moving to the Twin Cities. I was flattered to have been selected by the process they described. When I saw how pleased and enthused Betty was about the whole thing, I agreed to become Scoutmaster.

Our troop had a well-organized and dedicated committee. I knew most of the assistants because I had served as a patrol dad while attending camping trips with our first son. Jack crossed over from Cub Scouts to the Boy Scouts six months ago. In fact, Betty and I were still having den meetings at our house for our youngest son Louis, a new

Cub Scout. The uncertainty I felt about my new position came from the image I had of my old Scoutmaster. How could I ever live up to those vivid memories of Mr. Greenlee?

Just the two of us sat down on the patio. Our two boys were up at the lake with the Olsons and their children for the weekend.

"Do you suppose the Olsons were a part of the plan?" I asked.

She handed me a tall glass of iced tea.

"Could be. They were indeed well rehearsed and had planned everything else very well. And, well, it just goes to show how badly they wanted you.

"Now, Louis, tell me what's bothering you. You seem unsettled."

"Honey, I have absolutely no concern that this is the right thing to do. I sort of made a promise to do this a long time ago. And, with your support, I know we can manage the time issues. I guess it's just living up to my image of being a Scoutmaster."

So with the image and memories of my old Scoutmaster coming to life, I took a deep breath and started to tell her the whole story.

Chapter 1

THE HOME

"Louis Benjamin Carter!" The words echoed through the house. "Get your things packed and get out here this instant. You'll miss your ride!"

"Yes, ma'am!" I answered with a measured formality.

When Mother raised her voice and used my middle name, there was no room for argument. I was just putting an edge on my hunting knife.

"I'm on my way."

I slipped the knife into its sheath and tossed it into my duffle bag. I fastened the snap and headed for the door. The year was 1963, and I was preparing to go on my first Boy Scout adventure trip to the Boundary Waters Wilderness Canoe Area. It was fondly called the "canoe trails."

I stopped for a moment and looked back into my room. My eyes went to a picture of my great-grandfather and me on my dresser. My great-grandfather, who was very elderly, had recently become quite ill, and I didn't want to be gone if something terrible happened.

Even with this worry hanging on my mind, I knew I had to go on this trip. The Boundary Waters was a special place for my Scout troop. It was a sacred tradition to go every other year. When a Scout reached the age of 15 or 16, he was allowed to go. No one turned it down, and this was to be my year. Stories about the adventures were told around our local campfires and kept the younger boys interested in the Scouting program. There was a special bond formed between those who went on the trip.

I stopped one more time and looked back into my room. I was excited, yet when I looked again at Grandpa's picture, a tear ran down my cheek. It seems strange to me now, but I remember not wanting to go. My father had already paid for the trip, and all my friends were going. So I didn't have a choice. At age 16, I was now one of the "older guys," and I guess I had started to lose interest in Scouts.

I was a Life Scout and hoped to achieve the Eagle rank someday, but I wasn't sure all this Scouting stuff was important. Feeling like that may have been common for boys my age. There wasn't much I could do about how I felt about going on this trip. It wasn't the end of the world, but I didn't want to go on this or any other trip because of my great-grandfather's condition. I don't know why, but I had no interest in anything. It seemed like everyone, including my parents and the guys in my troop, were excited about this trip . . . everyone but me.

In addition to worries about Grandfather, I didn't feel like there was much excitement in my life. I wasn't a bad or a problem kid. In fact, my mom always referred to me as being such a good boy.

I guess I was just bored.

My family was like every other family on the street. Dad was a successful salesman, and Mom kept our house organized and clean as a whistle. Dad sold tools and building supplies, which kept him very busy, and sometimes he was on the road much of the workweek. Mom was always there at home after school, just like everyone's mother. She and Dad pushed me to excel in school, and I was a pretty good student, maybe slightly better than average.

It seemed to me there had to be more to life than going to school, coming home, doing homework, going to Scouts, or to whatever sport we were playing, and then doing the same thing the following week.

I have to admit the weekends were sometimes enjoyable. Our troop camped out almost every month on one of the weekends. Dad frequently went along to help Mr. Greenlee, our troop's Scoutmaster. On other weekends, things were great if Dad was home. We did interesting and exciting things on Saturdays. My dad liked to go places and do things rather than watch television like some people at that time.

Sundays often included a visit to my grandpa. He lived in a rest home, 25 miles from our house. It really wasn't far, but it always seemed like a long drive, and when I was little, it often felt like it took hours to get there.

Following church, we would drive up to the home. We ate lunch with some people from church and then went up to see Grandpa. I am sure we didn't see him every weekend, but it seemed like it. I had memorized the route and knew every farm, water tower, windmill, and silo along the way. I even named the horses we passed.

The old ivy-covered brick buildings Mom and Dad always called "The Home" smelled awful. However, the grounds were beautiful, with an amazing variety of trees, gardens, and walking paths. If Grandpa needed to be alone with the nurses, Mom, Dad, and I would go strolling. I always enjoyed those times.

I took Tom James with me a couple of years before. He razzed me for weeks about my weird relatives, the way the home smelled, and my being a half-breed Indian. I told him Grandpa was French Canadian, just to shut him up. What's the big deal about nationalities anyway? Who cares?

Tom was right about the smell. The home did smell terrible. I guess I eventually got used to it when I was little, but I swore I would never take anyone there again after being teased about it. It smelled like urine, and occasionally it stank like someone messed in their pants. Grandpa never smelled like he was unclean. Grandpa's problem was his breath, and it was pretty awful. He was missing some teeth, and it could have been from poor dental health.

Grandpa was very old and had recently stopped talking much. A few times, I remember he spoke of his father, grandfather, and others. He often went on and on about the "olden days." I remember it being uninteresting, and I didn't pay close attention.

Mom did most of the talking for us. She told him everything we had done since the last visit. Sometimes she had me tell about my school classes or our Scout campouts. He never seemed to pay much attention to anything we had to say, but Mom said it was important to talk to him. Maybe he was more interested than we thought. I remember Dad sitting very still with his head lowered, looking sad and bored.

To be more precise, Grandpa was my father's grandfather. My dad's father died before I was born. Grandpa was actually my great-grandfather, but I always called him Grandpa or Grandfather. It took me a long time to get this relationship straight in my mind.

I always thought of my family as average in height, skin color, and hair color compared to my school classmates. Grandpa was very dark-skinned and was short, like me. Grandpa was very wrinkled, and his skin looked like dark leather. He stayed tan all year. Mom said he spent too much time in the sun when he was young.

I often wondered if my dark hair and eyes came from my father's side of the family. It confused me more when Dad told me Grandpa was from the "part-Indian" side of his family. And, to make matters even more complicated, Grandpa had a different last name than ours. Could I be part Indian? Was Grandpa a full-blooded Indian? I often wondered.

Many of my friends bragged about their ancestors and nationality, and it made me stop and think. I liked to say I was mostly French Canadian, like those characters in the Howard Keel movie about the Royal Canadian Mounted Police. Mom said she was Norwegian and German. Dad never said much about his people. He only said he was English and French Canadian with a little Indian thrown in. Many guys in my class claimed they were part Indian. I don't think they knew of any real Indians in their family. Some claimed they were part Cherokee or Sioux. I guess they were "cool" Indians. I wasn't sure what Grandpa was.

Toward the end of July, we went to see Grandpa before I left on my trip up north. When we got there, Mom told him the Scouts were going to go on a canoe trip to Canada and then suggested I tell Grandpa about the journey.

Before I could start, he started to talk in a loud voice about people and things that made no sense. Some of the words were in another language unfamiliar to us, and some were like gibberish. The nurses had told us he often spoke a foreign tongue when he slept. Mom thought it might be French or, worse, Latin.

He became agitated and crossed himself several times. Mom always got after him when he crossed himself since we weren't Catholic. I guess she didn't want me exposed to Catholic things.

When it became evident he was not going to stop, Mom got worried and called the nurse. I figured he was interested in what I had to say because he seemed so energetic and full of life. After the nurse came in, she and Mom both thought he might be having a stroke. They decided it was time for a shot to calm him down.

Good grief, I thought, *he is over a hundred years old. What do you expect? I think he's excited about me going on this trip.*

But I kept my thoughts to myself. He looked at me with panic in his eyes as they gave him a shot. It took a few minutes for the injection to work, and Mom sighed with relief when he began to grow calm. After the injection, he became silent. I wasn't sure he was even aware when I tried to say goodbye, except he seemed to be pleading with his eyes.

After a short while, it became evident he was no longer aware we were there. The nurse told us he would sleep for several hours, so we decided to leave.

On the ride back, Mom and Dad were saying he was getting much worse. They didn't think he would last much longer. Mom asked Dad what could be done about his acting so Catholic.

"For crying out loud, he has been Catholic for over a hundred years," Dad said. "Why do you keep expecting him to change at this late date?"

They both became quiet. They didn't like me to see them argue. Not saying goodbye bothered me, especially given the desperate look I had seen in Grandpa's eyes before he went to sleep. Despite how strange he seemed at times, I felt like he and I had a strong connection. Sometimes he would look at me like I was his son.

I always believed he loved me. I felt a wave of panic come over me about the upcoming trip. So I asked my parents, "What will I do if Grandpa dies while I'm gone? What will you do? Will you come to get me?"

Dad looked at me in the rearview mirror and said, "Don't worry, Louis, he'll probably outlive us all. You are going to enjoy your canoe trip."

Chapter 2

THE TRIP

Two days of cornfields, fences, and small towns best described most of the trip. The corn was so high, I sometimes couldn't see anything but green. I tried to sleep because it was so boring. Our Scout group of 10 was traveling in two vehicles. Mr. Greenlee drove his vintage red 1956 Ford Country Squire eight-passenger station wagon with the Thunderbird V8 engine we all loved. Mr. Banwart, one of the troop committeemen, drove his blue and white 1960 Buick Invicta Estate station wagon.

We sang all kinds of songs to pass the time. Mr. Greenlee, our Scoutmaster, tried to get us to sing some of the "North Country" songs he had been teaching us. I think he was worried we would sing "99 Bottles of Beer " all the way to Canada and drive him crazy. So we practiced singing his favorites, "The Far Northland" and "The Paddle Song." Mr. Greenlee said they were the Canoe Base songs, and we would enjoy singing them after we got out on the trail.

But "The Far Northland" was a little hard to remember.

It's the far Northland that's a-callin' me away,
As take I with my packsack to the road.
It's the call on me of the forest in the north,

As step I with the sunlight for my load.

(Chorus)
From Lake Agnes, by Louisa, to Kawnipi I will go,
Where you see the Loon and hear his plaintive wail,
If you're think'n in your inner heart, there's a swagger in my step,
Then you'll know I've been along the border trail.

It's the flash of paddle blades a gleamin' in the sun,
A canoe softly skimming by the shore,
It's the smell of pine and bracken comin' on the breeze
That calls me to the waterways once more.

(Chorus)
From Lake Agnes, by Louisa, to Kawnipi I will go,
Where you see the Loon and hear his plaintive wail,
If you're think'n in your inner heart, there's a swagger in my step,
Then you'll know I've been along the border trail.[1]

It would have been possible to drive to the Base in one day. However, Mr. Greenlee said the Base expected us to arrive at two o'clock in the afternoon. So we stayed overnight at a police station in Cloquet, Minnesota, at the end of the first day. Mr. Banwart had made arrangements for us to sleep on the floor of the shooting range. We decided we could bend the story a little and tell people we had spent a night in police custody. Mr. Greenlee didn't think it was such a good idea.

Arriving at the Base in the afternoon was to give the departing crews time to leave and time for the Base staff to prepare for our arrival. We had an early breakfast at a café that the police officer in charge

---

1. "The Far Northland" is a traditional Canoe Base song.

recommended. Later we stopped for a short break at a roadside park by a lake about midmorning before shopping and lunch in Ely.

The scenery had improved by late the previous afternoon, and it became incredibly beautiful the farther north we traveled. The breeze at the roadside park was cool and crisp, unlike the hot, dry breezes of the prairies back home.

It was at this time I heard a loon for the first time. One of the guys thought the long wailing sound was a wolf. Mr. Greenlee told us it was a loon. He said they had many different calls, and we would recognize each of them by the end of the trip. The loon had a haunting sound, and I wanted to hear more.

We arrived in Ely in time to look around the town before heading out to the Base. Ely has a steep main street, and there was a neat store called Fisherman's Headquarters where we bought some fishing tackle. Our Scoutmaster, Mr. Greenlee, had made this trip before and told us what to buy.

He said we would catch northern pike, walleye, bass, and, if we were lucky, maybe some lake trout. I was anxious to catch some big northern like the ones I had seen in *Sports Afield*.

He said if we were catching walleyes, we should throw everything else back. I'm not sure what the big deal was with walleyes, but the store clerk agreed with Mr. Greenlee.

I bought a couple of medium-sized Red Devil spoons, a red and white Lazy Ike, and a KB Spoon. We all purchased several steel leaders and some lead weights with rubber in the center for attaching the weights to the fishing line. Dad had let me bring his old Shakespeare spinning rod and reel. He said to buy four or five bucktails for walleyes. I began to think the fishing part of this trip might relieve some of my worries about Grandpa. I loved fishing.

We bought maps and clear waterproof map cases. Mr. Greenlee told us our Pathfinder compass would fit into the map cases. He told us not to fold the maps until we decided where we were going so that the creases made by folding wouldn't obscure the area we would be

traveling. The maps showed all the lakes and the length of the portages between the lakes in rods. A rod equals five-and-a-half yards. It
looked like there was as much water as there was land in this place we
were going.

I liked Ely. Everyone spoke with a Minnesota accent, which included you guys this and you guys that and eh? We started to imitate the
way they spoke. As we headed out of town, Mr. Greenlee suggested
a quick lunch at Vertin's, a café next to the Forester Hotel. Vertin's
served good food, and it was very reasonably priced.

On the way out of town, Mr. Greenlee pointed out a laundromat on
the right farther down the street. He said it would be a good place to
stop and do a few wash loads after our time on the trails. He thought
our clothes would likely smell a bit rank.

Chapter 3

THE CHARLES L. SOMMERS WILDERNESS CANOE BASE

Mr. Greenlee drove the station wagon around the last bend in the road, which led to the Canoe Base's entrance. I saw a large sign. My eyes opened wide as I read the name Charles L. Sommers Wilderness Canoe Base.

I thought it was Summers Canoe Base and was so named because Boy Scouts went there in the summertime. I now realized Sommers was spelled with the letter o and not u. We later learned it had been his leadership to the Scouting program that allowed the Base Camp to be built starting during the winter of 1942.

The Scouts started canoe trips in this area in the 1920s from a base near Winton. The current Base is on the side of a steep and very rocky hillside where there are large white pines, red pine, birch, and aspen (called "popple" in Minnesota).

Young men wearing dark green Explorer uniforms met us in the parking lot. I figured they were at least 18 years old or more. They directed Mr. Greenlee to walk up the hill to the lodge, which contained the Base offices, to meet the director and our guide. They were very polite and said they were Swampers and hoping to be hired back on the guide staff next year.

As we stood in the parking lot with our gear waiting for Mr. Greenlee to return, I again heard the lonesome sound of the loon, which had touched my soul earlier in the day. In 20 minutes, Mr. Greenlee and our guide came striding back down to the parking lot to join us. The guide looked like he might have been pushing his twenties because of his full beard. However, he must have been younger since he told us he was in college in Virginia. He was wearing a dark green Explorer uniform with a white Sommers Canoe Base neckerchief around his neck. The only insignia he wore was his Eagle badge, his town and troop number, and a Paul Bunyan Region Ten emblem. His hair and beard were sandy colored.

Mr. Greenlee introduced our guide, saying his name was Fred Morton. Fred welcomed us to "Charlie's Place" and told us we had arrived right on time. Fred reviewed the things we had to accomplish during the rest of the day. He had a slight Southern accent, which was pleasant and welcoming.

Next, Fred told us to get our gear together and follow him. We were going to a place he called "tent city." He said we would spend our first night there and leave on our trip after breakfast. During the rest of the afternoon, we would go through our swim check and swamping practice first. Then we would pack food and gear, plan our trip, and attend a campfire with all of the other crews going out on the trail tomorrow after supper.

Fred recommended we leave any nonessentials in Mr. Greenlee's station wagon. Mr. Greenlee and Mr. Banwart helped us sort out a few things. Mr. Banwart was driving back home and then returning to get us at the end of our trip.

After stowing a few things in Mr. Greenlee's station wagon, we were off to tent city. Fred led us up a wooded trail. It was rough, rocky, and steep in places. He told us this would be much like the portage trails we would be on for the next 10 days.

Before leaving home on the trip, Mr. Greenlee had told us the portages were rough, and we would all need a good pair of sturdy lace-up boots. After walking on this trail in the Base camp, I was glad my folks had purchased a new pair of hunting boots for me. They were beautiful tan Redwing boots. They were darker after several coats of Huberd's Neatsfoot Oil. Mr. Greenlee also told us to break them in with lots of walks before the trip.

Tom was the one person in our crew who always knew everything better than anyone else. He ignored Mr. Greenlee and got his boots two days before we left home. We were not yet out on the trail, and he was already complaining of sore feet.

We found four-man wall tents with wood plank floors and mosquito netting when we got to tent city. Each tent had bunks, so at least the first night would be comfortable. Fred told us to stow our gear, get into swimming suits and boots as quickly as possible, and meet him at the Bay Post building. He also suggested we bring a towel and a shirt. He pointed, and I looked in that direction. I could make out a glint of sunlight off water through the trees.

Joe asked if our packs with all our personal belongings would be safe while we were away. Smitty answered before Mr. Greenlee or Fred could: "If our gear isn't safe at a Boy Scout camp, where would it be safer?"

Both grinned, and we started preparing for our great adventure.

Ten minutes later, we were down the hill at the Bay Post. I will never forget the sound of boots thumping on the extended wooden deck to the paddle issue room as we waited outside the service window. Fred told us we could either rent or buy one. Mr. Greenlee had told us to bring money to purchase a paddle if we wanted to keep it as a memento of the trip. I then realized I was changing my opinion of the whole deal because, suddenly, there was no question in my mind. I wanted a paddle!

Fred showed us how to pick a paddle, which came up between our chin and forehead in length. The paddles were made of ash and seemed well made. Fred held up a paddle and asked us to name each part. He looked pleased when some of us could name them: grip, loom, throat, blade, and tip. Mr. Greenlee was beaming with pride.

My observation of Mr. Greenlee was interrupted when Fred added in an authoritative tone of voice, "This is a paddle, not an oar. Oars are for rowboats. Paddles are used with canoes."

"Guys, always remember this is your only means of transportation," he continued. "Keep your paddles safe at all times, and don't ever lay them on the ground where they could be stepped on and broken. It's a long way back to the Base paddling with your hands."

Fred's strong directive was followed with a smile, and we all relaxed our tense shoulders.

The staff managing the paddle room was helpful. It seemed every selection we made was for the very best paddle available with the near-perfect grain. Finally, all of us had carefully made our selection. So, with a paddle in hand, we were directed to the waterfront.

The waterfront consisted of massive logs flattened on the top with rockfill behind them. The water was knee-deep off the log dock, and we were told it dropped off sharply about 20 feet out from where we would be standing. A crew from Georgia was leaving the waterfront and said the water was like ice. Since they were from the South, we figured they weren't as used to the cold water as us tough Northern boys. All of us had earned the swimming merit badge, and we weren't afraid of a little cold water.

Fred yelled out to a couple of guides sitting in a beautiful green wood-and-canvas canoe about 30 yards offshore. I looked at them and thought they were anchored because their paddles were in the water but hardly moving, and the canoe seemed to be stationary. I remembered how hard it was to keep a canoe still while working on the canoeing merit badge at our Scout camp back home. Fred told the guides to take a break while he finished the orientation. They both relaxed while keeping a paddle in the water. I figured an anchor rope must have been on the other side.

Without hesitation, Fred stepped into the ice-cold water, and Mr. Greenlee followed right behind him. Mr. Greenlee turned and motioned for all of us to follow. We made the plunge; that is, all of us except Tom. Mr. Greenlee had to admonish him, as Tom was whining about getting his new boots wet. Finally, we all stood in the water in a semicircle around Fred, who began reviewing basic paddle strokes.

"Everybody, grab your paddle by the throat with your left hand," he said. "Now place your right hand on the grip. Reach forward with the blade and pull it past your left leg. As your blade exits the water, bring it back to the forward position with the blade parallel to the water's surface. It's called 'feathering.' After about a thousand strokes, you will appreciate feathering because it cuts through the air like an airplane wing, and you won't be fighting against wind resistance. Now let me see you practice a few strokes."

Standing in knee-deep water, we practiced as the ice-cold water swirled about our legs. My loon friends seemed to be commenting on our skill with howls of laughter. Fred watched and both praised and suggested ways to improve our stroke.

"This is the primary power stroke, and a bowman uses this stroke most of the time," Fred said. "The other thing a bowman must master is performing the essential bow rudder. Can anyone tell me what a bow rudder does and give a demonstration?"

Three of us raised our hands, and Fred pointed to me. I explained how the bow rudder was for emergencies only. I demonstrated this by placing the paddle into the water with the blade in a vertical position with the tip aiming forward. I remembered this from canoeing merit badge class the previous summer back at our council's camp. I explained how the lower hand braces the paddle against the gunwale. Then I said, "The grip, on the other hand, should be held near the opposite shoulder. With this maneuver, a bowman can quickly pull or turn the canoe to the side where the paddle is placed."

Fred smiled and said, "You're exactly right." He stopped and looked at me and asked, "What's your name?"

"Louis," I replied.

"Well said, Louis! Everyone should remember that this action is an emergency move only."

"Fred, tell the guys what would constitute an emergency," Mr. Greenlee said.

"It might be a rock which can't be seen by the sternman, or it could be a deadhead, which is a log sticking up near the surface. We don't want to hit anything with our canoes, do we?" Fred answered.

The look on his face left no doubt in my mind. Our guide was quite serious about the care and proper use of his canoes.

"Who can demonstrate the J-stroke?" Fred asked.

All of us watched as Tom waded into the middle of the circle. He performed the J-stroke, much like the bow stroke. He turned the back of the blade toward him and then pushed the front of the blade away.

Fred narrowed his eyes and frowned with a troubled look. He looked at Tom and asked, "You are?" Tom moved back to the circle and almost wilted under Fred's gaze. He answered with a slight stutter, "T—Tom."

"Well, Tom . . ." Fred's face softened, and a warm smile replaced his perplexed look. "It's not uncommon to get the J-stroke turned around. You surely have the right idea, but let me show you how to get this simple stroke just right."

He turned and looked at us.

"Tom was right in that the J-stroke starts just like the bow stroke. However, carefully watch my paddle as I demonstrate."

Fred's paddle had an X or the Roman numeral ten on one side. He pointed it out and told us it stood for Region Ten of the Boy Scouts of America's twelve regions.

His paddle was darker than ours. Henry asked if the darker color was because it was made from a different type of wood. Fred told us it was ash just like ours, but he didn't like the varnish finish.

"Those of you that purchased your paddle may want to remove the varnish and replace it with several coats of linseed oil when you get home," Fred said. "After every use, wipe it with a thin coat of oil to waterproof it. It will darken it and create a smoother finish. Paddles that are used will have scratches and blemishes, which will be reminders of all the memories you'll have with them."

He placed his paddle in the water about an arm's reach ahead of his left side and pointed out the letter X was facing to the back. Those of us in front of him moved around behind him. As he reached the stroke's midpoint, Fred began to push the blade's backside away and out to the left with the X still facing backward. It didn't make a complete J. It was more of a curved L shape in the water. I had never noticed how simple the J-stroke was and felt I understood it for the first time. We all practiced it with 10 or 12 strokes while Fred watched and made a few minor corrections.

"Now, Tom," he said, "can you tell me the purpose of the J-stroke?"

"Isn't it to keep the canoe going straight?"

"Tom, you're partly right. An easy J-stroke will keep your canoe going straight. But what about a few hard J-strokes: what will that do for you?"

Fred looked at each of us as if searching for an answer to his question.

"Won't it turn you to the side you're paddling on?" Chuck answered, adding, "I'm Chuck."

Fred smiled as he answered. "Y'all have been studying. You're right, Chuck. The J-stroke will turn you to the side you're paddling on, and if you use a light J-stroke and power stroke combined, you will be able to hold a straight course.

"Now," he continued, "we will work on the last stroke I am going to cover today. There are a few other strokes to review later, but the next most essential is the sweep stroke. This one is used primarily by the sternman, and it will gradually turn the canoe away from the side you are paddling on. You start out as you did with the power stroke, only with a sweeping motion pushing out and around. You make an arc in the water. It will push you away from the side of the canoe you are on."

Fred demonstrated the sweep stroke several times and watched as we practiced for a few minutes. Then he said, "You can paddle your canoe in a figure eight using these two basic strokes and never change sides, even when you are solo. If you have a bowman, you can accomplish it with the bowman just using the power stroke. You will have plenty of time to perfect these strokes in the next ten days. Be sure to ask if you don't understand anything or need a review."

I thought about asking a question, but Fred stepped out of the water and quickly returned with his canoe. He slid it across his thighs and into the water from up on the log. All of our canoes had been placed on the racks close to the water. Smitty and Mike brought an aluminum canoe, as requested by Fred. He told us the Base used Grumman canoes made from aircraft aluminum. He had them carefully set it on the shore and explained that at Charlie's Place, we should always place our canoes bottom up unless they were in the water. He then had us gather around his beautiful wood and canvas canoe. He told us reviewing or learning the canoe parts is far easier with a classic Old Town or Seliga canoe. He said the Base still had a few Old Towns, made in Old Town, Maine. However, most of the wooden fleet was now the Seliga guide canoe, handmade by a local Ely craftsman named Joe Seliga.

All the Charlie Guides considered Joe Seliga's canoes to be the most magnificent canoes made anywhere in the world, and some called him the Michelangelo of wooden canoe builders. He built five wood and canvas canoes for the Base each year in the garage he converted into a workshop.

They were beautiful canoes made with cedar wood strips with wooden ribs of various shades of honey-colored cedarwood. They had a clear varnish or lacquer, making the beautiful interior surfaces shine. The seats were caned. They were painted dark forest green on the outside, which contrasted nicely with the Sommers emblems on both sides of the bow. I was in absolute awe of the exquisite craft.

Fred looked very stern as he said, "This, gentlemen, is not a boat! This is a canoe! I will be most disappointed if anyone should call any of my canoes a boat. Is this clearly understood?"

I looked around at the other guys, and each one was staring at Fred with their eyes wide. I made a mental note to keep that piece of information uppermost in my mind. I wondered about Fred's stern and gruff side and where his pleasant soft-spoken manner had gone. I was relieved when he grinned, but I think we all made a mental note not to call a canoe a boat.

It was easier to understand the canoe parts using Fred's wood and canvas canoe as an example. The first thing I noticed was the portage yoke, which replaced the center thwart in the middle. Fred seemed pleased when Chuck used the correct terminology in referring to it and the missing thwart. Next, he pointed out the gunwales, which were two long pieces of narrow wood about three-quarters of an inch thick, running on both sides of the tops of the curved ribs for the canoe's length.

I noticed the outside of the gunwale was much darker than the inside of the gunwale. Fred told us the exterior piece was made from mahogany and the interior was from white ash. He pointed out the canoe ribs and told us they were made of cedar and spaced exactly three-and-a-half inches apart from the bow to the stern.

Fred asked us to name each part of the canoe and was pleased we seemed to know all the parts. However, when he pointed to the wooden strips running the length across the ribs, none of us could come up with the name. He then told us it was called planking, and it provided an excellent contrast in both color and grain to the ribs. The planking was attached to the ribs with tiny brass nails. They were crimped on the ribs inside by a procedure performed by Joe's wife, Nora. The outer planking had the canvas stretched, sealed, and painted to protect the wood.

I looked at Fred's canoe as each of us ran our hands over it and recited the parts' names. The workmanship reminded me of fine furniture. Fred then told us that since Joe Seliga lived in Ely, many of the guides visited him on their time off to see the master at work. I began thinking that someday I wanted to meet this man who had the respect and admiration of such a terrific group of guys.

When he finished his lesson on the canoe parts, he showed us the aluminum canoe's details. They were the same except for the materials. I wondered why the guides used lightweight wooden canoes. I guess it was because those canoes were probably more fragile.

With both the aluminum and wooden canoe before us, Fred asked, "Can you see the difference in the materials?"

Tom said, "Yeah, we won't have to be so careful with metal ones. We can just pull them up on shore. You must have to be extremely careful with a wooden boat."

The rest of us, in unison, yelled, "Canoe!"

I watched Fred smile and then took a deep breath as the stern scowl crept back onto his face. He looked at each one of us as he said in measured words, "Guys, here at the Charles L. Sommers Wilderness Canoe Base, we treat all of our canoes like they were birchbark! Not aluminum, not wood and canvas, but birchbark! Some of the Grumman canoes we have here are fifteen or twenty years old and are still in great shape. The outfitters in town are lucky to get three years out of an aluminum canoe before it's ruined."

"Why do the Scouts' canoes last so much longer?" asked Dave.

"Part of the reason involves the fact we are standing here in knee-deep water," Fred replied. "Here at Charlie's, we 'wet-foot it' for the whole trip. We load and unload the canoes while standing in knee-deep water, just like the Indians and voyageurs did while loading and unloading their birchbark canoes. Your boots just got wet, and I guarantee they won't be dry for the next ten days. So don't even think about drying them. It won't happen. The second reason is, as of right now, I expect you to treat my canoes and all of my equipment like it was your mom's best china. Does everyone get my drift?"

We all nodded. It looked like Fred would be very strict, and none of us were about to question him. He was dead serious on the subject of the equipment and canoes.

He also showed us how one person could flip the canoe upon his shoulders by himself. It looked like one of those things easier said than done. Several of us tried flipping the canoe, and with a bit of help, a couple of us could "almost" do it. Fred smiled and said we would all be able to do it by the end of the trip.

All this was done while standing in the water and wearing our new boots. I now remembered very clearly what our Scoutmaster, Mr. Greenlee, said at one of our parent meetings before leaving for the Base. He made it a point to tell them our boots would be wet for the entire 10 days. I smiled as I remembered Tom having a fit over the idea of getting his new boots wet. He complained until the rest of us were tired of hearing him talk of it. After this session with Fred, getting boots wet was no longer a problem.

At the end of Fred's canoe talk, I did not doubt who was in charge of safety and equipment. I had seen two sides of Fred. One was very supportive and friendly. On the other hand, it was clear he could be very serious when needed. I felt like I wanted to see more of the genial supportive side of Fred. I suspected that we wouldn't see much of the serious side if we took care of the equipment and safety issues.

Chapter 4

THE BAPTISM

After standing in the water up to our knees during our paddling instruction, my legs felt numb from the cold. I noticed that Mike and Dave were shivering. Tom was looking apprehensive about what was coming next. So much for being tough Northern boys.

Since Joe was to be Fred's bowman, Fred took this opportunity to demonstrate how two people should carry a canoe. They carefully carried the Seliga canoe up onshore and gently placed it bottom up on the canoe rack. The Grumman was left in the water.

Fred and Joe rejoined us, and Fred called out to the guides who were still waiting about 30 yards offshore.

"I think this group is ready to swamp."

We were amazed when they both sat up together and were in front of us with a few effortless strokes. There was no anchor. They had been holding the canoe still with their paddles. I think we were all impressed with how they came in so quickly and skillfully.

Roy was a tall fellow and told us what was going to happen next.

"This is an opportunity for us to see how comfortable you are in the water," Roy said. "More importantly, we want you to know the procedure we use here at Charlie's Place if you should swamp for any reason."

The other guide, Bob, said during his three years on the staff, he had never had anyone swamp, but we need to be prepared.

"But if you swamp," Roy continued, "the first thing to remember is you should always stay with the canoe. You will have three Scouts, two packs, one tent, and three paddles in your canoe. Your canoe can support up to sixteen men holding the side in even the roughest water. It will not sink."

"After you tip your canoe and swamp on our command," said Bob, "we want you to get on opposite sides of the canoe quickly. Grab the paddles and stow them under the thwarts. Then, if this happens on your trip, you should grab the packs and tent and push them into the canoe. They will all float for several minutes before they sink because of the air spaces in them. When the gear is securely stowed, pull yourself into the swamped canoe. With the canoe full of water, grip the paddle by the throat and the loom. Holding it horizontal, pull it to your chest and pull yourselves toward shore. If it is windy, the canoe won't drift because it's full of water."

Fred pointed at Mr. Greenlee and said, "I would like you to go first and pick two of your crew to go with you."

Mr. Greenlee paused a moment and picked his previously selected canoe partners, Mike and Gary. The three got into the aluminum canoes and followed the guide canoe as Roy and Bob quickly paddled 40 yards out and away from shore. Roy turned the green guide canoe parallel to the shore, and as Mr. Greenlee's canoe came close, he shouted, "Now, swamp!"

I watched, and my eyes widened as they leaned toward Roy, and over they went! I knew I would soon be next, and I shivered as the boys came up splashing and screaming, "It's cold! It's cold!"

Mr. Greenlee got them settled down, and using the paddles as Bob had instructed, they all paddled on the left side to turn the bow back toward shore. Once they were facing shore, they paddled on alternate sides and pulled themselves back to the shoreline's shallow water. They were instructed to turn over the water-filled canoe and lift it to empty the water. It was now floating next to the shore.

Fred pointed the end of his paddle at me. I shuddered a bit when he said, "You're next. Pick two others to go with you." I picked Dave and Tom, my canoe mates.

I took the stern since I had my canoeing merit badge, and we made our way out to the green canoe. I tried to be as smooth as the guides. But I think we must have looked slightly awkward as our canoe did not go straight, and we banged our paddles on the gunwales.

When we were in front of the guide canoe, Roy yelled, "Swamp now!"

We put our paddles on the bottom of the canoe, grabbed the sides, and rocked. I was surprised at how fast we flipped the canoe over. When I found myself underwater, I felt like my head would split from the cold shock.

I wanted to take a breath but, instead, I quickly got my bearings and looked for my companions. The water was crystal clear, and I could now see Tom and Dave struggling to resurface with their heavy boots on.

They were on the same side of the canoe I was on. So after we all surfaced, I said, "You guys, stay put! I'm going to the other side so it will balance the canoe."

I took a deep breath and slipped beneath the canoe. It was unreal to be in such clear water after being in the murky lake water at our council's camp.

I decided I was going to be tough and not yell like the first group. Tom and Dave must have decided the same thing. When I came up from under the water, I only heard the loon's "laughing" sound along with my own quiet laughter. I felt invigorated from the cold shock, along with what I can only describe as incredible joy.

I did not feel cold at all. My mind focused on doing this swamping thing as well as I could. I moved back a bit to the stern. I saw Tom and Dave were about to get in on the other side when I said, "Hey guys, the stern is already pointing back to shore, so let's get in facing the shoreline so we don't have to turn around. Tom, you and I will steady the canoe while Dave gets in the middle. Then, Tom, you get in while I steady it, and then you guys keep her balanced while I slide in. Let's go!"

It worked, and we started to move to shore. Roy said, "Good move, fellas! Now I want the rest of you guys to use the same logic they used. It's the best way to do this drill."

When we got to shore, everyone said, "Good job, Louis!"

It really felt good. Mr. Greenlee grinned as he handed me my towel.

I looked at Fred and saw him smile at me. He looked up and then pointed to the two loons out beyond the green canoe as he said, "You had a couple of friends out there laughing along with you."

As I stood on the shore, holding my towel and watching the loons, I had the strange feeling I had done this all before. I felt that I was exactly where I was supposed to be at that moment.

Everything was suddenly so different! I didn't think boys were expected to see beauty. But I was suddenly and strangely aware of things I hadn't noticed before.

As my thoughts swirled with my newfound emotions, I looked out and across the lake. It was then that I noticed what I had thought to be the opposite shore was, in fact, a large island, and there were other islands I had not seen before. The trees became separate trees, not just patches of green. It was interesting how the rocks met the water in some places, and the trees seemed to blend into the water in other areas. The loons called with a different sound this time, and I noted the three other calls I had heard so far.

I even noticed how wonderful the air felt—so clean and fresh. I sensed a slight breeze and then smelled the scent of pine trees. I thought about all these new and wonderful smells and knew I would remember them for the rest of my life. I thought it strange as I stood there, as if in a trance, that the only smell I could remember well was the smell of the home when we had visited Grandpa.

Grandpa! The memory hit me like a thunderbolt. *Would he be there when I got back?*

I hoped so. The trip had barely started, and I already had so much I wanted to tell him.

"Louis, are you coming?" It was Mr. Greenlee. "Hey, are you going to stand there all day? You better dry off, or you'll get cold."

Cold? I had never felt better. Maybe I was giddy from the severe shock of cold water or the generous compliments that came my way when we got back to shore. No, something important had just happened. Everything was different. I was different. It felt like I had just turned a corner in my life.

Fred motioned for all of us to follow him up the hill to a large building. He said we were going to the Bay Post, and it was there we would pack our food for the trip. I followed but lagged, lost in my thoughts. I thought about the meaning of the word "swagger" I had heard in the song we had learned. I then thought about what had happened at the waterfront. I increased my stride with a feeling of pride and joy in each step.

Chapter 5

PLANING OUR ADVENTURE

I was so involved with not slipping on the rocky path with my wet boots that I didn't notice the large building until it loomed up in front of our group. We had approached it from the other side when selecting our paddles. This approach from the waterfront offered a much different and impressive view of the two-story facility.

Fred had us wait outside while he went in to see if they were ready for us. As we waited, I looked around and saw the large letters burned into the wood over the doorway. We had arrived at the BAYPOST.

Tom turned and poked me in the ribs and asked, "What's a Baypost?" We were soon to find out as Fred motioned for all of us to follow him inside on the bottom floor. I was expecting to see food, but instead I saw a large workshop area and 60 or 70 four-foot by four-foot locker doors made of heavy plywood. Fred pointed out his locker.

Fred opened it, and we all looked inside. It was four feet deep and contained tents, an assortment of packs, and other neatly placed items. I could smell the canvas of the packs, the well-oiled leather straps, and the familiar woodsmoke odor that clings to well-used camping gear.

"This is my locker, and its contents will be your home for the next nine days," Fred said.

He showed us several types of packs and said he would be telling us more about them after we packed food.

"Gary, since you are our permanent cook, I will place the three food packs in your care. After they are packed with food, you will see that they are all placed back in this locker."

Fred held up a large canvas A-3 Duluth Pack™ and told us it was a personal pack and would hold three crew members' belongings. Fred suggested we place the paddles diagonally in his locker.

We followed Fred outside to the wooden boardwalk leading to the deck on the second level of the Bay Post. We crowded through the doorway to the main room on this level. Once inside, we had time to look around the large room, which occupied most on this floor.

"Wow! This place is huge!" I heard Cliff whisper behind me. "Look at all those shelves and all of that food!"

I smiled. He was right. There was a lot of food, all stored neatly on shelves, bulk containers, barrels, and large sacks of rice, barley, and other grains.

I looked at one shelf and then at Cliff. His eyes were focused on neatly stacked rows of government-surplus cheese. Our camp back home used the surplus program available to schools and camps like ours. It was all great stuff, especially the cheese.

"I wonder how much of this we are going to take," Cliff asked as he stood in front of the seemingly endless array of products.

That question was quickly answered when Fred produced a detailed packing list for a crew our size. I noticed everyone now stood ready to do what came next.

While we were exploring the various food options, Fred had instructed Gary on the process he was to lead. After we had looked around, Fred told us, "As the cook, Gary is responsible for directing the rest of us to gather the food in the quantities called for on the packing list."

"We will put some items, like cereal, flour, cornmeal, and dried milk, in a plastic bag," Gary said. "Be sure and secure the plastic bag with a string, being careful to tie a bow or slipknot. Fred told me we would untie the bags many times, and we needed to make sure we could retie them after each use. The plastic bags are to be put into cloth bags and tied again."

There was a smorgasbord of smells in the Bay Post, including dried apples with a holiday aroma. The dried apricots had an odor I didn't recognize. Every food had a distinctive smell. Some, like the dried soup mixes, were full-bodied. Several cake mixes were in barrels, and the spice cake had an especially pungent odor.

I don't know why, but I closed my eyes and took in a deep breath through my nose. I could make out all the smells, and then my thoughts turned to Grandpa and the smells of the nursing home. I felt like something was wrong.

"I hope he's okay," I whispered. I thought about calling but remembered Fred had told us the nearest phone was over 25 miles away.

Then I felt a hand on my shoulder. I opened my eyes. It was Smitty.

"Hey buddy, are you all right?"

"I was worrying about Grandpa," I said. "But I'm okay."

"He'll be fine." Smitty patted my shoulder. "He's a tough old guy!"

"Listen up, guys."

I put my thoughts away as Fred spoke.

"I've told Gary to read the list very carefully as we plan our menus." Then to all of us, Fred said, "When you pack your food, be sure the food bags are correctly marked." Fred was now smiling broadly as he said, "Gary, have you got a surprise to show us?"

"Listen to this, guys, and I'm talking cooler than Duke!"

We all turned to Gary. He had brought our food packs from Fred's locker, and Fred gave him cardboard boxes that fit perfectly into the food packs. "Fred told me how to pack bread, and it's incredible."

Gary showed us a square piece of plywood and said, "This is the key to packing twenty-seven loaves into the space of nine loaves."

"Is this a magic trick?" asked Tom. "Okay, I give up! How do you do it?"

The crew was laughing.

Gary was grinning as he pointed to 27 loaves of bread on the counter, and he said, "Put the food pack on the floor next to the counter." Then he said, "Joe, please place nine loaves standing up on the bottom of the pack and then lay the plywood on top of the loaves."

Everyone was paying close attention.

"Now, push the plywood board down to compress the bread by two-thirds. Go ahead, and stand on the board, Joe."

Oh, how I wish I had my camera handy, I thought.

Joe stepped out of the pack and then placed another nine loaves into the pack. When he stood on the board this time, he held onto the counter to keep his balance. He repeated the process one last time until all 27 loaves were smashed down into the pack.

Henry asked, "How on *earth* do we separate all this smashed bread?"

Fred smiled and said, "We have been smashing our bread here at Charlie's Place for many years. It allows us to have peanut butter and jelly or cheese and salami sandwiches for lunch. Smashing doesn't diminish the amount of bread. It just means you have to peel the slices apart. Trust me, you'll get used to it."

Gary asked us to gather around the counter where he had placed the packing list Fred had provided. I was anxious to review it. I looked at the packing list, which included the foods and amounts for an average crew, defined as 10 Explorers, one advisor, and the guide.

Food Items	Number or Pounds
Apples	4
Apricots	3
Prunes	4
Raisins	4
Bacon	8
Corned Beef	10
Spam®	6

Salami	5
Cheese	5–6
Barley	1
Flour	14 (Fred had us double the flour.)
Macaroni	4
Potatoes	8
Rice	7
Spaghetti	4
Bread	2 loaves per man
Hol-Ry	8–10 boxes
Cornmeal	3
Bulgur	2
Oatmeal	8
Wheat Cereal	6
Cornbread mix	2
Cake mixes	2 per mix
Pudding mix	3 per kind
Gravy mix	1
Pancake mix	6
Baking powder	8 oz.
Cinnamon	2 oz.
Mapleine	2 oz.
Salt	2 lbs.
Black Pepper	2 oz.
Chili Powder	2 oz.
Cocoa mix	15
Lemonade	2 1/2
Soup mix	2 (each kind)
Milk (dried)	3 1/2
Milk (canned) (small)	5
Milk (canned) (large)	2
Butter	6
Coffee	2

Tea	1/2 (Fred had us double this.)
Peanut butter	4–5
Jam	4
Punch mix	5 boxes

Food Items	**Number or Pounds**
Dried onions	1
Dried split peas	3–4 pkgs.
Dried green beans	1 1/2
Dried carrots	1
Dried spinach	1
Tomato paste	10–15 cans
Lard	4–5
Sugar, white	12
Sugar, brown	14

Other Essential Items	
Ivory soap	3 bars
Chore girls	5
Toilet paper	4 rolls
Matches	1/2 box
Bon Ami soap	2 bars
Ajax®	1 can

The average total weight? About 240 pounds (more or less).

* * *

With Gary's leadership and Fred's supervision, we all participated as Gary assigned tasks to every crew member.

"How did Gary learn all this stuff?" I heard Smitty ask Henry.

"I dunno," Henry answered. "I think he's been studying about it ever since Mr. Greenlee told him he could be the cook several months ago."

"Well, I'm impressed!" I said. "I think Mr. Greenlee made the right choice."

After our food was packed into the canvas Duluth Food Packs, Gary directed us to take the food packs downstairs to Fred's locker. We checked out the Duluth Packs we would be using.

There were three sizes: A-2, A-3, and A-4. The Kettle Pack, an A-2, was already packed and ready to go, and Fred's pack was an A-2.

"The last crew cleaned and prepared the Kettle Pack for our trip," said Fred, "and we would do the same for the Scouts following us."

Fred handed an A-3 Duluth Pack to Cliff and Gary. A larger capacity A-4 pack was given to Tom. Fred explained, "Because of the number of Scouts in our crew, four of you will pack into this pack. Joe will join with Louis, Dave, and Tom."

Tom looked shocked and asked, "Won't this pack be awful heavy?"

I answered him. "Tom, you are always preparing to be in good shape for football after this trip. This pack will assure you will be a star player this fall!"

I saw Tom grin as he held his upper arm and flexed his muscles.

Joe asked what was in the Kettle Pack since he was in the Seliga with Fred and would be carrying it.

"The Kettle Pack could be called the equipment pack since it has all the hardware and tools we will need," Fred said.

"Like what?" asked Joe. I saw a worried frown on Joe's face. I figured he was thinking about the difference in weight. I know I was thinking about it.

Fred said, "Joe, the Kettle Pack is lighter than the food packs and weighs close to what the personal packs weigh.

"The Kettle Pack will contain a set of nesting pots sometimes referred to as the Trail Chef Cook Kit," he continued. "They make it possible for us to cook many different dishes and drinks at one time. For example, we often have cocoa, coffee, and tea, requiring pots for each. We may have a stew and a vegetable dish as well. We have seven pots, which vary in size from one to eleven quarts.

#1 = 1 qt. filled to rivets

#2 = 1 1/2 qt. filled to rivets

#3 = 2 1/2 qt. filled to rivets

#4 = 4 qt. filled to rivets

#5 = 6 qt. filled to rivets

#6 = 8 qt. filled to rivets

#7 = 11 qt. filled to rivets

Fred added that we also had

- a stainless steel reflector oven
- a large griddle
- cooking spoons
- spatulas
- can opener
- pot hangers
- hot pot tongs
- pie tins
- cake tins
- mixing bowls
- mountain kit
- spices and seasoning
- kitchen fly (sometimes called a dining fly)
- a friction top can for matches

"All those items are included in the Kettle Pack along with a three-quarter axe, a folding trenching shovel, a folding Sven saw, and a first aid kit," he said. "The reflector oven is carried in the front of the bread pack. We will review all this when we make camp on our first night."

Chuck asked if we had spares for anything we might lose.

"In three years, I have never lost any equipment," Fred said, reminding us to be careful that no items went missing at the end of each meal.

"Always check, before departing from a campsite, that no tools or utensils are left behind," he continued. "Pots and cooking gear should immediately be washed after each meal. We boil utensils at least once a day to ensure absolute sanitation."

I thought to myself, *With all this to consider, it's a good thing we have a guide along to keep all this organized.*

Fred had four tents in his locker and we took three with us. They were rolled up in canvas ground cloths, and Fred said we would learn to set them up at our first campsite. Fred told us we were lucky to have a "senior guide" since he was issued the new Voyageur tents for the first time this year. They were much lighter than the previous tents. The first- and second-year guides were still using the old tentage that weighed twice what the Voyageur tents weighed.

The canvas packs were made of olive-drab canvas and had thick oiled-leather straps attached with copper rivets. I took a sniff. They had a musty smell, and the leather smelled like the neatsfoot oil I had been putting on my boots.

Grandpa, I suddenly thought. *I have to stop worrying and trust that he will be there when I get home.*

Since we had packed our food and had all our necessary packs, Fred said, "Leave your paddles, the Kettle Pack, and the food packs here. Take the personal packs and go back to your tents to put on your uniforms. Leave the personal packs in your tents for now, and then let's meet at the lodge to have our crew picture made. After the photo and route planning, you will have some free time to visit the trading post and look around before dinner."

We all went back to the tent city to put on our uniforms, clean up, comb our hair, and take care of other needs. After those chores were completed, we headed down the hill to the lodge.

When we arrived, Fred took us around to the front. I don't know what I was expecting but what I saw took my breath away.

What a beautiful building! It was built in 1941and 1942 and was all log construction. Fred told us there were no nails anywhere in the structure. The logs were salvaged from a blowdown on the Echo Trail, and it was an example of the best of the old Finnish log-cabin builder's craft.

Fred introduced us to the Base photographer and asked him if he was ready for us. While we were being told about the lodge, Roy Conradi had prepared the identifying placard for our crew picture. He welcomed us and said, "Ah, a Sioux Council crew, one of the good ones!"

He then had us line up in front of the lodge and took our picture. He was amusing and was an expert at getting us all to smile at the same time.

Inside the lodge, there were large maps on which we could plan our trip. They were mounted on both sides of a large eight-by-ten display rack. You could see the whole wilderness area of Canada's Quetico Provincial Park and the Superior National Forest on the Minnesota side.

I found it hard to focus on anything but the interesting artifacts on display everywhere in this beautiful building. There were logging tools by the massive rock fireplace, above which was a mantle made from a split log. A thick chain draped across the hearth, which Fred said was an old logging chain. There was a rusty saw and some other tools, including a log-turner. A beaver pelt on a stretcher was hanging on the wall, and there was even a bearskin. Fred said the items on display were to show us the various historical periods that were part of this area of Minnesota and Canada.

I was so happy to see a picture of Charles L. Sommers framed and placed above the fireplace's mantle. He was quickly becoming one of my heroes.

Fred said he would tell us about the many Indian tribes of this area who were the first to occupy this irreplaceable land when we were out on the trail. We looked at a birchbark canoe at the back of the lodge by the big windows. There was a similar one outside the lodge.

We examined the canoe made of birchbark, with its hand-carved white cedar for the gunwales and ribs, strips of spruce roots to hold the bark to the frame, and spruce pitch (or resin mixed with tallow and charcoal) to seal the seams. Fred told us Chippewa or Ojibwe Indians of this area of Minnesota had made the canoes. He said the French voyageurs used similar canoes in the fur trade for several centuries, starting in the early 1700s and lasting up to the late 1800s.

He said we would be traveling on lakes and portage trails used by the Indians, the explorers, and the voyageurs. I asked who these voyageurs were, and he said we would learn more about them during the campfire all the crews in Base would attend that evening.

He took us to one of the large maps of the canoe country. We sat on wooden benches in front of the map. There were lakes all over the map. It looked very confusing.

He pointed to Ely and said, "I want to give you some perspective of distances," and showed us the road we had taken to the Base. The road ended at the Base, and then there was nothing until you looked up at the top of the map.

"This road across the upper part of the map is the King's Highway in Canada," he said. "Atikokan is the only town on the Canadian portion of this map. The Canadian border is only six miles from where we are sitting. The border runs across the lower third of this map."

It was a little overwhelming, but with Fred's description, it was making sense to me. I looked at each member of our crew. It was easy to see that there was both excitement and apprehension about the choices we were about to make.

Fred then asked us, "What kind of trip do you want to take?"

We all agreed we wanted to spend most of our nine days in Canada. We told him we wanted to get in some good fishing and wished to take a relatively rough trip. Fred stroked his beard as he considered the options that included our desires.

After a few moments, he said, "We might consider going up into Kawa Bay, where fishing has been good from all reports this year.

From there, we would also be able to go into Mack Lake, where some of the crews have caught some large fish." He pointed to the map and traced a route from Customs to Sunday Lake, Lake Agnes, Kawnipi, Kawa Bay, and up the Wawiag to Mack.

"Could we include a visit to Knife Lake Dorothy?" asked Mr. Greenlee.

We all looked confused until Fred suggested by continuing to the border at Saganagons, we could come back down Ottertrack and Knife. We agreed it seemed like a good plan. We liked the idea of traveling on Agnes, which was by Louisa. We had been singing about those lakes on our trip up to the Base. Fred said we would have many days to be proud of since there would be many portages and some rough going. Tom said, "The rougher, the better!"

Fred asked Mr. Greenlee to pick two members of our group to serve as our table servers. Mike and Henry quickly volunteered, and Fred gave them directions to the dining hall. The rest of us continued to ask questions and look closer at the route we had selected.

The time passed quickly, and there was a bell ringing in the distance. We had a plan!

At 5:50 p.m., we followed Fred on a steep and rocky path to the dining hall. As we approached it from the steep trail leading up from the lodge, I was again shocked. After seeing the lodge, I shouldn't have been surprised. The dining hall was very impressive, fitting beautifully into the surrounding terrain. It was built out of pine and had an enormous front porch. It was so rocky some of it had been constructed on solid rock, and some of it was on concrete supports.

I admired a nearly completed stone wall in particular. It was apparent that the Base was a work in progress.

Over a hundred Scouts, Explorers, and leaders were on the porch of the dining hall or on the steps waiting to go in. A large bell somewhere near us on the hill rang again to call us to dinner. It was precisely 6:00 p.m.

With all the activity we had just had, they sure didn't need to call twice. A young man dressed in a white jacket and hat came out of the dining hall and asked us to enter and sit by crews. Our own "waiters" met us when we arrived inside and told us about how the meal would proceed. It was pretty well organized.

Before we ate, we all said the Wilderness Grace.

"We will say this grace before every meal," Fred told us.

For food, for raiment,
For life and opportunity,
For sun and rain,
For water and portage trails,
For friendship and fellowship,
We thank thee, O Lord.[1]

Our dinner consisted of beans and wieners. We ate family-style and had plenty of seconds. Our waiter led us in organizing the utensils when we were done, and then we left while the table waiters washed the tables with soap and water. Some of them swept and helped clean up. In no time, they rejoined us at the lodge before our campfire program.

We had time to go to the trading post, a little store with Scout stuff, a few gifts and souvenirs, and more fishing gear. I wanted to get Mom and Dad a gift, and I saw many things that might work. I decided to get Mom a metal cross. I was going to wait, but the guy who ran the shop said, "These crosses are almost gone, and they have been on backorder several times over the summer. The crosses are made of German silver, and the one you like is called the Cross of Lorraine."

"Is it real silver?" I asked.

---

1. Traditional grace used by Sommers crews.

"It closely resembles real silver in sheen and texture," he said. "German silver is made from a combination of nickel, copper, and zinc."

The cross had a double crossbar and was of French design. A little paper folder said both the voyageurs and the Indians they traded with prized the silver crosses like these. Mom was very religious, so I bought her the cross.

Chapter 6

CAMPFIRE

Following dinner and the quick trip to the trading post, we went back to our tents as Fred had told us to lay out our personal equipment on our bunks so he could be sure we had everything. Mr. Greenlee looked over our gear and said it all looked okay to him. He then added, "But let's wait for Fred to see what he recommends we take and what we leave behind."

Dave said, "I think I hear him coming."

I threw the tent flap back and saw Fred striding our way.

"Hey guys," Fred called out as he entered our section of tent city. "Everyone gather 'round. We need to have a little talk."

"What have we done now?" asked Dave.

"I don't think we've done anything," I answered. "He's smiling."

"Okay, guys," Fred began. He was smiling, but he had a straightforward, businesslike tone to his voice. "The next ten days will be some of the roughest you will ever experience. The gear we take with us must be looked upon from the standpoint of weight and not just need or convenience.

"For instance, if you all bring a toothpaste tube, you will bring most of it back, and you will carry the weight the whole trip. Why don't you consider each three of you sharing a tube and then take another look at your gear to see if there are other things you could share."

"Makes sense," Henry said.

I looked around, and everyone nodded their head and headed for their tent.

During a meeting before the trip, we had already decided who would be in each canoe. Tom, Dave, and I were a team and went back inside our tent to take another look at our gear. Fred had planted the idea of saving space and weight.

"Wouldn't one or two flashlights and some extra batteries be better than three flashlights?" Dave asked.

"Dave, go check this question with Fred. This could be a safety issue," I said.

Dave came back into the tent, smiling, and told us that Fred thought it was a good idea and suggested two.

"I'm gonna leave my pillow and use some clothes or my rain jacket for a pillow," Tom said.

Dave and I both agreed one towel each would be enough rather than the towels our moms sent.

"My mom packed a clean pair of underwear for each day," I said, holding up the plastic bag filled with my underwear. "I think two pairs for the whole trip will be plenty. I stepped outside and checked with Mr. Greenlee. He said it would be okay for everyone as long as we agreed to wash the spare pair every day or two."

"Let's take one bar of soap for the three of us," Dave said.

Fred had been checking with each team and overheard Dave's idea. He smiled as he said, "You guys are getting the idea. But if you have a choice, make it Ivory soap since it floats. Almost every trip, I see a bar of soap get loose while a Scout is washing, and it goes to the bottom of a deep lake. Before you cut back on too much, remember, do not skimp on socks! Your feet will be wet every day, and you will find a dry pair to wear with your camp shoes most welcome."

It was fun repacking. We were amazed at the things we had decided we didn't need.

As we were putting the last items into the pack, Fred said, "It's time for the campfire. Let's go to the campfire together, and then y'all can take another look at packing afterward. Y'all might pick up a few ideas from the campfire program."

We arrived for the campfire at the lodge a little before 7:00 p.m. Fred joined the other guides standing near the fireplace. I smiled as I noticed the camaraderie between the guides.

Our crew sat together. Mike exclaimed, "Holy cow! Have you ever seen so many older Scouts in uniform in one place?"

It was exciting to see Scouts and Explorers from all over the United States. Eleven other crews were going out at the same time we were.

When the program was about to start, all of the guides sat down at a long log table to the right of the fireplace. They looked splendid in full uniform since they were older than we Scouts. A few of them seemed a lot older, but it may have been because some of them had thick beards.

At precisely 7:00 p.m., a tall slim guide made the Scout sign for silence and called the meeting to order. He introduced himself, saying, "My name is Ron, and I'm a third-year guide from Georgia."

His crew cheered. He was one of the few guides who had not grown a beard. He introduced each of the other guides, and their crews cheered as their names were called.

After all the guides had been introduced, he introduced the Canoe Base Director, Mr. Clifford J. Hanson. Ron told us he was the Boy Scouts of America's Region Ten deputy director.

During the summer season, he ran the Canoe Base operation. I noticed he was also wearing the Base uniform, which was the green Explorer uniform. Mr. Hanson wore a red wool jacket, as did many of the guides. I guessed him to be about 50 years old, and he welcomed us to the Charles L. Sommers Wilderness Canoe Base. Boy, was he enthusiastic!

I looked at the picture above the fireplace. He told us Mr. Sommers was a businessman from Saint Paul. He and some of the other Scouting volunteers made the Base possible.

"Mr. Sommers, Carlos Chase, Frank Bean, and a few other people found and developed this site for the Base," he said. "The wilderness programs began operations in 1923 and were initially operated from Winton, a little town you passed on the way out to this location."

He then told us about the history of the border country. It was strange that my heart began to race when he said, "The Indians living in this area have changed over the years. The first Natives we know about were the Forest Sioux and their ancestors. As Europeans pushed westward, the more warlike Chippewa or Ojibwe drove the Sioux out of northern Minnesota and the Canadian woods into western Minnesota and the Dakota plains in the early 1700s. Many of you may see some of the many Indian paintings estimated to be at least three hundred years old. You will see them on the rock cliff in sheltered areas not covered with lichens. Those earlier native residents used fish oil and iron oxide as they painted them."

He laughed and added, "I wish I could find some house paint that would last as long.

"The first Europeans to visit this area may have been Viking Explorers, and legends to that conclusion abound," he continued. "However, history tells us the earliest to enter this area was the French explorer La Vérendrye. And there were probably other unnamed explorers before him. The French were looking for furs and trying to find a northwest passage.

"The voyageurs were the most constant travelers through this area for hundreds of years. They were the paddlers who brought trade goods to the Indians and then brought back furs for their employers, the French, the English, and the Scots. They were flamboyant in their colorful shirts and leggings, woven sashes, scarves, and jaunty caps.

"Now most of you Scouts," he noted, "are taller than the average voyageur, for they were usually short in stature. They were seldom more than five foot seven since space was a significant factor in a business that used birchbark canoes to carry its entire product. Strength was more of a requirement, and the tales of their feats on the portages are almost unbelievable. They had to carry two packs of ninety pounds each, and some were known to have transported even more. They also had to paddle for several hours before sunup and, on two meals a day, paddle until late at night. Nevertheless, they survived dangerous rapids, mosquitoes, and bears while singing all the way from Montreal to Lake Athabasca and from the MacKenzie River to the Arctic Circle."

After the stories about voyageurs had me sitting on the edge of my bench, he said, "You come here as boys, but you will come back from the trail as young men. You will work harder than you have ever worked before. You will get sunburned, mosquito bit, and have sore muscles you didn't even know you had. On about the third night, you will wish your mother was here to tuck you in between some clean sheets. And that goes for you advisors too! But then you will start to feel proud, and you will find the strength you didn't know you had."

It sounded kind of scary and encouraging at the same time. I was drawn to these stories, and I wanted to hear more.

When Mr. Hanson finished, he turned the program back to Ron, who taught us a few songs. First, he sang "The Far Northland" with the other guides. What a voice! Then he asked all who knew it to join in. Our crew already knew it and joined the guides with gusto.

Next, we sang "The Paddle Song." Our crew had learned it when we started planning for this trip, but it was a new song to some of the Scouts.

"First, we will sing it through, and then we are going to sing it three more times," said Ron. "The first time, we try to imagine we are on the shore watching some canoe men approaching, so we sing it softly. Then, as they paddle nearer, we sing louder as they pass in front of us. The last verse will taper off as the voyageurs paddle out of sight."

Our paddles clean and bright, flashing like silver . . .

Swift as the wild goose flies . . . dip, dip, and swing

Dip, dip, and swing them back, flashing like silver . . .

Swift as the wild goose flies . . . dip, dip, and swing.[1]

It was fun to sing. I imagined those old voyageurs dressed in their finest outfits of colorful shirts, leggings, woven sashes, scarves, and jaunty caps as we sang.

Before Ron sat down, the other guides asked him to sing a song about Ireland called "Galway Bay." As his clear tenor voice filled the lodge, I felt it was the prettiest song I had ever heard. This guy could have been a professional singer and sung anywhere.

Another guide, named Terry, got up and came to the front of the room. He told us about fishing.

"You are going into some of the best fishing waters on the continent," he said. "You can expect to catch four types of fish: northern, lake trout, smallmouth bass, and walleye."

He next described the fishing tackle.

"You will need steel leaders, and I can't stress their importance enough."

He said our guide would teach us more, but we needed to communicate as we caught fish so we wouldn't catch more than we could eat each day.

Terry introduced a big guide named Mark, who joined him in showing us how to pack our three-man packs. Terry held and steadied the pack. Fred had given us advice and instruction, but it was better to see a pack become filled with three guys' gear. As Mark explained and demonstrated, I began to review what I was taking one more time.

---

1. "The Paddle Song" is a traditional Canoe Base song.

They showed us how to pick up the heavy Duluth Packs, and I learned something new for the hundredth time in one day.

"Always pick up and carry packs by the 'ears' or excess canvas on the sides until you are ready to portage," he said.

Mark showed us how to put a pack upon your back by placing the pack on your right thigh while holding the pack's top steady with your left hand. With the straps facing you, he explained, you slide your right arm through the strap on your left and slide it to your shoulder. Then you slip your left arm behind your back and slide it through the remaining strap. Once your arms are through the straps, you can adjust the pack for comfort.

"Never, *ever* pick up a pack by the straps," he cautioned us. "The leather straps are to hold the pack to your back, and should you break a strap, you will find it most unpleasant to have to carry it in your arms rather than on your back."

Ron returned to the front and introduced a guide named Voldi, a big blond fellow.

"Now we are going to learn a real voyageur song . . . in French," Voldi said. "Many of you will know the song but probably don't know what it means. It's an old French song. It belonged to France and went with Canadian soldiers during World War II. The song is called 'Alouette,' and many of you will recall Alouette, gentle Alouette.

"It's about a gentle lark, and the singer is telling us how he will prepare it for cooking as he plucks its feathers from the various parts of the lark."

Voldi sang the first verse and said he would lead each additional verse, and we were to repeat it and then all join in very loudly on the chorus. Voldi pointed to the part of the bird on himself as we sang each part. I had sung it in school, but I never knew anything about the song, nor did I ever have so much fun singing it.

(Chorus)
Alouette, gentille Alouette

Alouette, je t'y plumerai
Je t'y plumerai la tete (repeat)
Et la tete, Et la Tete
Oh . . .
(Chorus)

Je t'y plumerai les yeux (repeat)
Et les yeux, Et les yeux
Et la tete, Et la Tete
Oh . . .
(Chorus)

Je t'y plumerai le bec
Et le bec, Et le bec
Et les yeux, Et la tete
Oh . . .
(Chorus)

Je t'y plumerai le dos
Et le dos, Et le dos
Et le bec, Et les Yeux, Et la tete
Oh . . .
(Chorus)

Je t'y plumerai le cou
Et la cou, Et la cou
Et la dos, Et le bec,
Et les yeux, Et la tete
Alouette, Alouette
Oh . . .

Alouette, gentille Alouette
Alouette, je t'y plumerai

When we finished, we all clapped and cheered just for having had such a good time. Voldi was a good song leader, and I was sure his crew would have a great time. These guides all seemed to be nice guys, and they always showed such high regard for one another.

Mr. Hanson closed the campfire program with some final wise words about enjoying the wilderness and the need to protect and preserve it. He was about to lead in singing "Scout Vespers."

Just as we were about to sing, I heard a loon call out on the lake. It caused me to look out the windows on the right side of the lodge. I could see the sun must have been below the horizon. The sky was a beautiful red color. I couldn't see the detail of the sunset because there were aspen trees outside the lodge. But I could see the red through the quivering leaves as we sang. It was something I will never forget.

Softly falls the light of day,
As our campfire fades away.
Silently each Scout should ask:
Have I done my daily task?
Have I kept my honor bright?
Can I guiltless sleep tonight?
Have I done and have I dared,
Everything to be prepared?[3]

Our troop sang "Scout Vespers" at the end of troop meetings, and I guess most of the other troops and posts did too because it was beautiful. After vespers, we all walked back to the tent city in silence. It had become very dark except for the starlit sky above. I felt very much at home in this wild new place.

When we arrived back in tent city, I checked my gear one more time and then crawled into my sleeping bag. In my mind, I reviewed

---

3. "Scout Vespers" is a traditional Scouting song.

all the things I had learned that day. I said a prayer and thought, *Thank you, God, for all I have experienced today, but mostly I am thankful that Dad and Mom made me come on this trip. I have the feeling it is going to be the best adventure of my life. Bless and protect Grandpa and keep him well.*

I desperately wanted to see him when I got home. My thoughts and prayers went on for a long time.

Several times during the night, I heard the loons calling out on the lake. I was surprised at the variety of calls and knew I would come to recognize their meanings. Loons seem to call at all hours of the day and night. It was a good sound. I closed my eyes and soon fell asleep.

Suddenly, it was morning, and the loon's call woke me just before Mr. Greenlee yelled, "Daylight in the swamp!"

Chapter 7

BEGINNINGS

When I stepped out of my tent, I heard the loon again. It had been the last sound I heard before sleeping and the first sound I had heard upon awakening. Mr. Greenlee must have been noticing my fascination when the loons called as he said with a smile, "Louis, the loons are anxious for us to get on the trail."

"I think you're right," I said, nodding in agreement and thinking about the day before when we swamped the canoe. Fred had also commented on the loons communicating with me at our swamping.

It was neat to have two of my heroes paying attention to my interest in the loons.

Before breakfast, we rolled our sleeping bags and packed our personal packs. We were up early enough to take care of our morning chores and have our last use of a modern toilet until our return.

At breakfast, we again saw the other 11 crews as they filed into the dining hall. Everyone I spoke to seemed excited to begin the trip. Their guides were busily going over last-minute preparations with them. Wow! What a change! No one was dressed in uniforms. Like us, everyone had changed into trail clothes.

We were wearing comfortable trail clothing. I thought we looked pretty dapper. Some guides wore flamboyant clothing like logger shirts, leather vests, or suspenders. A couple of them were wearing voyageur sashes like the ones Mr. Hànson had mentioned. Our guide, Fred, was wearing a green beret and a leather vest. He wore light-colored cotton pants and leather boots like mine. He looked like a guide! Perhaps even like a voyageur.

Breakfast included pancakes and syrup, bacon, eggs, toast, and all the peanut butter and jelly we could eat. There was orange juice, coffee, and milk available to drink. Fred told us, "Enjoy the milk since it will be the last fresh milk until we return. We will take powered milk but only for cooking."

None of us talked very much during breakfast. I think everyone must have been intent on getting started.

After breakfast, Fred said, "Set all your gear outside of your tents, sweep them out, and then we will gather at the waterfront in fifteen minutes with everything ready to go."

Fred had his pack with him at breakfast and helped us to stay focused as we walked the short distance to tent city to clean our tents.

After the cleaning was well underway, Fred said, "Louis, I want to make sure my Grumman canoes are together near the waterfront. Which two fellas would you suggest I give the numbers to so they can go down to locate my canoes and move them?"

I recommended Joe and Mike.

Judging from the number of canoes I saw when we swamped, there must have been hundreds of canoes down at the waterfront. Joe and Mike must have quickly found ours because all three were together on the racks near the docks when we arrived. Those carrying the personal packs must have soon found Joe and Mike with our canoes.

Mr. Greenlee had a key to Fred's locker and took Tom, Gary, and me to the Bay Post to get the food packs and the Kettle Pack. Chuck and Mike were in charge of paddles. Tom, Gary, and I made one more trip to the locker to get the tents. It didn't take long to gather all of our gear and put it next to the canoes where Joe stood by the personal packs next to them.

Before we had left home, we had decided on the canoe teams and had made sure we were balanced with a good canoeist in each canoe. I was selected as a good canoeist because I had earned the canoeing merit badge. Joe and Mike moved the three Grumman canoes into the water.

That's when Fred said, "Let's all get our feet wet!"

Fred stepped into the water, and we all followed. I noticed Tom stepped in without hesitating. He must have forgotten about his new boots.

"Now we need to tie all the fishing rods inside the canoe under the thwarts. Do you all know the basic Scout knots?"

He smiled when we all answered yes at the same time.

Fred demonstrated with Joe's and his rods. He had plenty of paracord for that purpose. We set about securing our rods, and when we had finished, Fred went around and inspected each one.

"Good," he said and walked over to the food packs. "Now load the food packs with the straps to the outside so you don't catch the front buckles on the gunwales when you unload them. Secure them with the paracord. Connect the cord's ends with these metal clips, which attach to the D-ring on the other end."

When the food packs were loaded and secure, we loaded the personal packs. Again Fred emphasized that the straps were to be to the outside.

"Both packs go behind the portage yoke, and each canoe will then have a tent placed under the yoke. Now, never, *never* sit on the yoke! The yokes are made with thick oak, but you will have difficulty portaging a canoe without a yoke if you should break one."

Fred continued, "Here at Charlie's Place, only two people paddle in each canoe. The third person rides, sitting on the bottom of the canoe facing forward, and he may lean on the tent and the yoke if he wishes. His paddle is to be stowed beside him."

Chuck pointed at the bow seat and asked, "What about the bags under the seats?"

"Thanks for asking, Chuck! There are two personal flotation devices or life vests, as most people call them, one under the bow seat and one under the stern seat. They are in bags and tied securely under the seats. I always tie them with a slipknot so they can be removed quickly in an emergency.

"Chuck, you are assigned to ask me that question again before we depart Customs later this morning since we may need the life vests when we get to Bailey Bay," Fred added.

Finally, we were loaded and ready to go with four canoes, Fred, Mr. Greenlee, and nine Scouts. Three of the canoes were Grumman aluminum canoes, and Fred's was the beautiful green wood-and-canvas canoe. I again wondered why he got the lightweight wooden one, and we got the metal ones.

I paddled in the stern in my canoe with Tom in the bow and Dave in the middle.

"You might want to change paddlers when we arrive at Customs at Prairie Portage, about six miles from here," added Fred.

He grinned and said, "You will learn a lot about canoeing in those six miles."

Finally, we pushed off, but before we left, Fred called out, "Kettle Pack."

"Here," Joe answered.

He said "good" and then proceeded to call "food packs," answered by "here" three times.

Then he called out "tents," and again, there were three replies.

"Everyone has a paddle?"

The answer was yes from everyone.

"Then let's shove off."

And we were on our way.

Fred moved out with what seemed like effortless strokes. In only a moment, he was 50 yards in front of us. We all paddled hard to try to catch up to him.

It seemed like we were all headed for one spot at the same time. In only two minutes, two of the canoes touched, and the guys hollered, "Watch it!" and "Stay on your own side. You'll swamp us."

I moved away from the main group to avoid any collisions. I noticed Fred was still pulling away. Mr. Greenlee just sat in the middle of his canoe and smiled while Mike and Gary yelled at each other. Fred slowed down and waited for everyone to catch up. When we all got close enough to hear, he asked, "Are you ready to review what we learned yesterday?"

Everyone, including me, seemed to be ready for a review.

We hadn't yet gone 300 yards, and we were running into each other and yelling. Fred sat still in his canoe and said, "Remember, it's the sternman who determines direction with the use of the sweep stroke and the J-stroke. The bowman provides power, and you are always to paddle on opposite sides. The sternman may ask for a change of sides, and the bowman should also ask for a change of sides when needed. But always request a change so you don't swamp by both digging in on the same side."

Then Fred's tone of voice became serious, and he said, "I hope you are here to see the wildlife of the Boundary Waters. The birds and animals can be the finest part of this adventure we are about to have. Yelling will scare them away before we get to them. Even the loons will stay away from a noisy group."

Then he smiled and said, "Let's start again."

Taking Fred's advice, we started again, and this time we made much less noise. After another few minutes of practice, all of us seemed to be paddling better. Fred continued to maneuver his canoe among us and help those who were having problems.

I watched him carefully and copied him. Everything he taught us seemed to work. After paddling for another hundred yards, we stopped for a short rest, and I had time to focus on my surroundings rather than on my paddle strokes. I looked at the lake ahead and then turned my head and noticed the shore in the distance sliding by. Next,

I looked back and saw the rippling wake behind the canoe. Now it struck me all of a sudden that I was indeed on the canoe trails.

But I was a little upset with myself because I had wanted to remember everything from the first moment.

Well, the start was memorable indeed.

As we were about to round the first point of land jutting out into the lake, I looked back in the direction of the Base. I couldn't see it. I could see where it was, and I could see a crew pushing off as we had, but I couldn't see anything of the Base. It blended into the green forest and all the land around it. I noted how the islands and the shore looked so I would recognize it when I returned. I was already planning to be in the lead when we returned. I watched Fred as he effortlessly paddled his canoe and decided that I wanted to be a guide like him as soon as I was old enough.

Wow, we haven't been on this trip for ten minutes, and I was already planning my future!

As we rounded the point, I could see for a long distance ahead. There was a long straight shoreline to the right and islands and an irregular shoreline to the left. It was beautiful, and my friends, the loons, were back at it. They were making happy-sounding calls, almost like a peal of laughter.

Tom asked if I was ready to switch sides, and we did. I have always been much better at paddling on my right side, but I continued to paddle on my left. I had to think about every stroke because I was more practiced on my right. I noticed Tom was significantly stronger on his right, and we were now moving faster. I considered this discovery and decided that it would be wise to become proficient on my left side since most people are naturally stronger on their right.

Fred slowed, and I was sure he watched me paddle for a while. All he said was, "Remember to keep the lower arm straight and to feather the paddle. You are both doing great."

I felt my face flush as I watched him paddle ahead. We had gotten a compliment from Fred!

Tom must respond to praise as well because as he looked back over his shoulder, he said, "Louis, just let me know if anyone starts to catch up with us."

We continued to paddle, and soon I saw we were approaching two islands on our left. Fred pointed in their direction and said, "Those are called Twin Islands." I noticed people camped on the island on the right.

We stayed to the right, but with an audience watching us, we focused on paddling skills. As we passed the island, a teenage girl called out to us, "Good morning, Scouts!" Dave cupped his hands and responded with a friendly "hello!"

We paddled for half an hour after passing the Twin Islands. As we approached the end of Moose Lake, Dave, who had been studying the map, said, "It looks like there is a narrow waterway between this lake and the next with a small island in the middle coming up. We are in the lead, so which side of the island should we take?"

I looked ahead and could now see a couple of old dry cedar spars sticking out of the water from the right. They looked like they had been there for years. So I headed to the left of them. I looked back at Fred, who was helping Mike with paddling stern in Mr. Greenlee's canoe. He nodded approval to my decision.

New Found Lake started on the other side of the opening between the lakes. It was similar to Moose Lake except for a large island on the left side close to the lake's end.

"Guys, that is called Horseshoe Island, and there are several campsites around it," said Fred.

I could see it had several bays on the map, and it looked like a perfect place to explore and fish.

"Fred, is Horseshoe Island a good place to camp?" asked Tom.

"I have never camped there, since I always plan to be well past Prairie Portage on my way out and incoming crews seldom camp this close to the Base on the last night of their trip," Fred replied.

I followed along on my map and noticed you had a choice to make about a half mile beyond Horseshoe Island. You could continue to the left through Sucker Lake to Prairie Portage or veer to the right to Ensign Lake and stay on the Minnesota side of the border.

As I approached the point between the two water-path options, I remembered the words of a poem by Robert Frost, which I had memorized and recited many times.

"The Road Not Taken"
by Robert Frost

Two roads diverged in a yellow wood,
And sorry I could not travel both
And be one traveler, long I stood
And looked down one as far as I could
To where it bent in the undergrowth;

Then took the other, as just as fair,
And having perhaps the better claim,
Because it was grassy and wanted wear;
Though as for that the passing there
Had worn them really about the same,

And both that morning equally lay
In leaves no step had trodden black.
Oh, I kept the first for another day!
Yet knowing how way leads on to way,
I doubted if I should ever come back.

I shall be telling this with a sigh
Somewhere ages and ages hence:
Two roads diverged in a wood, and I—
I took the one less traveled by,

And that has made all the difference.[1]

I remembered how my American Literature class had discussed this poem and especially the lines

Oh, I kept the first for another day!
Yet knowing how way leads on to way,
I doubted if I should ever come back.[2]

In my mind, I knew that phrase was wrong for me.
I was pushed into a decision to take this journey on the canoe trails. Initially, I was not happy to take the path less traveled by most boys my age. And now, in just under two hours, I was confident I was on the right road.

I shall be telling this with a sigh
Somewhere ages and ages hence:
Two roads diverged in a wood, and I—
I took the one less traveled by,
And that has made all the difference.[3]

The choice to take the water path to the left led to the Quetico. I was sure that "road" would indeed make all the difference.

Our crew was paddling better, and we had been traveling for what seemed like several hours when Fred slowed to a stop.

"We are about to reach our first portage," Fred said, "and I want to use this as an opportunity to show you exactly how to unload the canoes and take a portage. Prairie Portage is where we go through

---

1. Robert Frost, "The Road Not Taken," Poetry Foundation, accessed September 9, 2021, https://www.poetryfoundation.org/poems/44272/the-road-not-taken.

2. Ibid.

3. Frost, "The Road Not Taken," Poetry Foundation.

Canadian Customs. You have covered the six miles relatively quickly, and I feel good about your ability to complete this whole trip with ease."

We were all grinning ear to ear, and Mr. Greenlee added, "I agree with Fred."

"This was a famous portage in the voyageur days because it was a good stopping place before heading to Basswood Lake and the Basswood River that led to adventures and riches beyond," Fred said. "Local Indians would come here to trade furs with the voyageurs, and many lived around here. We are now on the 'Voyageur's Highway.'"

In a more serious tone, he continued, "There are falls and rapids on the left side of the portage. You can hear them now if you listen. We must stay along the right-hand shore and not bunch up. This will be one of the easiest portages on our trip, but it's a good one to start with."

Fred and Joe reached the portage first, and by the time our canoe touched the shore, they were already out of their canoe and placing their gear on shore. The landing was shallow, and the bottom was gravel and sand.

As we all pulled up, Fred said, "Listen up, please! Each bowman should step out into the water as soon as the water appears to be only a foot deep."

All the guys in the bow of the canoes managed to get out without tipping over.

"Now, bowmen, steady the canoe and walk it as far as you can so the sternman can get out. Remember to stay bent low and hold the gunwales as you step out. Now both of you steady the canoe so the centerman can climb out, and remember you will likely be a little stiff from sitting for almost two hours."

As we all stood in the water, Fred said, "In this case only, place the packs up on the shore. This portage will be a demonstration exercise. The pack carriers will usually put packs on their back before we walk out of the water. Because this will be our first time flipping canoes, I want you guys to learn to do it together. Usually, it is a good idea for one pack carrier to lead off, followed by the man carrying the canoe and then the next pack carrier. That way, you cross the portages as a team and help each other if need be."

Each canoe crew had already decided who would carry what, so we were anxious to get started across the portage. Fred instructed the canoe carriers to move to the center on the canoe's left.

"Now watch me flip my canoe up on my shoulders," said Fred. "Stand in the water and at the middle of the canoe so it is right in front of your legs. You don't have to lift it far. Bend your knees and then pull it up on your thighs with the gunwales far as you can. While holding the yoke with your left hand, slip your right arm between your legs, under the canoe as far as you can. Now bounce a little and flip it up and over onto your shoulders. The yoke pads will be on both sides of your head. With your hands holding the inside of the gunwales, you can be off on your first portage."

He then went through it again. It looked so smooth. It was as if he had just put on a big hat.

"Before you go, watch and listen as I show you how to put your canoe back down," Fred added. "When you reach the other side, you will find a nice wide beach, which is not typical. Walk out into the water until you are sure the stern will not hit anything when you flip the canoe back down. When you flip it back down, just reverse the process. Be sure to catch it on your thighs before you just smack it into the water. Think of these canoes as birchbark and handle them that way."

He then flipped the canoe back down with practiced ease and slid it gently into the water.

Fred then said, "Let's all try it, but I want each of the pack carriers to stand on either side of you canoe carriers to help you."

Tom and Dave stood by my side, and I tried my first flip of our trip. I followed Fred's instructions, and everything worked, except I asked the guys to help me a little to get it up to my shoulders.

Not bad for the first time.

I could hear some of the guys having trouble when Fred said, "Louis, go on across. Just follow the trail and remember to walk out into the water. When you get your canoe down, rest it on the shore and help Tom and Dave with their packs. Have one of them help you to turn it over on the beach. Make sure the packs are placed on the shore next to the canoe and, when the others are across, have them do the same and keep the crew together."

Wow, I am going to be the first to cross, and I'm in charge.

I started across the trail and found it easy walking. It wasn't long before my neck hurt something terrible. The yoke was on my neck. I bounced the canoe backward, and then just the pads were on my shoulders.

Much better!

The canoe was not as heavy as it was awkward, and I found I had to pull down on the gunwales to keep it from tipping back. I tried to adjust my yoke's position again, and then the canoe was balanced even better.

The trail went uphill, made a turn, and was flat and even for walking. It didn't seem like a long time until I saw the next lake's water, and the trail started to slope downward. I reached the lake and did as Fred had asked. Out in the water, I stopped and took a deep breath before I flipped the canoe down off my shoulders to the water. It didn't go very well, and I slapped it down pretty hard. I was about to try to figure out what I did wrong when I heard Tom.

"Louis, did you make it okay? Please help me get this pack off. It weighs a ton."

As the crew began to appear, I noticed they looked a little bedraggled, and Henry said, "I hope the rest of the portages aren't that tough!" He must not have been listening to Fred's description of this being our easiest portage.

I looked across the bay and saw what appeared to be a small store and a single billboard with the word FITGERS written in large bold letters.

"What the heck is *Fitgers*?" Tom asked.

Fred heard Tom's question and said with a smile, "Tom, this will be the last sign we will see, and Fitgers is a regional beer, which is sold at the little trading post across the way." He added, "Some people think it means 'hello' in Canadian."

We all laughed, and I thought of all the clever ways to use that information when I got home.

"Fellas, I don't want to hear you hollering Fitgers at all the folks we meet," Mr. Greenlee said. He pointed to his lips and said, "And this is not a smile!"

Chapter 8

LOST TREASURE

The rest of the crew started to arrive from our first portage a few minutes behind Tom. I kept all our crew's gear together near our canoes.
When Fred and Mr. Greenlee arrived, they seemed quite pleased that
the first portage had gone so well and that the canoes and gear were
together in one area.

Fred had us call off the gear to make sure all of it had made it over
the portage.

"Guys, if you leave a pack, tent, or even a paddle behind at a campsite or following a portage, we would have to backtrack and would lose
valuable time," Fred said. "I'm proud of you guys and am sure you will
be a fast crew on the much more challenging portages ahead."

Dave asked, "Will there be lots of sandy beaches like this where we
were going?"

Fred chuckled and said, "Guys, this was the easiest portage we will
have on this trip. Most of them will be rocky, muddy, and longer. The
only other sand beach you see will be where we might camp tonight."

"Fred and I are going up to the Customs Station to do some paperwork," said Mr. Greenlee. "Louis, would you please come with us?"

"Sure," I answered.

As we left the beach area, I turned and looked back. Fred had left Smitty in charge of watching the gear and keeping the crew together. However, I was concerned about why I was being singled out.

When we were out of earshot, Mr. Greenlee turned to me and said, "Fred and I have discussed the two jobs left to fill. Gary is the permanent cook, and the only jobs not yet filled are quartermaster and crew chief. We have decided that we would like you to be our crew chief."

As we walked up the incline to the Ranger Station, Mr. Greenlee continued, "Fred and I have been watching all the crew members. We both agree you have displayed the best attitude and leadership skills. I'm very proud of you, Louis! Does it sound like a plan?"

I was shocked and proud at the same time. I did not know what else to say to this but managed to get out, "Sure thing!"

I looked down the hill at the crew, and a twinge of worry crossed my mind as I remembered Joe's mother had expressed how she had hoped Joe would get to be the crew chief.

"We still have the quartermaster slot to fill," added Fred, "and by tomorrow morning, I am sure you will have figured out who that should be."

My mind was swirling with thoughts of my new responsibility as we walked up to the Canadian Customs Cabin. There we were met by Vic, the Customs official. He greeted Fred with an outstretched hand. As they shook hands, I judged him to be about 30 years old. He was short, with sandy-blond hair. He seemed to know Fred very well and greeted Mr. Greenlee and me, saying, "Welcome to Canada!"

Vic and Fred filled out some paperwork for a tour permit, and Fred also wrote down a plan A and a shorter plan B for our trip. I overheard Fred say he was sure plan B would not be necessary since the crew was already moving more quickly than expected. I wasn't sure I was supposed to hear, but it made me determined to live up to Fred's expectations.

"Fred, the North Bay bears are still causing trouble," cautioned Vic.

"We will not be traveling through North Bay," Fred replied, "but I will warn any other groups we see."

Bears? What's this about problem bears? I recalled reading a scary article in Field and Stream *about a bear attack in Alaska.*

When we got back to the canoes, only Dave was there, watching our gear. Fred asked where the rest of our guys were. Dave pointed to the east side of the beach and said, "All the guys are over with that other crew looking for beads."

"Ron must have gotten on the water before us," said Fred. And sure enough, we spotted their gear stowed neatly over to the right near some trees.

"Two years ago, Ron found some trade beads in a washout over there and always comes early to look for trade beads before they get picked over," Fred continued. "I'll keep an eye on the gear while y'all go over to the site for no more than fifteen minutes."

I was anxious to get back on the water, but Fred also said, "We are a little ahead of schedule, and Ron will probably tell you more about the fur trade."

As we walked up to the site, Ron displayed the trade beads and told our guys about them. He had a Southern accent, different from Fred's.

"Because this was a frequent trading spot for Indians and voyageurs, there were lots of beads spilled during the process of unloading and preparing the trade goods," Ron said. "Hundreds of years later, we find that it's a good time to find more that have been uncovered after heavy rain. Last week we had a real gully washer."

I thought he must be a good storyteller because his descriptions were fascinating.

Since no one was going through Customs, Vic came over to the site and said, "When Ron first found beads, I told him the voyageurs traded with Indians on this very site. Sometimes trade goods and especially beads were spilled in the grassy area above the beach. They would likely have never been recovered."

I tried to imagine the sight of short voyageurs and Indians trading. Then I walked a short distance away from everyone. I figured it would be hard to find much with all this going on. As I looked down at the coarse sand and gravel, I spotted something blue, so I bent down to look closer and found my first bead. It was small. However, I was very excited. I sat down and started to run my fingers through the sand. As I dug, I found four larger beads with larger holes and irregular shapes. I also cut myself on a sharp piece of black glass.

The cut wasn't bad and did not bleed much. I picked up the black piece of glass and wondered if it was really glass. I held it up to the sun. It was so dense I could not see through it.

I took it over to Ron, who seemed to be an expert on such things. He looked at the beads and said, "You have some superb specimens." He also looked at the glass I showed him and said, "This is obsidian and probably a flake from when someone made an arrowhead or blade of some sort. Obsidian was traded with faraway tribes. This piece could have come from as far west as Wyoming or as far south as Mexico."

I couldn't believe I had found such treasure, trade beads from the voyageurs, and a piece of obsidian from faraway Indian tribes! I went back to my place and looked for more beads but didn't find any. I found a piece of flint considerably larger than the obsidian. It appeared to be an arrowhead that had broken.

Fred came over to look at my discovery and said, "Why don't you put your beads on a string to keep from losing them?"

He gave me a length of thin round black leather. He said it was left over from some cord he purchased in town after buying his voyageur cross. I noticed he wore his cross around his neck. I put the cord in my pocket and decided to do the same thing with the cross I had purchased for Mom, and I would put the beads on either side of it.

When we walked over to the rest of our crew, Fred said he had read a good deal about the canoe country's history in the staff library back at the Base.

"You appear to appreciate this country, and I can suggest some books if you would like. I am sure you can find most in your library back home," he said.

"Yes!" I said. I was excited and wanted to know more.

"Any of the books by Sigurd F. Olson would be an excellent place to start," Fred said, "and I have one of them called *Listening Point* in my pack if you would like to read a little."

I couldn't wait to see it. Fred suggested some evening, when everything was done, I could read a few chapters to see if it was of interest.

Fred and I moved closer to the crew, and Fred told me we had better get going. I yelled, "Okay, guys, saddle up, and let's get those canoes loaded!" We all took a few moments to say goodbye to our new friends in Ron's crew.

Ron looked at me and gave a thumbs up. None of the guys had found as many beads as I had found. I gave Ron the first blue bead since it wouldn't fit on the leather thong.

"Don't you want this one?" he asked.

"I have a plan for my four biggest beads but not this smaller one," I said. "I appreciate your helping me find all these cool treasures, and I want you to have this one. It's so different from the others."

He took it and then gave me four matching beads and said, "I've got a lot of these. I'll be pleased to keep yours, and you add these to your collection."

We all walked back up the beach to our canoes, moved them to the water, and started to load our gear. As we were about to shove off, Fred asked me to call out the gear, and I did with a bit of help from Tom. I got all the packs right but couldn't think what was next when Tom whispered, "Don't forget the tents."

Fred chimed in: "Louis, from now on, it's your job to see our gear stays with this crew until you select a quartermaster."

We headed out and away from the shore, and I took a look at my map to see if I could see where we were. I found Prairie Portage and could see we would soon be coming to a large bay called Bailey Bay. I could see by the map it was connected to many other bays, and I saw the North Bay Vic had mentioned. I was glad we weren't going to go there. I wanted to see a bear, but I didn't want it to be a problem bear.

About halfway across the smaller bay, I looked back at Prairie Portage. I could see the Canadian Customs sign and the orderly buildings there. I kept trying to imagine the big voyageur canoes turned upside down on the beach, the piles of trade goods, and the voyageurs over near where I had found my beads. I imagined an old Indian working on an arrowhead and the frustrated look he must have had when he broke the part below the notch and then threw it away.

Maybe it was time for him to join the rest of his tribe and use the traders' metal ones. Perhaps it was time for a gun. Trading must have been exciting for everyone!

"Louis, where the heck are you going?" yelled Dave.

I was about to ram Mr. Greenlee's canoe! With a hard sweep stroke, I managed to miss it.

"Keep your eyes on the road," said Mr. Greenlee, laughing out loud.

"Sorry, guys, it won't happen again," I said, coming back to the present and smiling. Still, I was a little bit embarrassed.

Chapter 9

PORTAGES

After our near mishap with Mr. Greenlee's canoe after Prairie Portage, we continued through the first small bay on our way to Bailey Bay. It appeared more extensive than the lake on the other side of the portage.

Fred was ahead of us, and I watched how easy and smooth he made his paddle strokes. His canoe moved in a straight line, and his J-stroke was more of a slip stroke. I wondered how he did it and decided to watch carefully and ask him about it when we got to our next portage. He looked so cool. I was also going to ask him how he got to be a guide. I had already decided being a guide was definitely what I would do when I was old enough.

Both Tom and I were paying close attention to our maps, and Tom said, "There is a large island ahead before we get to that huge bay."

Before we left the shelter of the island, Fred slowed and waited for us to gather together.

"Bailey Bay can be pretty windy," he said, "and the waves are frequently huge. Sometimes we get large swells, especially in the afternoon. It's only about eleven a.m., and it may not be too windy yet. If it is windy, I want everyone to stay together. I will head into the waves at a slight angle. Y'all do the same thing. The most important thing I want you to remember is, don't get caught sideways in big waves."

Fred and Joe padded hard to get well ahead of the rest of us. After a few minutes, they slowed, and Fred told us we were fortunate that the wind would not be much of a challenge, saying, "If the wind had been worse, I would have had us put on the life jackets."

As Bailey Bay came into full view, I could see why he cautioned us. The bay was enormous, and although the wind was not yet particularly strong, whitecaps were beginning to form. It looked like we would be lucky and get by Bailey Bay without much dangerous wave action.

"What would constitute a situation where we would have to wear our life preservers?" Chuck asked.

"We are a long way from needing them," said Fred. "If I had seen unsafe high waves, I would have declared us windbound, and we would have waited back on the island until evening to cross the bay when the waves were safe for a crew with our level of skill."

It was undoubtedly choppier and more difficult to paddle. Still, I imagined what a higher wind and waves would be like. We stayed to the right along the side of the bay and came to a smaller bay. From there, I could see a place ahead which looked like it might be another portage. Fred headed that way, so I must have been right. I looked at my map and noticed this portage was called North Portage.

Tom was still paddling bow since waves and wind would not be a good situation for our most inexperienced paddler. Dave had responded well to our decision and said, "I hope I can paddle when we get to Sunday Lake."

"Dave, count on it," I said. "Tom, would you paddle stern when we get to Sunday Lake?"

"Louis, why don't you continue until we stop for lunch? You did a great job of coaching me," Tom answered.

We found another easy landing when we got to the next portage, although the bottom was muddier than the last. I was looking at the map and could easily see this would be a long portage.

Before I did the math to convert rods to yards, Fred said, "I am going to start across first." He added, "Louis, would you and your team come next and remind everyone to load and unload the canoes while standing in the water?" I told him we would.

"About halfway across the portage," he continued, "you will see some canoe rests where you can lean the bow of your canoe and get it off of your shoulders for a few minutes. You pack carriers must stay close to your canoe carrier to inform him when a canoe rest is ahead and help him if necessary."

I watched Fred send Joe on ahead with the Kettle Pack and paddles. Then he slipped his personal pack on before he flipped his canoe with ease. I hadn't noticed he carried a smaller A-2 pack with the canoe.

Well, of course, the wood canoe was probably lighter than the metal ones we carried.

When it hit his shoulders, I could hear the water splash on the ground with a whoosh as what little water that had collected from his wet boots rushed out. I was sure I could be that smooth with a bit of practice. Fred trotted to catch up with Joe, and they both disappeared on the trail where it became more wooded.

"Louis," said Mr. Greenlee, "you and your team go on next, and we will bring up the rear."

Everyone was looking at me as I faced the second flip of the trip. I took a breath and tried to do it just like Fred. The flip went all right until I got it to my shoulders, and then the canoe went forward, and the bow lightly thumped on the shoreline. It produced a loud bang inside the canoe. I pushed up on the gunwales and got it balanced, and Mr. Greenlee said, "Pretty good, Louis. You're getting the hang of it."

Dave was waiting up ahead, and Tom was behind me as we started up the trail. Tom had the food pack, which he said weighed a ton, and we were on our way with Dave falling in, right behind me, carrying the larger A-4 personal pack and the tent.

I asked who had the paddles.

"Stop worrying," said Tom. "I have them."

"How long is this portage?" asked Dave.

I noticed Fred didn't mention the length. I had looked at the map and knew it was at least a half mile in length.

Dave was the youngest of the crew and smaller, so I said, "Oh, it's longer than the last one, but it's not bad."

It was relatively easy walking as boots and moccasins had worn the trail for centuries. I began to wonder about these rocky and rugged portages Mr. Greenlee had referred to. As I walked along, I noticed a cloud of mosquitoes. They were stirred up, and they seemed to be attracted to my ears. The buzzing was irritating.

Tom was griping about them and kept brushing them away. I knew he was getting tired when he asked, "Where are these rest stops Fred mentioned?"

My shoulders were starting to hurt, and I found if I adjusted the canoe forward or back, it helped. I was also wondering about the rest. It seemed like we had gone a long way when Tom said, "There's a canoe rest. Do you want to stop?"

To ease the ache in my shoulders, I said, "Yes."

Tom guided me to the rest, a sturdy pole tied about eight feet above the ground between two trees. When I got into position, he helped me place the canoe's front tip on the well-worn horizontal pole, and I was able to step out from under it. It felt incredible as I stretched my sore muscles. Tom sat on the ground with a thud. He had not removed the food pack. He wiped the sweat from his face and groaned, "Wow, this food pack is heavy!"

Dave sat down next to him but took off the larger-sized pack and the tent he had balanced on top of it.

I looked at the canoe rest and spent a few minutes studying how it was made. I saw that someone had lashed a three-inch diameter pole between the trees. It looked like a Scout lashing project. I was glad it was there as I rubbed my sore shoulders.

"This portaging is a lot harder than I thought," said Tom.

I had the feeling there were going to be rougher portages ahead.

After a short rest, we heard the next canoe banging on trees some-where on the trail behind us. I heard Cliff yell, "Is this the right way?"

Tom tried to get up but fell over on his back from the awkward weight of his pack. Dave and I had to help him get back up.

Tom must have noticed that Dave's A-4 pack was the largest of all the personal packs with four people's gear in it.

"Dave," he said, "let me take the tent for a while. I'm getting accus-tomed to the weight of the food pack."

With no argument from Dave, Tom grabbed the tent and put it on top of his food pack.

I whispered to Tom, "You're a champ, and I look forward to seeing our best lineman in action this fall." I got under the yoke, lifted the canoe off of the rest, and we were again on our way as Dave yelled to the team behind us, "A canoe rest is just ahead!"

After another long but thankfully easy walk, Tom called out, "I can see the water. Next lake is just ahead!"

I was relieved since my shoulders were burning, and I was exhausted.

Fred and Joe crossed more quickly, and by the time we got to the lake, they had already loaded the Seliga, and Joe was holding it away from some rocks. Fred asked how we were doing, and, of course, I said, "Excellent."

I was nervous about flipping my canoe since I was so tired. But as I walked out into the water, Fred was there to talk me through it. It went better this time, and I hardly made a splash as I placed it into the water. Fred said, "Excellent indeed."

I had almost forgotten that I wanted to ask Fred about the modified J-stroke I had observed. When I referred to it as a slip stroke, Fred said, "Bingo! That's what most of us guides call it. We could call it an incomplete J-stroke or a partial J-stroke. Anyway, I have noticed you are already using it without realizing it. You will find it eventually becomes your most used stroke."

Fred suggested we take a short break and then go back to help others get across the portage. He said he would stay and assist the rest of the canoe carriers in getting their canoes into the water. Before we went back to help, we loaded our canoe, and Joe held both his and our canoe while standing in the water between them.

Tom, Dave, and I started back across the portage to help the other guys. Fred had told us not to carry their loads but just to encourage them. We did and found the others were not as happy with the experience as we were. They were, however, glad to learn the portage was coming to an end. When we had seen and encouraged everyone, we jogged back to the water, and Fred told us to paddle out a short distance and wait while everyone got their canoes loaded.

About 50 yards from shore, Fred said, "Welcome to Sunday Lake!"

We hadn't gone much farther when we heard Gary, from Mr. Greenlee's canoe, yell, "Shoot, I dropped my cup!"

Fred said for everyone to come up close, and he would show us how to get a drink without a cup. He also told Gary he would fix him up with a cup in camp that night.

Fred had us gather near his canoe and said, "Guys, by bringing our paddle up above our heads with the lower edge of the blade to our mouths, we can get a good drink from the water on our paddle." Some of it ran down the front of our shirts, but it worked.

"Does the water needed to be purified?" asked Tom.

"Don't drink the water up close to shore," Fred replied. "However, out twenty or thirty yards or so, it's fine. Now use your head and never drink the water in a beaver stream or where one enters a lake. If you see a dead animal floating in the water, avoid getting water for any purpose near it."

With Dave paddling bow, we were on our way. Mr. Greenlee asked Fred about lunch. Fred pointed and said, "Toward the center of the lake and on the right is a nice campsite on a point where we can eat without blocking either of the portages if other travelers come from either direction."

Dave had a pretty strong power stroke, and I said, "You have a powerful stroke! Be sure you remember to keep your lower arm straight and feather your paddle."

It wasn't long before I could tell he was also much stronger paddling on his right side as each stroke sent little whirlpools back as far as the stern. Dave asked to switch sides twice before we reached the island, where we stopped for lunch.

Fred asked to have the canvas bucket we had packed on the top of a food pack filled with water away from shore before we stopped so the water was clean. It was a good, soft, mostly sandy landing where we could pull the canoes up without being unloaded except for the food pack with the lunch supplies.

We found a big flat rock with a view where we could sit together. As we sat waiting to eat, everyone had their version of the portage trail to tell. I had observed Tom and knew he had struggled with the food pack. However, I loved his description when he said, "I thought the portage was a breeze. I hope there will be some of those muddy ones we heard described. After this trip, I won't even need football practice."

"I'm proud to be in the middle of this beautiful lake, but I must admit I felt like I wanted to bail out of this trip on that last portage," Henry said. "But here we are, and I'm looking forward to proving that I can do things I never dreamed of doing."

Before we ate our lunch, we all said the Wilderness Grace together. Some guys didn't seem too enthusiastic about thanking God for the portage trails, and what the heck is *raiment*?

Mr. Greenlee heard the comments about the grace and asked us, "Fellas, who can tell me what 'raiment' means?"

Tom asked, "Does it have to do with rain gear?"

Henry raised his hand before Mr. Greenlee could respond.

"It's an old-fashioned word meaning clothing, garments, or apparel," said Henry. "I guess it could include rain gear worn over one's clothing."

"That is as good a definition as I have ever heard," said Mr. Greenlee. "Now let's discuss portage trails. What is the purpose of a portage?"

"The French define it as carrying place," said Fred.

"It also means the act of carrying canoes, boats, and gear or trade goods overland between waterways or to avoid the danger of rapids or a waterfall," added Chuck.

Mr. Greenlee continued, "Our fellow Scouts who go to the Philmont Scout Ranch pray,

For food, for raiment,
For life, for opportunity,
For friendship and fellowship,
We thank thee, O Lord.[1]

"Up north, we add, sun, rain, water and portage trails:

For food, for raiment,
For life and opportunity,
For sun and rain,
For water and portage trails,
For friendship and fellowship,
We thank thee, O Lord.[2]

"Up here, we travel on water, and the portage does two things: it connects those waters, and it gets us around trouble or danger," he added. "You will appreciate the portages on the Falls Chain."

That's when Henry said, "Let's eat. I'm good with portages, and raiment is a cool word. But right now, I'm hungry!"

---

1. Traditional grace used by Sommers crews.
2. Ibid.

We had already assigned cooks for the day, and Gary was the head cook for the trip. Fred worked on this lunch with Gary and was explaining every detail. I watched them measure punch mix into the bucket. Fred called it "Red-Eye" and added, "But it's not always red."

Everyone got a peanut butter and jelly sandwich. Gary and his crew used their hunting knives to spread the peanut butter. We had squeezed the bread down thin, and it was sometimes challenging to pull apart without ripping. I guess it still had the same amount of bread in each slice, even though it was flatter than a pancake. We also got a few pieces of Hol-Ry crackers with a little slice of salami and some cheese.

As we finished our lunch, Mike asked, "Fred, how long are the next couple of portages?"

Fred got his map out and showed us where we were and where we were going. After doing the math to convert rods to yards, we realized we had a three-quarter mile portage followed by a half-mile portage ahead of us. From there it would be a short distance to our campsite. Fred said we would stop at Louisa Falls and perhaps camp there.

We packed up and got back on the water. The lunch break made us all feel better, and it seemed to me everyone was paddling better. Dave continued paddling bow, and he was pretty good. Tom took over the stern, and I sat in the middle.

Sunday was a lovely lake, and Fred said, "Next time you come this way, remember, the fishing is always good here on Sunday Lake."

It didn't seem like more than a half hour before we approached the next of the Meadows portages.

"This one, though longer," said Fred, "is easy walking like the last one."

As we prepared to portage, I was pleased to find I could flip the canoe without a problem.

"You did that perfectly, Louis," said Tom.

Both my canoe partners put their packs on like pros. Tom had the paddles, and Dave had the tent on top of the A-4 pack.

This time, I had better control of the canoe's position and enjoyed the sights as I walked along this trail. Toward the end, I felt like I should make a quick rest stop so I would be better prepared to flip the canoe down at the next lake. I was sure I could make the next one without rest. The biggest problem I had was the pain in my shoulders and neck. I was learning to keep adjusting the canoe to keep it from hurting so much.

This portage was long but uneventful. My biggest challenge was dealing with the pain in my neck from the yoke. However, it was so much better than the first two portages.

Tom announced the lake was in view, and Dave was as relieved as I was. After putting our canoe in the water and loading it, we again left it with Joe as Fred prepared to assist with the other two canoe teams.

Again, we walked back and encouraged the others who were not far behind. Some of the guys complained about the portage's length but were pretty proud as they reached the end. I called out the gear, Fred smiled, and we were on our way to the last portage.

Meadows Lake was tiny and didn't give us much of a rest from portaging. The landing was smooth but muddy. Tom and Dave told me they wanted to make this portage with no rest, though we had already portaged over a mile today.

We started across, and I thought I might be able to catch up with Fred. I walked as fast as I could, and halfway across, I wanted to rest. Tom paused at about that same time, looked back at me, and said, "Come on, Louis, you can do this!"

Dave must have looked exhausted, too, for he added, "Dave, you may be younger than we are, but you are strong like your dad."

As we picked up the pace to the end of the longest portages of perhaps the whole trip, nothing more was said.

When we saw the sparkling water through the trees at the end of the portage, we were excited and proud. Fred and Joe acted like they had been waiting for a long time. Then Fred said, "You fellas almost caught up to me. Are y'all up to helping again?" We were tired, but after we loaded the gear, we went back.

As we walked back along the trail, I figured that you end up with more energy when you accomplish a challenging task . . . like crossing the portage without a rest. It certainly seemed to be the case up here in this North Country anyway. I felt Fred's compliments helped too. I told Dave and Tom of my theory and suggested we congratulate the other guys on how well they were doing when we saw them.

Although all the rest of the guys looked tired, our compliments and encouragement seemed to help. Tom said, "We are starting to sound like my football coach!"

We were all pretty happy when everyone was across. Fred acknowledged our accomplishment, saying, "You have now completed the three longest portages on this trip. Others will be tougher or harder walking, but these three were the longest."

Everyone was happy with that news. I reminded Chuck to call off the gear, and we were on our way.

Agnes was as beautiful as I had expected. Dave must have felt the same way, saying, "We have been singing about this lake, and now we are here!"

Tom was still paddling stern, and Dave was our bowman. We were now in Lower Agnes, and the wind had come up a bit. Fortunately, it was coming from behind us, and with its gentle push, it made paddling much easier.

We moved up the lake with noticeably increased speed. It wasn't long before we slowed as Fred pointed to the right and said, "Louisa Falls."

Chapter 10

FIRST CAMP

As we paddled away from the portage and entered the lower end of Agnes Lake, I looked ahead and to my right. I could see a large waterfall off in the distance. I looked at my map and saw the words Louisa Falls, and Fred led us in that direction.

"That's Louisa Falls," he said, pointing as we got closer. "And it looks like the campsite on the left side of the falls is empty. We'll camp there for the night."

As we came closer to the waterfall, we could hear the roar it made as the water from Lake Louisa fell 40 or 50 yards into Lake Agnes. Fred asked to have the canvas bucket filled with fresh water while we were well away from shore. It was a narrow waterfall about 15 feet wide. We pulled up to the landing area. I was happy to see the smooth sand and pebble beach-like area rather than rocks and boulders.

Fred walked up into the campsite to look it over while Joe held his canoe. The rest of us stood by our canoes and waited for them to tell us if it would be suitable. As I watched them inspect the campsite, it reminded me of my dad and mom. They always looked at motel rooms before we rented one on family vacations. I watched him walk around the campsite and then disappear behind some trees and brush.

In a few moments, he came back into view and called for Mr. Greenlee to come up.

Then he said, "Louis, you come, too. The rest of you stay there a minute."

I followed Mr. Greenlee up the slight rise and into the campsite. As we came close, Fred said, "We have a decision to make."

He did not look happy as he walked us back to where he had just come from and pointed out some garbage strewn around. It consisted of some crushed cans, ripped-up paper, and some torn cloth sacks.

"A bear raided the last group camping here," he said.

I looked around and saw the large tracks in the moist earth. I had seen bears in zoos, but to see paw prints in the wild and know the bear might be back in the trees watching us was a scary thought.

After we had looked around, Fred said, "This happened yesterday or maybe this morning. It looks like they were a tourist group because these are not our Base's supplies. We could camp here and likely receive a visit from a bear tonight, or we can camp across the lake and come back over to swim after we get set up. Another option would be to swim in the falls now and then cross the lake to an excellent campsite I had planned on using if this one was taken. The only catch is other groups will be heading for campsites, too, and we may not get the closer one across the lake. There are lots of other campsites, but it would take a while to get to them."

Fred and Mr. Greenlee both looked at me. Mr. Greenlee asked, "Louis, what do you think?"

What do I think? Hey, this is serious stuff. There is a bear around here, and they want my opinion?

I stammered a little and said, "I think the guys would appreciate a swim here at the falls, and then we could head over to the campsite. I think some guys might not want to paddle back over here if we go to our campsite. They are pretty tired."

"I agree," said Fred. "Dell?"

That was the first time on this trip I had heard Mr. Greenlee's first name used. He often suggested other adults use it. Mr. Greenlee agreed and asked me to explain our plan to the crew.

This is weird. A few days ago, I didn't want to go on this trip, and now I have adults asking my opinion and then asking me to explain the decision to the rest of the guys.

I noticed the crew looking around with anxious looks on their faces when we went back to them and our gear. I think they had seen Fred when he saw the bear sign and may have already figured there was a problem. I told them the whole story and our plan. They all swallowed and nodded in unison. They looked frightened.

"Are there a lot of bear raids?" asked Tom.

Fred told him there had recently been a lot of trouble with "tourist bears" that weren't afraid of people in the Basswood Lake area, especially in North Bay. I remembered Vic had mentioned North Bay.

"The best protection against bears is a clean campsite," Fred said. "Remember, this is a wilderness area, and there are lots of bears, wolves, moose, and other potentially dangerous critters. I have seldom had visits from bears in a camp. Usually, they are easy to scare off because they are wild and don't want to be around us except for our food."

"Wolves?" asked Tom.

"I know there are wolves," Fred replied, "but I have never seen one. I've heard a few reports of sightings from other guides, and we occasionally listen to them at night, but it is very unusual."

I noticed some guys were looking even more upset than before and figured we didn't need to dwell on bears and wolves anymore. I asked Fred where we should "park" the canoes while we swam. Everyone laughed, and Fred suggested we unload and leave them and the gear there at the campsite.

"Since we have food packs, should we split up into two groups and stand bear watch just in case?" asked Tom.

"You guys are good," said Fred. "Excellent idea, Tom."

Tom volunteered to take the first watch. Several others agreed to stay while the first group went up to the falls.

I thought, *Wow, Tom actually volunteered to work before play. What's happening to us?*

I went with Fred and the first group. Mr. Greenlee stayed with those on the first watch.

On the way to the falls, Fred said, "You guys are lucky to have Mr. Greenlee as a leader." I agreed and started to think we needed to get some kind of gift for him to say thanks.

Louisa Falls was impressive! There was a natural bathtub about halfway up, and it was big enough for six or eight people all at one time. The guys had already started to undress when Dave said, "We need to get our suits, don't we?"

"Dave, this is *wilderness*," said Henry. "There won't be anyone to see us. We can just skinny-dip." He looked at Fred. "Can't we?"

"You're right about the wilderness," Fred replied, "but there is a portage trail on the other side of the falls, and you can't hear anyone coming with the noise from the falls. Let's wear our swimming trunks."

We were undressed and in the falls within a minute. While we took our turn guarding the gear, I asked Fred where the other campsite was. He pointed across the lake and said it was up the shore a short distance on the left. He told me it had a sand beach and that wide sandy beaches were very uncommon in this rocky country.

"There is another good sandy beach on Sturgeon Lake. I like to camp there because you sometimes find arrowheads and flint chips from the Indians who once camped there. They often made their villages by the sand beaches because it was easier on their birchbark canoes."

I showed him my broken arrowhead and asked him if he would tell the whole crew about the Indians of the area after dinner, and he said he would if I asked him. He suggested maybe we could have a campfire before turning in.

I thought about what Mr. Greenlee had taught us back home: "Scouts always leave a place better than they find it."

I got the other guys and went back to the raid area to clean up the trash caused by the bear raid on the campers who had been there before. It didn't take long to clean the site, and we took what we had collected down by the canoes, then went back and walked around the campsite to see if we had missed anything.

Back in the woods, I saw a pack with several rips in the front. Whoever owned it had left in a hurry leaving their new A-3 Duluth Pack behind. There were a few items in it, and before I looked into it, I took it down to Fred. We opened it and found a new three-quarter Plumb axe, a folding saw, some eating utensils, and many dirty clothes.

"Well, well," said Fred, "here is a cup for Gary. Now what can this pack and gear tell us?"

"They were on their way in from their trip," I said, "and they were adults judging from the size of the socks." I opened the sheath on the axe and said, "This wasn't a Scout group either, because the edge of this axe looks like they were chopping rocks."

Just then, Mr. Greenlee and the guys walked back into camp. Mr. Greenlee smiled when he noticed the garbage gathered and piled near the canoes.

"I see we've done our good turn for the day," he said.

Fred chimed in. "Louis and the guys cleaned up after the bear. They also found a pack with some gear left behind by some folks who must have been in a big hurry to leave."

Mr. Greenlee said, "I guess I don't need to give my speech about leaving things cleaner than you found them," and Fred said, "I think these guys have learned the concept very well."

I got the giddy feeling again, and I think I caught Mr. Greenlee wink at Fred. I took it to mean they had been waiting to see if we would clean up the mess. I think our folks might be surprised and proud of this strange behavior. It wasn't just me either. We were all being more courteous and, well, thoughtful.

"We have something to discuss before we head over to the camp-site," said Mr. Greenlee. "What do we do with the garbage, and what do we do with the extra gear?"

"The paper will burn along with the scraps of food," said Fred. "The cans will be packed out with the rest of our cans, all of which we will take back to Base."

"I think the ripped pack should belong to Louis since he found it along with the gear," said Tom. To which I responded, "I'm concerned the owners might come back, and I would like to see if we could get it to them."

Fred weighed in, saying, "Judging from the dirty clothes, they were on their way back in from their trip." He said we would check with Vic on our way back in, and if someone hadn't reported it lost, it would become mine.

We loaded up and paddled over to our new campsite on the other side of Lower Agnes. Fred, Mr. Greenlee, and I walked up to the campsite, 10 or 12 feet higher than the sandy beach. We looked over the site and found no problems or any signs of bears. Fred told me to start getting our gear out of the canoes and up into the campsite. The guys were exhausted and more than happy to get to camp since we had taken three tough portages, swam in the falls, and cleaned a campsite.

Fred came over and asked me to have the food pack and tents set out.

"Keep the guys in close so I can give some training on how to set up our first camp," he said.

I remembered the canoes were to be placed well out of the water and upside down. It didn't take long to get everything in line and to gather the guys for Fred's instructions.

Fred and Mr. Greenlee went back into the woods while we were unloading and walked back into camp as we finished unloading the canoes. I think they had been talking about how the trip was going and how we were functioning as a team.

"Let's all gather around here so I can go over a few things about set-ting up camp," said Fred. "First, I want you all to know y'all did great on your first day. I am sure we are going to have a terrific trip. Some basics will help you have a better experience, and the first one is first things first! By that, I mean before we fish, swim, or anything else, we always set up camp, and everyone helps. Today we swam first because of the circumstances back at the falls. That won't usually be the case. This campsite has an excellent beach for swimming and washing, so let's get moving so you can enjoy it.

"You all have jobs for the first day listed on the chart you filled out," he continued. "Suppose everyone does their job quickly and efficiently . . . in that case, the camp will be set up correctly, and we will have plenty of time for relaxing fun.

"Firemen, get out and gather plenty of driftwood and deadwood from downed trees for tonight and tomorrow morning. The last group left the wood you see stacked by the fireplace, and we will always leave the next group enough firewood for their first meal. It's simple trail courtesy."

The fireplace was made out of rocks carefully stacked and balanced in a squared-up semicircle about two-and-a-half-feet high. It was smoke-blackened on the inside and built on a rock slab so there was no danger of a fire spreading. The fireplace's interior was clean and damp from when the previous fire had been put out, probably a few days ago when there had been heavy rains.

Gary had been chosen to cook for the whole trip. As the guys ro-tated through the schedule, they would all get a chance to assist with cooking. According to Fred, "The Base staff and guides have written an excellent cookbook just for Sommers. It was designed around the particular food we have with us. We can change the menu around based on the weather and our luck at fishing. Part of the first day's duties for the cooks is to plan our menu for each day of the trip, using the mimeographed menu planning sheets."

Obviously, we had lots of options and lots of great-sounding meals from which to choose.

I asked Fred what I should be doing, and he said, "Louis, you have been doing great in encouraging the guys, and I am tempted to answer you by saying keep up the good work. However, you have responsibilities, including several meetings with Mr. Greenlee and me each day to discuss the trip's progress and process. We will also discuss any problems and make sure we all get what we should from the journey. You should work with the different task groups so you become familiar with the whole process. By the third day, Mr. Greenlee and I should be like excess baggage in the advisor's role. Remember, you can call on me anytime, and I am sure it is true for Mr. Greenlee too."

I asked if there was anything I could be doing better, and he said, "You are ahead of the curve at this point. I'll let you know when and how you can improve."

I think I understood what he meant. Mr. Greenlee said he was impressed with the crew that day, and we both agreed.

I told them I had given the quartermaster job some thought.

"Chuck is the most organized person I have ever known," I said, "and I would like to appoint him to be our quartermaster to keep track of the gear and to call out the equipment before leaving camps and after portages."

Mr. Greenlee agreed, saying, "Louis, you are correct. I don't believe I have ever had a more organized Scout in this troop."

Fred showed his agreement with a thumbs up.

Fred then asked me if I had been up here before because I seemed very much at ease, and I told him I had never been to northern Minnesota. I told him I felt very much "at home" for some reason, adding that I would like to discuss working here when I'm old enough.

Fred looked at me and nodded. I thought I saw a hint of a smile when he said, "I'll explain the process of applying to work at the Base and introduce you to Mr. Hanson when we get back, if you still feel that way. We will have lots of time to talk during the rest of the trip."

I felt good about our brief chat and headed off to find Chuck and help Gary with the menu planning. On the way, I stopped by the dishwashers. Mr. Greenlee was going over the pots and pans' soaping procedure. He was telling the dishwashers that soaping the outside of the cookpots would make cleaning them much easier. The most important thing to remember, he said, was never getting soap on the inside of the pot, or we would all get "the trots." We had soaped pots on our troop outings, too, so this wasn't new. But being out in the wilderness made it seem much more significant.

I saw Chuck and motioned him to join me. I knew Chuck was organized, but I always believed he was intuitive, for he frequently anticipated needs. Before I had the chance to say the words, he said, "Yes, I would be glad to be the quartermaster. I wondered why that slot was left open. Consider it filled unless I have misread your actions."

I had recruited a quartermaster without actually saying the words!

"Chuck," I said, "do I need to go over the responsibilities with you?"

"Nope. I've got this and will not let you down, Louis. Thank you!" he said.

I smiled to myself and moved on to the menu planning.

I went over to where Gary was huddled in conversation with his assistants. By the time I got there, they were nearly finished with the menu planning for each day of the trip. Gary had been reading the cookbook while he was the middleman in the canoe and not paddling all morning so that he would be ahead of the game. He had me look at it, and it looked fantastic. I grinned and told them they were doing a great job, hoping to make them feel as good as I had felt when Fred or Mr. Greenlee complimented me on my actions.

Gary asked how the soaping was coming when Henry arrived with the first of the soaped pots. He told Gary they had been careful not to get any soap in them, and they should be careful to do the same.

"Nobody wants to get the trots out here in the boonies, ya know," he said.

Gary and the guys laughed and asked me who was supposed to get the water. I remembered the guys with the water bucket had filled it back at the falls with the understanding we would camp there. I became concerned we might have left the bucket back at the other campsite since I didn't recall checking to see if we loaded it. I felt panicky about making a mistake since it was my job to verify we had all of our gear up to a few minutes ago.

Chuck pulled the bucket from behind him and said, "Are we looking for this?"

It was full of water.

I asked how it had gotten here, and he said, "It was my responsibility all along, wasn't it?" I felt kind of silly and relieved at the same time.

I left the group and found Fred just about to send the firemen out to take care of another chore, which was their responsibility. I heard him tell them, "The digging of the latrine is a critical and important task. It needs to be back in the woods about a hundred fifty yards and definitely not near the water. And, since we will only be here for a day, it doesn't need to be very large. So come back to the campsite and get me when you are finished. And don't build any fancy seats."

Fred and I came back to the center of the campsite, which, according to Fred, was very level compared to most.

"Next," Fred said, "I'll show everyone how we will set up the tents, and we need to get everyone together to hear this."

After I had brought everyone together, Fred explained the process for setting up the tents.

"Usually," he said, "the ground is pretty rough and rocky. The tent locations or sites are normally pretty obvious since they are the only flat areas around. Here on this campsite, there are lots of tent sites where there is reasonably flat ground. We always need to check to see that no branches or dead trees could fall on a tent. Always look up before you set up your tent. Spend a little time imagining the tent site in a heavy rainstorm. Will the tent site drain, or is it in a low spot?"

We had new Voyager tents, and he carefully showed us how to set up this type of tent.

"With the Voyager tent, the first step is to lay out the ground cloth," he said. "This provides an opportunity to look over the ground and pick out the loose rocks and sticks. If you can, lay it out with a tree a few feet in front of where the front door will go. If you have a tree in front and a tree in the back, you have a prime tent site. If you have just one support tree, that's fine. If you have just one tree or even no trees, we can still deal with it using an 'A-frame.'"

We had noticed there were no stakes like we used in our sandy loam soils back home. Fred explained the ground was so rocky, we couldn't use traditional tent stakes.

"Up here," he said, "we use thick wire stakes about seven inches in length, with the ends bent into a triangle to which you could attach a line. But only when the ground is soft enough between the rocks. Then you can use them like the stakes you would usually pound into the ground."

I looked at the tent and lines coming from the tents and wondered how we would do it. I didn't have to wonder for long.

"There are generally big rocks around good tent sites," Fred said. "They are used to place on a stout stick put in the four corner loops and would more than hold the tent if you can't easily push or pound stakes far enough into the ground. Many campsites are rocky, and pounding stakes is sometimes not practical. Always pull the tent out and 'rock' or stake the four corners before thinking about the uprights." He also explained the mosquito netting always stays zipped and the flaps tied until the tent was fully set up.

We got the first tent laid out, with two rocks put into place, using the thick wire stakes on two corners. Then we raised the front, which was about four feet from a tree. We tied it off with a taut-line hitch so we could adjust the length of the rope. The rear of the tent did not have a nearby tree. So we used the long poles leaning against a nearby tree. Fred told us he always warned crews not to cut up and burn the "tent poles" sometimes found in campsites.

We lashed the two poles into an "A," passed the tent rope over it, and secured the end of the line with a big rock. By adjusting the height of the A, we could get the right amount of height to support the tent.

With this all completed, we opened up the netting and pulled out the ground cloth. Fred showed us the sod cloth, a foot and a half of waterproof flap sewn all around the tent's inside. The sod cloth was carefully spread on the ground, and the ground cloth was placed over it. The system provides for the water to run under the sod cloth and the ground cloth. Fred told us to set up the other two tents as we had the first while he watched.

When we had finished setting up the tents, Fred said, "I am impressed with your knowledge and skill with the basic Scout knots."

Mr. Greenlee grinned.

Mike came back from digging the latrine and said, "I saw chickens back in the woods."

Fred smiled and said, "Mike, they were probably grouse and are not to be part of our food plans."

Most of us had family members that farmed. Mike did not.

"They were probably Red Pine Chickens," said Henry, "also known as grouse."

We all had a good laugh, and Mike looked relieved. Henry always seemed to be thoughtful and concerned for others' feelings.

Mike put the folding camp shovel against a log near the fireplace. Fred picked it up and asked us to gather around. When we had assembled, Fred said, "Our first camp set up has gone very well, and we will always have lots of free time when everyone does their job."

He held up the waterproof bag with four rolls of toilet paper in it. "These few rolls are all we have," he said, "and they are to be kept dry at all costs. The 'paper bag' is to be kept on the top of the Kettle Pack so if we have the 'call of nature' and the bag isn't there, we know the latrine is in use."

"Do we have a seat of some kind?" asked Henry.

"We could lean against a log," said Fred. "Or, better yet, this shovel makes a great seat."

He set the folding shovel blade at a 90-degree angle and placed it under one butt cheek. "Now you have a three-legged stool using your feet as the other two. It's just a matter of taking careful aim at the latrine hole."

Most of the crew stood with mouths open in astonishment. Fred continued with a reassuring smile. "Seriously, guys, this works, and it's the seat I always use."

He waited a moment, and then he said, "Seriously, we need to make these four rolls last for nine days. So watch how much paper you use. There is no corner store to run to if we run out."

"Is that all?" asked Henry. "I need to give it the first try."

As he headed out in the direction Mike had pointed, Fred called out to him, "Don't forget to flush."

Henry stopped with a grin, and everyone laughed.

"I'm serious, Henry. Kick a little dirt over your deposit. It's how we flush."

We all went about our duties getting the camp ready while the cooking crew worked on supper. It seemed like in no time at all, Gary called out, "Supper will be ready in about twenty minutes."

Mr. Greenlee suggested, "Let's all wash up with a short swim and move your sleeping bags and personal gear into your tents."

Everyone took this time to move in and clean up before dinner. Most of us decided to take a brief swim.

Chapter 11

FIRST EVENING

Our campsite had one of the few sand beaches in the entire Quetico Provincial Park. Although it was almost 7:30 p.m., it was still light, and it would be several hours before dark. The beach sloped out very slowly, and we had to wade out quite a distance to get into water deep enough to swim. The water was crystal clear, and I could see the bottom. I started to look for anything that wasn't sand. I only found some clamshells.

Then I remembered what Fred had said about finding arrowheads at the sand beach on Sturgeon Lake and began to search for them. Now everything seemed to look like an arrowhead but turned out to be small stones and pieces of shell. Finally, Mr. Greenlee came down and suggested we might want to get our soap and wash up while we had the chance. Several of us followed his lead and soaped and then dove into the water to wash off the soap.

When I surfaced, I had soap in my eyes, and it stung so much I ducked back underwater and swam with my eyes open. I figured it would wash the soap out of them.

While swimming underwater, my eyes felt better. As I was coming up to take a breath, I looked down and thought I saw an arrowhead. I had to come up for a breath and then went back underwater to get it.

For a moment, I couldn't see it. I panicked because it looked exactly like an arrowhead.

I took a deep breath and then decided to wait until the sand I had stirred up had settled. I took another breath and then very carefully submerged again. There it was! I had it in my hand. I almost took a breath of water in my excitement as I stood.

It was a nearly perfect arrowhead. It had a smoother finish unlike the sharp broken point I had found on Prairie Portage. I decided it had spent a considerable amount of time on the bottom of this sandy cove on Lake Agnes to have been worn smooth. It must have been either a missed shot at a deer or some other animal on the shore, or it could have been from an arrow shot at a fish.

Hey, if the arrow had been shot and hit or missed, it would still float with the shaft made of wood, wouldn't it? Maybe it was a good shot that didn't kill the deer, and the hunter, in losing the trail, never found the deer he wounded. Perhaps the deer had lived for a day or two and died while drinking water in pain from its wound. Ah! That's the best explanation.

I imagined the scene for each of the possible descriptions.

I felt the pain of the deer, which had been shot. I felt the utter disappointment of the native hunter who was upset with himself, having been unable to track a wounded deer when suddenly I saw snow . . . it was winter, and the native hunter desperately needed the deer to feed his family and tribe.

I followed the dramas of life and death in this very bay when . . .

"Hey Louis, your feet are going to wrinkle up like raisins if you just stand there all evening."

It was Mr. Greenlee. I looked around, and the guys were all dressed and standing on the shore with their plates in hand.

Good grief, how long have I been standing here dreaming about this arrowhead and its stories?

Wow, I felt silly wading back to shore alone. When I got out of the water, I quickly grabbed my towel and put on my clothes. I then walked over by the guys, who had gathered around the cooks. Gary had already started explaining the procedure for serving the meal.

I walked over and stood by Mr. Greenlee and tried to listen to Gary when Mr. Greenlee took me aside and said in a soft whisper so only I could hear, "You must have been deep in thought. Were you anywhere interesting?"

I showed him my arrowhead and told him I imagined how it came to be in this little cove.

"I would like to hear your theory," Mr. Greenlee said. "Maybe you would share it when we have a little campfire later this evening?"

I agreed and made a mental note. This might have been a time to chew me out for being late, but, instead, it was made into a positive experience. I again felt unique and good about myself because of a brief comment from Mr. Greenlee.

I'll remember to do likewise in my role as crew chief.

The dinner was excellent. Gary and his team had boundary stew, rice pudding, hot cocoa, and cornbread for dessert.

"What's in the stew?" I asked Gary.

"It consists of dehydrated potatoes, barley, dehydrated onions, corned beef, a can of tomato paste, powdered milk, a cup of dry peas, and some powdered eggs," he said. "Fred also told us to cook two pans of cornbread and to save one for lunch tomorrow."

After supper, we cleaned up, washed dishes, and then sat and enjoyed the quiet as together we watched the sun's rays slowly disappearing on the opposite shore. I looked out upon the scene, the water's mirror-like surface in our cove and the near calm surface out to the lake's center. The reflection of the trees and hills across the lake made the water awash in gorgeous colors. The trees on the nearby shore to our left were distinct in their detail as reflected in our cove.

It was beautiful . . . and then, it started.

First, one loon called, and then came an answer. I looked out and saw a single loon in the distance. It was calling to a loon that was apparently out of sight.

Fred came over and sat down next to me with a cup of coffee. He didn't say anything for quite a while. Then he put his hands together and blew through his thumbs. It made a long loon-like wail and even matched the pitch as the note went up and back down. I was shocked at how real it sounded.

Our visiting loon was now flapping its wings and standing on the water. Then he settled back down and started to move slowly in our direction.

"Fred, how did you make that call?" we all said in unison.

Fred showed us how to place our hands to make the loon call. We all forgot the loon and started to practice this new art form. Joe and Dave gave up when they could only get a stream of air. Smitty and I could get a pretty good sound, and I felt I could sound as good as Fred with some practice.

I looked for our loon and couldn't see any sign of him when suddenly, he popped up out of the water, creating a round ripple. He made a laughing sound, and we all sat quietly, watching and listening.

Smitty nudged me and pointed behind us. I turned around and looked. I saw he was also looking at the beautiful sunset taking place. However, I could only see the colors because of the trees. I looked up and saw the last blue of the sky with long clouds trailing to the west. The opposite shore was washed in the reds, purples, and the colors of the sunset. I closed my eyes for a moment and tried to make this into a memory. I wanted to remember it forever.

I quietly asked Fred if we would ever be camping on the east side of a lake to see the full sunset.

He said, "Guys, the best is yet to come."

It was almost dark when Mr. Greenlee said to get our bedrolls set out in our tents and then come back over for a little campfire. Our troop was really into campfires, so this was definitely a natural thing for us to do. Fred told us to put on some mosquito lotion. As we walked back in from the shoreline, it sounded like a B-17 warming up somewhere back in the woods.

"The mosquitoes are awful at this campsite," said Fred, "so we may want to stay down by the lake and not have a fire."

Mr. Greenlee looked at me as though he needed my approval, and I said, "Sounds good to me."

Because Mr. Greenlee checked with me, the guys all looked at me as though I was in charge, so I said, "Fred, would it be all right to build a small fire down by the lake?"

"It will be okay as long as we clean up and leave the site like it never happened," he replied. "Remember, we need to leave an ample wood supply for the next campers."

I assigned Chuck and Mike to get some additional wood and asked Gary if he could make some hot chocolate without too much trouble. He said he would, and I said, "Let's meet on the beach and get started in ten minutes or so."

Mr. Greenlee said, "You read my cue."

"I hope it was all right to take charge like that," I said.

He smiled and said, "You betcha. That's why you're the crew chief."

I asked him if he had a plan for the campfire. "Fred and I have a few things to say, and then we could sing a couple of songs," he said. "Remember, I would like to hear the stories of your arrowheads."

I said, "Great." Then he said I should do the honors and lead the campfire if I felt up to it. "Sure thing," I replied.

What am I doing? I don't usually get up and lead things like this. But I had said sure, and now the guys were already lighting the fire and gathering, so I don't even have time to get nervous.

Okay . . . this is up to me. The fire is going, and the hot chocolate has arrived. How do I start this thing? The hot chocolate smells terrific, so I'll thank Gary first and then . . .

Smells?

Grandpa! What about Grandpa? Dear Lord, Please keep him safe and healthy!

As my thoughts drifted around my memory and worry about Grandpa, I heard the loon call from far out on the lake. I thought of the loon calling and wondered what he was thinking. I closed my eyes a moment.

"*Louis . . .*"

The loon seemed to be calling to me.

Chapter 12

CAMPFIRE STORIES

"Louis . . . *Louis?*"

The words jarred me from my dream.

"Louis, you may start the campfire."

It was Mr. Greenlee, and then I was suddenly speaking. The words were coming out of my mouth, but it sounded as if someone else was saying them.

"First, I want to thank some people. Guys, so far, this has been the neatest day of my life. I hope you are having as great a time as I am. It wouldn't be happening if it weren't for Mr. Greenlee. Thank you for bringing us on this trip. I'm sure glad I came. I also want to thank all of you for pushing me. Gary, the food was great tonight. I think we all agree we picked the best cook in the troop. I am very proud of everyone and the way we all pitched in and got camp set up. Now, Mr. Greenlee and Fred have a few things to say, and then we can sing or whatever you want."

Mr. Greenlee stood, walked up by the fire, and said, "I'm very proud of all of you. I believe we have gotten off to a good start on the first day of our trip." He then said something good about everyone in the crew, adding, "I'm pretty sure we have been assigned the best guide on the

Canoe Base staff." Fred looked a little embarrassed, and I noticed his slight smile.

Mr. Greenlee always seemed to have a friendly way of talking with us and quickly pointed out the good things we did. I guess it may have been why we were always trying to live up to what he expected. Now Fred had some living up to do as well. Mr. Greenlee then turned to Fred and asked if he had any comments or suggestions for improvement.

"This is my third year as a Charlie Guide, and so far, I am impressed with this crew," he said. "You guys are working together and are picking up important things quickly. If everyone will just consider all the gear as yours and treat it in that way, you will have an outstanding trip. Then consider this wilderness area as yours and treat it with that same respect. I want to help you get everything you want out of this voyage we are on."

Then he said, "I am so impressed with our Scoutmaster. Mr. Greenlee, I wonder if you would tell us about that well-used KA-BAR® knife you carry."

As soon as Fred mentioned the knife, I remembered I had thought about it many times but never asked about it. The blade was about seven inches long and had a stacked leather handle. The blade was dark, as if it had been blued. It was always sharp, and I noticed Mr. Greenlee sharpened it nearly every evening when we were out camping.

I thought I saw Mr. Greenlee take a deep breath as he took a moment and looked out across the lake before he began to tell us about the knife. At that moment, I remembered he had told us about being a Marine in World War II.

"This knife was issued to me shortly after I became a Marine," he said.

He took it out of the well-worn leather sheath and looked at it as he spoke.

"Guys, I don't usually say too much about my experiences in the war because it was a time when I lost a lot of close friends and saw a lot of things I hope you will never have to see. I guess I was a feisty young man when I signed on to fight. It was in the middle of the war, and it looked like our country needed all the help it could get."

A log on the fire shifted, fell to the side, and sent sparks in the air as he paused. He was still looking at the knife when he began. "Remember when Fred told us to watch out for our gear? Well, if I learned one thing in the Marines, it was our lives depended on the condition of our equipment and that it was always where it was supposed to be when we needed it."

Mr. Greenlee's son, Dave, said, "Dad was one of the first to land on Iwo Jima. He knew all those guys you see holding up the flag in the famous picture on Mount Suribachi."

You could have heard a pin drop. None of us were aware of that. Fred looked impressed.

"Dave is right," said Mr. Greenlee. "We were among the first to hit the beach at Iwo Jima, and we spent a lot of time on our bellies just trying to get to cover on the first day. The Japanese had us pinned down most of the time, and it took us a day just to get up to where we could operate without bullets flying over our heads all the time. The ships offshore pounded the enemy positions, and after a few days, we were finally able to make some progress. This old knife was a handy piece of equipment, and it never let me down."

"Did you shoot any Japs?" asked Tom.

Mr. Greenlee didn't answer for a long time. He just looked into the fire with a look that said he was in deep thought. No one said a word, and then Mr. Greenlee looked up, cleared his throat, and said, "The Japanese were tough little fighters. I guess I might have shot a few. In battle, you are not always sure who shot whom. I can tell you my fellow Marines and I shot many Japanese soldiers when it was all said and done.

"Tom, during the war, we called them Japs and other inappropriate things as you just did," he continued. "I felt a lot of hate for them.

Because of all the buddies I lost, some of them close friends, sometimes right beside me when they died, I guess I hated them at the time.

"As a Marine, I learned to respect bravery. It takes courage to be the first to hit the beach. But there was a lot of courage displayed on the other side too. Most of them never gave up, even when it was of no use to fight anymore. They were fighting for what they believed. None of us could help but feel respect. All these years later, you will not often hear a Marine who lived through that time call them Japs."

Everyone became quiet again. I heard the loon call from out on the lake. I think we all got the point.

As we stared into the fire, the call of the loon faded.

Mr. Greenlee continued in a quiet voice, "As Scouts, you guys have promised to be brave, and I am sure you would go to war and fight just like I did. The fact is, I fought in hopes you wouldn't have to. I hope we can get this old world to learn to talk, respect, and live with each other. I think if all the boys in the world would learn and live by our Scout Oath and Law, maybe knives could just be for cleaning fish."

There was a long pause. I watched Mr. Greenlee stare at his knife, and I thought I saw a tear glisten in the reflection of the firelight and roll down his cheek. Finally, he looked up and said, "Maybe we can talk about this again sometime. But right now, I want Fred to tell us when we will get to some good fishing."

Fred was looking at Mr. Greenlee and seemed at a loss for words like the rest of us. Mr. Greenlee broke the silence and said, "Fred, I was about your age when all this was going on, and some of my Marine buddies were just a few years older than these Scouts. We did what we had to. I would rather have been able to do what you are doing right now. It is every bit as important. Now when do we get to fish?"

Fred told us some of the best fishing would be tomorrow when we made our next camp and then every day after that.

"There are fish in Agnes, but I like to get up to Kawnipi before I think of fishing," he said. "Agnes can get pretty windy, and the wind always seems to be against me. Kawa Bay and Mack Lake will provide some excellent fishing. Every overnight, when we make camp, we will have the potential for good fishing. Of course, it means you have to get out and work at it. These fish aren't going to jump into the canoe.

"But that's enough fishing advice for now. I think Mr. Greenlee has something to say."

Mr. Greenlee stepped in and said, "I think our crew chief has a little story to tell us. Louis, are you ready to tell us about the arrowheads you found?"

I was still stunned from learning about Mr. Greenlee's experience as a Marine. But all of a sudden, there I was, talking again.

"Mr. Greenlee's knife caused him to remember a time in his past. There were a couple of lessons in his story I will never forget. I have a couple of little blades I found today in my pocket."

I reached into my pocket and took them out for all to see.

"They are arrowheads, and Mr. Greenlee caught me daydreaming about both of them.

"The first one is this small and broken arrowhead I found on the beach at Prairie Portage. I have been very interested in all the stories we have heard about the Indians and the voyageurs, and I was caught up in my own thoughts as I looked at this first point. I wasn't recalling my own experiences like Mr. Greenlee was. Instead, I imagined the times this arrowhead has seen in the distant past. Because this one is broken, I think an old Indian made it back when the voyageurs were trading for furs with metal arrowheads, knives, axes, and other useful trade goods. The new metal trade goods made the skill of arrowhead making old fashioned.

"When I nearly ran into Mr. Greenlee's canoe this morning, I had just looked back at Prairie Portage. I imagined what it must have looked like back in those voyageur days. There were Indians in their buckskins and voyageurs in their colorful clothing and their leggings. I could see an old Indian who made this arrowhead throwing it away, unhappy with himself. I believe he was thinking to himself, *Maybe we need to start using the new metal ones.*"

"Louis!" It was Mike. "How do you know it wasn't made correctly and broken in battle or something neat like that?"

"I guess it could have been broken that way. But I think it was a mistake because the point is very sharp, and the break is back where it would attach to an arrow. The notch is okay on one side, and it's broken off on the other. But that's just what I think."

"How about the one you found in the water this afternoon?" asked Mr. Greenlee.

"Well, I found it while getting the soap out of my eyes. I was afraid I had just imagined it for a minute, and then I went back down under the water and there it was. As you can see, it is a perfect arrowhead."

"So what's the story on this one, Louis?" asked Tom.

"Well, at first, I thought this one was lost when the hunter made a bad shot. He didn't kill the deer he was trying to shoot. I was thinking it had been shot, only wounding the deer. I figured the deer probably lived several days in excruciating pain and ended up dying while trying to drink when it had become sickly from the wound. I was imagining there was a very frustrated hunter who spent the best part of the day looking for a wounded deer that just kept moving on every time he came close."

"Why do you think it was a wounded deer and not a missed shot that put the arrow in the water, Louis?" asked Tom.

"I thought of that. However, with as much work as it takes to make an arrow, I believe a hunter would have gone after an arrow that would have floated with the wooden shaft. If you have the archery merit badge, you will have learned about the old way of making an arrow, and it is a difficult and time-consuming job. If the shot were in this cove, the hunter would probably have had a canoe over here where we are camped."

"Fred, do you think Indians camped here where we are?" asked Henry.

"Without a doubt, they did, Henry," Fred said. "This site would have been very popular with the sandy beach. Louis, what gave you the impression this is the story of this particular arrowhead?"

"Well, there is no sharp edge to this one at all. It is very smooth, and although the shape is perfect, it has been worn like it has been in the water for a long time. Our next-door neighbor at home polishes agates in a mixture of sand and water kept in motion with a motor. I think this arrowhead has been on the sandy bottom of this cove for a long time, being polished in this way over time.

"When Mr. Greenlee and most of you saw me out in the cove," I continued, "I was lost in thought, thinking about what it must have been like to have lived back then. I guess I felt like a wounded deer and then like a frustrated hunter as I imagined the arrowhead's story when suddenly it started to snow . . .

"Then I saw what I think *actually* happened."

"Snow! Louis, what happened?" asked Dave. "Are you going to finish the story? What about the snow?"

I looked at Mr. Greenlee, and he looked like he was waiting, so I picked up where I left off.

"It happened just before a hard winter began, and the hunter was devastated to have only wounded the large buck. The arrow had lodged in a fleshy area of the leg. The deer was not injured enough to bring him down immediately. The arrow's shaft eventually broke off, and the arrowhead was left lodged against the thick bone in the thigh. As the wound healed around it, the deer was left with a lump and a pronounced limp. As the winter wore on, the deer foraged as usual and moved only slightly slower than other deer.

"The buck escaped death at the hands of the hunter," I continued. "Then, as the temperatures dropped in the severest part of the winter, his slight slowness and limp marked him as the next victim selected by a wolf pack. After being stalked for much of a day, he was driven onto the ice in this very cove, where he no longer had trees and rocks to protect his flank. During a valiant fight with antlers and hooves, the exhausted deer received a powerful bite on his injured leg. Soon another wolf applied a bone-crushing bite to the once-powerful buck's neck.

"With both wolves whirling like rag dolls, the deer spins in his attempt to dislodge his attackers. However, the fight soon ends as the powerful jaws, still holding fast to his neck, cut off his air supply. He drops to his knees and falls to his side. The blood from both the wound to his leg and his jugular reddens the snow. As the deer stops thrashing in his final death throes, the wolves pause for a brief moment as if to gaze with admiration on the brave adversary before beginning their much-needed meal.

"After the hunters eat their fill, others of the pack move in to dine, and soon the pack's half-grown pups are left to begin their ritual fighting over the remaining meat. As one wolf pup chews on a leg bone, he bites down on something very hard, and he tastes his own blood as he breaks a tooth on the dark stone embedded in the bone and sinew of the deer's leg.

"After the wolves move back to the shelter of the thick cedars along the shore, the ravens complete the cleaning of the last bits of meat. For several hours scavengers of all types compete as the bloody scene of the battle becomes just a discolored area of snow on the vast expanse of snow-covered ice. Only scattered bones and some scraps of hide and hair remain.

"As the last tiny scavengers complete their work, snow again begins to fall and buries the remaining evidence of the drama ending the life of the once-proud buck.

"The wolves, the ravens, the jays, and other scavengers are well fed," I added. "The wolf pack will survive for another week before they must kill again to survive in this cold and inhospitable land.

"A wolf pup curls up with other pack members for warmth and finds contentment in his full stomach. He has already forgotten the life-giving meal as he licks his muzzle for the last bits of dried blood.

He works his tongue against his teeth and pauses at the new sensation of the broken tooth before he drifts off to sleep.

"And that's what I think happened to cause the arrowhead to be at the bottom of this sandy cove."

Everyone was quiet for a while, and then I said, "If you see me lost in thought again, just throw something at me and bring me back."

"Louis, I think we will just let you dream if you promise to share your stories with us again," Mr. Greenlee said. "I think I agree with your assumptions about both arrowheads. Fred, what do you say?"

Fred said he agreed with Mr. Greenlee, and I felt a twinge of the giddy feeling start to come over me again.

"Guys, how about a song or two, and then let's hit the sack," I suggested.

Mr. Greenlee offered to lead us in a fun song about the "Good Ol' Mountain Dew." He then led us in singing "The Far Northland." He was a great song leader, and his voice reminded me of Gene Autry's. When we finished, Tom asked if we could also sing "Scout Vespers," and we all joined in as he led it.

Talk about strange, I didn't think Tom had a serious-minded bone in his body, and here he was leading a solemn song. What's happening to this group?

As we were putting out the fire, Fred very softly said, "Everyone, look up."

The sky was incredibly clear, and I don't think I had ever seen so many stars. I was thinking about Mr. Greenlee, my folks, and Grandpa. I prayed Grandpa would still be alive when I got back. I really wanted to tell him about this day. We all stood and looked at the stars for a while, as the loons called again. I guess we all had our own thoughts because nobody said a word. After a while, we all moved off to our tents.

Chapter 13

FIRST NIGHT ON THE TRAIL

There had been a few mosquitoes down by the water, but the gentle breeze and the smoke from the campfire had helped keep them away. We walked up the rise to our campsite. The pesky bugs were everywhere and biting. Fred had us spray mosquito repellent into our tents and zip the netting before our campfire so they would be bug-free when we went to bed. The trick was to get them off of us before we entered the tents.

We settled into the tents after brushing off all the mosquitos we could. I was in a tent with Mr. Greenlee, Smitty, and Fred. We had just enough room for our ditty bags and some essentials like our camp shoes. Mine were Gokey double-soled moccasins. Our clothes and rain jackets became our pillows. We tied the tent flaps back, and Fred slept by the mosquito netting. Mr. Greenlee was by the back wall. I was between Smitty and Fred.

We must have let a few mosquitos into our tent because each of us slapped those landing on us. There were not too many because, in no time, we heard no more except for the low din of those still outside the tent.

Some of the other tents were using their flashlights and yelling about each mosquito's location. Mr. Greenlee didn't say anything for several minutes, and then he said, "It's time to hit the rack, guys. Put out the lights, or you won't have them when you really need them. If you lie still, you will feel them and can slap them when they land. Lights out! Now!"

The camp became silent except for an occasional slap. Fred called out to everyone, "All you guys by the mosquito netting, don't roll into the netting or sleep with your arm against the netting. The mosquitoes will think you're a buffet."

"Sounds like the voice of experience," said Mr. Greenlee.

"Yeah, you just do it once," said Fred. "And I would rather tell them the first night and spare them the experience."

In less than five minutes, Mr. Greenlee was softly snoring, and I think Smitty was asleep as well. A loon called from out on the lake.

Fred whispered, "Say goodnight, Louis."

I was exhausted and hardly noticed a rock under my leg. I was so tired my last conscious thought was to ignore the stone and move my leg if it seriously bothered me.

I don't know how long I had slept, but when I awoke, it was pitch-black in the tent. Fred was not there by the netting. I figured he was out taking a leak, although he had warned us to all take care of such chores before getting into the tents. I looked through the mosquito netting and saw a little light outside where our cooking fire was, and I could see Fred blowing on the coals to produce the flames. I sat up and watched as he blew. He stopped and looked up at something in the darkness. I couldn't see anything, but I guessed it was a bear.

We had put all of our food packs under an aluminum canoe and placed pots and pans plus several canoe paddles against it. The idea was to provide a bear alarm, and I guess we were all so tired only Fred heard it. I watched as Fred stood up and walked toward the darkness and something I could not see. I put on my clothes and camp shoes, slipped out of the tent, and went over to where Fred stood just beyond the fire with a paddle in his hand. I could hear the bear moving off through the brush.

Fred came back to the fire and looked surprised to see me standing there.

"He's gone for a while," he said. "I'm going to brew some tea. Would you like some?"

"That would be great," I said. I had never had tea when I wasn't sick with a cold or the flu. Fred put on a pot to boil and then came over and sat on the log.

"Was it the same bear that tore things up at the campsite by the falls?" I asked.

"I can't say for sure, but it's probably the same one," he said. "Once a bear starts raiding campsites, they especially get into it. I had hoped he would still be on the other side of the lake."

"Will he come back?" I asked.

"I've only had a few bears in my time doing this, but I think he will be back. Our best bet is to keep a fire going and hope we can bluff a bear."

"Were you trying a 'bluff' when I came out?"

"Yes, and so far, it has worked. I don't want to start banging on pots to wake up all the guys."

The tea water was ready, and Fred got the black tea bag from the top of a food pack. He measured the tea into the pot. In a few minutes, he sat down and handed me a cup.

"Fred, Mr. Greenlee was talking about bravery during the war at the campfire tonight," I said. "I think a guy who will stare down a bear is pretty brave too."

"Thanks. But I don't see you shaking in your tent. And I think you had a good hunch as to what you were getting into when you came out to help."

The tea was pretty good. Mom always made it with milk and sugar. This was just plain black tea.

"Tea was a much more common drink than coffee in voyageur times and was preferred by lots of explorers and backwoodsmen," said

Fred. "It was easier to pack, weighs much less than coffee, and the British always made sure there was plenty of tea."

It was good to sit and visit with Fred. I asked him how often bears were a problem.

"Back in the Basswood Lake area," he said, "it is frequently an issue because some fishermen come by motorboat into those areas and bring more than they need. Sometimes the camps get pretty messy and attract bears. Our crews try to get beyond Basswood the first night, just as we did. When we go back to Customs, I'll let Vic know of this and pass the word back at Base. Let's just hope he doesn't come back tonight."

"What time is it?" I asked.

Fred pulled out a pocket watch and said, "It's four thirty a.m. We have been at this for a good half hour. It's going to be a short night in the sleep department. The mosquitoes must have gone to bed a while back because there haven't been any since I got up."

I looked up and noticed the stars were no longer visible. Fred was looking too and said, "I think it will be raining by morning, so we may as well put up the dining fly so the guys can eat and pack beneath it."

We spent the next 10 minutes putting up the fly using the trees in the center camp area. After the dining fly was secure, I stepped out from under it, looked at the sky, and took a deep breath. Fred was right. I could smell the rain coming, and my thoughts turned back to Grandpa.

I told Fred all about Grandpa and how I was concerned about him still being alive when I got back. The smell of rain in the air started me thinking about him. During the first day of this trip, I had experienced a lifetime of adventures to tell him about, including a bear.

The hollow hissing sound startled us both, and Fred stood up and looked into the woods beyond the fire. He turned back to me and said, as he picked up a piece of wood and threw it on the fire, "I've heard they do that when they are angry or panic stricken. Stoke up the fire, and I'll get a pot to bang on if we need to. If he gets dangerously cranky, wake the guys and paddle out in the canoes. We will leave him with the food. Let's hope he will fall for a good bluff again."

I got the fire going and saw Fred was standing on the other side of the fire. I could just barely make out the bear about 15 yards from Fred. It had its head down and was walking sideways and making that horrible hollow hissing noise.

Fred calmly said, "Louis, look all around and see if you see a cub. This bear seems very angry and could be a mother with a cub."

I looked and didn't see a thing and told Fred.

"Then here goes a bluff. Hope I've got a change of underwear," he said.

I got the joke but didn't laugh because I was scared stiff. I think the humor was for my benefit.

The large stick was burning brightly at a knot, and it stayed lighted as I walked up next to Fred. Fred was softly saying, "Git!" to the bear. The bear stopped about 20 feet out and started to back up as we approached. Then it turned with a snort and ran off into the woods.

I looked at Fred, who was looking at me.

"Were you planning to set him on fire or serve him some tea?" he asked.

I looked down, and I had the burning stick in one hand and my cup of tea in the other.

"I wasn't actually planning to do *anything*. I just sort of got here before I had a chance to prepare a plan."

"Well, I'm glad I've got a brave crew chief because I am sure we made a better bluff together."

We went back to the log by the fire and poured another cup of tea. Mike came out and sat with us.

"Is anyone else awake?" I asked.

"I don't think so," said Mike.

Then he said he had been watching since I stoked up the fire. "I didn't know it was a bear until you walked over by Fred. Holy cow! It was a big bear! I thought I was going to see you guys get eaten. What were you saying?"

I don't think Mike believed us when Fred said, "Just, 'git.'"

"Mike, you were pretty brave coming out to join us," I said. "Will you walk around to the tents and see if everyone is asleep? Then, come back, and we should move some firewood under the dining fly because it feels like it's going to rain."

While Mike was making the rounds, Fred said, "Are you still interested in doing this when you are old enough? I'll sure recommend you since you passed the bear test."

I felt the giddy sensation start again and felt proud at the same time.

"Just pack an extra pair of underwear for bear scares," said Fred with a chuckle. "You may need it."

By the time Mike got back, it had started to rain, and we gathered under the fly. The corner of the fly was shielding the fire from the rain. As we were moving all the wood undercover, I noticed a dim light in the east. I thought about the bear and took a deep breath.

I had just had the best adventure of my life.

Chapter 14

"BLUE SKIES"

As the three of us stood under the dining fly and watched the rain continue in a slow, steady drizzle, when Mike asked, "Fred, should Louis and I bring all of the food packs under the tarp so the cooks will have an easier time with the breakfast preparation?"

Fred grinned and said, "Mike, you're thinking ahead. I'm impressed."

I judged it to be close to five-thirty when the rest of the fellas started to stir. Gary was the first one out of the tents and said, "Wow, I'm surprised to see the dining fly is already up. I thought I would be the first one up and could get breakfast going." Mike handed him a cup of tea.

Fred suggested we help Gary get some hot cocoa going and then said, "Gary, how about fixing oatmeal for breakfast? It will be easier and quicker to prepare in the rain. Fix some of the fruit stew as well."

Mr. Greenlee was the next to appear and had Fred's and my rain jacket with him. "It looks like you were up before the rain started," he said. "Louis, let's get everyone up so we can get packed and maybe even take the tents down before we eat."

Gary handed Mr. Greenlee a cup of hot tea and, after a sip, said, "Gary, we are going to keep you if you continue with this good behavior."

Soon everyone was under the tarp and planning the packing and the chores for the morning. Fred reminded everyone the toilet paper was all we had and chuckled as he said, "Be very careful to keep the precious papers dry on your morning trip to the latrine."

Mike asked, "Aren't you guys going to tell everyone about the bear?"

Everyone stopped talking, looked up with a startled expression, and, in unison, said, "The bear! What bear?" Everyone was talking at once.

"Fred and Louis were up all night keeping a bear away," Mike said, "and I saw them chase it off. Fred had a paddle and cooking pot and told it to 'git!'

"Then Louis walked right up to it with a torch and a hot cup of tea. You should have seen that bear run."

Everyone was standing with their mouth open, even Mr. Greenlee. "Is this true?" he asked.

Fred explained, "I thought the bear across the lake would stay over there, but I'm sure it was the same bear. He woke me up a little before four o'clock, and I scared him off without any trouble the first time. Louis came out as the bear was running off, and we sat and drank tea while we kept the fire going. He came back, and just when I was about to bang on a pot to scare him off, Louis walked right up next to me with a burning stick and his cup of tea. I was relieved the bear decided to run off again."

Mike chimed in in agreement. "I saw the bear, and it was mad and growling, and it was no cute, cuddly teddy bear."

Everyone became silent, and then Fred said, "Let's get going before he comes back for breakfast and the cup of tea he missed."

Mr. Greenlee agreed and said, "We can hear more of the story later when chores are finished."

I walked over to where the bear had been and started to look at the tracks. Mr. Greenlee came over and looked at them with me. I pointed at the tracks and said, "I'm sure it was the same bear. I saw the tracks at the other campsite, and these look the same."

We turned and looked at the distance from the fire.

"Louis, that's only about twenty feet. The bear was very close," he said. "I am very proud of you. It was a brave thing you and Fred did. But, as crew chief, you don't need to be taking risks. This was pretty close to be staring down a wild and angry bear."

"Mr. Greenlee, I was just helping Fred. He is the guy with the nerve, and last night you said guys who were a little older than we are were staring down the enemy on Iwo Jima. What's the difference? Someone needed to help, and I was there."

"Louis, you got me on this one. Just be careful, and don't tell your mom all the details if you ever want to come up here again!" He chuckled. "Now, what's the difference? I'm not sure. But if I had to choose another beach or a close encounter with an angry bear, I might just take the beach."

I'm sure he said that just for me. Then he smiled and said, "Let's get packed."

We walked back to the tarp, and Mr. Greenlee put a hand on my shoulder. "Let's just have an average day today, okay?"

While Dave and the cooking crew worked on breakfast, the rest of us got busy. When we were packed and had the tents down and folded, we were called to breakfast. We all ate under the tarp after saying grace. It was chilly, and the hot oatmeal and fruit stew really hit the spot. Gary served the cornbread he had initially been fixing for lunch with butter and jelly. After far too many questions about the bear, I changed the subject.

"Fred, I was looking at my map. We have a long way to go on a huge lake. What do we need to be aware of?"

"Well, guys, you're a pretty bright group." He was smiling at Mike. "What do I think we need to keep in mind today? I'll just say it will probably rain all day. The good news is big old Lake Agnes will be calm for a change, and rain makes for excellent traveling weather."

"Why would getting wet in the rain make it excellent traveling weather?" asked Tom.

Fred replied, "The alternative is staying in camp while it rains. Traveling in the rain has several advantages. It makes everything look like a beautiful Monet painting. It's far better than losing a day and moping around feeling sorry for ourselves. We can't do anything about this rain.

"We can, however, paddle through it," he continued. "The only thing we can control is ourselves, which means we all have a choice to make. We can choose to be miserable, or we can choose to have a good time. Instead of complaining, we can sing. Instead of whining, we can laugh and put our backs into paddling our canoe like the voyageurs."

"I knew you would make me feel better," Tom said. "Are you planning to be a football coach, Fred?"

"Won't the guys in the middle freeze if they aren't paddling?" interjected Henry. "Should they sit on something to keep warm?"

"With such a long paddle ahead, sitting on something like the edge of the tent would not be such a bad idea," said Fred. "It's not freezing, but it is in the low fifties, and it will feel cold. Those of you in the middle, make sure you stay dry, and since we are on a sandy beach, y'all can 'dry-foot it' until our first portage."

He concluded with a reminder. "Guys, lots of people get grumpy when it rains. I think the Quetico is at its most beautiful in the rain. Enjoy a beautiful lake and a great day. Let's pack up and be off."

As Fred carried his canoe down to the water, he was singing "Blue Skies."

It's a strange song to sing in the rain, but it certainly is cheery.

As we loaded the canoes, the rain let up a little, and Chuck called off the gear. He and I made one more trip up to the campsite and found a cup someone had missed. When I got to my canoe, both Tom and Dave were ready to paddle and suggested I rest since I had been up all night fighting with bears.

Tom was not the best sternman, and I had assumed I would paddle stern all trip. This would be an excellent time for him to learn. Then I suggested I paddle in the bow and let Dave take over when we made our first stop. I felt wide awake and felt like I could coach Tom to paddle stern if I were in the bow. Since Dave had a surplus rain poncho, I figured he would stay warmer than either Tom or I, who had shorter rain jackets. I was grateful for my jacket as the rain started to increase.

Tom did great with a bit of coaching and caught on fast as I told him when to sweep or pull a hard J. We started to lag, but Tom and I wouldn't have the last place, and we quickly caught up.

Agnes was gorgeous as we passed by high cliffs on our left. The rain seemed to give everything a different perspective. As Fred had said, Agnes is indeed a beauty.

After what seemed a long time paddling in a steady rain, I noticed the wind was coming up a little. Since the lake was narrow in this area, the wind didn't bother us much. The lake seemed to become even more narrow, and then we rounded a corner. Dave said, "Wow, look at the size of this lake."

We had just hit the main body of Lake Agnes. Now the rain was not as heavy and seemed to be ending.

"So much for my career as a weatherman," said Fred. "The wind is going to be right at us."

As we paddled out into the central part of Agnes, I took a deep breath. I looked up from the map and my eyes took in its size. It was huge, and to make matters worse, the wind hit my face and steadily increased.

We were aware Agnes was a big lake since we all looked at the map before leaving the first camp. I guess we weren't quite ready for the real thing. I wasn't sure this was the time for Tom to be in the stern and for me to be in the bow, but he seemed to be getting the hang of it, and we all have to start somewhere. Before we got into the wind, Fred had us all gather near his canoe.

"Guys, this is going to be a challenging paddle, but with the performance you've shown me so far, you're more than up to it. There are a couple of things we need to review before we get into the wind.

"Number one: feather your paddles. I noticed most of you are careful to do that, and today you will especially appreciate why we push the point. Number two: you will be feeling like you are making slow progress when we are actually moving at a pretty good clip.

"Don't let yourself get down. In fact, this is a good time to do some singing, and thirdly, we need to stay close. Don't get spread across the length of Lake Agnes. Louis, you and Tom lead out and stay ahead. I'll bring up the rear."

"Fred, will we ever be able to take a break?" asked Tom.

"We will stop near where Silence Lake joins Agnes about halfway up and on the left," Fred replied. "There is a protected landing there, and we will be ready for a break by then. Oh, and when your arm gets tired, remember to talk it up and tell the other paddler before you switch."

Fred also looked us over and had a few canoes adjust the tent forward so we were all slightly lower toward the bow. If you were heading into the wind, I assumed it would make sense to be a little low in the bow.

"Louis, should we switch? You're best in the stern," Tom said.

"Tom, you have been doing great, and I think we will be just fine."

"Yeah, but we have to stay in the lead."

"Don't you worry; I'll keep us in the lead. You just navigate, and I'll keep us ahead of the crew."

It's funny, but I feel stronger than I thought I was. I have never thought of myself as strong since I am usually one of the shorter guys for my age. But on this trip, I feel and think strong. It feels good.

As we started up the lake, both Tom and I had our map cases out. As Tom studied his map, I noticed he gradually cut across to the other side where Silence joined Agnes. We could see precisely where Fred wanted us to go, and I was determined to keep us in the lead. It wasn't long before Tom needed to switch sides, and it also felt good to me. He was doing well, although he occasionally made some loud banging on the edge of the canoe. I kept wanting to look back to see if everyone was keeping up just as Tom informed me they were. Then he said, "Louis, go ahead and look back. I'll keep us balanced."

Wow! Tom is thinking of safety and cares about my concern as crew chief. This is really weird.

It was a hard paddle, and I was grateful Tom always seemed to need to switch at about the same time I was wearing out on the side I was paddling. We had to slow down a couple of times and let the guys in the back catch up to us. Fred paddled his canoe in and out among us so he could give pointers and encouragement to everyone. He told Tom as he came up alongside, "You're doing great and headed just right. Keep it up."

I felt jealous someone else could handle the stern and then thought it didn't erase the feeling of jealousy until I realized Tom was now feeling as good as I did yesterday. We all needed to learn, and if I wanted to be a guide, someday I needed to learn how to make people feel good like Fred made us feel.

To be a guide, being a strong paddler is not as important as being a good teacher and coach.

Agnes is such a long lake. I watched the shoreline pass slowly because of the headwind. I paddled harder, sometimes wondering if we were making progress. The waves slapped against the bow in hypnotizing rhythm, and time seemed to be passing slowly, so to pass the time, I found myself looking around.

My eyes came to rest on the bottom of the canoe. There were Canadian stickers all over the inside of the bow. There was one for each year the canoe was used in Canada. Our canoe had stickers dating back to 1951.

I was just a little kid then.

The bottom was scratched where boots had scraped the sand about the aluminum. There was sand, a few tiny pebbles, and little bits of bark rolling about in the thin layer of water at my feet. My rear end was getting sore and cold, and that last cup of tea was having its effect, so I knew I would need to stop reasonably soon. I looked to the left and could see a prominent rock outcrop where we were heading.

"I hope that rock is the point Fred described," Tom said. He looked over his shoulder and then reported that Fred had nodded yes in the direction we were heading.

When we arrived in front of the rocky point, Tom pointed to the top of a large rock and said, "That will be a perfect place to jump from if the water is deep enough."

Fred motioned us around the point, and I noticed a landing on a small gravel beach with lots of reeds around it. When Tom guided the canoe up toward the shore, I stepped out before the canoe touched the shore. I started to stumble and had to hold on to the canoe and stretch a moment. My legs were so stiff it was hard to walk.

I turned to the incoming canoes and said, "Guys, my legs are stiff, and I almost fell. One foot was asleep. So remember to exit carefully and watch out that your legs aren't asleep."

I directed the guys to get the canoes up out of the water after unloading the gear. I assumed that we wouldn't want to leave them in the water with the wind blowing as hard as it was. If it wasn't the correct thing to do, Fred didn't say anything. I remember he had said, "Care for them like they are birchbark, and they will never let you down."

Everyone was exhausted and rubbing their legs. Mr. Greenlee said he felt like his rear end was dead. Everyone laughed, and then Mr. Greenlee said we were a good bunch of paddlers.

After everyone was out of their canoes, Tom walked away from the group and motioned for me to follow. When I went over to him, he showed me his hands and asked, "Louis, did you get any blisters on your hands?"

Tom's hands had some nasty-looking blisters on his palms and thumbs. A couple of his knuckles were bleeding from banging on the canoe.

As I looked, I recalled Mr. Greenlee's advice before the trip. He had suggested that we twist a cut-off broom handle in our hands while watching television to develop some calluses. I even got a little blister while watching *The Ed Sullivan Show* one Sunday night.

"Gosh, Tom, why, didn't you tell me?" I asked.

He replied, "We were asked to stay in the lead, and I didn't want to let you guys down."

"You didn't! But don't hurt yourself to prove a point."

"Yeah, like you and the bear last night."

We both smiled, and I had gained a new respect for Tom. Fred asked me to walk with him and Mr. Greenlee down to the shore while the rest of the guys looked over the rocky point. I told them about Tom's blisters and bleeding knuckles.,

"Most of us guides are very familiar with treating blisters," said Fred. "Then again, most Scouts stop what's giving them blisters before they become serious. I'll fix him up as soon as we finish talking."

"How do you think the morning went?" asked Fred. "Sorry I got my weather report wrong."

Mr. Greenlee laughed and said, "I was very impressed with the paddling, and I think it's your little reminders and encouragement that kept us going, Fred."

"We will be in some strong headwinds until we get to the end of the lake," said Fred. "It's not dangerous, just strenuous paddling." Then he added, "It's a little early for lunch, but the guys worked hard getting here. Let's not ask for lunch to be prepared and just see what the cooks do."

"I'll bet Gary has already started," said Mr. Greenlee.

We went back over to the crew. Gary was already getting the lunch materials out, and the helpers were going out for water with the canvas bucket.

Fred and Mr. Greenlee just grinned.

The cooks gave everyone a slice of the hard salami and cheese with some Hol-Ry crackers since we had expended a lot of energy. We also had a handful of raisins per person.

While lunch sandwiches were being prepared, Fred and I moved in close to help Tom with his hands. Tom's hands weren't as bad as I thought they would be, and Fred suggested we wait until evening to drain the blisters.

"Sometimes, they go down on their own. But, for now, I'll clean the knuckles with a little Phisohex."

I told Fred I would keep Tom riding in the middle so he could rest his hands. I added, "I'll also help him with getting on his pack on his back at the portage."

Fred looked up at the clouds and said, "The sun is coming out, and there's nothing like the sun to speed the healing."

After lunch, we checked out the campsite. Fred said it was a pleasant campsite because of the excellent jumping rock. The water was clear, so you could see the drop off was free of rocks. We were all kind of excited about wanting to swim and dive.

I was just about to bring it up with Mr. Greenlee when Fred said, "Ya know, with all the speed you guys have, we could probably use a longer break. What say we take a little swim?"

It didn't take long before we were jumping off the rocks, swimming, and enjoying the sun, which had just come out from behind the clearing clouds.

Some of the guys were having trouble getting up the nerve to jump, so we found a "low-board" area for them. Soon they were moving to the "high board." We were having such a good time swimming that several guys mentioned it would be a great place to camp. I reminded them we were only halfway to our planned stop and chosen campsite.

The cold water and brisk wind helped change our minds, and it did not take long before we were ready to call it quits, get back into our trail clothes, and get moving up the rest of Agnes. It also didn't take long to get loaded and traveling again.

The weather was still cool, but the sun breaking through the clouds made it much more comfortable. Everyone had stowed their rain gear in their packs. Fred said to keep it handy in case the rain started again.

The sky became partly cloudy with low, fast-moving clouds. However, it looked like the sky above was clear, and it would soon be a bright and sunny day.

I was back in the stern since Tom's hands were banged up. Dave said he was glad to paddle since he had nearly frozen to death while riding in the middle during the rain and wind.

"My military-surplus poncho kept me dry," he said, "but I was still cold, just sitting."

As we paddled away from the campsite and into the lake's main body, the wind continued to blow steadily and briskly. It quickly became evident we would be paddling directly into it. Dave groaned as he dug his paddle hard into the water with each stroke.

"It's one of Murphy's Laws that the wind is always against you on Agnes," said Fred with a smile.

We paddled with renewed enthusiasm. It felt good to be back in the stern again, although the headwind meant the minor corrections I needed to make headway had to be made with a more demanding stroke. I hit my thumb on the side of the canoe and realized how Tom must have felt if he was continually doing it all morning. After asking for a switch, Dave said, "It feels good to be paddling!"

"Yeah?" said Tom. "It feels good to sit."

Shortly after those comments, I saw a flash up ahead. It was like a flashbulb had just gone off in the distance. Then I saw the canoes far ahead coming in our direction. I looked at Fred, and he had already spotted them.

"It looks like another Charlie crew coming in from their trip," he said.

They were all paddling in unison and moving in good order. I was impressed with their expert strokes and how they seemed to be in unison with each other. Not only had they been out for a week or more, but they were paddling with the wind. Lucky guys!

Suddenly someone up ahead yelled, "Hol-Ry!" and Fred replied, "Red-Eye!"

I was excited to see another Scout unit that had been out for six or seven days. It did not take long before I saw the green canoe and three aluminum canoes with Sommers logos on their bows.

I knew about Hol-Ry. They were the crackers we ate with our sandwiches at lunch. I guessed it was also a greeting between guides, and "Red-Eye" was the correct response.

Cool!

As they came closer, we could see they had been out a long time because they were "brown as beans," as my mom would have said. They all had smiles on their faces as they paddled with practiced precision.

The guy I guessed was their crew chief asked where we were from as we all paused in the middle of North Agnes. He said they were from Kansas City, Missouri, and their guide was a fellow named Tom. He had dark hair and a beard and was from Amarillo, Texas. He had a cartoon woodpecker smoking a cigar on his paddle.

He and Fred spoke quietly, and I assumed they were conferring about bears, fishing, and campsites. We were holding onto a canoe with one of the Missouri crewmembers and talking about our trips. Tom told the guys in the canoe next to us about our bear and how the guide and I sat up and kept it away. They looked at me with a look that made me feel kinda cool.

They were nice guys and said they had been west to Darky and Argo lakes, then up to Sturgeon. They camped on Russell for two days. They were heading to Louisa Falls for the night, and they were making good time. It must be nice to have a tailwind!

They were due at the Base tomorrow. Fred suggested they might want to push on into Sunday Lake since there was a "campsite bear" around lower Agnes.

The other guide said, "We may just do that!" Then he yelled, "Hey, Crew Chief! Come on down and feed that ol' bear some tea and birthday cake with candles for me too."

Fred was smiling. I guess he had told him about our bear, and I felt proud to be included in the report. We shoved off, said goodbye, and started to paddle the last part of the north end of Agnes.

We were making good time even with the headwind. I hoped we would look as good as the other crew by the end of our trip. Since several of our teams had changed paddlers back at the lunch break, we were not as smooth as they were. I knew watching the other crew paddle was having a positive effect. I watched as everyone was trying to make paddling look as effortless as they had.

We paddled for another half hour and finally reached the portage at the end of Agnes. Finally, all of us were ready to walk for a change of pace.

Agnes was a big lake and had become almost calm as we got closer to the shore. I looked back and noticed how different she looked with the whitecaps going the other way. I could hear the wind whistling through the pines, but it was calm down at lake level because the trees and hills above us protected us in the little cove. I assumed I was to take charge of the portage and did so, reminding Chuck to make sure all of the gear was accounted for before starting across the first portage of the day. I noticed the map said the portage was 80 rods. Our first portage at Customs was 40 rods and was easy compared to the Meadows portages yesterday.

"This should be a cakewalk, guys," I said, looking at Fred to see if he agreed. He smiled and didn't say anything as he got Joe started on his way across the portage.

I watched Fred as he prepared to flip his canoe. I carefully studied his moves as he effortlessly rolled the beautiful green canoe onto his shoulders. A little water had collected in his canoe. I loved the way it sloshed to the ground as the yoke landed on his shoulders. He gave the canoe a little bounce and then began to "dog trot" up the trail.

Since I was next to portage, I was determined to master flipping my canoe and carefully thought through the process. Dave and Tom quickly picked up their loads, and Tom started across the portage. I realize everyone in the crew watched as I took a big breath before I began what I hoped would be my best flip of the trip.

Standing across from the yoke, I pulled the canoe up on my thighs. Then I reached through my legs as far under the canoe as I could. With my left hand, I reached across and grabbed the gunwale. Properly crouched and feeling well balanced, I rocked slightly and rolled the canoe to my shoulders. It landed perfectly.

Finally!

Getting it right felt terrific. I adjusted how the yoke felt by bouncing slightly and started across the portage. Several of the guys yelled, "Way to go, Louis!"

I yelled back, "Thanks! Remember to check all the gear."

After I was sure I was out of sight from the rest of the crew, I decided to try a dog trot like Fred. I jogged for about 20 yards and then decided it was too rocky to be moving quickly. This portage was very rocky and was still wet from the morning rain.

After jogging, I was beginning to catch up with Tom. I slowed my pace so I wouldn't crowd him. He was moving along okay, and there would be other times to practice jogging when the trail was drier and smoother. At least I hoped there would be smoother portages on this trip. I was beginning to see what Fred had meant about the trails being rocky.

It felt good to be walking, and I noticed that I had developed a swinging gate because of the concentration required on the rocky path. It was necessary to place each step since there was no level ground. In some locations, it was outright treacherous. Because I was concentrating and carefully placing each step, I found it necessary to look up only when I could see a relatively smooth area ahead.

After a slight rise, we began the easy descent to the next lake. This lake would probably be considered a pothole since its total length was perhaps a little more than the portage we had just completed. I walked out into the water until it was nearly to my knees and set the canoe down with a minimal splash.

"You're getting it down pretty good," said Tom as began to load his gear into the canoe.

Dave was right behind us, and we were on our way out to wait with Fred and Joe. The rest of the crew came across without incident.

I said, "Since this is our first portage for the day, let's call off all our equipment and make sure we have everything, Chuck."

Everything was there, and it seemed like only a few moments before we had paddled across the lake and were at the next portage. Fred suggested that Mr. Greenlee, Mike, and Gary start over the portage first. He said this would be another moderately short portage but to mind our footing since it was still wet. After they had moved on across the portage, Fred sent the others across.

As they walked out of sight, Fred said, "Louis, you're doing a great job as crew chief, and I think your attention to detail of always checking for the equipment is excellent. However, part of what we are trying to accomplish on this trip is providing everyone with leadership opportunities. Your selection of Chuck for quartermaster is perfect. Yet you have reminded him to check gear twice today, and I think it's time to let him do his job. What do you think?"

"Fred, I see what you mean. You are right. I'll try to let all the guys function once I have assigned a task," I said. "I hope you don't mind if I make suggestions from time to time. You're doing a great job, and maybe you can consider this just a little fine-tuning."

I was thrilled Fred had taken the time to coach me and told him I appreciated it.

He said, "We had better get going. Think you can catch up with the crew?"

"I'll be right behind you," I said.

Fred rolled his canoe up with his typical ease and was on his way. It helped me to watch him flip his canoe again because I picked up on a little more of the technique each time.

As I started across the portage, I figured Fred must have slowed his pace, because I quickly caught up with him. I remembered I had wanted to ask him about the canoe he used. I presumed that it would be lighter and easier to carry since it was made of wood. The guides also carry their own 30- to 40-pound pack in addition to the canoe.

When we arrived on the other side of the portage, we had to wait to put our canoes down while the rest were loading their canoes. It was at this point I learned another new skill from Fred. While waiting, I told Fred the yoke felt much better while walking than when I was standing still. He agreed and said, "Try to lift the bow as high as you can, and lean it against a branch while placing the stern on the ground behind you. It will serve like one of the canoe rests we saw on the Meadows Portages. You can get a little relief and rest that way."

I found a solid branch, tried it, and found it a great suggestion. I decided to share it with others as the opportunity arose. The next lake was about a mile long, but it was relatively calm since it was narrow and the wind was coming from the side. We stayed along the right-hand shore and made excellent time on the small lake.

About halfway across the lake, we saw one canoe with a man and woman paddling toward us. Since we were grouped close together, we all heard the hushed exchange between them and our guide. It was merely a quick hello and a smile I would describe as friendly.

With so little conversation coming from Fred, everyone else merely nodded or said a quiet "hello." After we were out of earshot, Fred slowed his canoe and said, "Thanks for being quiet. Many people come here for the quiet and solitude one can find in the wilderness. Sometimes people spoil it by making a lot of noise."

Just then, a beaver slapped his tail on the water and caused us all to look where only ripples remained.

"See what I mean?"

We continued to the lake's end and made the next portage in record time. We had reached Kawnipi, an enormous lake with many bays.

We entered the lake through a long narrow inlet. As we moved to more open water, it didn't seem like a massive lake at all. I looked at the map and noticed we would only see as far as Rose Island, which appeared to be almost a mile across and more than a mile long. Fred had said we would be camping on a small island just below Rose Island.

Fred pointed to the island where we were to camp and said, "Is anyone up for a race?"

We all took off with a great burst of energy, and I watched as Fred rapidly pulled ahead, leaving us far behind.

We had a great time racing to the island, and this time, Cliff, Henry, and Chuck were the first of the crew to arrive. Of course, Fred had already unloaded his canoe and was standing on the shore waiting for us.

Chuck was the biggest guy in our crew and very strong. With him paddling in the bow, he and Smitty made an excellent racing team.

When we got to shore, we unloaded our equipment, and Fred asked me to join him and Mr. Greenlee for a brief conference while we looked over the campsite. Fred asked if there were any issues we needed to discuss before we had the crew set up camp. I wondered if he had seen any bear signs. Fred told me that, although bears are excellent swimmers, they prefer not to swim out to small islands this far out from the main shore. Fred suggested we get together after supper to discuss the rest of the route and assign the Scouts responsible for our Sunday worship service. Mr. Greenlee said, "Okay," and I agreed.

I walked down to the landing, where the crew was still moving gear, and made sure everyone knew who was doing what regarding the camp duties for that day. The latrine crew was Chuck and Mike. I asked Mike to help set up the tents so I could help Chuck with the latrine and have a chance to talk with him about his new assignment. As we walked back into the woods to dig a latrine, I told Chuck I was sorry to have reminded him of the job he had already accepted.

Chuck said, "I noticed, Louis, but I figured we are both new to our jobs. No need to be sorry."

Chuck has always been a friend I could trust.

As we were walking, I noticed the fresh smell of the woods. Chuck said many trees on that island were cedar trees, and I remembered

Chuck was always good at identifying trees and plants. So I said, "Please feel welcome to share your knowledge with the crew." He smiled broadly and said he would.

After we had finished digging the latrine hole, I noticed the lake through the trees. We walked to the north side of the island and found the most spectacular view I had seen so far on this trip. I could see the narrows between Rose Island and the mainland shore on the left. Both the mainland and the island rose far above the lake level, and the view was something to remember. Chuck told me he felt the same way and said he wished he had his camera with him.

"Let's come back with our cameras," I suggested. "In the meantime, I'm going to take a life picture right now."

"What's a 'life picture?'" Chuck asked.

"A practice I invented on this trip," I replied. "There are already several moments I will never forget. In every case, I focused on the details of what I saw in order to remember it later."

"Like what?" Chuck asked.

"The view of the lake just after we swamped back at the Base is a scene I will never forget," I told him. "The picture I imagined when looking back from where I almost ran into Mr. Greenlee just after leaving Customs will also be one of my life pictures."

"That's a neat idea since you don't even need a camera," said Chuck. "I'll have to try it, but I will get a real picture of this too."

On our way back to camp, we came across a dead cedar. We decided to pick up some firewood. I loaded Chuck's arms with firewood, and he headed back to camp. Alone, I became more aware of the much stronger odor of the aromatic cedarwood we had broken apart. I picked up a piece and smelled it.

Grandpa! The smell led my thoughts to Grandpa. *I sure hope he is doing okay.*

Just then, I realized collecting life pictures without a camera wasn't something new for me. All of a sudden, lots of images of Grandpa flashed before my eyes.

I remembered something else as well, and I started to worry. Fred had mentioned we needed to begin to prepare for the church service on Sunday. How was I going to plan one?

Mom was the real religious one in our family. Dad and I just went along. I went to church every Sunday, but I'm dreaming half the time. I wasn't sure I could even remember a Bible verse.

What the heck are we going to do?

Grandpa came back to my thoughts, and I remembered the uncomfortable situation we have in our family. Mom is a Methodist, and Dad was raised an Episcopalian. Our family is Methodist. Dad always goes to our church and seems to enjoy the fellowship. I guess he became an official Methodist when he married Mom.

Grandpa is actually my great-grandfather and was born in 1858. He has always been Catholic, and Mom has always seemed down on his faith. Dad said his dad, my grandfather Carter, was Catholic as a boy, but his wife, Grandma Carter, made his father change when they married. They met in England during the First World War, and she made him become a member of the Anglican Church and change his surname to Carter. I remember she didn't like Catholics or anything French.

I don't remember Grandma and Grandpa Carter very well. But I do remember Grandma Carter didn't seem to like my great-grandfather very well. I guess he embarrassed her. I think it was partly because he was Catholic. I don't know; it's just all very confusing. Mom loves Grandpa but always trys to get him to stop acting Catholic, which makes Grandpa sad and upset. Every time anything religious comes up in our family, Mom controls the conversation.

My big concern now is I had just remembered Tom is Catholic. Mr. Greenlee, Dave, and Joe are Baptist and go to the church that charters our Scout troop. Cliff and I are Methodist, Chuck and Mike are Lutheran, Gary is Episcopalian, and Henry is Jewish.

Good grief! How do we put on a church service with all those different faiths? Don't Jews go to church on Friday or Saturday? How did I get to be the one in charge of all this anyway?

"Louis!"

Someone was calling my name. It was Chuck.

"What happened to you? I have been back to camp. I was worried you had fallen into the hole or something."

"I'm okay, Chuck. I was just thinking about some things."

"Let's get some more of this cedarwood. Fred talked about doing some baking tonight since split cedar is good for a reflector fire," replied Chuck.

"Sounds good to me," I said, and soon we were on our way back with another good load of wood.

Chapter 15

ROSE ISLAND

When I got back to camp and had deposited my armload of wood with the rest of the firewood, Fred pointed out a spot on the south side of the island, saying, "Mr. Greenlee and I are ready to have a planning meeting."

I looked up and saw Mr. Greenlee standing near the water's edge.

"I'll be there as soon as I finish stacking the firewood," I answered.

I finished stacking the wood, brushed the bark off my arms, and thought, *I wonder what this is all about?*

I followed Fred, and when we got there, we sat on a large rock overlooking the water. Mr. Greenlee began, "Well, Fred, I guess the trip we planned will be a little too easy for this group. What do you think?"

"I agree," he said. "I am going to suggest we add one more side trip to our plan. I believe tomorrow, and for the next few days, we will be able to do some serious fishing in some very productive spots. However, I recommend adding a little side trip to Blackstone before heading down the border to see Knife Lake Dorothy. We need to buy these guys a root beer on our way back to the Base."

"Do you think we can do it? It's a little out of the way," I said, looking at the map.

"I am sure we will be able to do it. Blackstone has some excellent fishing. We will probably be able to make some other side trips if the weather cooperates," replied Fred.

I looked at the map again and traced the route change.

"It looks good to me," I said and then asked, "May I ask a question about something else?"

"Of course," they answered at the same time.

Mr. Greenlee said previously it was only Thursday, and we had plenty of time to discuss the service. I was extremely nervous about ever seeming to argue with Mr. Greenlee but decided that I should bring it up since I was so concerned with our group's mix.

"Mr. Greenlee, I was just thinking about the service and, well, sir, I'm worried! I'm not sure how to handle a religious service with a group like ours. Besides, I'm not sure I can remember even one Bible verse."

Mr. Greenlee smiled and said, "Louis, I think you are about to learn a valuable lesson about leadership. When I have a task at work or when I had a task to do while in charge of Marines, I always found there are not only folks who can do most things better than I can, they are often waiting to be asked to help."

"Yeah, just like Chuck," I said, "when I asked him to be the quarter-master and be responsible for the gear."

"That's right, Louis," said Mr. Greenlee. "Let's talk about the group and see if we can come up with a couple of guys who can do the service. Everything happening isn't your job. It's your responsibility to see that it happens, but good leaders also learn to delegate as much as possible. Okay?"

Fred chimed in: "Louis, I probably didn't mention it, but I have some trail church-service books the Base provides. I'm sorry if I shook you up when I asked you to take care of the service."

I certainly was relieved to learn of the books.

"Louis," said Mr. Greenlee, "you've mentioned your concern about this being a mixed group. Tell me, what do you mean by a 'mixed group?'"

"Tom is Catholic, Chuck and Mike are Lutheran, Gary is Episcopalian, and all the rest are Baptist . . . except Cliff and me, who are Methodist. Oh, and Henry, he's Jewish," I replied. "How do we do a worship service for a group like ours? Don't Jews go to church on a different day? I wouldn't want to force Henry to do a Christian thing if it's against his religion. It wouldn't be right. Would it? And do Catholics worship with Protestants? And don't they have to eat fish and stuff?"

"Slow down, Louis," said Mr. Greenlee. "You have all the right concerns. Now here is a little test for you to consider. What is the twelfth point of the Scout Law?"

"A Scout is reverent," I answered.

"And . . ." said Mr. Greenlee, "what's the rest?"

Oh boy, I have memorized all that, but what did it say?

"Let's see . . . it says a Scout is reverent toward God and is faithful in his religious duties. And he respects the convictions of others in matters of custom and religion. Is that close?"

"Yes, it is, Louis, and you're right about Henry. He is Jewish. I would like you to think about this dilemma as you see it. Talk with some of the guys about how we can have a worship service in line with the Scout Law."

Fred started to say something about the books. Mr. Greenlee broke in and said, "Louis, you discuss it with the guys, and then we will get back to looking at the books.

"Fred," he continued, "how does that sound to you?"

"Sounds good," Fred replied. "We have plenty of time. Let's see what you all come up with before we firm it up."

This deal is still mine until I talk to the guys about a church service, I thought. *Now how do I cause that to happen? I'll ask Smitty.*

Mr. Greenlee then changed the subject and said, "What about fishing? Are we there yet, Guide?"

Fred laughed and said, "Well, as they say in Ely, you betcha! Kawnipi has some productive fishing. With the tremendous time we made today, we should be able to do some fishing after an early supper. Tomorrow we are just going to paddle up into Kawa Bay, set up camp by noon, and fish the rest of the day. Other crews have been doing very well in both Kawa Bay and McKenzie Bay. I'm still excited about a fairly short day to Mack for some serious fishing there as well, okay?"

"Sounds good to me . . . Louis?" said Mr. Greenlee.

"Me too! Is there anything else we need to talk about?"

"Well," said Fred, "I was watching the guys head out to the latrine this morning and notice most of them made the trip with the toilet-paper bag. Sometimes guys will get constipated on a journey like this and can get pretty miserable. That is why I suggested some fruit stew this morning. Help me keep an eye on the rest of the crew. If you see someone getting grumpy or quiet, it sometimes indicates a problem."

"I've noticed pretty steady visits to the latrine," said Mr. Greenlee, "but Joe has been uncharacteristically quiet."

"Well, let's just keep an eye on him," said Fred. "Now, if it is all right, I want to discuss some fishing tips with the guys before we start."

"Sounds good to me. I love fishing tips," said Mr. Greenlee.

After we had finished our meeting, I went to see what we were having for dinner. Gary was well into preparing fried Spam®, potatoes, and gravy, and he said we would be eating soon. Meals were one area of this trip which was absolutely no worry.

I saw Fred was with Chuck and Joe, who were getting some wood ready for the baking after supper. They had set up a little axe-yard area away from the rest of the campsite. Fred showed them how to split off uniform pieces of the cedar just right for keeping a constant fire going in front of the reflector oven.

They were using the contact method for splitting wood. We had learned it from our troop leaders but didn't use it much back home. Most of the wood we used was hardwood and challenging to split. We always tried to pick up wood small in diameter whenever we could. Most of the wood up here in the north woods was a softer wood and easy to split. I complimented the guys on being able to split the wood into finger-sized pieces.

"It's what Fred asked of us," said Gary. "It was good to review the contact method, which involved placing the axe blade on the length of wood to be split and then striking with the axe, remaining in contact with the wood at all times. We sure don't need any axe cuts out here in the wilderness!"

I moved away from the work area to speak privately with Joe.

"How's it going, Joe?"

Joe said he was enjoying the trip and liked being in the same canoe with Fred, but he said, "Fred has been kinda' quiet when we are underway."

I thought, *Ah! That may be why Joe seems quiet to Mr. Greenlee.*

"Let me know if you need anything," I said.

Joe smiled and went on with the firewood project.

Cliff was getting his gear stowed in the tent. I thought I might start my church-service chats with Cliff since he was my closest friend. It seems funny Cliff (or Smitty, as most people called him) was my best friend, and this was going to be the first talk we had on this trip. Smitty and I were close friends, and the thing I liked about our friendship was, we didn't have to be together all the time. We respected that we liked different things and didn't have to do everything together. We frequently talked about serious stuff, and I knew he would be the best place to start. So I walked over and said, "Hi, Smitty, got a minute to talk?"

He smiled and began to walk to the big rocks on the north side of the campsite. I followed, and he said, "You're doing a good job, Louis. I knew you would like all this if you came along."

I remembered he was a big part of why I didn't put up too much of a fuss about coming. His folks had a cabin in northern Minnesota, and he kept telling me I would love this place. It's funny when someone knows you so well.

"Ya know, you are kind of a star on this trip," he continued.

Gosh, I hoped he wasn't thinking I was getting cocky or something.

"Well, it all just sort of happened," I said.

"I was watching and could see you change in a day," he said. "And I'm glad."

I could tell he wasn't jealous or anything. He was just happy for me.

"Smitty, I've got a problem I wanted to ask you about."

"Shoot," he said.

"Well, Fred and Mr. Greenlee want to have a church service on Sunday, and I just don't know how to approach all the other guys. With Tom being Catholic and Henry a Jew, I'm just concerned that we have something good and not step on any toes. Ya know?"

Cliff looked out over the lake and said, "Why don't we just have a meeting, like a patrol meeting, without Mr. Greenlee and Fred, and talk about it. I'll help you, and actually, I don't think Henry will be a problem. Most of his friends are Christian, and he is used to hearing Christian prayers and such things."

"That's just the problem, Cliff. We probably aren't the best kind of friends if we always assume he just goes along with us. Scouts are supposed to be reverent, remember? We're expected to respect others who are different from us in religious matters. Isn't that the way you learned it? Why does Henry always have to be the one respecting our faith?"

"Yeah, you're right, Louis," he said. "I still think we just need to have a meeting and talk about it. If I were you, I would get a handbook and read the twelfth law and then discuss how we could have a service respectful to all."

"Good! Then that's what we will do," I said. "Cliff, how are you enjoying the trip?"

"I'm getting into it now," he said. "I was kind of feeling maybe you were mad or something. However, I also figured you have enthusiastically gotten into this leadership role, and you've been off thinking by yourself a lot. But then, I just figured you had a lot on your mind."

"Cliff, I do have a lot on my mind, and things are happening so fast, I can hardly keep up. I don't know if I told you, but Grandpa could not even talk when I left. I'm afraid he is going to die while I'm gone, and it makes me anxious. He is on my mind all the time, and I am collecting things to tell him. He's over a hundred, ya know."

"I wasn't aware your Grandpa was so bad off," said Cliff.

"Pretty bad," I said.

I knew Smitty had heard all my theories about Grandpa; in fact, he was the only friend I trusted enough to visit the home with us.

Cliff then said, "Louis, sometimes very old people who are ready to die hang on until their families gather around them. My grandma waited until all of her kids and grandkids could see her, and then she died peacefully shortly after. I think because you have always been close to your great-grandfather, he will be there when you get home. Besides, you can't do anything about it while you are out here, so I hope you will find a way to keep it from messing up your trip. He wouldn't want that, would he?"

Smitty always had a way of putting things into perspective.

"Ya know, it was when we told Grandpa about this trip that he reacted by speaking in a loud voice and using words we didn't understand. Everyone thought he was having a stroke. They gave him a shot to calm him down. Maybe he was just excited for me. What do you think? Gosh, I hope he is there when we get back."

I had tears in my eyes, and Smitty put his hand on my shoulder.

"I think he will be, Louis. He is a pretty tough old guy."

We sat quietly, looking up the channel between Rose Island and the mainland for a while. What a view and what a friend.

I had become pretty emotional remembering my last visit with my Grandpa. I felt I needed to change the subject, so I said, "What do you think of this canoe trip so far? Isn't Fred the neatest guy? I am thinking about applying to be a guide when I'm old enough."

We sat for another five minutes looking in the direction of the narrows between the mainland and Rose Island. Then Smitty said, "Yes, sir, I could get into all this. Let's talk with Fred, and maybe we could both apply."

I figured that, like me, he was lost in thought.

"It's something else up here, isn't it?" he said.

"Smitty," I said. "It's probably time to eat. We'd better get back to camp. I'm hungry."

When we got back to camp, Gary had already started serving. We got our plates, and everyone went down by the water to eat so we could avoid the mosquitos as the wind had died down.

Henry said grace, and I remembered we needed to have the meeting we had discussed. The guys enjoyed the food, and I grinned at Mr. Greenlee, who was eating fast as the rest of us. I guess we were both hungry and anxious to get out fishing.

"Let's all pitch in on dishes so we can all get out fishing as quickly as possible," said Mr. Greenlee. "Fred, is there anything we need to review before we catch all the fish in this lake?"

"Yes, there are several things I want everyone to hear," said Fred. "One is we don't want to catch too many fish, only what we can eat. And that means we need to communicate our progress and ensure we don't all come in with a canoe-load.

"When you are out fishing, signal to the other canoes and let them know how you are doing. It doesn't need to be anything elaborate. Just wave and hold up fingers to communicate numbers.

"Another thing to remember is how the various fish act. Northerns are loners, and if you catch one in a spot, there probably won't be another close by, but stay in the area since you're in good northern habitat."

"How about the walleyes?" Mike asked.

"Walleyes tend to be in groups, and if you catch one, stay put and keep trying," continued Fred. "They like points where the water is cool and moving. They will generally be deeper than northern, although northern are found in deep waters as well.

"When you catch a northern," he continued, "remember they have lots of sharp teeth and will bite you if you put your fingers near their mouth. If you get a good-sized one, remember what Terry Gibson, the guide at the campfire, told you. Bring them up beside the canoe, bring your hand up behind them, and grab them behind the eyes. If you get a huge one you are going to keep, grab them by the gills. Remember, if you plan to throw one back, always wet your hands when you handle them, and don't bugger them up while removing the hook.

"Now, speaking of hooks, be careful with your casting. Talk to each other so you don't hook one of your buddies. If you should get a hook in you, remember your first aid training, and it would be best to get Mr. Greenlee or me involved in removing the hook. Never remove the lure if you have to cut the barbs off of a treble hook. If you don't have a cutter, I have had a little experience in these operations and a side-cutting plier. Guys, the main thing is to have fun while being careful and to remember to not catch more than we can eat.

"Now let's get to it. After we fish, Gary and company will make some pies or cakes for dessert, and now I am ready to catch some breakfast!"

It was early evening, and there were still three hours of sunlight left. Tom, Dave, and I got our fishing gear together and headed out onto Lake Kawnipi. As soon as we were away from the shore, we slowed, and I suggested we first troll around the island. We set up our gear by putting on a steel leader and the lure we thought would be best. Dave used a black and white Lazy Ike, Tom used a Red Devil, and I put on a red and white Lazy Ike.

We started to troll around our island, and Tom and I tried to keep a consistent speed, which was similar to the slow trolling speed of a small outboard used on fishing boats back home. Everyone in our group had fished with their families. The most significant difference was how clear the water was up here and the kinds of fish for which we were fishing.

The water was calm, and the sun felt warm as its rays came from low in the western sky. We rounded the east side of the island and could see the view of the narrows. The sun on Rose Island and the shore in the shade looked very different from just an hour ago when I saw the same panorama. The channel between the landmasses was bright with the reflection of the light on the island.

We paddled into the shade of our island when Dave said, "I've got one!"

I told Tom to keep paddling while I quickly reeled in, and then I resumed paddling while he brought in his line.

Dave was busy reeling in his catch, and Tom asked, "Dave, did you set the hook?"

"Yes, Tom, and please keep the canoe moving slowly."

"Do you know what kind of fish you've got?"

"No, not yet."

"Is it big?"

"I don't know. It could be. Gosh, could you just let me do this without having to answer lots of questions?"

Dave then said, "It's a northern and a good-sized one too. Dang!"

"Tom, stop paddling so I can help Dave get the fish up to the canoe," I said.

Dave had the fish within five feet of the canoe and held his fishing rod in his left hand. He was trying to bring the fish up past his right hand. As he reached out and grabbed the steel leader, the fish gave a violent shake as it came out of the water. It was a big one, almost as long as my arm. It splashed water on all of us as it hit the water. Then . . . it was gone. Dave was holding the leader and an empty lure.

"NUTS!" yelled Dave. "It would have been the biggest fish of my whole life. I can't believe it got away!"

"Well, you've got witnesses," Tom said, "and I'll swear the fish was twenty pounds or more."

"What did I do wrong? I didn't expect to get one this big in the first five minutes."

"Dave, I think perhaps you didn't set hook very well," I said. "Or maybe the hooks were in a weak spot that couldn't stand the strain of twenty-plus pounds shaking around. Anyway, I sure see why Fred said to pick the fish up. I guess he meant not by the leader. Sorry, Dave . . . are you ready to try it again?"

We started trolling again, paddling around the island. Ten minutes later, Tom hooked one. It was a short fight, and he landed him without a problem. It was a northern but only half the length of Dave's. I estimated it weighed about 10 pounds. He seemed disappointed until I reminded him of the size of bullheads, crappies, and bluegills we were used to catching at home.

Tom had a stringer. We put the fish on, tied it to a thwart, and continued our quest. As we reached the south side of the island, we saw Mr. Greenlee's canoe. We waved and held up one finger. He gave thumbs up and then made a zero. He pointed to the campsite, and we saw Fred and Joe casting from the shore. They indicated they had one, and then Fred nodded toward Joe. We quickly paddled over to Mr. Greenlee's canoe and told them about Dave's loss on the island's northwest side.

Mr. Greenlee said, "If that fella was hungry, he is probably still hungry. What say we all cruise over there and see if he is still in the neighborhood?"

We did, and Dave and Mike both caught a walleye out some distance from where Dave had lost the big northern. Mr. Greenlee said they were the perfect size for eating. He had his camera along and got pictures of the guys with their catches. Later, we saw the other two canoes over toward Rose Island, and they waved and signaled they had three fish between them. We figured we could catch two more with the seven fish reported. We accomplished this within 15 minutes. We signaled for everyone to stop fishing since we had enough for a meal.

Tom and Dave caught all the fish in our canoe. Still, I did not feel sorry about not catching a fish since I enjoyed keeping the canoe moving and in position for the others. I had also learned a few things, which I would remember when I had a big one on my line.

We headed back to camp and counted the fish. We had nine fish altogether, with three northern, one bass, and five walleyes.

Fred asked everyone to gather so he could show us how to clean the fish. First, he told us it was imperative to take the fish guts and skins far out into the lake and sink them so we didn't create an odorous mess attractive to bears. Next, Fred showed us how to clean the fish so the fillets were removed with as much meat as possible. The method he demonstrated also left the skin and most of the bone left behind in one piece.

Fred used his knife, a Finnish Puukko with a blue handle and a brass horse head on the hilt. It had a relatively thick blade for a fillet knife. However, it was so sharp it worked beautifully.

Fred made one cut along the backbone of the northern. He then opened up the belly from the anus to the gills. By slicing close to the bone along the spine, he separated the still-attached first fillet. Following a cut behind the gills, he left the fillet attached to the tail. He then flipped the fillet skin-side down on his paddle, and using the tail to pull, he placed his knife down toward the skin and pulled and sliced the skin from the meat.

When he finished the same procedure on each side, he had two nice fillets, and all the rest was in one piece. He said it was now our turn to learn while he and Mr. Greenlee helped.

We all got to try our hand, and for the most part, it went well. A few of the guys forgot and cut the fillet away from the tail. They had difficulty trying to separate the meat from the skin without the tail and skin to grasp. This process was different than the way we cleaned the fish at home. We usually left the skin on and scraped the scales off.

After cleaning up the mess, Smitty and Henry paddled out with the remains and dumped them into the lake. When they got back, they washed their canoe so it wouldn't smell like fish.

The sun was starting to set, and we were able to enjoy another beautiful sunset. Gary had put on the coffee and hot chocolate. He and Fred had decided to make a cake instead of pies. As he mixed the cake mix, I became concerned about how the cakes would be level in the pans and went up to watch the baking.

Mom and Dad had recently put in a new electric range, and I remember it took the installer a while to get the unit level. Mom was quite concerned about it being perfectly level so that her cakes would be perfect.

When I got up to the fire, I told Fred about how I was worried about how we could get a reflector oven level, and he said, "Well, watch, and I will show you guys how to level a reflector oven here at Charlie's."

Gary brought the reflector oven out, and Fred showed us how to find a good place for a reflector fire. There was a nice flat spot next to the rock fireplace. Previous folks must have used the same place because there were still some flat rocks to provide wings on both sides of where the fire would go.

Fred set up the stainless steel reflector oven, and it was a little different than the ones I had seen before. Once set up, it was like the open end of a V, facing the fire, which had not yet been started. The thin steel reflective surfaces were spotless and polished. The top reflector was hinged at the top, so you opened it from its bottom edge. Inside, there was a metal grate where the cake pans or pie tins would go. The metal grate had to be level.

"Gary, please get a small bowl and fill it about half full of water," said Fred. He placed it on the grate and said, "Take turns and look down into the bowl."

We did and could see the grate was high on one side and low on the back. Fred took some small flat rocks and raised the legs and the bottom of the reflector until the water was perfectly level in the bowl.

"Gary," he said, "I am ready for the mix you have prepared. Are the cake pans ready?"

"I put a thin coat of lard into each pan and then shook a dusting of flour over the lard," Gary answered.

"Good," Fred said. "Go ahead and pour in the cake mix and set the cakes aside while we get a fire going."

Fred had us gather a pile of the thin split cedar, and with one match, had a few of the pieces burning. It didn't take long to have a good fire. Fred showed us how to stand the cedar upright against the fireplace so the flame surface was vertical and directly across from the oven.

I know Mom always had the oven set at various temperatures for everything she made. I asked Fred, "How do we judge the temperature of a reflector oven?"

"That is exactly what you do," he said. "You *judge* the temperature. If you put your hand in front of the oven and count, you will usually jerk it out at about three, which is about three hundred degrees and just right for baking."

We all tried it. Everyone jerked their hands out from in front of the oven in about three seconds.

"The only problem with this job is if you bake a lot," Fred observed, "you don't have much hair left on your hands by the end of the summer."

The cakes were in the oven, and Gary watched to see when he needed to add wood to keep the fire consistent. I went down to the lake and sat with the guys while we waited for the cake. We had covered the fish fillets with water in the largest pot and added a little salt to keep them overnight. Fred said that it had been unusually chilly, so he was confident they wouldn't spoil during the night.

We were all pretty tired from the long haul up Lake Agnes, so we decided to go to bed after cleaning up after eating the cake. It wasn't long before we were eating the best spice cake with frosting I had ever tasted. I expected to be a little hungry on a 10-day camping trip, but so far, the food was excellent, and I never expected to have a dessert this good.

I guess everyone must have been tired because we didn't talk much except for a few fishing stories while eating our dessert. Tom and I told the crew how Dave had almost landed a huge northern, and everyone claimed they would soon have one like his.

While the guys were getting their tents ready and washing dishes, Mr. Greenlee, Fred, and I talked about the day. It was just after dark, and we were exhausted.

"How is our church-service planning coming along?" Mr. Greenlee asked.

"I'm not as worried after talking with Smitty," I said.

Apparently, that resolved the issue, as he said, "I think it's been a great day, and at this point, I'm looking forward to some shuteye."

"I'm pleased with Gary as a cook," interjected Fred. "He is one of the best I've seen this early in the trip. Chuck has already spoken to me about ideas of how to keep track of the gear. This crew is tops!"

Mr. Greenlee moved off to the tent. Fred and I sat listening to a couple of loons singing out on the lake. I told him about my talk with Smitty after getting to camp.

"Smitty and I are both interested in guiding someday and would like to talk with you about how to go about applying."

"I would be glad to discuss it with you," said Fred, "and I'm glad to hear Smitty is interested as well."

After that, we just sat for a few minutes. Fred may have noticed I had become quiet because it wasn't long before he said, "I think I am going to leave you with the loons and join Mr. Greenlee and Smitty in the tent."

He stood, turned back to me, and said, "Please greet your Grandpa for me," and walked back to our tent.

I waited for the loon songs to begin again. It wasn't long before a loon made the long low wail I had already come to love. I was enthralled. I put my hands upon my knee and rested my chin on them.

The slight smell of fish was still on my hands. As always, lately, when I encounter the odor, it took my thoughts to Grandpa. I said a short prayer asking God to watch over my family and especially Grandpa. Then I added, "Fred sends his regards!"

When I was about to get up, I felt like someone was watching me. I looked around, and Smitty was sitting alone about a dozen feet behind me.

"Hey, Smit, how come you're sitting back there?" I asked.

"I figured you were probably thinking about your grandpa and wanted to be alone with your thoughts."

That's what I always liked about Smitty. He was there when you needed him but not hovering.

He moved down next to me and said, "You doing okay, Louis?"

"I sure am, and I think you are right about Grandpa. I think he is waiting for me to come home and will be there when I get back." Then I said, "Thanks for being such a good friend."

"Always," said Smitty.

When we got back to the tent, Mr. Greenlee was already snoring, and Fred whispered, "Leave the mosquitoes outside if you don't mind."

We settled down in our sleeping bags, and I continued to listen to the loons. If there were any rocks or sticks under the ground cloth, I didn't notice. I tried to retrace the events of the day. I must have fallen asleep before I got to our lunch stop because the next thing I knew, I heard Gary and Henry moving the canoe covering the food packs. It was dawn, and I knew they were preparing our fish breakfast.

Chapter 16

THE TEST

I unzipped the netting and flipped back one tent flap on my way out. I felt a little stiff as I stretched to stand at my full height. I suddenly realized I could not see more than eight feet in front of me.

I paused and listened to the sounds of breakfast. Gary and Henry were speaking in low tones. I carefully worked my way to the sounds near the cooking area. Gary and Henry were getting ready to light the fire.

"How about this fog?" asked Gary. "It's like a London fog. Maybe we will find that guy looking for Lord Baden Powell in London back when Scouting started there. What was his name?"

"I recall reading about how Scouting came to America in the front of the *Handbook for Boys*," Henry responded. "In 1909, a Chicago publisher, William D. Boyce, was in London on business. He was having a difficult time finding an address during an especially thick fog. Mr. Boyce was surprised when a boy approached him and asked if he could be of service. He told the boy where he wanted to go and was surprised when the boy saluted him and said, 'Follow me.'

"When they reached the address, Mr. Boyce reached into his pocket and offered the boy a shilling. He was even more surprised when the boy refused it, saying, 'No, thank you, sir. I am a Scout. Scouts do not accept tips for doing good turns.'

"Mr. Boyce said, 'Good turns? Scouts? . . . What are Scouts?'

"The boy told him and showed him the way to Baden Powell's nearby office. There, Mr. Boyce found out about the Boy Scouts and decided that American boys would benefit from this program.

"On February 8, 1910, Mr. Boyce and others interested in the idea formally incorporated the Boy Scouts of America in the United States. So it was that Baden Powell started Scouting during his military service in South Africa. It was an idea for training young men in outdoor skills and came to America because of a good turn. Today, Scouting is a worldwide movement."

I was impressed by Henry's recollection of the story I had read and heard several times.

"What was that boy's name?" I asked.

"He is known as the 'Unknown Scout,' and we can thank him for Scouting and all it means to us over sixty years later."

Henry then chuckled and said, "We'll be lucky to find the latrine this morning."

It hadn't rained during the night, but everything was damp from the thick fog. Henry was whittling on some of the cedar wood we had left over from the baking fire. He was making some fuzz sticks to expose some dry wood to light. It wasn't long before he had a fire lighted.

Larger pieces of wood were added to the now growing fire in the fireplace, a two-foot-high semicircle of rocks carefully stacked to support a pole across the broadest part. The inside was about two feet deep and three feet wide.

While Gary worked on the fire, Henry carried the cooking pots down to the lake to soap the outside of the pots needed to heat some cocoa and coffee water. I heard some of the other guys stirring and thought I had better make my trip to the latrine. I had to stop and think about how to get there even though I was involved in digging it.

I grabbed the shovel and the toilet-paper bag as I started my trip through the wet foliage. It was darker in the dense woods, and the fog seemed thicker. I had to stop several times. I found the path we had taken to get to the downed cedar tree. I knew it was close to the latrine. As I made my way, I noticed the ferns and moss on the downed logs, and I could smell the pungent odor of the cut cedar.

Surrounded by the pleasant aroma of cedar, I said out loud, "Hi, Grandpa!"

I was grateful for Smitty's insights during our talk yesterday.

I think Smitty is right. Grandpa is alive!

As I made my way back through the trees and fog to where I heard the crew fixing breakfast, I noticed the sky was lightening through the fog with the approach of dawn. At one point, I thought I could see through the trees and to the lake beyond. At least, I knew there was a lake beyond. All I could see was dense fog. I wondered how we would navigate if this fog didn't lift before we started.

When I got to the campsite, it looked like everyone was up. I handed the paper bag and shovel to Chuck, who took the bag without hesitation and headed toward the woods.

Mr. Greenlee was urging Gary to get the coffee going. Fred was mixing some cornmeal with a bit of flour. Henry helped by mixing powdered milk to dip the fish into before Gary rolled the fish in Fred's coating mixture.

"Should we start getting the tents down, or do you think the fog will lift and dry the wet dew off of them?" I asked Fred.

"Louis, it will be foggy all morning, and we will just have to shake the dew off the tents and roll them wet," he replied. "Let's get the guys packing so we can get going as soon as we have a fabulous breakfast of fish and pancakes."

I got the guys who weren't cooking to start the packing and explained how Fred had asked us to shake off the tents before rolling them.

When I got back from talking to the tent crew, I watched Gary at work, following Fred's instructions on cooking the fish. He dipped each fillet in the thick milk and then rolled it in the cornmeal and flour mixture.

"Fred was a big help," he said. "He suggested a little salt and pepper should be added to the mixture. The frying pan has a blend of butter and lard. This is going to be a breakfast to remember."

The pieces of fish sizzled as Gary placed them into the hot frying pan. It didn't take long to fry each piece of fish.

When the fish were ready, Henry announced, "I've got two dozen lovely pancakes ready when you are."

Fred was helping by mixing white sugar, brown sugar, water, and some Mapleine imitation maple flavoring. It smelled and even looked like maple syrup.

Fred put a spoonful of butter in and said, "Betty Crocker would approve of this meal."

Henry volunteered to lead grace, and we all joined him in saying the Wilderness Grace. Nobody stumbled on the words "portage trails" this time. I think everyone had looked at the map and realized we had no portages today.

We all started eating fish, pancakes with butter and syrup, and some fruit stew. I sat with Joe, who I had noticed was still a little quiet and uncharacteristically somber. I asked him if he was doing okay, and he just said, "Yeah, not too bad."

I said, "But?"

And he said, "But *what*?"

"Joe, you have been very quiet, and I just wondered if something was bothering you," I said. "I noticed you didn't make the trip to the latrine this morning, and I'm not sure if I saw you make the trip yesterday, either. How about it?"

"Gosh, Louis, the crew leader is supposed to watch our trips to the john?" asked Joe.

"Well, no, but Fred told me to watch to see if any of us are out of sorts because it sometimes means they are constipated. He said it happens on some trips because of the change in diet, and just 'going' on the latrine is a problem for some guys.

"How about it, Joe? Have you made the trip yet?"

"Well, no, not since we left home. But, Louis, I don't want the whole group to know. What do I do? I'm feeling kinda sick this morning."

"Have you been eating the fruit stew, Joe?"

"Nah, I threw it to the fish yesterday. I don't like the stuff."

"Joe, sometimes we have to take medicine and eat stuff we don't like. Fred said the fruit stew always helps keep the guys regular, if ya know what I mean. If I were you, I would eat several helpings of it this morning. It would go well with the pancakes and syrup. If I get a cup, will you try it?"

"Yeah, but don't tell anybody, okay?"

Good grief! I'm starting to sound like my mother.

I got some more fruit stew for Joe and took it to him. Mr. Greenlee saw me and smiled an approving look. I think he knew what I was up to, but he didn't say a word.

"My compliments to the chefs!" said Mr. Greenlee. "This was an excellent breakfast. Fish fried in butter and pancakes so light you could sit on them."

"Fred first shows us how to cook everything and makes it look easy," said Gary.

"But the art is in the actual cooking, right?" said Mr. Greenlee.

"It is indeed an art," said Fred. "Some guys take the directions and still mess it up. You guys are doing great!"

I looked over at Joe. He looked at his cup of fruit stew with a frown on his face but took a few bites and then looked at me and winked. When he finished what was in his cup, I filled his cup with the last stew from the pot and said, "It's all yours."

I asked him to help with the dishes so he could spend a little more time eating while the guys finished packing. I then went to help move gear and to get the guys started on the pots and pans.

When I walked over by Fred, I spoke to him about Joe, and Fred said, "I noticed your several trips to the fruit stew."

I told him Joe told me he was embarrassed.

"Do you think maybe we should switch Tom or Dave with Joe so he could ride in the middle?"

"I think Joe would do better paddling," Fred said, "and besides, we have the Kettle Pack with the toilet paper in my canoe if he needs to pull over for a quick stop in the woods."

Half an hour later, we were ready to depart. Fred asked us to ensure we had all of our gear since the fog was still thick, and it would be easy to miss something. However, there was good light coming from above, and I figured the day would be clear as soon as the fog lifted.

"Okay, guys, this is a test!" Fred announced. "Since we can barely see a canoe's length in this fog, we will have to navigate by map and compass. Let's all get on the same section of the map and plan where we are going and how we will get there.

"First, does everybody see where we are right now? We all agreed on which of the small islands just south of Rose Island we were on. Now what direction do we want to go if we want to get to the right-hand turn into the main channel of Kawnipi?"

He gave us some time to consider this challenge. Everyone agreed with Chuck that traveling 60 degrees, or just east of northeast, would take us up to the channel.

Fred concured.

"Guys, you are correct, and as you can see, we will need to stay on the right-hand shore and make sure we don't turn into one of the little bays by mistake. We need to round the point and then head where?"

"It looks like we need to bear to the southwest at about one hundred thirty-five degrees, and after we pass those small islands on the left, hug the left-hand shore," said Chuck. "Then we need to pass the entrance to McKenzie Bay and, still hugging the left-hand shore, make our turn into Kawa Bay."

"Chuck is correct," said Fred, and then he added, "We will need to remember we will have to trust our compasses with the fog so thick. We will also need to stay in a close group and try to stay in sight of each other. If you drift out of sight, call out so we can get you back on course."

"Is everyone clear on the plan?"

It was Mr. Greenlee, and he sounded like this was serious.

"This is going to put all those drills with a map and compass to the test. Only we don't get a camporee ribbon for this one."

"What do we get?" asked Tom.

"We get to camp in Kawa Bay and fish all afternoon if we do this right," said Chuck. "Otherwise, we can be all confused and waste time touring all the bays of this big lake. It looks to me like there are about ten big ones and scads of little ones."

Chuck was usually quiet, and I was pleased to see him in his element with the map reading.

I moved over by Fred and said, "Should we let Chuck, Henry, and Cliff lead today? Cliff is especially sharp on map and compass reading. Chuck will probably be an engineer someday. I'm surprised he didn't bring a slide rule and a protractor."

"You're getting the idea of delegating, Louis," said Fred. "During my first few trips, I had to be in the lead all the time, and then an advisor gave me the delegation and leadership talk. I still get a little nervous about turning over some of the good stuff, but it would be entirely my trip instead of the crews. In answer to your idea, if it is okay with Mr. Greenlee, let's do it, and you make the assignment."

I looked for Mr. Greenlee, and he was right behind me. He just smiled and gave a thumbs up.

Mike and Chuck were headed out to cover the latrine before packing the toilet paper and shovel into the Kettle Pack.

Mike called out, "Anyone else need the important papers before we pack them up?"

Joe yelled, "Hold on a minute. I need to make a call on Mother Nature before we get going."

Mr. Greenlee grinned at me as Joe quickly walked out of sight. In a few minutes, he returned with a big smile, tossed the bag to Chuck, and handed the shovel to Mike.

"It's all filled back in," he said.

I gave Fred a hand with his canoe and noticed it seemed heavier than the metal ones we paddled.

I've still got to talk with him about his green canoe.

"Well, it's eight a.m., and if we pass this test, we will be in camp before noon," said Fred. "Let's get ready to be underway, and remember to keep it quiet so we can hear each other."

We paddled out 25 yards and waited for everyone to gather in close. When we got together, Fred said, "Louis, who do you want to navigate this fine morning?"

"This morning, I would like Cliff, Henry, and Chuck to lead out and navigate for us," I said. "Fred is going to bring up the rear. Remember what he said: In a few yards, we will not see where we have been or where we are going. Bowmen, you must stay alert to rocks, logs, and anything we might hit.

"Fred, Mr. Greenlee, anything else?"

"We need to be as quiet as possible, and all our senses need to be on alert since it looks like we will just barely see the length of our canoes for a while," he said. "Louis, anything else?"

I smiled and said, "Smitty, take us to some good fishing in Kawa Bay. I need to catch a big fish or two."

I was happy Smitty was in the stern. He had been pretty quiet so far, and I wanted Fred to see my neat friend.

He appeared to be checking his map and directions. Then Smitty pointed and said, "This way!" and started paddling.

The lake was perfectly calm, and we were moving at what seemed like a pretty good pace, but being in such a thick fog was strange, as there were no visual references. I could only take a wild guess at our speed. Fred had said we would be moving at about three miles per hour. I figured we would be making our turn to the southwest in about 25 minutes. As we moved along with only the sounds of paddle strokes and the wash of water against the canoe, I realized I hadn't heard a loon in some time.

Maybe they are quiet in the fog. When I get back, I am going to read up on loons.

I figured we had traveled 15 minutes, and we should be reaching a small point by the small bay on the lake's southern shore. I could faintly see the first shore and felt we were right on target. We heard a beaver slap his tail, and it sounded like it was off to the right and back in the bay. If I was correct, it confirmed we were where I thought we were.

As we made the turn, I watched my compass, and when the bow pointed to the southwest, I sighed in relief as Smitty stopped the turn and headed us in the proper direction. It was then that I heard a loon and felt much better. The fog had still not lifted, but my eyes were becoming accustomed to the constant grayish light. In some places, it was like a watercolor painting where the artist had used more light gray at the bottom and scrubbed it into a smooth consistency on the upper part of the canvas.

Tom said, "This must be what it is like to be flying through a cloud."

As we crossed the channel and moved to our left, we soon saw the small island Fred had said would tell us we were on target. Soon there was another island dimly visible, cinching our location.

Good going, Smitty!

Now we could faintly see the shoreline on our left. We stayed out far enough to miss any rocks, yet we could see the shore as a hazy greenish shape. Occasionally, we came to pockets of what seemed to be clear air, and we could clearly see the shore for a short while, and then we would slip back into the thick fog.

I was staying to the rear and off to the right of our four canoes. We were right beside Fred's canoe, and the other two were evenly spaced.

With the shore as a dark backdrop of vertical green trees rising from the gray rocks, I imagined that our canoes might have looked like they were filled with travelers of another time from somewhere out in the fog. I was mesmerized by the thought and began to imagine the early travelers through the area. The stories told by Mr. Hanson and the others at the campfire were replaying in my memory.

Suddenly, Smitty raised his hand, and faintly said, "Whoa."

Up ahead, we could see an animal swimming across the channel. We kept moving but were ready to slow down if we were going to disturb its progress. It was a bull moose, and his magnificent antlers were moving from side to side as it swam.

Fred quietly said, "Keep back so we don't scare him. Just let him cross so we can have a good look."

Mr. Greenlee was pulling a camera from his pack, and Mike and Gary were trying to get him in line for a picture. My camera was buried in our Duluth Pack, and I vowed I would keep it near the top, even on foggy days, from now on.

After Mr. Greenlee had taken a picture or two, we all slowed and let the moose continue undisturbed. He was trying to reach the shore to our left, and we were moving him more parallel than he probably planned. When the moose reached the shore, there must have been a rocky beach because he made quite a clamor as he charged from the water and up into the brush. We were in the water directly in front of him. He stood still and looked at us. Suddenly he shook his whole body and massive antlers. He slowly turned away from the water and disappeared into the dense woods.

No one said a word, and we all sat still as if lost in our thoughts.

After a few moments, Fred broke the silence and whispered loud enough so all could hear, "Gentlemen, that is as good as it gets! Some crews never see a moose and especially not up close. Smitty, thanks for spotting him, and I thank all of you for being a quiet crew. We will likely see more like him since we will be traveling in moose country for the next few days. Remember, quiet is the key."

He then told us Smitty and his mates kept us right on track, and we were across from the bay, which could lead us into Murdoch Lake, which was another route back to Agnes. First, however, we would proceed past the mouth of McKenzie Bay on our left. Then in a little more than a mile, we would make a left turn into Kawa Bay.

When we started paddling again, I looked up toward the sky, and it looked like the fog was thinning. I looked to my right and could easily make out the shoreline. There wasn't much detail, but it was undoubtedly clearing. I was sad to see the dissolving fog as it erased the vivid pictures of voyageurs and Indians I had imagined as we paddled through the heavy fog.

When we rounded the point and entered Kawa Bay's wide mouth, the fog had nearly cleared, so now we could see across the entrance. It was calm and very still except for the occasional lonesome loon calls I had heard earlier. It was now becoming a constant calling back and forth. I felt like they were calling to me.

I figured it must have been midmorning. As I looked up to check the sun's location, I saw a clear blue sky surrounded by fading fog. It was mystical to see all the fog banks still drifting and slowly dissipating down at lake level.

I stopped paddling and asked Tom to dig into the pack and get my camera. I didn't want to miss getting a picture of the mist rising on Kawa Bay.

Chapter 17

KAWA BAY

As the fog began to disappear, I felt a slight sadness. The morning had started with a great deal of apprehension as we paddled from the safety of the campsite and into the fog, leaving the visual world behind. We had become covered by a gray blanket, which made everything seem surreal. I had found my thoughts were easily transported to visions of voyageurs and Indians. Yet it had not taken long for the fog to become a comfort, like a snug blanket, as the three of us in our canoe passed through the thick fog, and we became confident in our navigational skills. Now the comforting blanket was lifting, and I felt a little bit exposed yet excited as the entrance to Kawa Bay was right in front of us.

The sky had become brighter, making details more well defined. Looking at the map, I judged Kawa Bay to be rather long, about four miles in length. As we paddled into the bay, it became easier to glance at the map and note our progress as we passed the points and inlets making up the shoreline. By memorizing small sections of the map, I found that I could move quickly through this country defined by the shape of the land and its relationship to the ever-present waterways.

We had not seen another living thing except for the moose and the loons since we had left our morning campsite. I wondered if other travelers in the Quetico had stayed back in their campsites or if perhaps we were in an area not traveled as much. I thought about the many hundreds of square miles in the Boundary Waters Area where one could travel from lake to lake by canoe and portages. I could see how one could go for days without seeing other people. Plus, we were already 35 miles from the border where most folks cross.

The hour it took to cover the distance from the bay's mouth, where we began to lose the fog, to our destination seemed to fly by. I was lost in thoughts of the past and also trying to memorize sections of the map. I was making a conscious effort to take in every detail of the landscape as we paddled. I became aware of what might be described as only "lots of lakes, trees, and sky" by some was a diverse and ever-changing panorama.

I noticed the continually changing patterns of various trees as fascinating. The rocks, with the ancient and living lichens creating designs on the surfaces, were different and unique at every turn of our progress. It was easy to imagine images of the Natives, the explorers, the voyageurs, and the loggers who had seen these same sights. It made me feel a type of kinship. I thought about how Mr. Hanson had described the voyageurs and how he had imagined them keeping themselves entertained as they paddled those endless miles.

Looking up ahead, I was glad to see Smitty conferring with Fred. Our lead canoe was heading to our destination for this, our most leisurely day of travel.

The campsite was on a horseshoe-shaped island. I glanced down at my map and confirmed the campsite to be on the island's southwest side. I knew it would be easy to look out across the lake and to the west, which I hoped would give a gorgeous view of the setting sun if the sky remained clear.

The campsite seemed to be larger than our last one, and it sloped to the water. The front of our chosen campsite appeared to be a large flat rock surface starting where the soil and plant growth began and extending down to the water's edge. The rock was cracked, and there were both large- and medium-sized boulders sitting where they had come to rest at the end of the last ice age. Just past the central part of our soon-to-be campsite, the shoreline became very lush with reeds and cattails, which continued as a long and curving bay. It looked like a place one would find fish.

While the rest of us waited offshore, Smitty and Fred walked up into the campsite. They must have been checking for bear signs, just as Fred and I had twice before. I felt a twinge of jealousy as I watched them conferring together as Smitty was now getting the personal attention from Fred, which I had once solely enjoyed. I thought about it and decided it wouldn't be fair for me to be the only one to feel special. I began to admire how Fred spent some individual time with each crew member and related to us all.

Another thing to remember.

The campsite must have met with their approval as Smitty waved to us and gave the signal to unload.

As Tom, Dave, and I moved our gear to the shore, Fred caught my eye and motioned toward Smitty and gave me a thumbs up. I was glad that Fred had communicated with me. His simple thumbs-up motion said that my suggestion of a leader for the day had been an excellent choice. Or at least, it's how I took the quick nonverbal communication.

I'm going to remember to use nonverbal communication like that when I'm a guide.

I felt a little awkward being part of the group and not the leader as we stood at the campsite, looking it over. However, I knew Smitty and his small crew must be feeling the same pride I had experienced on similar occasions. Mr. Greenlee and Fred were both lavish in their praise of our navigation through the fog.

I asked Smitty to share how they stayed on track with just a compass and the map. As Smitty started to describe the process, I felt happy about him being in the limelight this time.

After a quick overview, I was taken aback when Smitty passed the explaining of the detail of compass points and calculations to Chuck. Chuck beamed while explaining the details of the process. As Chuck got deeper and deeper into the details, I looked at Mr. Greenlee and saw him smile and nod his head at Fred. I understood as Chuck was the least verbal of our group. Now he was performing well in front of the entire crew.

It wasn't that Chuck didn't talk much. He could talk your ear off about a physics project. Chuck just didn't socialize as easily as most of us. He would rarely hang out and chitchat unless it was about a subject, usually scientific, in which he was interested.

His explanations were probably more detailed than required. However, if anyone didn't understand degrees, compass points, and how to figure them, they did now. I was a little surprised he didn't pull out a drawing compass, a protractor, and a slide rule. Smitty was grinning at me as we both realized we had unleashed the public speaker in our friend.

Smitty motioned to his shirt pocket. I took it to mean Chuck looked funny without his pocket protector, three pens, and a couple of mechanical drawing tools. It's neat when friends can communicate. We weren't making fun of him. We were excited to see Chuck on the pedestal where we had both stood.

I've got to figure out how to get everyone "up there" on this trip, I thought.

After Chuck's dissertation, he and everybody else looked at Fred and Mr. Greenlee for further instruction or comments. In unison, the response was our leaders and everyone else in the crew looking right at me.

I guess I was still the crew chief.

I looked down and noted my shadow was a small tight circle around my feet. I determined it was close to high noon and said, "Guys, I don't know about you, but I've had a morning I'll never forget with the fog, and we saw our first moose. It's close to noon, and I'm anxious to spend some time trying to catch the biggest fish in this lake. However, work before play. Let's get camp set up quickly while

Gary gets lunch ready. Then we'll have the whole afternoon to fish and swim."

I looked at Mr. Greenlee and Fred. They responded by moving to their packs with the rest of the crew. It was amazing how fast we set up camp. I helped Joe set up two tents, and Dave and Tom set up the other. In less than 20 minutes, we had set up our camp. All our gear was secure, and then we gathered on the rock near the water where Gary had sandwiches, cheese, Hol-Ry, and Red-Eye ready. While we ate, Fred reviewed a few fishing tips and pointed out some of the best spots near our campsite.

"Mr. Greenlee, how close was Louis on it being noon?" asked Joe. "Do you have the exact time?"

I knew what was coming and rolled my eyes at Smitty, who had a grin on his face. Both of us looked at Mr. Greenlee's son, who was looking down at the ground as he tried to control a laugh. Most of us knew what was coming. Some of us had learned not to ask the question unless we wanted to make an impression on new members.

Mr. Greenlee smiled, looked at his watch, and began.

"Well, Joe, I am greatly humiliated and deeply embarrassed that due to unforeseen circumstances beyond my control, the hidden working mechanisms of my chronometer do not exactly coincide with the great sidereal motion by which time is generally reckoned. Therefore, I cannot state with any scientific measure of the accuracy the exact time. However, without fear of being too far wrong, I will state, with some degree of certainty, it is two ticks, three minutes and forty-seven seconds past the hour of twelve o'clock noon, Central Daylight Time."

Joe apparently forgot only new Scouts ever ask Mr. Greenlee the time, and then they ask only once. By the time Mr. Greenlee was finished, the whole crew was laughing, including Fred.

"I'll have to memorize that one to add to my list of answers to common questions on the trail," Fred said.

I've heard him say that so many times, I think I can repeat it word for word. Mr. Greenlee has a lot of other fascinating quotations and folksy sayings. I'm going to write them down when I get home.

After a hearty laugh, Fred reviewed a few more fishing tips. Although we were all anxious to get out fishing, Fred's information caused some serious discussion about who would catch the biggest fish for the evening's dinner.

"Let's make sure we put all the 'keepers' on a stringer to keep them alive until we are ready to clean them," Fred said. "Remember not to catch more than we can eat this evening and tomorrow morning for breakfast. Let's keep it to no more than four fish per canoe.

"Some of you may want to explore some of Kawa Bay, so take your maps and stay aware of where you are. It isn't too hard to get turned around when you are concentrating on fishing."

"It looks like it may be a pretty hot afternoon, so let's review some safety rules," said Mr. Greenlee. "Just because we are out in the boonies doesn't mean we can ignore what we have learned about safety. But because we are out in the boonies, we need to be more careful. What's the rule if we want to swim?"

"We need to use the safe swim defense plan we learned at camp Lewis and Clark last summer," said Henry.

"Which means?" asked Mr. Greenlee.

"Well, it means we need to have a good swimmer along if we want to take a dip while we are out. Right?" Henry replied.

"Fellows, I want you to divide up, so someone who has both safe swim defense training and a lifesaving merit badge is along with if you plan to stop to take a quick dip to cool off. I know all of you want to have a group swim session here at the campsite late this afternoon. You may get tired of fishing all day. Although for me, it's hard to envision getting tired of fishing. I would also like Fred to give us some canoeing instruction so everyone can complete his canoeing merit badge before we get back from this trip."

"Won't a ten-day trip by canoe automatically qualify us for the canoeing merit badge, Mr. Greenlee?" asked Tom.

"Tom, how would you feel about boarding a plane with a pilot with lots of flight time but hasn't yet passed all the Federal Aviation Administration requirements for his pilot's license?"

"I wouldn't like it in a plane twenty or thirty thousand feet above the ground," said Tom.

"Or how would you like to hear your doctor who is about to operate on you say, 'I actually don't have all of the training for this. But I have spent a lot of time around a hospital.'"

"I see what you mean," said Tom.

Mr. Greenlee continued, "Well, like it or not, people have expectations of us when we are Scouts. And if—no, *when*—you become an Eagle Scout, the public expectations are even higher. People expect a lot from you when you are a Scout. Now, with all this in mind, do you think it's appropriate to cut corners on the requirements?"

"You're right, Mr. Greenlee. Fred, can you work with us on our canoeing merit badge?"

"Sure thing, Tom. I carry a copy of the canoeing merit badge pamphlet and some other reading material. Just let me know when you or anyone is ready to read up on the requirements."

Mr. Greenlee surely had a way of making his points.

I'll file his logic away for use when I'm a Charlie Guide.

Within a few minutes after our lunch discussion, we finished planning our afternoon of fishing. Smitty, Henry, and I teamed up, and we headed out with Smitty in the stern. Henry was paddling bow, and I took the middle.

Some of the guys were heading southwest toward the narrow channel we had just come through. We decided to fish around the island and then up toward the mouth of the Wawiag River.

Smitty and I had talked earlier. We figured we could work on our church service and communicate with Henry about including him and his faith in our worship-service plans.

Smitty and I had been fishing many times since our dads were avid outdoorsmen and liked hunting and fishing. We had been pheasant hunting together with our dads, but we had never been fishing together.

Chapter 18

GOOD COMPANY

The canoe moved on the water with ease. Smitty and Henry paddled in perfect unison. Their paddle strokes were becoming more efficient each day. The only sound was that made by the swish of the paddle in the water. Neither one of them banged their paddles against the gunwales. I watched each stroke and smiled as each of them feathered their paddles with practiced ease. They had learned fast.

I sat in the middle of the canoe. It gave me a different perspective from my usual place in the stern. For one thing, I was much closer to the water. As I looked over the side and watched the water silently slide by, I thought of Grandpa, and for some reason, a thought crossed my mind: *Grandpa would like this!*

It was odd sitting in the middle, not paddling from the stern position. The stern paddler was the one in charge. He guided the canoe, set the stroke rhythm, and read the map, deciding on the course. I had given that responsibility to Smitty, my best friend. I enjoyed the role I had as crew chief. Still, I knew everyone needed to experience the responsibilities of being a leader. I looked back at Smitty, and he smiled at me.

Friends share, I thought.

A few minutes later, Smitty broke the silence. He spoke in a tone that was a lot softer than usual.

Perhaps he doesn't want to scare the fish, I thought. *Or maybe he feels the same way I feel about loud noise.*

"Louis, why don't you and Henry troll while we circle our island first? I will keep us moving while you get your lines out."

"Sounds good to me," said Henry, speaking in the same hushed tone of voice as he put his paddle down without banging it against the side of the canoe.

Smitty kept us moving at a slow even speed while Henry and I got our fishing gear ready. I chose the red and white Lazy Ike, and Henry picked a medium-sized red and white Dare Devil spoon.

I let my line out on the starboard side, and Henry stayed on the port side. I suggested Henry not put out quite as much line as I since the Lazy Ike moves about a lot and could tangle with his line. When we were all set, Henry resumed paddling, and we moved along at a steady trolling pace as we headed around the north side of our island.

Henry asked, "Louis, are you glad you came? We were kind of worried before the trip. You didn't seem too excited about coming."

"I didn't realize it was so obvious, Hank. How did you know?"

"Someone asked Mr. Greenlee about your waning interest at a Green Bar meeting you missed a few weeks before the trip. He said lots of guys lose interest in Scouts about the same time they get interested in girls, cars, or sports. He said we should encourage you to stay with it. We had thought we would push you to be our next senior patrol leader since you did such a good job as patrol leader with the Fox Patrol.

"What happened, anyway? You got a girl or something?"

"Well, I don't have a girlfriend. Cars are okay. I just got my learner's permit, and cars are just transportation. I guess I just lost interest in everything; even track was kind of boring last spring. It's hard to imagine I might have missed all this. I think this is the most exciting thing I have ever done. I am glad you guys and my dad pushed me. How about you?"

"Oh, yeah! This is unreal for me too. I had no idea there was a place like this, just a state away. Isn't Fred a nice guy?"

Just then, I felt a strike on my line and quickly gave it a solid jerk to set the hook. Smitty said, "Hank, reel in. Louis has a fish!"

By the time Henry had his line in, I could see I had a good-sized northern. It made a graceful leap and violently shook the lure. I could understand why they suggested the steel leaders.

"Any suggestions on how to make sure I don't lose this one?" I asked.

Smitty suggested I let him wear himself out by fighting for a while before bringing him in. The fish's head broke water again, and I could hear the sound of the lure and leader as he fought. I remembered I could easily set the drag on the reel and quickly set it with a little less drag so the fish could run while I kept constant pressure, moving it slowly toward me.

Smitty and Henry were doing an excellent job of keeping the canoe sideways to the fish. I appreciated the help. It seemed like a long time before I reeled him up close enough to see what I had. It appeared to be just over two feet, and I was sure it was a keeper.

As I brought him alongside the canoe, he thrashed again, and I let him run a bit more before I brought him up close to the canoe. I asked the guys to steady the canoe as I got up on my knees in order to be a little higher to land him.

I remembered what had been said about bringing your hand up from behind. Wetting my hand, I quickly grabbed the fish behind the gills as firmly as I could.

The fish was hooked with the rear treble hooks of the Lazy Ike. The rest of the lure was out of its mouth. I was glad to see the lure because it meant my fingers would not find a sharp barbed treble hook back by the gills.

I held the fish up, and although it was still struggling, I had a good grip and was in complete control. I placed my fishing rod against the thwart.

The next job was to get the hook out, and Henry produced a pair of long-nose pliers his dad had given him. I grabbed the treble hook and, with a quick twist, removed the hook. Now we could look him over, and although it wasn't quite as big as the one we had lost the previous evening, it was a very nice-sized fish. I estimated its weight to be 10 to 12 pounds.

Henry grabbed the stringer and said, "Here, let me help you," and slid it back to me.

I slipped the stringer up through the gills and out its mouth. Then I slid the probe on the front of the stringer into the ring at the other end and had the fish securely tethered. I tied the stringer to the yoke, making sure my fish was in the water so he would remain alive and fresh while we continued fishing.

I asked Smitty if he wanted me to paddle so he could fish. He said he wanted to continue as we were. He looked at the map and suggested we troll over to where the Wawiag River enters Kawa Bay. We trolled past another good-sized island on our right, and Henry caught a little bass near the second island. He decided to throw it back since it was small.

When we got up to the river's mouth, we stopped to try casting in front of the river entrance where the water would be moving. It was very calm, however, and there wasn't much current from the river. We were able to fish without moving much at all. Smitty now got into the act and was trying a jig to see if there were some walleyes.

It felt good to sit and drift. Smitty and Henry threw side casts, and I used an overhead cast to get reasonable distance with Dad's old Shakespeare rod and reel. After a dozen casts, I asked Henry if we could talk to him about the church service that was still my responsibility.

Henry said, "Sure, what's to discuss?"

"Well, Hank," I said, "Mr. Greenlee asked me to make sure we have a worship service, and I have been worried about how to proceed with such a mixed group as we have in this crew. You know, we have Baptists, Methodists, Lutherans, Episcopalians, a Catholic, and you."

"Guys, it looks to me like we have a bunch of Christians and one Jew," said Henry. "But I belong to lots of groups where I am the only Jew, and I am used to it. This year I am the chaplain in my High-Y group. Don't worry about me."

"Hank," said Smitty, "that is exactly what I said when Louis and I first discussed this back at Rose Island. Louis said it wouldn't be very Scout-like not to include your faith, and now we want to figure out how we can do this service and obey the Scout Law for being reverent. It says, 'A Scout is reverent . . . He is faithful in his religious duties, and he respects the convictions of others in matters of custom and religion.'[1] We want to figure out how we can worship while respecting each other's diverse beliefs. Will you help us?"

"Well, sure. What do you have in mind?"

"First off, don't you guys have church on Saturday rather than Sunday?" I asked.

"Well, we don't call our sanctuary a 'church,'" said Henry. "We refer to it as a 'synagogue' or a 'temple.' But it's true that we do observe the Sabbath. The Sabbath begins at nightfall on Friday and lasts until sundown on Saturday. However, as a Jew, my whole life is a continual act of worship. I try to keep God always before me. Actually, in the Hebrew, Shabbat or Sabbath comes from the verb *shavat*, to rest or cease. It's a holy day of rest observed by Jews and some Christian denominations on the seventh day of the week and most Christians on Sunday.

---

1. Boy Scouts of America, "The Scout Law," in *Handbook for Boys*, 5th ed., ed. Ted S. Pettit (New Brunswick, NJ: Boy Scouts of America, 1955), 27.

"My parents and I discussed my going on this trip. They agreed Mr. Greenlee is a fine man, and as long as I quietly observe my prayers every day and spend some time in reflection on the Sabbath, I would be okay. They encouraged me to take part in our Sunday service and be respectful of your faith. So it doesn't look like we have a problem, does it?"

"I think we . . . or at least I . . . have a problem," I said. "Ya see, I just learned something about your faith and would like to know more. I don't think we are respectful of your faith if you are the one who always has to be respectful of our faith. And we aren't learning either. As a matter of fact, I don't know much about the Catholics and Episcopalians either. I would like to put together a service where we can worship in our own way and yet learn from each other."

"Guys," said Smitty, "why don't we have two services? Henry, couldn't you lead us in a Sabbath service Friday or Saturday evening? We, or those who want to, can learn from you? And then we can have a Sunday morning service as well. Hank, could you do a Sabbath service? Would you?"

We were both looking at Henry. He looked surprised and maybe even a little shocked as he said, "Smitty, Louis, you guys are the first Christians who have ever asked me anything but dumb questions about the Jewish faith. You guys are serious about this, aren't you? And isn't attending the worship services of other faiths against your religion or something? I went through all kinds of schooling while preparing for my bar mitzvah when I was thirteen. I guess I could lead in a Sabbath service and make part of it a discussion of the questions I anticipate I would get."

"Then let's do it," I said. "I'll let Mr. Greenlee and Fred know what we have planned. I am sure it's going to be okay with them. It's our crew, and it's A-OK with me.

"Smitty, I would like you to give leadership on the Sunday service. Fred said he has some worship booklets for us to use. We need to get started since it's Friday already. I am not usually excited about church stuff, but this is going to be neat."

Smitty and Henry were both looking excited as well. I threw my line again and started the slow return of my Ike. Smitty and Henry did the same with theirs, and then it occurred to me: "Henry, what about kosher food and stuff? Can you eat everything we have? How about fish and Canadian bacon?"

"And what exactly does kosher mean?" asked Smitty.

"It's the term to describe any food that complies with strict dietary rules in Judaism. These rules are called 'kashrut.' Not all Jewish people observe the rules of kashrut by eating kosher food. For those of us who do, it is a way to show reverence to God and feel connected to our faith.

"Kosher comes from a Hebrew word meaning 'fit or proper,' continued Henry. "It refers to what Jews are permitted to eat and that it is properly prepared. My mom runs a kosher home, and although everything is typically tasty, sometimes I would like a sandwich made out of plain old white Wonder Bread. Mom bakes everything. We don't eat bacon. But I don't have a problem with much else."

"Why can't you eat bacon?" asked Smitty.

"In Deuteronomy, it says only animals that have cloven hooves and are ruminant are permitted (Deut. 14:2–21 King James Version). Kosher also means they are killed according to the traditional rules set down by the ancient rabbis and cleaned to remove any traces of blood. There are just a few places at home where we can get kosher food."

"What about fish?" I asked. "Obviously, you can catch them. Are they okay?"

Henry replied, "We can't eat fish that doesn't have fins or scales. Those we catch here are fine. And if I don't get to catch some soon, I am going to be disappointed."

"Okay, let's just fish for a while," said Smitty.

We all cast again, and it was quiet for a while as we tried our best techniques for attracting fish.

After a few more tries, we moved up closer to the mouth of the Wawiag. Henry caught a nice walleye on the first cast, and Smitty landed one a few minutes later. We all switched to bucktail jigs, and within a few minutes, I had a nice walleye as well.

"Aren't we supposed to keep it to just four fish per canoe?" said Henry.

"Yup, four fish is right," said Smitty. "Let's paddle up the Wawiag to see what it is like."

Henry and Smitty paddled up the river for a mile or so. I noticed the land along the river was very flat, and the trees were not the pines and cedar to which we had become accustomed to seeing. They seemed to be deciduous trees similar to the ones at home. I saw some ash and some larch I recognized but figured I had better ask Fred about this when we came this way tomorrow.

As we headed back to the bay, I had an unnerving feeling about the Wawiag. I wasn't afraid, but I had a disturbing sensation of being watched. It was as if someone was staring or about to reach out and touch me. I looked all around but saw nothing.

I asked Henry and Smitty, "Do you guys feel funny?"

They both said no, so I said no more.

When we were about 100 yards from the entrance to the Wawiag, I looked back to where we had been to see if someone was in view. No one was there, and the eerie feeling was gone. However, I had a nagging sadness as if I was missing something. I found myself turning my head and looking back several times. What was it? I did not know.

A moment later, my throat began to tighten as a sensation of panic came out of nowhere.

Grandpa! I thought. *Has something happened to you? Are you gone from me?*

I fought to push the thoughts from my mind, and then I remembered Smitty's words when he said, "He is a tough old guy." Relief replaced the panic. I knew he was safe.

I will see you again, Grandpa!

As my thoughts returned to the lake and fishing, I heard Henry humming. It was the tune to "The Far Northland." It helped me shake off the feelings I had just experienced.

We paddled out of the mouth of the river and back into Kawa Bay. I was taken aback by the beauty of the lake and its surroundings. The water had become calm. It was beautiful. I looked up at the clear blue sky and noticed the very high, feathery cirrus clouds coming from the northwest. Dad called them mare's tails. I tried to remember what high cirrus clouds forecast but couldn't recall.

Smitty and Henry must have been enjoying the midafternoon scenery as well because we said nothing on our smooth paddle back to the campsite. I was excited that we had four nice-sized fish and hoped the rest of the guys were as lucky.

When we got back to the campsite, I noticed Fred and Mr. Greenlee looking at the sky and were speaking with their heads close together as if they were in a serious conversation.

We put up our canoe and left the fish in the water with the stringer tied to an overhanging limb. Three of the guys were back and asking about a swim. We could see the other canoe within sight of our camp heading our way. We had 14 fish with three good-sized northerns, three smaller northerns, three bass, and five walleyes. We would eat well tonight.

After everyone was back, Mr. Greenlee wanted to take a crew picture before we cleaned our fish. We lined up quickly with our prizes. He took a picture of everyone holding their catches by placing his camera on a large rock and using the timer. Most of us had cameras, so following the crew picture, we took photos of each other's fish with each fisherman's camera. I had one taken with my camera of Henry, Smitty, and me with our catch.

After the photo session, most of us gathered at the shoreline to clean the fish. At the same time, Gary and his crew began preparations for the meal to come.

My first cut into my large northern caused me to carefully review in my mind the demonstration, which Fred had given us back on the island. I looked up and saw him watching the crew members. I sensed he was watching me. I desperately wanted to complete this job with no coaching if possible.

I made a long cut down the back and another up the belly. Then I cut behind the gills and sliced the meat away from the rib bones. It was a nice thick fillet. After repeating the process on the other side, I flipped the first fillet, still connected by the skin to the tail, onto my paddle blade with the skin-side down. I set my knife at an angle and carefully separated the meat from the skin by working from the tail to the gills. I kept tension by gently pulling the tail section I was cutting close to the skin. The process Fred had demonstrated was working perfectly. Fred moved on with no comment. I pretended I didn't notice. But I was beaming inside.

When Fred was gone, I looked up and saw Smitty and Hank grinning. Smitty said, "Funny how no comment can also be a compliment. Let me do the next one and Hank, then you."

I would have been glad to clean all the fish, but then the guys wouldn't have learned anything.

What a meal we had! Our cooks fried the fish in butter and lard after rolling the fillets in the mixture of cornmeal and flour Gary had mixed. We had green beans, and I would have never guessed they were freeze-dried beans. They were sliced like Mom fixes them, with a hint of minced onions. They were just right and went well with the Spanish rice. Since it was early in the evening, we all sat and visited about our fishing adventures. There weren't too many of the "one that got away" stories since it was evident not too many did.

While we were talking, I noticed Fred kept looking at the western sky.

Suddenly I felt cold air moving over us, and Fred said, "Time to batten down the hatches, y'all. There's a storm a-coming."

I looked behind me, and there was indeed a big front moving toward us. Then I remembered Dad always said mare's tails usually meant a storm was coming. I promised myself to be more attentive to the weather in the future.

As I looked at the threatening clouds, I could not help but think they had a sort of beauty in contrast to the blue sky above. However, the dark bottom of the enormous cumulonimbus clouds told us rain and the wind were coming. For the second time on the trip, I could smell the rain, and as had become my habit, the odor reminded me again of Grandpa. I was beginning to feel like he was with me all the time.

"We probably have as little as ten minutes before the storm starts, so we need to move quickly," said Fred. "It looks like this storm could have high winds judging from lumpy bottoms of the clouds." He then pointed and said, "There, do you see what I mean?"

Mr. Greenlee concurred: "I agree, Fred. Back home, we would be headed to the basement."

Fred typically involved us in developing a plan of action, but in this case, with time being so short, he took charge.

"Gary, you and your crew secure all the food packs and bring up an aluminum canoe to put over them. Tom, organize your team and check all the tents to see all knots are well tied and secure. Then put larger rocks on all the stakes and then put up the dining fly lower in front.

"Dishwashers, y'all gather up all of the dishes and, for now, put them under the canoe by the food packs," he continued. "Make sure there isn't anything left out to blow away. Firemen, gather a good supply of dry wood and put it underneath a canoe so that we will have some dry wood, and tinder should get a good soaking. Also, put out the fire so it doesn't blow. Louis, you and Mr. Greenlee help me get the canoes placed where they won't be windblown or damaged. Let's move. Now!"

Everyone moved to his task. Fred, Mr. Greenlee, and I went to the canoes at the shoreline.

"Fred, it would have been nice to discuss and plan our preparations," said Mr. Greenlee. "However, I agree it doesn't look like Mother Nature has provided us with much time. That was well done! Sometimes one doesn't have time for discussion even with an exceptional group like this."

I figured that was said for my benefit. However, I agreed with Mr. Greenlee. With time constraints, a leader can't afford to take the time to be democratic in an emergency.

We moved all of the canoes up from the waterfront, following Fred's directions. Then we placed them in sheltered spots where the wind could not get under them. We also checked to make sure no trees could fall on them.

Fred asked me to give him a hand with his Seliga. I was surprised to find it much heavier than the aluminum canoes. We carefully chose a spot where it would be safe, and then Fred checked to make sure no trees or branches would fall on it. He was very protective of the gear and especially his beautiful wood and canvas canoe.

We had no sooner gotten things battened down when the wind started to blow, and the first drops of rain began to fall. We all put on our rain gear. Fred told us we could wait this out in our tents or under the dining fly. Then he said, "Actually, you can stand anywhere you wish, just not under a tree that could fall if it really starts to blow."

I walked down near the shoreline to watch the incoming weather. At home, I was always safe inside when a storm came. I remember going to the basement once when there were tornado warnings.

I had never stood outside and watched an approaching storm like this one. I looked back, and everyone else was in the tents except Fred, Mr. Greenlee, Smitty, and Henry, who stood under the dining fly. I gave Mr. Greenlee an "is this okay?" look, and he nodded his approval.

Chapter 19

THE STORM

I'm not sure why I wanted to be alone in the middle of a storm. I knew as far as being safe was concerned, I was as secure as the guys in the tents. The thin canvas might keep them dry, but I didn't mind getting wet. I don't know why I wanted to experience the power of this thunderstorm, but I wanted to be out in the open, at the edge of the lake. I needed to be here.

I knew this North Country could be considered a lonely place. Compared to back home, the number of people per square mile was insignificant. The separation between those traveling in the Quetico makes it seem the small groups are entirely alone on the planet. However, I was with a small group of friends, a great Scout leader, and an excellent guide on this trip, so I was never really alone. Still, being in a group with friends close by made me want to be alone for a while. So I stood apart and watched the rapidly approaching storm.

I looked up at the oncoming weather and was awestruck as the clouds I could see boiled and swirled. I knew they swelled thousands of feet into the air above me. I imagined what it was like among and above the clouds. The rain started with a sudden pelting fury. The drops were cold as they hit my bare face and legs.

I was glad I had my long pants tucked safe and dry in my pack. I was very grateful for my hooded waxed-canvas rain jacket. The wind was starting to pound, and soon my jacket seemed as though it was glued to my chest. Now and then, the wind gusts were strong enough to rock me, and I became captivated by the flashes of lightning. The sound of thunder grew increasingly louder as the storm moved upon me. It was incredible!

Somehow, I didn't feel frightened at all. I was overwhelmed as I watched and sensed the powerful display. I searched for a word to describe the onslaught of one of nature's most violent forces. This was raw nature at its most overpowering. Only I had the same feeling I had in the morning fog. I was being embraced.

By . . . what?

I couldn't think. I could just feel, and then suddenly, I thought, *Power*, as the words of the Lord's Prayer came to mind.

"For thine is the power and the glory" (Matt. 6:13).

Was I feeling embraced by God?

I've long said I couldn't remember a single Bible verse, even to Mr. Greenlee, as we discussed our worship service. Still, all of a sudden, the words to the first verse of a familiar hymn came to mind:

O Lord, my God! When I in awesome wonder
Consider all the works Thy hand hath made.
I see the stars, I hear the rolling thunder,
Thy power throughout the universe displayed.[1]

With this display of power above and around me, I felt minuscule and insignificant. But as I stood there with the wind pushing against me, my mind began to race.

---

1. See Stacie Marshall, "How Great Thou Art," Godtube, accessed September 10, 2021, https://www.godtube.com/popular-hymns/how-great-thou-art/.

I go to church nearly every Sunday. I have heard other people speak of knowing God or having a personal relationship with him. I like church and have even said I love God. But I have never, if truth be told, experienced the things of which I have heard others speak.

Suddenly, my thoughts were interrupted by a deafening thunderclap that shook the ground as the storm raged about me. It was tremendous, yet I stood defiantly against the overpowering forces, committed to experiencing whatever came next.

My thoughts yet again turned to God. I remembered just hours before, while fishing, my friends and I had a meaningful conversation about our respective faiths.

I know I believe, and I am loyal by my attendance at church. I put some of my allowance in the small white offering envelope each Sunday. I am comfortable talking about God, and it was good to share with Henry. Henry seemed so devoted to his faith. He was more than faithful and loyal, he was committed, and maybe commitment was what was missing for me.

The lightning struck again in the vicinity, and I could smell the sharp, fresh aroma of ozone in the air.

Grandpa! How I loved that old man.

My thoughts turned to my mother. She seemed to almost hate and sometimes rejected Grandpa's Catholic faith because it wasn't like ours. I began to think, *If Henry, a Jew, and I can respect and nourish each other's faith, why can't my family do that for Grandpa's?*

I vowed to reconcile the conflict in our family. I would start by learning more about Catholics as I had just today learned about the Jewish faith.

The worst of the storm passed, and although it was still raining heavily, the wind had let up, and the thunder seemed to be in the distance. Suddenly, I sensed someone was behind me, and I was sure it was either Smitty or Mr. Greenlee. I had not finished my thoughts, and whoever it was respected my space and didn't speak.

My thinking now turned to a plan to bring respect and honor to the faith of my grandfather. The idea was simple. We—Mom, Dad, and I—would talk of reverence. I will share the simple statement I had learned in the program in which they had encouraged me to participate.

The storm finally started to subside, and as I watched the lightning flash in the distance, I whispered to myself, "A Scout is reverent. He is faithful in his religious duties, and he respects the convictions of others in matters of custom and religion."[2]

I'll tell them I've learned I can be faithful and committed to my belief in God while respecting others' right to be different. And if I can do this with my Jewish friend Henry, why can't my family do it with our own?

Instead of trying to change Grandpa, making him feel his faith is rejected, why can't we encourage, celebrate, and support his belief? I wondered if Grandpa has had a visit from a priest in a long time.

I'll arrange that, and I'll get Mom to help me as soon as I get back. It would be good for her.

I felt a hand on my shoulder but wasn't quite ready to acknowledge my companion, who had been standing with me.

I then thought how strange it was to be having thoughts like this while standing in a raging storm.

Rather than fear, I was feeling embraced, surrounded, and very much loved. I determined that the "embrace" I was feeling was God's way of speaking to me right then and there. The feeling was love, and the message was to share the love and bring people together.

Rather than feeling small and insignificant as when I started this ordeal, I now thought of myself as empowered and committed to doing, as I knew I was being called. I was having a conversation with God, and it included answers. This was an authentic prayer! And it was like the words of the hymn were written for this moment.

2. Boy Scouts of America, "The Scout Law," in *Handbook for Boys*, 27.

When I in awesome wonder, consider all the works,
Thy hand hath made.
I see the stars, I hear the rolling thunder,
Thy power throughout the universe displayed.[3]

Indeed!

With the storm passing, I ended my prayer with an audible "Amen."
I had just prayed my first real prayer.

I turned to see who had been my companion. Nobody was there.

The rest of the guys must have still been in their tents. I saw Mr. Greenlee, Fred, Smitty, and Henry were still standing under the tarp. They stood looked like they needed permission to join me, so I smiled, and they came down to where I was standing.

"We were worried about you," Henry said, "but Mr. Greenlee said the only difference in where you were standing and where we were standing was one thirty-second of an inch of light green canvas. What were you doing anyway?"

I didn't answer right away. I paused to think, and then I said, "I apologize for not acknowledging whoever came down here to join me."

Smitty replied very deliberately, "Louis, nobody ever left the canvas."

Then he asked Henry to join him in checking on the guys in the tents. With a look of understanding, Fred immediately followed.

Mr. Greenlee stood with me and did not say anything. After a few moments of silence, I said, "Mr. Greenlee, I was feeling someone behind me. And later, someone touched my shoulder. I was sort of praying, and now I am feeling a little. . . ."

"I figured it might be something like that, Louis. I have had a couple of similar experiences. While praying at an awful time on Iwo Jima,

---

3. See "How Great Thou Art," Godtube.

I felt hands on my shoulders, and nobody was there. The guys beside me were dead, and nobody else was close by."

"What did you think it was?"

"Well, I was praying for my family one by one and then the guys beside me. I was asking for strength to do my duty and that I would survive the battle raging all around me. I have experienced 'the touch' a few times since, and I think it happens when we actually connect with God. Maybe we are touched by the Holy Spirit or the spirits of other people. Perhaps we are touched by God himself. I don't know. I just know God is real, and once you become friends, you will never be alone."

Then Mr. Greenlee put his hand on my shoulder and said, "We can talk about this again if you'd like. You may have some more thinking to do, so I'll get Mike started on dessert if you don't mind."

Mr. Greenlee knew I still had some things to straighten out and probably didn't want me to lose my train of thought. Smitty was within earshot, so I called out, "Hey, Smit," and he came right over to me.

He always knew when I needed time alone and when I needed to talk.

Chapter 20

CONVERSATIONS

I turned around, and Smitty stood as if he was watching me with understanding. He nodded his head and pointed to a large boulder near the water's edge and out of earshot of the rest of the crew.

Together we made our way to the boulder and sat down in silence. I looked at the sky and noticed clearing in the west. The sun was close to the horizon and was shining through the clouds. I wondered what the loons had done during the storm as I had not heard them for a while. It was then I heard a lone tremolo call.

Smitty was the first to speak: "I'll bet that's their rejoicing call!"

Then I heard Chuck yell, "Will you look at the rainbow?!"

We both turned and looked behind us. The rainbow arched from horizon to horizon. It was the most brilliant rainbow I had ever seen. Smitty and I both chuckled as the rest of the crew, including Mr. Greenlee and Fred, gathered to hear Chuck's detailed explanation of the physical properties causing the rainbow.

Watching the rest of the crew gather around Chuck, Smitty looked at me and said, "Hey, Louis, what's going on?"

I knew he was referring to the recent episode during the storm, and I tried my best to explain. "Well, I'm a bit overwhelmed. The whole day has been sort of—"

I couldn't think of the word I wanted.

"Well," I continued, "both weird and fantastic, ya know?"

"What do you mean?"

"First, it was the weather. We started the day in a dense fog, and when it finally lifted, I had experienced the most fantastic morning of my life. We navigated in the fog by trusting our compass and maps, and, I don't know, I just felt very close and connected with . . . I guess . . . nature. Did you?"

"Yeah, I enjoyed the experience too," said Smitty, "but it was a lot more than that, Louis. What else?"

"As the fog lifted, I was sad to see it end. I had become utterly lost in thought as you led us to our campsite in Kawa Bay. I have been doing that a lot lately. I noticed every little detail of the scenery. I kept thinking of the voyageurs and Indians and what it must have been like before good maps and all the modern gear we have today. I don't know about you, but I can't ever recall doing this much thinking. It's better than a movie. It's so . . . so—"

"Real?" asked Smitty.

"Yeah, this is a real adventure, and we are right in the middle of it."

Smitty smiled in agreement as he looked at me and raised an eyebrow.

"And?"

"Even lunch with Mr. Greenlee was something I'll always remember with his time gag and the way we discussed the issue of being too easy on passing requirements. Instead of just saying no, Mr. Greenlee and Fred explained why, so it made perfect sense to everyone, even Tom. And when did peanut butter and jelly on smashed bread, dry crackers, and watered-down punch come to taste so good?"

Smitty nodded and then said, "Go on."

"I thought our fishing trip with Hank was incredible. How many guys talk about their faith in God while they are fishing without an adult along?"

"That conversation with Hank was amazing and helped me to sort out some things I have been thinking about," said Smitty. "I can't wait to hear what Henry will have to share with us on Friday evening."

"Remember when I asked if you guys had a funny feeling as we were paddling out of the Wawiag?"

"Yes, I do."

"Well, I honestly had a feeling that we were being watched or like someone was there. I have no idea what it was. I wasn't afraid at all, and it actually made me feel sad as we left the area by the mouth of the river.

"Smitty, am I going nuts or what?"

Smitty just smiled and waited for me to continue.

"I thought maybe it was just because I was so worried about Grandpa. I keep telling myself what you and Dad said about him being a tough old guy."

"Louis, you have a lot on your mind with worrying about your grandfather and your crew chief responsibilities. Also, I don't think you were expecting this trip to be as much as it has turned out to be."

"No lie! I still can't believe I didn't want to come less than a week ago."

"And?"

"Next, the storm comes in, and I find myself standing out in the middle of it, praying."

"Praying?"

"Yes, praying!"

"And you felt someone was with you."

"Right. Someone touched me and put a hand on my shoulder."

Smitty looked at me for a long time and then said, "And you feel like it's too weird, and nobody would believe you."

"Well, have you ever experienced anything like that?"

"Not even close, But I believe you."

Smitty then asked, "What about the prayer? And I will understand if you would rather not talk about such a personal thing."

"Smitty, I have always been surprised and upset by my mother's total lack of respect for Grandpa's Catholic faith. I know she loves him. But she reacts negatively to everything about that faith. He can't even cross himself or say a blessing without her saying, 'GRANDPA!'"

I had to wipe the tears from my eyes.

"During the storm, I developed a plan to try to convince my mother to change her behavior toward Grandpa in my conversation with God about what I consider to be a family dilemma."

Smitty said, "Maybe the touch you were feeling was God's way of saying, 'Good plan, Louis! Go for it!'

"If I were God," he added, "it's what I would be saying!"

We both sat quietly for a few moments. Then he said, "I hope I will connect like that someday. I always thought prayers had to be formal and have lots of thee-, thy-, and thou-type words. I guess real prayer is more of a discussion telling God how you feel and listening for answers."

Someone cleared their throat and said, "Ahem! Hey guys, the cake's done. If you don't come on up and eat, we're going to eat it for you!"

We both turned to look and saw the whole crew was standing with plates and pans of cake.

Gary said, "Ready for some cake, guys?"

Smitty and I exchanged glances, and I whispered, "Thanks, Smit."

Smitty turned toward the waiting crew and said, "Come on down. There is going to be a Canadian sunset on this channel."

Gary brought a pot of hot cocoa, and Joe carried the cake tins with yellow cake and white frosting. It was baked perfectly. I made a mental note to pay more attention to cooking with the reflector oven.

As we sat enjoying the dessert, cocoa, and the sunset, I noticed Mike was sitting a little apart from the group, not entering into the conversations. Mike was slight in build and seldom drew attention to himself. Of all the guys in our troop, he came from the poorest family. His father rarely came to any of our meetings or events. His mother worked as a cleaning lady. He was the only boy in our troop whose mother worked outside of the home.

The troop had some extra funds due to an enormous pancake supper we put on each year. I had heard Dad talk to Mom about the fact the troop was able to help with camp fees whenever there were financial problems for Scouts. I was confident Mike had benefited from those funds.

After a few minutes, as the guys were still relaxing and commenting on the sunset, I said, hoping to engage him in expressing himself, "Mike, are you enjoying the trip so far?"

"Yes, it's nice," he said. But he said nothing more.

I watched him for a few moments as he looked out across the lake and to the sunset beyond.

What is he thinking? I thought. *What can I do to get him to fit in with the rest of the group?*

While I was trying to think of ways to get him to talk, Henry asked him, "Mike, what one thing have you enjoyed the most so far?"

That's when I learned yet another thing from Henry. When you want someone to talk, you don't ask questions that can be answered yes or no. You probably won't get much of a response.

Mike continued to look out on the still waters of Kawa Bay. He didn't answer right away, and I thought he wasn't going to answer. A loon broke the uncomfortable silence, and then Mike said, "Well, I really like it when we set up camp and get to walk back into the woods to collect firewood or dig the latrine."

Tom interrupted him with a laugh, saying, "You mean digging the latrine is your favorite thing?"

"No, I just like being back in the woods when we do," said Mike. "I like being back there where we dig it. I like the way it feels back in the woods where it's still and quiet."

"The way it feels!" exclaimed Tom. "What do you mean by that?"

Mike paused, put his hand on his chin, and turned his head to look toward the campsite and the darkness of the woods beyond. It took him a few moments to answer, and then he said slowly, "The first night when I was collecting firewood, I walked way back away from the campsite. Every time I was about to pick up some downed wood, I saw some better wood up ahead, and every time I stopped, I noticed that the woods kept getting prettier and prettier."

I noticed that everyone was silent as Mike spoke.

"I like the way the moss grows on some of the trunks of birch trees which have fallen and are on the ground rotting," he continued. "It's like one thing dies and becomes the home to the lichens, ferns, and moss, helping break it down into the fertile soil. It then becomes nourishment for other trees and forest plants.

"I was looking at one tree, a pine of some sort, and it seemed dead at the bottom with lots of bare branches. It was green at the top when I looked up, and then I noticed the tree next to it was different, with heart-shaped leaves that shimmered and glistened. Looking up at the sky through the trees from deep in the woods looks different from seeing it from out on the lake. I don't know. I just like the way I feel when I'm in the woods."

I looked at the other guys as Mike continued his descriptions of the sights, sounds, and even the deep woods' smell. They were all listening, and Mr. Greenlee looked pleased and proud.

I was glad to realize I wasn't the only one noticing the beauty of this North Country. I knew every kid who came to this country had to see all the beauty. However, if they did not talk about it or share how it felt to them with a group of trusted friends, no one would know. I suspected most would consider it uncool to express such things to others. I was saddened to think how thoughts and feelings kept inside are soon forgotten. I vowed to remember this lesson of getting the crew to talk at some point each day. The key was to ask the kind of open-ended question Henry had asked Mike.

The ever-present loons now began their evening songs. We all sat quietly and listened. No one spoke a word. I looked at Mike. He had his eyes closed and a smile on his face. At that moment, I knew he had become a part of the group.

As the sun drifted closer to the horizon, Mr. Greenlee thanked Mike for sharing his thoughts. He suggested everyone take a turn in sharing the one thing they liked most about our trip so far.

Chuck was the first to speak.

"I love the opportunity to put into practical application the scientific principles we learn in school."

No surprise there.

Gary spoke next and said he loved being the head cook and appreciated Fred's excellent direction and coaching.

No surprise there either.

Joe said he liked being in the canoe with Fred and enjoyed being in such a beautiful place and a handsome craft. He described the workmanship he saw when he looked across the bow of Fred's Seliga. He also described the dozens of Quetico Provincial Park stickers, carefully placed between the ribs in the canoe's bow.

I need to remember to check those out.

Tom said he enjoyed the outstanding food, the hard portages and that he hoped for more. But, he said, "I expect to be in great shape for football when we get back."

Dave spoke next and said, "I thoroughly enjoyed the fishing, both the catching and the eating."

Henry liked the sounds of the wilderness and the absolute silence you could experience out here.

"I enjoy getting to know everyone better," said Cliff. "I also like that I have time to think about and work out some important things in my mind."

He didn't share what the things were, but I had an idea what he meant.

"Louis," Mr. Greenlee asked, "what about you?"

I had to think because I had been listening and watching the others quickly. I had been pleased and surprised at the seriousness and maturity of the answers of the other guys. I wanted to share some of my spiritual feelings for this day. Still, I decided I wasn't quite ready to share something so personal with anyone but Smitty and Mr. Greenlee.

"I have enjoyed being able to experience this leadership role and being able to learn from Fred and Mr. Greenlee," I said.

Mr. Greenlee smiled at me and then turned to Fred and said, "How about you, Fred?"

"One of the things I like best about being a Charlie Guide is having the opportunity to meet, work with, and learn from some amazing advisors," Fred replied. "I also learn from some sharp young Scouts from all over the country."

He turned to where most of us sat and said, "First, I want to tell you that your Scoutmaster is as first rate as they come. Now, to answer your question. What do I like best about the wilderness experience? Well, I love this country. I love everything about it. However, it is really about the people, the team, and what a small like-minded group of individuals can accomplish and the places they can go when they set their minds to it."

Fred looked at Mr. Greenlee and said, "You're next."

Mr. Greenlee cleared his throat and said, "The thing I have enjoyed the most about this trip is what we just did. It tells me you are seeing and experiencing just as I hoped you would. You know I enjoy my work tremendously. My company is doing great. But what gives me the most satisfaction is seeing you guys grow and become young men. Someday you may be asked to be a Scout leader. I hope you will."

I had already decided I was going to be a Charlie Guide like Fred. I wasn't sure I would ever be the kind of man I saw in Mr. Greenlee, but I sure hoped I would be ready someday.

Mr. Greenlee said, "Before we head to the hay, Fred, let's review the rest of the trip. Are we on schedule, and are these guys up to the voyage we have planned?"

Fred grinned and said, "We may have planned too easy of a trip for this crew. I have been thinking about a little change in plans and suggest we drop in on Blackstone Lake to add some hard portages for Tom and some superb fishing for Dave. We have another easy day tomorrow with an exciting paddle up the Wawiag River into Mack Lake. The next day, we could change course and take a beaver stream. I've always wanted to try and travel down to Kennebas Falls. I hear you can paddle all the way down once we get past a few portages from Mack.

"Joe, would you get my map on the seat of my canoe so I can show you what I have in mind?"

Joe quickly got the map, and in the fading light, Fred showed us how we could adjust our route to include Blackstone Lake. We all poured over the map, asking questions about fishing and camping spots. Fred said this would add some harder portages, and Tom said, "Let's do it, and the harder, the better!"

I looked around at the crew, and their looks told me that everyone agreed. I chuckled, remembering a few days ago, Tom was the one who didn't want to get his new boots wet.

Everyone stopped talking for a few moments, and we sat listening to the night sounds start. I heard an owl hoot from somewhere across the lake, and as I turned and looked toward the east, the darkening sky started to glow with the rising of the nearly full moon.

Fred broke the silence and said, "If the weather is clear in the next few days when the moon is at its fullest, we may be able to do a little night paddling."

I expected Tom to start asking questions, but everyone remained quiet. After some nervousness about starting out in a thick fog, we had come to trust Fred. Maybe we had come to believe in and trust ourselves.

Chapter 21

THE WAWIAG

Friday morning, I woke up early and paused as I opened the netting of our tent. The sky had become light, and I could see out across Kawa Bay. It was as smooth as glass, and there was a delicate mist rising from the warm water reacting with the cooler air. It wasn't fog, for I could see everything above the mist distinctly. However, the mist rising from the bay was thick enough to make the surface obscure. The trees and features on the opposite shore seemed to rise like ghosts in the mist.

It was chilly and invigorating as I stepped out of our tent. I was the first one up, although I was sure Fred was awake. I bumped him on the way out of the tent, but he didn't stir. I was convinced he was transferring more responsibility to me by staying in our tent and pretending to sleep.

After rubbing my eyes, I held my cupped hands over my nose, inhaling the clinging smell of the fish we had cleaned last evening. As usual, the odor caused my thoughts to turn to Grandpa and yesterday's conversation during the storm. I turned toward the lake and said a short prayer of thanksgiving as I looked upon another of the loveliest views I had ever seen. It was like I was saying good morning to an old and good friend. I was feeling warm even though this was the coldest morning of the trip thus far.

I walked to the canoe, sheltering the kindling and firewood we had put under it before the storm. While getting the small friction-top can of matches from the Kettle Pack, I also grabbed the toilet-paper bag and the shovel. I was feeling like I would need them as soon as I got a fire going.

As soon as the fire was well established, Gary approached and said he and the rest of the cooking crew would be happy to take over and get things rolling.

I excused myself and walked back to the latrine. I remembered Mike's comments on how pretty his walk was. I paid closer attention to the various things he had pointed out. He was right, and I was pleased. Maybe everyone was feeling what I was feeling for the beautiful details of this place.

On my way back to the campsite, I met Henry, who was waiting for the "precious papers," as he called them. He didn't seem in a hurry, so I asked him if he had given any thought to the Sabbath service we had discussed.

"There for a while," he said, "I thought we were going to have one last evening."

"Yeah, it got pretty serious, didn't it? When Mike started talking, I thought we surely are ready for this service."

"Louis, something happened when you were standing out in the storm yesterday. Do you mind if I ask what it was?"

"I started out just wanting to see and feel the storm. However, it turned into much more. It turned into a conversation with God, a real prayer. As I was thinking about fixing an old family situation involving my grandpa's religion, I felt like someone was behind me, and then there was a touch. It was so real, and I'm still a little confused. When I found none of you had come down to join me, I was kind of shaken. Ya know what I mean?"

Henry nodded his head, saying, "I understand. And if you don't want to talk about it, I will understand that also. But can I help you with the situation?"

"Well, it's just that my grandfather is Catholic, and I certainly don't like the way my mother and others in the family treat him regarding his faith. They are kind to him, and I know they love him. But they are always trying to get him to stop crossing himself and to change his religion. It makes Grandpa feel bad."

"Boy, as a Jew, I can relate to your grandpa's situation. What made you want to deal with such a touchy subject now? Isn't this the grandfather who is over a hundred years old?"

"You're correct. He is about a hundred and five and is quite ill. But I still want to help him be happy. Our conversation yesterday started it! It's about respect and reverence. I was thinking of a plan to help my mother be more respectful and supportive of Grandpa's faith."

"I can't begin to tell you how much I respect what you want to do, not only for your grandfather but also for my faith and me as well. If more people in the world thought as we do, World War Two might never have happened.

"Louis, I hate to change the subject," he added, "but the matter which brought me here this morning is now a little more urgent. I'd best be heading up the trail."

I smiled as Henry quickly headed back through the dew-covered foliage and thought to myself, *How often do you have a conversation like that on the way to the 'john'?*

When I got back to camp, Gary had the coffee ready, so I found Fred's and Mr. Greenlee's cups. I started to fill them but stopped when I noticed they were not up yet. I thought about it a moment. Then it occurred to me.

They're letting us run things this morning, and that is what we will do!

I gave the two coffee cups to Dave and then asked him if he would enjoy changing roles with his dad, so I asked him to call out, as was the custom.

He grinned and bellowed, "Daylight in the swamp! Come on, guys, we are burning daylight!"

In two minutes, Mr. Greenlee exited his tent, smiling broadly. Dave handed a steaming cup of coffee to him and then to Fred.

After the Wilderness Grace, we dined on a breakfast consisting of scrambled eggs, Canadian bacon, and a small portion of fruit stew and Farina, a cereal much like Cream of Wheat®. There were a few pieces of fish left, and I noticed Henry had those instead of the bacon.

The cleanup process and packing seemed to take less time than ever before. I think the crew realized there would be more daylight left for fishing and swimming if we got underway earlier.

Henry and Tom sat together, and I wanted to assign a task before starting the final cleanup.

"When we get back to the Base, there is a closing campfire in the lodge, and I recall at the opening campfire, we were told that each crew should be prepared to present a skit or song," I said. "I can't think of two guys better at such things than you two. Will you guys please come up with a song or skit and rehearse the crew well before we get back?"

"Consider it done!" Tom said.

Everyone else was moving with haste to take care of their assigned tasks. It seemed like little time had passed before we cleaned up our cooking and eating gear, packed our personal packs, and took down and rolled our tents. We set our equipment near our canoes, which had been placed in the water, ready for loading and departure. Tom and Mike gathered and left a generous supply of firewood for the next campers and filled in the latrine after the last call for anyone possibly needing to make the trip. After Chuck called off the gear checklist, we loaded and began our journey up the Wawiag River and then to Mack Lake.

As I looked back at our Kawa Bay campsite, I decided this was to be one of my life pictures. Not because it was remarkably beautiful, as most views in this country are breathtaking. Still, because of the conversations I had in this place, I wanted to remember it.

I recalled the conversations with my friends, especially Smitty, Henry, Mr. Greenlee, and now, my newest and best friend. I have always believed in God and have gone through the church motions, but now I feel like I have a real connection and a true friend.

When we were underway, everyone came together a few hundred yards from the campsite. Fred slowed his canoe and said he wanted to talk to us.

"We will see some very different country along the winding Wawiag River," he said. "Although we will be paddling against the current, we probably not notice unless we stop. The river is slow moving, and there are no rapids between the mouth and our exit to Mack.

"Stay alert to the trees," he added. "We will see several varieties we haven't seen in the country we have traveled through thus far. I also suggest we travel quietly to increase the likelihood of seeing wildlife along the river."

We crossed the distance from our campsite to the Wawiag quickly. I was pleased to see every canoe was moving together in a straight line. There was no zigzagging this morning, and each sternman seemed to have mastered the combination of strokes which would hold a proper course to the point we all had as our objective.

As we approached the island near the river's mouth, I again had the feeling someone was watching me. I saw nothing on the island except for some ravens visibly perturbed by our approach. They noisily scolded us during our passing. Everyone watched the ravens except Smitty. He was looking over at me as if to see if I was all right. I smiled, and he turned to look at the large shiny black ravens before we paddled beyond the island.

Before entering the Wawiag, Fred again slowed and had us assemble close to his canoe. He reminded us to be alert, keep an eye out for wildlife, and notice the change in the type of trees along the Wawiag. He said we would occasionally stop, and he would ask us if we could identify the various varieties. He added that this was the only area he knew of where we would see deciduous trees, which were more common farther south on the prairies.

"Guys, if you paddle in silence, we can see the various and plentiful wildlife in the area." He also suggested we use hand gestures to communicate as much as possible.

I suggested everyone keep an eye on the map to determine our location by the turns in the river I had noticed.

Fred laughed and said, "During another time when I came up this way, I overshot the cutoff to Mack Creek and didn't realize I had missed it until we came to a set of small rapids some distance beyond."

I noticed Mike was paddling stern with Gary and Mr. Greenlee, so I suggested he be the navigator and get us to the creek which led into Mack. Fred nodded his agreement. Mike looked very pleased and asked to confer with Fred. Fred pulled alongside him for a few minutes as we all drifted very slowly backward. I'm sure they consulted the map and discussed how to determine the Mack Creek cutoff's approximate distance.

I was paddling stern and was glad to be back where I was most comfortable. Tom was my bowman. With the slow movement of the river against us, we were imperceptibly drifting backward. We found sculling very slowly seemed to hold us in place. As Mike and Fred discussed the map and the navigation process, I studied my map and planned to follow every inch of the way.

While carefully analyzing the map, I again sensed I was being watched. After yesterday's experience with the storm, I tried to determine if this feeling was the same.

It was different.

It wasn't a scary feeling, and it wasn't uncomfortable. It reminded me of how I feel when I wake up at night, and without seeing them, I know my parents are in the house. I looked at the rest of the crew, and they were all looking at the lush green banks and the different trees. Nobody else seemed concerned or uneasy.

As Mike pushed away from Fred's canoe and started up the Wigwag, we all fell into place. Our canoe was bringing up the rear. I began to feel more at ease as we began to establish a steady pace. I still had the sense of being watched or accompanied from afar. Yet, although unnatural, it was a comfortable feeling.

Everyone followed Fred's recommendations, and we crept along, watching and listening. As we made progress up the river, I noticed the trees and brush. The greenery extended to the waterline, and in some places, the usual rocky shoreline was completely absent. It seemed almost tropical. Besides our canoes and their contents, there was nothing to suggest we weren't traveling through a time even before the voyageurs.

Dave whispered, "Dinosaurs, anyone?"

I became lost in thought. I remembered what I had heard from Mr. Hanson, who vividly described the Indians and explorers who first traveled and lived in this land.

Tom suddenly said, "Louis!" and I came back to reality as I realized we were about to collide with the rest of our armada, which had paused.

As we came together and drifted with the current, Fred pointed toward the shore and asked, "Who can identify those trees?"

Dave pointed out ash trees, and Tom identified some larch.

"Those are some tall elm trees like the ones on my street," said Mike.

"Why aren't there any evergreens?" I asked. "I've seen lots of varieties everywhere else. Why not here?"

"In my studies, I have learned there are accumulations of ancient sediment along the Wawiag," Fred shared. "Some of the low-lying regions have cranberries, which are a favorite of the Native people. Louis, the deciduous trees we see here along the river are at the northernmost limits for their species. This is a most unusual area because of that fact."

We moved on, disturbing a family of ducks with some half-grown ducklings as we steadily made our way upstream.

During our stop, I had asked Mike how the navigation was going, and he said, "It's hard to keep track of our progress."

Fred smiled and said, "Although accurate, the maps aren't detailed, and navigation along the Wawiag requires noting when significant direction changes occur. I have been confused, too, Mike. You're doing fine."

He then told us the Boundary Waters Area had been scraped to bedrock by the last ice age's glaciers. Upon receding, the glaciers had left the huge boulders and the sediment common to this region.

"The Wawiag once filled the whole valley created by the runoff from the melting glaciers," Fred continued. "Over time, as the water volume subsided, the sediment formed the levies, which now border this much more gentle river. Navigation can be challenging, as the river, which was once a raging torrent, now meanders its way through this ancient valley."

He told a funny story about a ranger report that a tourist group had presented, saying they had seen a few burros along the Wawiag. It turned out the observers had seen some moose calves and thought they were burros. The rest of their bird and plant life report was probably considered in question by the rangers. They likely did their best to keep a straight face during the very humorless story.

We continued along the lush green banks and observed the water was like the color of tea. I noted that Mike and Gary had slowed after a few more twists and turns. Mr. Greenlee had his camera ready to shoot a picture.

With a few more strokes, I could see a cow moose. She looked only mildly disturbed by our arrival and was apparently not concerned enough to move out of sight. We could see the ears and the top of the head of a calf, and it became apparent how someone might think they were looking at a donkey or burro.

I had remembered to keep my camera near the top of our pack, and Dave handed it to me. The cow seemed to move for a better pose. I was now ready, and I could see the calf's head and neck as I snapped a picture of the pair.

As we continued upstream, we saw several deer. Occasionally, the sound of birds made it seem as though we were in a giant birdcage. Dave leaned back and said, "It's so tropical you'd almost expect to see Tarzan swinging through the trees along here."

"Yeah, right. Jane, oh Jane, where are you?" said Tom as we continued along in silence, following a good chuckle.

I had been carefully watching as we made our way along the winding river. Sometimes the dense brush and large overhanging trees made it difficult to keep a sense of direction, and I found myself frequently checking my compass.

After two hours of deliberately slow progress, I saw Mike slow and turn toward the right shoreline. He was looking back at Fred, and Fred gave him a thumbs up. My calculations had been correct. We had reached the point where we would turn off to Mack.

Mike's canoe disappeared from sight as they entered the very narrow Mack Creek. We all followed in turn. The water in this stream was more transparent than the water in the Wawiag. Beautiful grass-like plants were growing along the bottom and slowly waving at us as we navigated the narrow stream. It took a short time to reach Mack Lake, from which the water in this little stream flowed. We had to step out of our canoes to walk through a shallow part before entering the lake.

As we entered Mack Lake and left the close confines of the stream and the enclosed feeling of the Wawiag behind us, it made me feel like I had suddenly entered a whole new country. We were back in the kind of territory we had been traveling in for three days. I was glad to see Mack was another lovely lake, for this was to be our home for a long day, and it would permit some significant fishing.

Mike and Fred stopped side by side, and I watched them talk for a few moments. They motioned for me to come close, so I pulled up nearby. Fred pointed out several camping sites.

"I like the island campsite," said Mike.

I agreed, saying, "The island campsite on the lake's westerly side will likely provide another sunset to remember."

Mike looked at me as if needing permission to continue in the lead. I nodded for him to proceed. I looked at Mr. Greenlee, and he just smiled as if to say, *You're still the crew chief, even as you share the opportunity to lead.*

Chapter 22

MACK LAKE

The rest of the crew waited as Mr. Greenlee, Fred, Mike, and I checked over the campsite for a few minutes before giving the okay to unload and set up camp.

When we came back to the canoes to start unloading, Gary said, "You guys remind me of my folks, checking out the motel room before deciding to stay when we were on vacation."

Everyone laughed. I guess everyone's parents conducted a room inspection before agreeing to stay in a motel. Then he asked Mike if the bathroom was okay.

Mike grinned and said, "It will be, and don't forget to flush!"

We had made good time traveling up the Wawiag and Mack Creek. I looked up at the sun and judged it to be late morning, and we decided to set up camp before lunch. Everyone sprang into action, and in no time, we were started.

Some lessons had been learned during yesterday's storm. Those who set up the tents paid particular attention to drainage and carefully checked all the knots. I noticed there always seemed to be a lot of large rocks around each campsite. As the tents were set up, I walked around and made sure they had been carefully placed to ensure the stakes, used with our Voyager tents, would not pull out if we should have another storm like the last one with such strong wind.

Gary and his crew carefully examined the fireplace. They spent some time adjusting rocks and making sure there were no weak or unstable areas in the semicircle of rocks that the smoke from previous cooking fires had blackened. Some other campers had left behind a wooden crossbar. It was in good shape with just a little darkened wood from the heat of previous fires. Fred had told us we would have pizza that evening, and we would need a good reflector fire for the reflector oven. I wanted to be a part of the process and assist.

I noticed the fireplace had been thoroughly cleaned out and no ashes remained, only the bare rock outcrop on which the structure was built. Joe expressed surprise at the firepit being clean.

"What does that tell us?" asked Fred.

Joe thought and said, "Well, I guess it would mean there hasn't been anyone here since the day before yesterday, at least. Yesterday's storm would have washed the fireplace out and left it clean as a whistle."

Everyone nodded in agreement and remained silent, offering no other suggestions. Joe grinned at being allowed to solve the mystery by himself. Fred could have given the obvious answer. I was impressed because he chose to build someone up rather than show off his own knowledge. Fred's skills of observation must have been well honed after several years of guiding.

"I see that there is still a little bit of bark left on the crossbar, which the previous campfires have not burned off," Gary observed. "Joe, would you take the crossbar to the 'axe yard,' give it a good scraping, and then wash it off, please? We don't need any bark in our food."

Joe agreed and went to work.

Fred knelt down by the fireplace. As Gary and I came up close, he said we needed to prepare another smaller fireplace only as wide as the reflector oven to set up our "pizza parlor." He pointed to the side of the existing outside wall, and as we could see by the fire and smoke stains on the rocks, the location had been used before.

"I wonder what happened to the rocks that must have been here before?" Gary asked.

"They're probably some of the rocks you found scattered about and used for setting up the tents. Rocks seem to move about a campsite as the various needs arise," said Fred.

"Why don't you look around and see if you can find some large flat rocks about the size of a briefcase so we can have nice even sides for this pizzeria," he continued.

Gary and I headed off to find our rocks.

As we walked along the shore looking for the perfect rocks, I asked Gary how he liked cooking and how hard it was to follow the various recipes in the trail cookbook.

"First of all," he replied, "the best part is getting to work with Fred. He was pretty quick to turn over the responsibility as soon as I demonstrated I could follow directions and understood the references to measurements. I'm sure glad my mom involves me in cooking at home.

"The second part, which makes it fun and easy, is the little white cookbook. It was written for these canoe trips and is related to the specific equipment we have with us. I am going to try out some of these recipes at home. I hope they work in an electric oven."

We found two superb rocks that would fit nicely and headed back to camp, each of us carrying a flat rock weighing 15 pounds or more. Fred was pleased with the rocks we found, and we started to get them placed and stabilized as sides to the oven. Mine was thicker on one side and was flat, indicating it was once twice its size and had broken in two at some point in the distant past. We set it in place and, with a few small rocks wedged to steady it, completed one side of the project.

Gary's rock was a little heavier than mine and didn't have the nice flat side upon which to rest it. We decided we would have to balance it against the fireplace and secure it with other rocks on the inside and outside edge to hold it in place. Fred could see we had the concept well in hand and went over to Mr. Greenlee, who was looking for a good "shaving tree" with just the right amount of morning light to hang his metal shaving mirror.

Joe and I went looking for a few more perfect rocks to complete our project. We both had an armload when we heard Gary yell, "Ouch!"

I dropped my rocks near the fireplace and was first to reach Gary. He was holding his left middle finger, and blood was running over both hands. I told Joe to get Fred and Mr. Greenlee and then get clean water over there.

I had Gary sit and asked him to let me see the cut. He said, "Darn," as he moved his uninjured hand away. It looked like he had cut his finger to the bone between his middle finger's first and second knuckle.

"Hold it tight to stop the bleeding and try to relax," I said. "You're going to be all right."

Actually, I was worried about the dangerous-looking cut.

Mr. Greenlee and Fred arrived, and I told them about the status of the wound.

"Keep it together and just try to stop the bleeding with direct pressure at this point," said Fred. "I'll be right back."

"You're doing fine, Gary," said Mr. Greenlee. "Take it easy so we can clean the wound and get you fixed up."

While Fred was getting his first aid kit, I asked Gary how he had cut his finger.

"I cut it on that darn rock I found," he said.

I looked at the rock, and the side Gary had been placing against the fireplace had blood on what looked like a very sharp edge.

"As I was rolling it into place, it sliced into my finger," Gary continued. "I was holding the side against the fireplace. The edge is sharp as a razor, and the weight of it caused the cut. I was afraid I had cut my finger clean off at first."

Fred arrived, and Joe came back with fresh water in a large pot. Fred told Gary to keep the pressure on but to let him guide his hand. Fred instructed Joe to pour the water over Gary's hands with a cup while he held the cut closed. Once the blood was washed off, Fred said, "Okay, Gary, we need to see what we have here, so I am going to take over holding the cut closed, and then we need to wash it with this Phisohex soap."

The wound was no longer bleeding heavily. Fred carefully moved his finger from the injury and opened it to see how deep it was. After a quick examination, with Mr. Greenlee looking on, he washed the whole area with the antibacterial wash and then flushed the wound.

Mr. Greenlee asked Joe to hand him the adhesive tape in the first aid kit and a couple of matches. He then prepared to make a butterfly stitch. Fred continued to hold the cut closed and had me again wash the wound and his hand with the soap and then fresh water. I asked for more clean water, and the bucket was gone before I completed the sentence.

All of the crew was now gathered in a circle around us, trying to get a look. Mr. Greenlee looked up at them and said, "Let's everyone watch, and I'll show you how to make a butterfly stitch."

He had already grabbed a canoe paddle and had placed about five inches of tape on the clean, dry surface. He then took his knife and cut four inward diagonal cuts. There were two on each side, with the cuts slicing inward. The inner points were about three-quarters of an inch apart on the long surface and about a quarter of an inch apart at the center. The result looked like a butterfly with a one-inch body. He then pulled the tape off and folded the "wings" in so there was now adhesive tape with a quarter-inch nonstick bridge between the sticky areas.

"I sure hope that paddle isn't the one we cleaned fish on," said Gary with a laugh.

Of course, the paddle had been dipped in the water a thousand times since we might have cleaned fish on it, but the humor helped relieve the tension, especially since it came from Gary.

Mr. Greenlee asked Joe to strike a match and hold it steady while using the heat to sterilize the non-sticky area between the adhesive surfaces. Joe then dried Gary's finger with a sterile gauze pad from the first aid kit. Then Mr. Greenlee carefully attached the butterfly bandage to the top of the finger. Hence, the non-sticky, sterilized section came across the cut and held the wound together. He made sure the cut came together and didn't overlap and then, with a slight bit of tension, pressed the other sticky surface to the area below the cut. He covered the wound with a fresh folded gauze pad and taped it with additional pieces of adhesive tape.

Gary now looked a little white with the procedure completed and said he felt a little "shocky" and should probably lie down with his feet up. Chuck already had a sleeping bag laid out and a pack at the end for him to put his feet on.

Gary rested a few minutes, and then said to Fred, "Okay, Doc, how bad did I cut it?"

"You and your sharp rock cut it to the bone," Fred replied, "but it doesn't appear you cut any tendons. I'm sure there is nothing broken, just a nice clean cut."

"If we were home," added Mr. Greenlee, "we would take Gary to the doctor for stitches, but if Gary will keep the finger immobile for the day and let it heal, he will be just fine."

"Can I still cook?" asked Gary.

Fred told him he would need to direct others for a few days but that he was still head cook.

By now, it was close to noon and time for lunch. Joe took charge, and Tom offered to help with the preparations. Mr. Greenlee, Fred, and I sat with Gary for a few minutes and had him drink a cup of water.

Mr. Greenlee said he was very impressed with how everyone pitched in and helped, anticipating the needs, and Fred said, "I think it shows how well trained these guys are in first aid." He added that it was good we had the whole afternoon so Gary could get the healing process started.

We had lunch in no time, including salami, bread, jam, dried apricots, and Red-Eye. Everyone was talking about their fishing plans. I had planned to fish with Smitty and Henry, work on the church service for Sunday, and help Henry with the vesper service we agreed to have that evening. However, I decided to stay in camp and keep Gary company instead.

Fred went to his small personal pack and brought back a hardcover book in a plastic bag. I remembered Fred had mentioned a book he brought along, and I had asked him if I could read some of it. It would be a perfect way to pass the time while keeping Gary company. The book was by Sigurd F. Olson and was titled *Listening Point*.

Fred handed me the book and said, "This is one of those books you can read over and over again. Sig Olson is an incredible writer who lives in Ely, Minnesota."

I asked Fred if he knew him since he referred to him as "Sig."

"I do," he replied. "Sig and his wife, Elizabeth, enjoyed visits from Charlie Guides."

He suggested I read a little after the guys went out fishing. "Then skip to page sixty-one before you continue. I've marked the passage I love."

Everyone made their fishing arrangements, and Mr. Greenlee was pleased he and Fred would be fishing together in the Seliga. Smitty and Henry agreed we would touch base on the church service after they returned from fishing. Henry said he was all set for his worship service.

Gary agreed he needed to stay quiet since he was still feeling a little shocky from his injury. He urged me to go fishing but seemed pleased I was staying in camp with him. Mr. Greenlee said they would remain in sight of the campsite, and a holler would bring them back in a hurry.

After everyone else paddled out to fish, Gary and I sat on the large sloping rock which led to the water's edge and provided an excellent view of the lake's western side. It was high noon and must have been 80 degrees, a little warm for this North Country.

Gary was still looking a little puny, so I got a couple of sleeping bags and fixed him up with a place to rest where he could recline against a personal pack and put his feet up. We visited about the trip, and Gary again related how much he enjoyed being our crew's cook. Gary was in a shady spot and soon was napping. I figured it was the best thing he could do and found a comfortable place to sit and read.

I looked over the book Fred had loaned me, and I noted it was well worn. The cover was torn and repaired with scotch tape in several spots. It was signed "Sigurd F. Olson" on the first page inside the cover.

I looked at the illustration on the cover. I flipped the pages, noting each chapter had a pen and ink drawing illustrating the concept described in the chapter's title. The illustrations by Francis Lee Jaques were beautiful and captured scenes already looking familiar to me. On the first page, Fred had written lightly in pencil, "See page two hundred thirty-eight. It says it all."

I turned to that page and found the following paragraphs marked carefully in pencil:

"And so it must be for all of us who have known the backcountry. No little sanctuaries along the fringes of civilization ever quite suffice. We must know the wild and all it entails, the bite of the tumpline on the portages, the desperate battling on stormy lakes, the danger and roar of rapids and falls. We must know hunger and thirst and privation and the companionship of men on the outtrails of the world, for all these things are inseparable. When after days or weeks of travel, we modern voyageurs find ourselves on a glaciated point a hundred or a thousand miles from any town and stand there gazing down the length of some unnamed lake listening to the wild calling of the loons and watching the islands floating in the sunset, there is a fierce joy in our hearts."[1]

I went back to the beginning and started to read. By the time I had finished the introduction and first chapter, Sigurd F. Olson had become my favorite author. I reread the passage Fred had marked, and I went back to where I had left off and began to devour the book.

---

1. Sigurd F. Olson, *Listening Point* (New York: Knopf Doubleday, 1958), 238.

This man captured the spirit of this country. He described the sights, the sounds, and the feelings of being in this lake country that made me feel like I knew him. I wanted to know him and vowed to meet him someday.

I remembered Fred had said to go to page 61 before I got too far into the book. I turned to the beginning of Chapter 8, "LAUGHING LOON."

The first paragraph was marked and read, "The canoe was drifting off the islands, and the time had come for the calling, that moment of magic in the North when all is quiet and the water still iridescent with the fading glow of sunset. Even the shores seemed hushed and waiting for that first lone call, and when it came, a single long-drawn mournful note, the quiet was deeper than before."[2]

I was sure Fred had marked the passage long ago. However, it seemed to have been chosen just for me. I had come to love the loons. Everything about them!

I had goosebumps as I quickly turned the page and noted this chapter fully described my favorite bird, the loon. I immediately turned back to the beginning and began to peruse every word of this extraordinary book.

---

2. Ibid., 61.

Chapter 23

FISH STORY

After being happily lost in my reading for hours, I checked on Gary and found him asleep. I was careful not to wake him, but he awoke when I stopped to stand next to him. He looked up at me and said, "Rats! I'm sorry to keep you back here in camp." I told him of the reading I had been doing and suggested he might enjoy it while his injury healed.

I handed him the book after I brought him some Red-Eye.

"If you are okay, I think I'm going to try my hand at fishing from shore for a while. How's it going?"

"I'm fine," Gary said, yawning. "I think I'll go back to sleep."

"Call out if you need me," I said as I got my fishing gear and selected a Lazy Ike lure. "I'm not going far."

I went to the water's edge and cast my line. I looked up and saw Mr. Greenlee and Fred fishing near the opposite shore. They waved at me from the Seliga, which blended with the shoreline because of its green color and made it hard to spot at first. I responded with a slow wave and gave a thumbs up to indicate that Gary was okay.

After a couple of dozen casts, which only produced a few fingerlings following my lure, I decided to try a medium-sized red and white Dare Devil. As I finished placing it on the steel leader, Mike, Dave, and Chuck came around the point, moving as though they were in a canoe race.

"We have what might be a significant problem!" Mike yelled. "We caught a sick fish and think there might be an issue with the other fish in this lake."

Mr. Greenlee and Fred must have seen or heard them because they were already rapidly headed our way. I assisted the guys with landing their canoe and then saw the fish they were concerned about on the stringer. It was an immense northern and would have weighed 30 pounds or more judging from the head's size near the water's surface. The body was like a three-foot snake and only a fraction of the size it should be. It was still alive, with just its gills moving in and out.

"Mike caught this on the opposite side of our island," said Chuck, "and if this fish has some disease, we figured we had better call in the fishermen. The rest of the guys are right behind us, and some have some pretty nice fish."

Within a few minutes, Mr. Greenlee and Fred arrived and asked what the commotion was all about. We had already yelled and told them nobody was hurt or in trouble.

Mike showed them the fish, and Mr. Greenlee looked worried as Fred waded in to have a closer look.

"This guy is either very sick or is somehow starving to death," Mr. Greenlee said. "Where did you hook this fish?"

Mike said the hook was on the lower lip's front edge, and he thought he had a big snag as the fish didn't fight at all.

"It came in like a log," he said.

"Should we kill it or what?" asked Dave.

"No! Let's see if we can figure out what's wrong and then decide what to do with it," Mr. Greenlee said as he opened the fish's mouth and peered inside.

He then looked up and around.

"Where is Henry and that thingamajig for getting hooks out?" asked Mr. Greenlee.

Henry, Smitty, and Joe arrived right behind the Seliga, and Henry brought the heavy wire tool we had used while fishing. Mr. Greenlee handed it to Fred, and he opened the giant mouth.

"Just as I figured, it has a large lure lodged in its throat."

"Can we get it out?" asked Dave.

"This old fish isn't going to give us much trouble, and with this neat tool Henry has, we may just be able to get the lure out and give this fish a new lease on life," said Fred. "Louis, go to my personal pack and get the bag with the first aid kit. It's right on top since we just used it. The bag I keep it in has a miniature Puukko inside."

I went to his pack and immediately returned with the small knife with the stacked birch handle and a small brass horse head on the hilt.

Fred took the knife and said, "I keep this knife sharp as a razor, and it's only for emergencies like cutting out fishhooks. Usually, it's for people, but it looks like this tough group of fishermen wants to get this guy back where he belongs."

Fred was standing in water up to his thighs and was supporting the monster fish with the thin body as tenderly as if it were an injured person. That picture may be the most profound memory I have of him.

The whole crew gathered round to watch and help as Mr. Greenlee steadied the fish while Fred forced open the mouth, which was filled with sharp teeth.

"Louis, bring the knife and stand by to help."

We kept the fish in the water, and Chuck suggested moving it to keep the water flowing over its gills. With its mouth open, we could see a large treble hook far inside of its mouth.

"He has a huge KB Spoon filling its throat," said Fred. "It must try to feed, but it can't swallow anything. And he must have been this way for weeks to lose this much body weight. Louis, hand me my little pliers in the small sheath on my belt next to my Puukko."

The small pliers had a side cutter on one side, and the word SARGENT stamped into the handle. He cut the lure off the treble hook using the side cutter by cutting the little ring attaching it to the treble hook. Mr. Greenlee drew out the spoon, which was five inches long and almost two inches wide. The ring at the front end of the lure still had six inches of heavy nylon line on it with a little swivel connecting it.

Fred handed the pliers to Mr. Greenlee, and he held the treble hook steady while Fred cut it out of the cartilage in the fish's jaw. He had to saw a bit where it was under what appeared to be bone or firm cartilage. Mr. Greenlee released Henry's thick wire device holding the fish's mouth open when the hook was removed.

Fred moved the fish back and forth to move water over its gills and then held him up for us to see. He was well over 36 inches long and was at least four inches between the eyes. His body girth was like a 10-pound northern's, about a third of what it should be. It had used up most of its own fat and body weight to survive and was perfectly docile as we gave it a quick look.

Mike waded in, wet his hands, and touched the fish as if to say goodbye. Then Fred gently pushed the fish away. He floated for a moment, and I was afraid he would not be able to make it on his own. Suddenly, with a few flips of his tail, it was gone.

The whole crew just stood, and you could almost feel the unspoken prayer that the fish would recover.

"Dr. Morton and Nurse Carter," said Mr. Greenlee, "I think our patient will make it. Well done! Guys, I have no concern the rest of these fish you've caught are safe. We could use a few more, so those who want to keep fishing, let's get after it. We are burning daylight."

Nobody moved. Mike said, "Mr. Greenlee, we just saved a badly injured fish, and I'm not sure I want to fish anymore."

"Ah-ha," said Mr. Greenlee. "Let's everyone sit. I think it's time for a talk."

Everyone sat around Mr. Greenlee on the large sloping rock.

"Mike, by not wanting to fish anymore, did you mean ever?"

"Well, seeing the injured fish and the way everyone became concerned and pitched in to help . . . well, I just feel different about fishing after that," Mike replied.

Several guys nodded.

"I am incredibly proud to see the caring and concern you all feel for that poor fish we just saved," said Mr. Greenlee. "If I'm reading Mike correctly, you're all feeling sad for a hurt creature and want to prevent any more hurt. Is that it?"

Everyone nodded.

"Fellas, ya know, at the plant, we kill hundreds of cattle and hogs each day and prepare them to become hamburgers, steaks, bacon, and all the products your mom purchases at the Piggly Wiggly," said Mr. Greenlee, who owned a packing plant. "Animals, plants, and everything we eat were once living beings before they became dinner for us. We go to great lengths to treat the livestock humanely and kill them quickly and with as little pain as possible. Guys, animals, like fish, are part of what we humans eat.

"As Scouts, we promise to be kind, and I'm proud of the way we worked with the intent to save the fish's life," he continued. "Every week at our packing plant and feedlots, injured animals are treated and cared for even though they will be killed for processing. We care for them, and I've seen men risk their lives protecting animals which they will later kill for food. That is kindness, caring, and respect.

"Harvesting food is what we humans do, but how we do it is what determines the kind of people we are."

Everyone seemed to be considering what had been said, and then Chuck said, "We are a part of the food chain. With the skills and technology we have developed over thousands of years, we are considered to be at the top. I was sure concerned about our fish and was sincerely hoping it would live to fight another day. I guess I would always want to help the helpless and injured, and that includes animals. I'm still going to fish and eat fish. I will just be much more careful to do it right and be respectful in the process."

"Guys, remember when we talked about landing fish?" asked Gary. "You were instructed to wet your hands before touching the fish so you didn't disturb the fish's protective film. It's a kindness to help ensure that those we put back aren't injured as a result of our handling them."

Mike broke in: "I'm ready to get back out fishing. Who wants to go?"

Soon the whole crew was out fishing except for Gary and me. Gary rested, and I read some more. After all the excitement over the fish, Gary fell asleep quickly, and I made sure he was not running a temperature and was breathing normally.

Yikes, the things we learn from our mothers!

After I had read two more chapters, the canoes started to return and, once again, we had more than enough fish. We had a helping for everyone that evening, plus plenty for breakfast.

Gary woke up and seemed excited to be the executive chef and direct his helpers. I went to help clean fish with Henry, Chuck, Joe, and Fred. The rest of the guys set about helping to get dinner ready.

After the fish had been cleaned and delivered to the cooks, Fred asked me to help him prepare the dessert. We were having apple pie, and I was excited about learning to make a pie in the reflector oven.

Dinner was spectacular, and it seemed the food got better each day. Although we had planned to have pizza, the excellent fishing changed the plan. The reflector oven was used for a couple of perfect apple pies instead. The cooks made a delicious pot of macaroni and cheese. I think it may have had more to do with how hungry we were with nearly constant physical activity, but everything was tasty. The guys also made a yellow cake for the next day's lunch.

Gary seemed to be feeling better. Mr. Greenlee caught me off to the side where nobody could hear us and said, "Gary will soon be feeling much better. Then the most significant challenge may be to keep him from infecting the wound before the cut has a chance to heal."

"I'll personally watch over Gary. I think he should continue to just advise and direct others in the cooking duties—not only to protect the wound but also to keep any germs or infection from contaminating our food," I said.

"Agreed," said Mr. Greenlee.

Mr. Greenlee didn't tell me anything about keeping the wound covered or changing the dressing in the morning. Still, as I described the plan for Gary's care, he once again expressed his agreement with a big grin. I guess he figured if he, the first aid counselors, including two doctors from our troop, had done their job, I would know what to do. His nonverbal agreement and trusting smile made me feel good.

Henry came over when it appeared our private conversation was completed and asked if he could check a few things with us.

"I am ready to lead a Sabbath lesson and am wondering if we could do it after we eat our dessert," he said.

"Sure," I said. "Can I do anything to help you prepare?"

"Thank you, Louis! I think I'm prepared. Please have everyone gather down near the water by the big boulder after we wash our dishes."

Chapter 24

SABBATH

After eating dessert and washing dishes, everyone started to gather as I had asked. When everyone was present, I told them Henry would lead us in a Sabbath service, as was the custom in his Jewish faith.

I was impressed everyone was washed up and had even combed their hair. As we walked down to the edge of the water, I commented to Tom about how everyone had cleaned up.

He said, "Well, we are going to church, and cleaning up is what you do. It's part of being reverent!"

We came together and gathered around in a semicircle facing the lake and the setting sun. Henry, who could never be accused of being shy or at a lack of words, stepped to the center and raised his arms with his palms facing up and began, *"Barukh ata Adonai Eloheinu, melekh ha'olam."*

No one said a word as Henry stood in silence. A loon broke the quiet with a call from across the lake. Henry looked at each one of us and then said, "That is the way we begin our service of the Shabbat or Sabbath. This sunset is the beginning of the Sabbath day. It was the day the God rested when he created the earth and heavens. In English, it translates to 'Blessed are You, Lord our God, King of the universe.'

"I feel very humbled to have been given this opportunity to lead a brief service to fulfill my religious obligation," Henry continued. "However, when asked to do this by Louis and Smitty while fishing on Kawa Bay, I must admit I was at a bit of a loss about what to do. So I will begin where this all started, with the twelfth point of the Scout Law, which is 'a Scout is reverent!'" Henry held up a copy of the *Handbook for Boys*.

"I asked to borrow a Scout Handbook so I would get this precisely right, as we have all learned the definition of the twelfth Scout Law is."

Henry opened the book and began.

"'He is reverent toward God. He is faithful in his religious duties and respects the convictions of others in matters of custom and religion.'[1]

"I then read further, where our handbook provides more, and found this: 'Reverence is that respect, regard, consideration, courtesy, devotion, and affection you have for some person, place, or thing because it is holy.'[2]

"'The Scout shows true reverence in two principal ways.

"'First, you pray to God, you love God, and you serve him. Secondly, in your everyday actions, you help other people because they are made by God to God's likeness. You and all men are important in the sight of God because God made you. The "unalienable rights" in our historic Declaration of Independence come from God.'

"'That is why you respect others whose religion and customs may differ from yours. Some fellows think they are smart by telling stories or making fun of people of other religions or races. All your life, you will be associating with people of other beliefs and customs. It is your duty to respect these people for their beliefs and customs, and to live your own.'"[3]

---

1. Boy Scouts of America, "The Scout Law," in *Handbook for Boys*, 26.
2. Ibid., 39.
3. Ibid.

Henry closed the book and continued, "I thought of the discussion with Mr. Greenlee on our first night. Maybe if we all lived by the twelfth law, knives would just be for hunting, fishing, cooking, and whittling."

Tom raised his hand as though he wanted to comment.

"I want to invite you to ask questions after my lesson, but right now, let me continue," said Henry, acknowledging Tom. "On this trip, I have found that every day, I see living sermons from y'all (Henry smiled at Fred) and our leaders."

Henry paused to collect his thoughts, and I was sure he was about to ad-lib an original idea.

"Just a few hours ago, I saw all of us involved in the most beautiful example I have ever seen of the sixth Scout Law, which is 'A Scout is kind.' I'll read it to you. It says, 'A Scout is kind. He is a friend to animals. He will not kill nor hurt any living creature needlessly but will strive to save and protect all harmless life.'[4]

"You have heard me refer to kosher food, which comes from a Hebrew word that means 'fit or proper.' It relates to what Jews are permitted to eat and how it is properly prepared. I won't go further into this but want to add that when we kill animals for food, we want to ensure the animal is killed quickly and in such a way it feels little or no pain."

One of the things I liked about my friend Henry is that he could put things in perspective. Everyone was listening intently as he continued.

"When our whole crew gathered this afternoon to try to save the fish we were worried about, you all gave by example a sermon on kindness to me. It made me proud to be your friend. You all, I mean 'we,' exhibited kindness and used the skills we have learned in this organization. I felt like all of us loved and cared for that fish as we watched it swim away. All of us wanted it to survive. I had tears in my

---

4. Boy Scouts of America, in *Handbook for Boys*, 26.

eyes, and I saw some tears in several of your eyes also. I think all of us try to live by those laws, and those laws will guide us in our lives.

"Now I would like to close with this thought from the story of Queen Esther, which is found both in the Hebrew Bible and the Old Testament of the Christian Bible. Although she is the queen of Persia, even she cannot approach the king unless he has called her to the throne. To do so is punishable by death. She decides she must go to the king anyway and try to convince him to spare the Jewish people. She sends her uncle Mordechai a message to ask the people to fast for her safety. She closes her letter with the bravest words in the Torah: 'Then I shall go to the king, though it is unlawful, and if I perish, I perish' (Esther 4:16).

"We are told people cannot approach a king because he wants to protect himself and control his schedule. That is true of many leaders. Now I would like us all to think of the kind of leader we will be. I hope I will be like Fred and Mr. Greenlee.

"Do we sometimes do things to keep people from approaching us? Ask yourself, am I kind and welcoming to everyone who comes to talk to me? And do I pay attention to what they are saying? Do people know when they call on me with a problem, I will be understanding and try to help? If I am rude or thoughtless in responding to someone, I may not hurt them physically, but I wound their spirit. I am so impressed by how everyone in this crew is open, kind, and supportive of my faith and beliefs. I am so grateful I came on this adventure.

"By being open to other people, 'calling' them to us, we have a chance many times every day to be helpful, friendly, courteous, kind, and reverent.

"Let us pray:

May the Lord bless you and protect you:
May the Lord show you kindness and be gracious to you:
May the Lord bestow favor upon you and grant you peace:
May this be God's will. Amen. (Num. 6:24–26).

"Shabbat shalom! I wish you peace on this Sabbath!"

Several of us answered, "And also with you."

No one said a word as we sat quietly for several moments. I was about to speak when Mr. Greenlee said. "Henry, that was very well done! I love your message. Sunday morning, we will have a service led by Smitty and Louis. I'm looking forward to our continued worship right after we are packed and ready for a relatively long day on the trail."

"Can we ask questions and discuss some of this?" asked Tom.

Henry answered, "I'm counting on it. Tom, do you have some questions?"

Mr. Greenlee grinned and gave his "go ahead" look.

"Since the Sabbath starts tonight and runs through Saturday night, are you okay with working all day tomorrow?" asked Tom. "Aren't you supposed to rest on the Sabbath?"

"My parents talked to me and said they were pleased I was going on this adventure. They said they feel good about Scouting, noting that Mr. Greenlee is a good man, and they are grateful for his influence," Henry replied. "They also insisted I observe my daily prayers and fully and respectfully participate in every aspect of the trip, including your prayers and religious services.

"I think they will be pleased and perhaps even a little surprised when I tell them we held, and everyone participated in, a Sabbath service. We always try to observe the Sabbath, but my parents wanted me to make my own decision about this, because I'll have to make these decisions for myself once I leave home."

Mike asked about dietary laws, and Henry explained, as he had while fishing with Smitty and me. I noticed everyone, including Mr. Greenlee and Fred, seemed very interested in his answer and everything else Henry shared.

As it became dark except for the starlight and the nearly full moon rising in the sky, the whole crew seemed peaceful and reflective. We were enjoying the pleasant evening when Tom observed, "Tomorrow we should have a nearly full moon."

"This is called the last of the waxing gibbous moon," said Chuck, "and the full moon would be on Sunday night." He pointed out Saturday's moon would be described as full as well.

I shook my head and smiled.

Leave it to Chuck to know these details.

Chuck then suggested this would be an excellent time to sing "Scout Vespers" and led off the singing.

Softly falls the light of day,
As our campfire fades away.
Silently each Scout should ask,
Have I done my daily task?
Have I kept my honor bright?
Can I guiltless sleep tonight?
Have I done and have I dared,
everything to be prepared?[5]

Without prompting, we concluded by reciting the Scout Benediction, a tradition in our troop.

"May the Great Scoutmaster of all Scouts be with us until we meet again."[6]

And we all said, "Goodnight, Scouts!"

Everyone but Henry, Smitty, and I silently moved toward the tents.

"Henry, what do you think? I thought this was a marvelous and very moving evening," said Smitty.

---

5. "Scout Vespers."

6. Boy Scouts of America Troop Program Resources, "Closings," accessed September 13, 2021, https://troopresources.scouting.org/closings/.

"Mission accomplished!" said Henry. "Thank you, guys, for bringing this together. I wasn't sure about all this, but I feel like this was one of the best nights of my life so far. Thank you, my friends!"

I felt as if I should say something in response, but then I thought, *No—everything that needed to be said has been said.*

Chapter 25

KENNY CREEK

I woke up early and started a fire before anyone else began to stir. I put the coffeepot on and must have made some noise because Smitty and Gary soon joined me by the fire. Gary said he would get his cooking crew and direct them in preparing a good breakfast since we had a long day ahead. The cooks joined him.

After he got them organized, Gary told us his wound was getting better. I told him he needed to protect it and the dressing for another day or two, and he readily agreed.

"I've got good helpers," he said. "I'll let them do the cooking, and I'll supervise."

Smitty and I left Gary to think about breakfast and made our way down to the edge of the lake.

"I thought our Sabbath service went well," Smitty said. "And Henry did a remarkable job putting it all together. We all learned a lot."

"I'm looking forward to our Sunday morning service on Joliat Lake," I responded. "I hope the lake and our travels to Blackstone Lake are all we hope for. I think it will be the greatest challenge of the trip."

Mr. Greenlee and Fred joined us with their first cup of coffee. Fred said he wanted to review the day's travel down Kenny Creek and the Falls Chain we would navigate before Wet Lake and Joliet.

"We will have a most pleasant morning on a quiet beaver stream after a few portages and small potholes," he said. "Let's encourage the crew to again be as silent as possible since seeing moose and other wildlife is likely. When we get to Kenny Lake, we will pause to review the several sets of waterfalls we will encounter on our way to Wet Lake and Joliet. There is always danger around waterfalls. Everyone needs to follow directions during travel close to waterfalls to keep safe."

"Louis," said Mr. Greenlee, "I think this will be a good day to assign a navigator who hasn't had the duty yet. It's your decision. However, let's let Fred advise the process through the Falls Chain."

"Sounds good to me," I said with a nod. "I'll make the announcement after breakfast. I think I will assign one crew member for the morning and another for after lunch."

Fred chuckled and said, "Sunday, when we travel from Joliet to Blackstone, we will be in new territory for me, and we will need to use all of our skills. I have heard other guides say the Joliat portages are tough but possible. Since the route is seldom used, it will require close attention to map and compass and perhaps some bushwhacking."

"Bushwhacking?" I asked.

"It's the process of finding your way without well-traveled or obvious portage trails," Fred explained. "Since we have had lots of rain in recent weeks, there may be some streams we can paddle or at least float the canoes as we walk them through shallow water. I guarantee we will have an adventure few others will experience."

Fred and Mr. Greenlee left us alone and walked over to the fire to warm up their coffee.

"Smitty, I like the idea of delegating and especially the skill-based activity, like navigation," I said. "All the practice and compass games we played back home have paid off. So whom do you think I should pick for morning and afternoon navigation duty?"

"I was impressed with Mike the other evening," said Smitty. "Dave seems to be paying attention, and as the youngest in the crew, he might be a good choice for the afternoon segment."

"I agree and will announce those assignments at breakfast. Thanks!"

I walked over to the fire to check with Gary. The cooks were fixing French toast with syrup, fruit stew, and the fish left over from the evening before. The reflector oven was set up, so I asked Gary what was baking.

"I found a recipe for bannock, a type of heavy bread that will be done by the time we are finished and cleaned up from breakfast," he replied. "We will have it for lunch with peanut butter and jelly rather than the smashed bread. If it is as good as I believe it will be, we will make it again.

"I'm glad Fred advised us to double the amount of flour when we were packing food," he added. "We can make bread pudding some evening with the smashed bread not used."

Gary then looked at his hand and said, "My stupid wound seems to be doing fine, and it doesn't appear to be infected. But we should change the dressing after the dishes are done, right? We cleaned one of the empty plastic bags so we can put it over my hand to keep it clean and dry while traveling if need be."

"Sounds like a plan, Gary! Maybe we can have the pizza during our layover on Blackstone."

Breakfast was delicious, and I was amazed we still had a good serving of fish for everyone. Joe grinned as I watched him get a second helping of fruit stew. Gary was doing a great job managing the menu and cooking by directing and delegating the actual cooking to others.

It didn't take long to clean up the campsite; do the dishes, pots, and pans; and all the other chores. After we stacked the firewood, we packed the canoes for departure.

It had been a fantastic campsite, but we were eager to travel. I asked for everyone's attention in order to make a few announcements.

"This morning, I am asking Mike to navigate, and I would like Dave to navigate this afternoon. Both of you should spend a few minutes with Fred to review the route before we head out. After a couple of portages, we will be on Kenny Creek, which is a beaver stream that will take us to Kenny Lake and the beginning of the Falls Chain. You already know we will see more wildlife if we are quiet, and Fred tells me we will likely see a lot on the trip down the creek.

"When we get to the Falls Chain, there are several things you need to be aware of. There is always danger around falls, although we will be going upstream. We will use the well-marked portages, and Fred is very familiar with safe travel through this area. Pay attention and follow directions."

I looked at Fred and Mr. Greenlee and asked if there were other comments to be made. I got two thumbs up in reply.

After a 10-minute meeting with Fred, Mike and Dave indicated they were ready to go. So we started across Mack Lake to a bay in the southwest corner. Mack was a beautiful lake with some old-growth timber around it, and I vowed to return someday.

Our first portage took us to Munro Lake, a small lake south of Mack. It was a rugged and relatively long portage about a half mile in length. It began with a muddy bog that sucked at our feet. When we got through the bog, we had to negotiate a long steep hill. The path was not smooth but littered with rocks and boulders which we had to step over and around.

As we got closer to the lake, the path became steeper. I stopped and looked back and was happy to see everyone close behind. No one was complaining or had stopped to rest. I knew we were getting stronger and used to this portage thing. They took it as a walk through a park. I could not help but feel a sense of pride in my friends.

When Tom caught up to me, he took a deep breath and said, "Wow, I love it, and the tougher, the better. I'm going to be ready for football season this year, that's for sure!"

It was just a short distance to the next portage. We portaged along an overgrown stream that led us to an unnamed pothole, which I estimated to be about two acres in size. The pothole was an excellent place to take a short break.

"On a previous trip," Fred said, "we stopped for lunch, and a couple of the guys asked if they could fish while we waited for lunch to be prepared. They instantly caught walleyes. This little pothole produced enough walleyes for our dinner."

He smiled at me and added, "If you ever come this way again."

I smiled back.

You can count on it, Fred! It's on my list!

After a very short portage around some blockage in the stream, which flowed from the other side of the pothole, we entered Kenny Creek. We found ourselves in a pleasant, meandering beaver stream. There were wooded ridges within sight on both sides, and rock faces and outcrops were visible between the hills. Kenny Creek flowed through a flat valley that appeared meadow-like, stretching as far as we could see. Fred told us there might be a few pullovers at beaver dams. Depending on water levels, a couple of short portages might be necessary as well.

Though the stream flowed the direction we were paddling, there was little current. When we stopped paddling, we hardly moved. The meadow grasses and plant life reminded me of some of the undisturbed natural prairies I was used to back home in South Dakota.

I gave my Brownie camera to Tom, who was sitting in the middle. I asked him to take pictures of any wildlife. I had not taken many pictures since I kept putting my camera out of handy reach in our personal pack. I fully expected to return with a better camera when I became a guide.

Dave stopped paddling and got his camera out as well. When he did, I noticed the canoe slowed a great deal. Dave had become a strong paddler, and I had to paddle hard to keep us up to speed. I was glad when he put his camera down and picked up his paddle.

This creek did not seem to be popular with the loons. At least I did not see or hear any. However, there were a lot of other varieties of birdlife were everywhere. A family of wood ducks was the first to greet us. I pointed at a red-tailed hawk standing guard on a tall spar, which looked like a long-dead cedar tree. Fred had briefed us on some of the wildlife we would likely see along this route. He told us to expect to see hermit thrushes, various warblers, and nuthatches along with the ever-present herring gulls. I decided I should buy books on birds of northern Minnesota and the Quetico.

It wasn't long before Mike slowed his canoe and held up his arm, pointing to the right where some deer were feeding. Our passing didn't spook them, and it was an opportunity to see the family groups in detail. They seemed almost uninterested as four canoes passed. We were making good time in our progress down Kenny Creek.

Mike held up his arm on one of the many turns, and we all gathered near him. He pointed ahead to what seemed to be a motion or swirling in the water. Suddenly a bull moose raised his head with the green remains of stringy weedlike material hanging from his massive antlers. Water poured from his antlers, snout, and beard. He seemed unimpressed with his guests and continued his feeding.

"Well, he is bull moose number two," said Dave. "Impressive, eh?!"

After what seemed a long paddle, we came to a beaver dam. We quickly crossed with a drag over. We were cautious not to damage its intended use as we gently slid our crafts over the top.

"Amazing critters, nature's engineers!" said Tom.

Soon after our moose sighting, we came to another short portage around a blockage caused by silt and brush piling up against a fallen tree. We continued on the creek to an area that became quite marshy, and then we paddled into another small unnamed lake. The map showed we were near Kenny Lake, and the stream we were on broadened before leading into it.

We found a beautiful campsite on Kenny Lake and pulled in to have lunch. I noted Joe had pulled out and filled the water bucket well before reaching the shore. Fred noticed me looking and smiled, which I took to mean he was pleased he didn't have to remind Joe of this chore, as it had become automatic.

Kenny Lake was a pretty lake with Kennebas Falls at the northwest end and Canyon Falls at the opposite end. The map showed one could also take a 1,270-yard portage to McEwen Lake.

Someday I'll take that route.

We all sat together as the cooks fixed lunch. I complimented Mike on the morning's navigation. Fred was sitting next to Dave, and we all listened as he described the afternoon's journey, which remained ahead of us.

Chapter 26

.

THE FALLS

After lunch, I started feeling concerned. I had studied the map. I believed everyone had. We could hear the roar of Kennebas Falls in the distance, and it sounded powerful. It was clear we were in what could be considered dangerous waters with three waterfalls and a rapids to navigate. I noted we were going to be paddling upstream until the rapids into Wet Lake. Fred waited, and soon we were quiet in anticipation of his guidance.

Fred smiled and began.

"We will soon be traveling on the Falls Chain. Although I am not concerned with your skill and ability, I want to remind you to pay close attention to these instructions. Falls can be dangerous. It is important to become familiar with the maps we have available. They will show us what we need to know to travel safely. I suggest the word for the afternoon should be 'cautious'—not fear, just caution."

We all had maps out, and Fred gave us time to look at the upcoming three falls so we could follow along as he spoke.

"Each team should have the best sternman paddling stern," Fred continued. "We will come to Canyon Falls with a four-hundred-eighty-yard portage on the falls' right side at the end of this lake. If other folks are coming down, let them load up and get on their way before you proceed to the landing."

"Fred, will it be best to stay together through this process?" asked Chuck.

"Yes, we should. It's uphill around the falls, and it is very well traveled. On the opposite end, load as we always do but stay together by canoe teams so each canoe can load and paddle up the shoreline on the right. Then hold and wait for the rest of us. Each canoe team should make sure you have everything before you move on.

"Koko Falls is next with its five-hundred-sixty-yard portage, also on the right," Fred continued. "Use the same plan as I just described. The next portage around Little Falls will be to the left of the falls and, again, the same procedure. It's one hundred-eighty yards. Then paddle out and wait. When we are all across the three portages, we will have just one short carriage around some rapids going into Wet Lake, and it will be on the left as well.

"Guys, this is all very familiar to me. Dave, you may want to ride in the middle so you can follow the map and keep us on the right course. I don't plan to say anything more once we are underway unless you are about to make a mistake.

"Dave, you're in charge. Once we are on Wet Lake, it's all up to you. The portage to Joliat is not marked on the maps, and I have never been to Joliat Lake, where we will camp.

"I'm not sure about the portage and travel from Joliat to Blackstone. I know there is a way, but no one I know has traveled it. Although it is not marked on the map, the word has been passed down from guides before that there is a way. We will have to use logic, our compass, and probably bushwhack a trail."

"Two on the right and two on the left, right?" asked Dave.

Fred smiled and said, "You've got it. You and your canoe mates will be in the lead, so you guys study the map and then remember to talk it up with Louis in the stern when we are underway."

"Lunch is ready," said Gary, "and I hope you like our homemade bannock."

Lunch was excellent, one of the best of the trip. The bannock was delicious and much more filling than the smashed bread. Jelly and peanut butter were tasty on it, and it was also excellent with just butter. Red-Eye was beginning to be my favorite drink, and the various flavors were great. The yellow cake with frosting was a sweet treat.

Dave was a little concerned about being responsible for the safety and navigation during the most dangerous part of our trip. Tom and I reassured him he could count on us to help, but we were confident in his ability to perform this critical task.

As we departed our lunch-stop site, he suggested we head to the point with the island up ahead, saying, "The portage should be about a quarter mile and on the right after we round the point."

As we approached the falls, the sound became increasingly louder, and I was glad we had discussed this process before getting here. We reached the portage first, and there were no other travelers on it, so we quickly started on across. On the other side, we loaded up, and then Tom and I held the canoe as Dave went back to see if anyone needed help or direction. Soon Dave returned and said everyone was following the plan. We got into the canoe and moved up the shore a short distance.

We didn't see anyone on the Koko Falls portage. The sounds of both falls dominated our environment. The power of the water flowing through and over these ancient rocks was dangerous. However, there didn't seem to be an increased current unless you were close to the falls' top or bottom. I felt safe and secure even though I knew this was not an area for daydreaming.

As each canoe team arrived with big grins, it was clear that firm, caring leadership equals safety and calm in a place that could very well evoke fear. When the last canoes arrived, Fred and Mr. Greenlee were grinning ear to ear.

Without prompting, Dave said, "On to Koko, we go!"

The portage was half again as long as the last and went smoothly and without incident. Little Falls was right across the small lake.

We found a small group with two canoes having lunch. Their canoes were up in the trees so as not to block other groups. They expressed concern about the longer portage at Koko Falls.

I turned to Dave and said, "Dave, would you go over and talk to them about the portage? Smile a lot and take your map."

Dave calmed their frazzled nerves. I think having a younger member of our team reassure them seemed to help their confidence. Dave was all smiles at having had the opportunity to help a much older group of people and have them respond with respect and sincere thanks.

I remembered how I felt when Mr. Greenlee or Fred acknowledged my actions. I thought, *Maybe it's time to let Dave paddle stern for the rest of the day since he has stepped up to the navigation responsibilities.*

When everyone was across the portage, I asked Dave to paddle stern for the rest of the day. He was both enthusiastic and joyful as he took my place in the stern. Without prompting, he asked for a gear check and then led us to the rapids going into Wet Lake.

As we approached the rapids, Joe asked if we could shoot them. Dave thought the question was aimed at him and answered, "The map shows a portage, so we take the portage."

He then looked at Fred. I believe he thought he had spoken out of turn.

"Bingo, Dave!" Fred said. "That is exactly the right answer. When the canoes are loaded, we take the portage. Sometimes I let crews shoot easy rapids I determine to be safe and shoot-able after unloading the gear."

I noted the answer and made a mental note to discuss it with Fred at some point.

We all moved as one and quickly left the short portage behind us.

"It looks like one of those two tiny bays on the left would have the portage to Joliet," said Dave. "Let's pull ahead so we can guide the rest of the group."

Tom dug in, and we quickly left the crew behind. We checked the first little bay and saw nothing like a portage. We found the landing and a seldom-used and overgrown trail leading to our destination in the next bay.

The crew quickly caught up, and Fred said, "Great job, Dave! We are about to enter a realm where y'all know as much about it as I do. Are you ready for some adventure?"

Everyone answered in the affirmative.

"Okay, let's get on across this portage to Joliat and see if we can find a good place to camp. We may have to build one. There are no campsites marked on these maps or the maps back at the Base."

Rather than leading off, Fred suggested Dave check it out to see if it really was a portage.

With a huge smile, Dave returned with the news: "This is indeed a portage trail. However, it appears that it is seldom used."

It didn't take long to reach Joliat. We could see we were in a smaller bay from the map, and the more significant part of the lake was ahead after a narrows, which led to it. Dave asked for everyone's help in looking for a campsite. Joliat was as beautiful as it was secluded.

Chapter 27

JOLIET LAKE

We slowly paddled into the central part of the lake and then followed the shore to our right. I noticed a small island at the mouth of the first of two bays. Chuck held up his hand, and the rest of us paddled our canoes in close so we could hear.

There was very little wind, and we floated quietly as Chuck pointed at the lake ahead and said, "There is a point just beyond the second bay, and if there is a campsite or a place where we could make a campsite, it would be a good place for several reasons. Number one, we would have a great view of this lovely lake. Number two, we would be on the north side of the lake with clear views to the east, south, and west. Number three, we will have a full moon tonight, and it looks like it will be a clear night as well. Finally, from here, it looks like the point has a good landing with some openings beyond, and it wouldn't take long to build a fireplace."

I have always admired Chuck's logic, and everyone, including Fred and Mr. Greenlee, seemed to agree.

"Let's check it out!" said Dave.

"Dave, you are still in charge," I said. "Why don't you and Fred determine if this location will work?"

With that, we paddled over to the point and up to the shore. I steadied the canoe so Dave could get out as Fred and Joe did the same thing.

"Louis, why don't you let Tom stay and hold the canoe, and you join us in the walk through," said Dave.

After walking over the point, Fred said, "There was probably a campsite here at some time in the past. But it's clear it hasn't been used in many years. There are plenty of rocks to rebuild the fireplace. It looks like it was pushed in by someone or something."

"Could it have been a bear?" Dave asked as he turned around and looked behind him.

"No, I think someone pushed it in," Fred said. "It could have been a bear, but why would a bear do that? Louis, why don't you look around and see if there is room for setting up tents?"

I found that there were locations for at least our three tents, but it would require clearing tree limbs and other brush to make a flat sleeping surface. I asked Dave what he thought.

"If this site has been used in the past, it must have been in the distant past," he said.

"I've heard older guide staff speak of this lake," added Fred, "but no one claims to have camped here. Perhaps the evidence of use we see is from a group of voyageurs or an old Indian encampment. If we camp here, we will need to be careful and vigilant. There might be ghosts to deal with."

Fred looked around and smiled before he continued, "Without too much work, it appears this could be a suitable campsite. Louis, let's get started on our move-in. I'll be available if you need me, but I think this crew will develop a plan and execute it without much direction. It's still fairly early, and I'm dreaming of another fish dinner to eat with whatever Gary has planned. Other guides have told me that voyageur ghosts like fried fish."

I looked over at Gary, and he winked back at me and said, "Fried fish for the ghosts of Joliat Lake will be the main course if you guys get busy and catch some fish!"

Dave had done so well navigating, showing skill and judgment, that I asked him to tell the crew this was our home for the night and to get them started building it. Mr. Greenlee had a grin a mile wide.

"Louis," he said, "I appreciated you allowing Dave to lead."

"Sir, I learned about delegating from you!" I replied.

Joe stepped up as we were unloading and directed the placement of the four canoes. It required cutting some dead trees, which would soon become firewood.

"Where the woods are thick," he said, "there are many dead trees. Perhaps we should cut and save a few good poles to use as A-frames for the tents or the dining fly."

Wow! Everyone is thinking and taking action.

After the canoes were secured, Gary picked Joe and Mike to help him build the fireplace and suggested Joe cut a thin tree to serve as a pole to hold the pots and pans over the fire. He did, and I noticed he scraped off the bark so it wouldn't fall into our cooking pots and add flavor to our food.

Chuck and Henry went to dig the latrine. They needed the axe and saw to clear a path to the location. They picked a spot well back from the campsite and the lake. Dave, Tom, Smitty, and I started clearing areas to set up our tents. We found two good locations where we could use a tree for one end and an A-frame for the other. We had to dig out a couple of rocks to have spots for sleeping. Since there was lots of topsoil, we used some to fill in those holes. Tom found another place between two trees requiring the removal of several rocks. Henry and Mike joined in, and with five workers, we had the tents up and ready in no time. Chuck went to help Gary and his cooks.

I noticed Mr. Greenlee and Fred were sitting on a large log over-looking the landing area and the beautiful lake. I went down to talk with them and report on the progress of setting up camp. Mr. Greenlee said he and Fred had been discussing the crew's progress.

Just then, Henry, Smitty, and Tom walked by with their fishing gear and said they were headed out to fish. Chuck, Mike, and Dave were close behind them and said they were headed out to fish too.

"Dinner is planned," said Chuck, "but it isn't time to start fixing it yet."

"So, Louis, what did you think of today's travels?" asked Fred.

I replied, "Every day, the crew gets better, and I'm beginning to wonder if we planned a long enough trip."

As he pulled out the map so we could all see, Fred said, "We were about to discuss tomorrow's trip to Blackstone. This doesn't look like a great distance as the crow flies. However, I suspect it may be our roughest day yet, and you will all be thankful for the layover day on Monday."

He pointed out the route he envisioned and added, "Many of the creeks you see may be open with enough water to float a canoe with the rains we have had the last month. Then again, some of these creeks may be dry. In any event, plan to do lots of wading, pulling, and portaging tomorrow."

"How long will we be on the trail tomorrow?" I asked.

"I think we will eat lunch at the end of this longer little lake about half the distance we will travel," he said. "I hope to make Blackstone by midafternoon. However, it could be later. Let's hope there are open campsites when we get there."

I asked if it was a possibility that all the campsites would be taken.

"The portage from Bell is a rough one," Fred replied, "and the others look rough on the map. Therefore, not a lot of folks go into Blackstone because of the reputation of the portages. We will go out this route on the Northeast branch to Saganagons. From there to Ottertrack and Knife will be a good haul, but not like tomorrow will be."

"Fred, do you have any specific recommendations for tomorrow's journey?" asked Mr. Greenlee.

"Yes, I have a few suggestions," Fred answered. "First, Louis, I would like you and Joe to switch places as I think we will be doing a lot of consulting. Joe and your crew will be a good team. Second, remember, tomorrow will be all new territory for me. We need to stay together, but there are a few places where you and I will need to bushwhack ahead so the whole crew doesn't walk into a dead end and have to backtrack."

"I'll share the plan with Joe and my guys," I said.

Mr. Greenlee changed the subject by asking how our Sunday-morning worship service was coming along. I told him of our plans and how we even added a few verses of a hymn from memory.

Joe and Gary came by with their fishing gear. Gary came over and displayed his wound and said, "I think it is healing and ready for a little exposure to sunlight and clean water."

I agreed and wished them luck.

Fred looked at Mr. Greenlee and said, "How about it? Are you fellas up for a little fishing?"

With a warm smile, Mr. Greenlee said, "Let's get our gear!"

Fred asked me to get his Seliga into the water. I paused, and he said, "Louis, you can do it. Just be ready for a little more weight than the aluminum canoes. And you paddle stern."

Holy buckets! I was beyond excited to get to paddle the beautiful green canoe. I got my fishing gear but figured I would be happy to keep the canoe moving for Fred and Mr. Greenlee to fish while I paddled.

I got my gear and fishing rod, which the guys had left laying against our personal pack with my little tackle box right on top. As I walked up to the Seliga, Fred was untying his fishing rod.

"Well, let's get this show on the road, Louis," he said.

I pulled the beautiful craft up on my thigh, ran my right arm down between my legs, rocked it, and flipped it up to my shoulders. It worked. However, it was 15 or 25 pounds heavier than our aluminum canoes.

I walked it down to the water and waded out where it would be away from any obstacles to ensure a safe landing. I flipped the canoe off my shoulders and onto my thighs and, with a light splash, set it gently into the water. I held it steady while Fred and Mr. Greenlee boarded. I placed my left foot in the center ahead of the seat and pushed off as I settled into the stern seat.

Fred paddled bow while Mr. Greenlee sat in the middle and readied his gear. I suggested we move to the west side of the lake, circle an island that was a short distance from our camp, and then fish on into a large bay beyond. Mr. Greenlee caught a nice six-pound northern on the north side of the island. When we circled the island, Fred caught a nice bass with a lot of fight in him.

In the larger bay, we found an inlet where a stream entered. The stream had a strong current, and Fred said it was a good sign as it meant there was still a lot of water flowing in the creeks from the recent rains. Near the creek's mouth, we caught two nice walleyes and then decided we should head back. Upon arriving back at our camp, we learned the other canoes had had similar luck. We had 15 fish to cook for dinner and perhaps enough for breakfast tomorrow.

What a pleasure it had been to paddle Fred's canoe. It was silent as it moved through the water, and it was very responsive to every paddle stroke. I also learned the wood and canvas canoes are indeed substantially heavier than aluminum canoes.

As we unloaded, I told Fred and Mr. Greenlee, "I'm one of Charlie's Boys now, but I'm going to be a Charlie Guide as soon as I am old enough."

We ate another dinner with fish, only this time, we enjoyed Kala Mojka, a fish stew, and hot chocolate. Kala Mojka is made with fish chunks, dehydrated potatoes, rice, onions, tomato paste, and seasoning. We noticed Gary had fixed another batch of bannock in the reflector oven for lunch tomorrow, and there would be an excellent breakfast fillet for everyone as well. He and his crew also fixed a delicious butterscotch pudding for dessert.

After dinner and dishes, everyone tied their fishing rods into their canoes in preparation for a quick departure after our church service. Smitty met me at the log so we could check signals regarding the church service. The books Fred provided were a huge help for conducting the service. I believed that given the Sabbath service Henry led, we would have another meaningful worship service.

Everyone had now gathered at the log, and as we sat in silence, the loons began their evening serenade. Their motion created smooth ripples on the surface of Joliat Lake. The lake was calm, and as I looked to the west, I saw another beautiful Canadian sunset. Since there were no clouds, it was a brilliant sunset with pastel colors as I watched the setting sun slowly disappear below the horizon. I turned my head and looked to the eastern sky and was treated to the sight of a full and enormous moon as it began its slow evening rise into the sky above.

There would be no need for flashlights or even a campfire, for we were in for a most memorable light show exactly as our most ancient ancestors would have seen it. The silence continued, with occasional notes provided by the loons. Luna and loons.

What could be better?

I heard Tom whisper to Dave, "Do you really think there are ghosts?"

I saw Dave smile at him as he shrugged his shoulders. He did not say a word, but a loon called hauntingly from across the lake.

Mr. Greenlee broke the silence and said, "Back in my Marine days, I looked up at this same ol' moon and prayed I would someday see this sight with my family and others I loved. I have done that and want each of you to know that you are among those I love."

No one said a word, but I knew everyone felt the bond the same as I.

After a few more moments of silence, he continued, "You know it was just a few years ago, in 1961, when President Kennedy challenged us to reach the moon, land, and walk on it in ten years with Project Apollo. How are we doing? Well, last year, John Glenn became the first American to circle the earth, making three orbits aboard Friendship

Seven. Just this past May, astronaut Gordon Cooper circled the globe twenty-two times in Mercury capsule Faith Seven.

"When you look at the moon tonight, in August of 1963, know that it won't be long before we walk on the surface. Some of you could be among those who become space pioneers. I hope you will set big goals for yourself and make your dreams come true. You are indeed on the right track.

"Now, Louis, I wonder if you have any more stories to tell us."

"Mr. Greenlee, thank you for being our inspiration in so many ways," I began. "Being here on this remote lake, listening to loons with a full moon, will be something I will never forget. This trip has been full of adventure, and tomorrow may top it all.

"I was just thinking that my great-grandfather was born in 1858 and lived most of his life dreaming of something faster than a horse, and here we are speaking of space flight. Tomorrow we will be traveling into the unknown with only the technology and methods my grandpa would recognize. Thank you for this opportunity.

"Remember when Dave, Fred, and I checked out our campsite before we decided to settle in? Well, we found evidence of a fireplace. However, I noticed no blackened rocks, just rocks that were the remains of a fireplace deserted and pushed in. There were also several areas, back in the woods, where tent or shelter sites looked to have been cleared, used, and abandoned. New growth had nearly hidden the places."

"Louis, do you feel another story coming on?" asked Dave. "What do you think happened here?"

"In looking at the map, I noticed Joliat Lake seems to be remote because it is not on the way to anywhere. I see routes going through Wet Lake to Louisa via McEwen and routes up Knife and the Man Chain, bypassing Joliat and Blackstone. Blackstone has three ways in or out. However, it leads to nowhere. Before the European explorers came, both lakes would have been good places to avoid detection. I can't imagine why anyone would come to Joliet unless it were to escape or hide out. This site would be a great choice since a person wanting to be cautious or hidden could watch all the entrances.

"I remembered from the lore of voyageur times. The Hudson Bay Company and the North West Company were competitors and not always on friendly terms. That would be another reason for a place of refuge to hide out during those times. While looking over our camp-site, I wondered why the apparent tent or shelter sites were not over-grown with tall timber. I believe it would be because the trees of the time shaded the cleared locations. I think we may be the first to use this site since Indians camped here."

"Louis."

It was Mr. Greenlee.

"You may have the makings of a good detective or scientist with your sense of logic and observation. When did you develop these thoughts?"

"It was when we were clearing tent sites. I noticed the clearings, and I became lost in thought as I considered what we saw," I said.

"Your ideas certainly make sense, and, again, we enjoy your sto-ries," said Mr. Greenlee. "Even so, we have a big day tomorrow and will be using a seldom-used route. Since we have chosen a likely diffi-cult route, I think an early start is in order. I think it may be time for us to adjourn and head to the tents. Remember, we have a worship service after the breakfast dishes, so wear your Sunday best.

"Fred, anything else?"

Fred stood and told us he was, again, very proud of us, and he was looking forward to the morning service. "I would include prayers for strength and discernment as we journey over an unknown route.

"Louis?" he continued.

"And now may the Great Scoutmaster of all Scouts be with us until we meet again," I said.[1]

---

1. Boy Scouts of America Troop Program Resources, "Closings."

"Goodnight, Scouts!"

I stayed awake for a while after I got into the tent and into my sleeping bag. Fred zipped the mosquito netting shut but left the flap open. As I looked out at the campsite illuminated in the moonlight, I imagined a group of voyageurs preparing to bed down for the night. I heard a loon call, and just before I closed my eyes and fell asleep, I thought I saw movement in the changing shadows.

Maybe there are ghosts. Hmm, I think I'll keep that thought to myself.

Chapter 28

"IN THE RUSTLING GRASS, I HEAR HIM PASS"

I woke a couple of times before I fell into a deep sleep. Each time I looked out into the shadows in the moonlight filtering through the trees around the campfire, expecting to see ghosts. However, there were none. Each time I woke, I heard a loon call, and my thoughts turned to the touch I had felt on Kawa Bay and the unexpected "presence" sensation near the Wawiag.

Could what I thought I had seen at the campfire have been ghosts, or was it part of the same spooky feelings I had had that someone was watching or traveling with me?

I did not know.

Once I woke and thought about the morning worship service. Then my thoughts turned to our upcoming trip to Blackstone and that Fred had said he had never been this way before. I tried to imagine what he meant when he said we might have to bushwhack our way. I wondered how we would find the right path and not get lost in the wilderness and never be seen again. I wondered what it must have been like for the early voyageurs who traveled this way for the first time and had the same worries. They must not have had good maps like ours. How could they find the next lake and determine the direction they should travel? Did they have a compass? Did Indians guide them?

There were so many questions and so few answers. I looked out of the tent again at the shadows in the moonlight. I imagined a group of voyageurs gathered around the campfire, pointing and discussing what they would do next. Mr. Greenlee started to snore, and I suddenly felt calm. I closed my eyes and fell fast asleep.

I woke to a dark tent and stepped out after locating my camp shoes. There was a very faint light in the eastern sky, promising a clear day to come. I was so sure I would be the first one up that I was surprised to find Gary blowing at the tinder to encourage a flame beneath the water pot.

"Morning, Louis," Gary said quietly. "Looks like we will have an early start on our big day!"

I headed to the latrine and was handed a cup of tea upon my return. Everyone else was now up and moving to the morning tasks. Gary and his crew fixed baking powder biscuits, oatmeal and raisins, fruit stew, and heated the leftover fish fillets for breakfast.

When the biscuits were browned on the tops, Gary put bannock on to bake for our lunch. I could see why Fred had us pack extra flour.

Everyone must have been anxious to get started as the tents were taken down and folded before we ate. As I struggled to put my boots on over cold wet socks, I paused a moment and thought, *I have a lot to be thankful for, even cold wet feet. The worship service, I almost forgot! Today is Sunday!*

I took a deep breath as I laced my boots. I was glad Smitty and I had reviewed the religious-service books Fred had given us while we were on Mack Lake. They were provided to the Base by Region Ten of the Boy Scouts of America, headquartered in Saint Paul, Minnesota. There were both morning and evening services suggested, and we chose the morning version.

We had decided Smitty would lead off by introducing the format and passing out the booklets. With some sharing, everyone in the crew could follow the service.

Smitty would lead the call to worship, the doxology, and the ascription of praise. I was going to lead the responsive reading, the discussion, and the unison prayer. We had discussed the format several times, and both of us felt prepared.

A few hymns were provided in the back of the booklet, and we chose the hymn "America the Beautiful." We also decided to use "This Is My Father's World," a favorite hymn of many of us, which wasn't in the booklet. We had gathered several of the crew and wrote the three verses we could remember on the back of a blank menu sheet. Chuck has a fantastic memory, and with him involved, we were confident it was absolutely correct. Chuck wrote it down on four sheets from the journal he was keeping. We were ready, so we began.

CALL TO WORSHIP – (Read in unison)
The Lord is near to all that call upon Him; to all that call upon Him in truth; He will also hear their cry and will save them.

DOXOLOGY
Praise God from whom all blessings flow;
Praise Him all creatures here below;
Praise Him above, Ye Heavenly Host;
Praise, Father, Son, and Holy Ghost.

ASCRIPTION OF PRAISE
Leader: For the beauty and glory of the world wherein
            by Thy love, we continue to dwell.

Response: Lord, our Creator and Bountiful Preserver, we give
            Thee our praise.

Leader: For the blessings of food and the rich provisions for our comfort that comes from the sun and the rain and the soil of the earth at Your Command.

Response: Oh Lord, gratefully do we acknowledge Thee and give Thee our praise.

Leader: For our joys of devoting our physical strength and substance to Thee, the Giver, and Thy needy Children who wait for Your love at home and abroad.

Response: Oh Lord, our heavenly Father, out of whose open hand all our needs are supplied and from whom comes all our gifts and powers, we praise Thee and dedicate ourselves anew to Thee.

HYMN
"America the Beautiful"
O beautiful for spacious skies,
For amber waves of grain,
For purple mountain majesties
Above the fruited plain

America! America!
God shed His grace on thee,
And crown thy good with brotherhood
From sea to shining sea.

SILENT PRAYER
Let us each pray silently in our own way, thanking God for the privileges of Scouting and His protection and guidance during this trip; and asking help to fully see and appreciate the wonders of nature.

RESPONSIVE READING
Leader: A SCOUT IS TRUSTWORTHY: If he were to violate his honor by telling a lie, or by cheating, or by not do-

ing exactly a given task when trusted on his honor, he may be directed to hand over his Scout Badge.

Response: Ye shall not steal, neither deal falsely, neither lie one to another. And ye shall not swear by my name falsely, neither shalt thou profane the name of thy God: I am the LORD. Thou shalt not defraud thy neighbour, neither rob him: the wages of him that is hired shall not abide with thee all night until the morning (Lev. 19:11–13).

Leader: A SCOUT IS LOYAL: He is loyal to all whom loyalty is due, his Scout Leader, his home, and parents and country.

Response: Put them in mind to be subject to principalities and powers, to obey magistrates, to be ready to every good work, (Titus 3:1).

Leader: A SCOUT IS HELPFUL: He must be prepared at any time to save a life, help injured persons, and share in the home duties. He must do at least one "Good Turn" to somebody every day.

Response: But to do good and to communicate forget not: for with such sacrifices God is well pleased (Heb. 13:16).

Leader: A SCOUT IS FRIENDLY: He is a friend to all and a brother to every other Scout.

Response: Thine own friend, and thy father's friend, forsake not; neither go into thy brother's house in the day of thy calamity: for better is a neighbour that is near than a brother far off (Prov. 27:10).

Leader: A SCOUT IS COURTEOUS: He is polite to all, especially to women, children, old people, and the weak and helpless. He must not take pay for being helpful or courteous.

Response: Be not forgetful to entertain strangers: for thereby some have entertained angels unawares. Remember them that are in bonds, as bound with them; and them which suffer adversity, as being yourselves also in the body (Heb. 13:2–3).

Leader: A SCOUT IS KIND: He is a friend to animals. He will not kill or hurt any living creature needlessly but will strive to save and protect all harmless life.

Response: And be ye kind one to another, tenderhearted, forgiving one another, even as God for Christ's sake hath forgiven you (Eph. 4:32).

Leader: A SCOUT IS OBEDIENT: He obeys his parents, Scoutmaster, patrol leader, and all other duly constituted authorities.

Response: Obey them that have the rule over you, and submit yourselves: for they watch for your souls, as they that must give account, that they may do it with joy, and not with grief: for that is unprofitable for you (Heb. 13:17).

Leader: A SCOUT IS CHEERFUL. He smiles whenever he can. His obedience to others is prompt and cheery. He never shirks or grumbles at hardships.

Response: A merry heart doeth good like a medicine: but a broken spirit drieth the bones (Prov. 17:22).

Leader: A SCOUT IS THRIFTY: He does not wantonly destroy property. He works faithfully, wastes nothing, and makes the best use of his opportunities. He saves his money so that he may pay his own way, be generous to those in need, and helpful to worthy projects. He may work for pay but must not receive tips for courtesies or good turns.

Response: Go to the ant, thou sluggard; consider her ways, and be wise: Which having no guide, overseer, or ruler, Provideth her meat in the summer, and gathereth her food in the harvest (Prov. 6:6–8).

Leader: A SCOUT IS BRAVE: He has the courage to face danger in spite of fear, and to stand up for the right against the coaxings of friends or the jeers of enemies.

Response: For God hath not given us the spirit of fear; but of power, and of love, and of a sound mind (2 Tim. 1:7).

Leader: A SCOUT IS CLEAN: He keeps clean in body and thought, stands for clean speech, clean sport, clean habits, and travels with a clean crowd.

Response: He that hath clean hands, and a pure heart; who hath not lifted up his soul unto vanity, nor sworn deceitfully. He shall receive the blessing from the LORD, and righteousness from the God of his salvation (Pss. 24:4–5).

Leader: A SCOUT IS REVERENT: He is reverent toward God. He is faithful in his religious duties and respects the convictions of others in matters of custom and religion.

Response: The fear of the LORD is the beginning of wisdom: a good understanding have all they that do his commandments: his praise endureth for ever (Ps. 111:10).

HYMN
"This Is My Father's World"
This is my Father's world,
And to my listening ears
All nature sings, and round me rings
The music of the spheres.

This is my Father's world:
I rest me in the thought
Of rocks and trees, of skies and seas;
His hand the wonders wrought.

This is my Father's world,
The birds their carols raise,
The morning light, the lily white,
Declare their maker's praise.
This is my Father's world,
He shines in all's fair;
In the rustling grass I hear Him pass;
He speaks to me everywhere.

This is my Father's world.
O let me ne'er forget
though the wrong seems oft so strong,
God is the ruler yet.
This is my Father's world:
Why should my heart be sad?
The Lord is King; let the heavens ring!
God reigns; let the earth be glad!

As we finished the last words of the hymn, I paused a moment and then began.

"Guys, I don't know about you, but this is my favorite hymn, and it seems to fit beautifully with this trip we are on. I want to thank those who helped us write down the words, especially Chuck and his super memory. We are supposed to have a discussion at this point, and I

---

1. Boy Scouts of America, Region Ten, Saint Paul, MN: *A Scout is Reverent,* "Morning Service."

would like you to share your thoughts if you wish. It could be about the Scout Law or perhaps the ideas in this hymn. Who wants to start?"

Mike surprised me by offering to go first. He shared that the first part of the hymn, "And to my listening ears . . . All nature sings, and round me rings . . . The music of the spheres," captured his thoughts.

"Last night, we saw a perfect sphere, the moon, and the visible planets," he said. "We also travel on a sphere where, for me, all nature sings. I think the music of the spheres refers to the patterns of nature and all life itself. If we listen, we will hear."

There was a stunned silence after Mike finished.

I remember our discussion on Mack Lake and Mike's comments in particular. They were thoughtful and profound, but I never expected this.

Joe was the next to speak and said, "Whenever we sing this hymn in church, I think of my dad, and how much being outside, working, hunting, and fishing, makes me think of him: 'I rest me in the thought . . . of rocks and trees, of skies and seas; His hand the wonders wrought.' Dad always reminds me that being outdoors is the closest we can get to God and his creation."

"The reverence I felt last evening was something I will always re-member," added Henry.

Smitty spoke up next and said, "I have a feeling Louis would choose 'In the rustling grass I hear Him pass; He speaks to me everywhere.'"

And Smitty was right.

"Smitty is aware there have been several times when I shared a sto-ry," I said, "which for me was more like a vision. I have not identified the storyteller because they just seem to come to me.

"During the storm and several other times, I not only felt a pres-ence but also felt like someone was watching. It was often connected to thoughts of my great-grandfather, and sometimes I felt like he might have died and was reaching out . . . I hope that wasn't it. I seriously don't think it was.

"During the storm, the feeling was so intense, I believe I felt a touch. You guys all know I go to church, but there is something more going on for me on this trip. I still have some thinking to do about all this, but your thoughts confirming I'm not the only one feeling a presence is so helpful."

I waited a moment and then said, "Let's close with the unison prayer."

Our Eternal God, our Loving Father, we reverently bow before Thee in the quietude and beauty of these morning moments amid the glories of thy handiwork. We thank Thee for thy presence with us, for the wholesome fellowship among us, for the new friends, for the inspiration of our leaders, and this great brotherhood to which we belong. Grant to us the nearness of Thyself as we seek Thy presence in worship, that we may be more like the pattern Thou hast shown us through Scouting. Amen.

Chapter 29

JOLIAT "PORTAGE"

After our church service, Mr. Greenlee walked over to Smitty and me and said, "That was well done! I'm proud of you two."

Fred asked us to gather with all of our gear by the lake next to the canoes. We had packed our gear and cleaned the campsite before the worship service, leaving it ready and waiting with an ample firewood supply for the next group of canoe-country voyageurs. Tom and Dave went through the campsite one more time to be sure nothing was left and then joined us.

We gathered around Fred as he said, "Before we start this adventure, I want you all to have your map folded to today's journey with the compass in your map cases. We need to stay together, and although Louis and I will go ahead to explore the route from time to time, we will always return to tell you of our findings. I doubt we will find anything but game trails to explore. So please stay alert and communicate. Thank you for this early start and the beautiful beginning of the day with an excellent worship service.

"Louis and Joe have changed places so Louis and I can guide us in this adventure. You guys have proven your ability to navigate, so I expect you to help us pick the best route. Your thoughts and ideas will be both welcome and essential to our success."

And so it began . . . the day we tackled the unknown . . . the portages to Blackstone Lake.

It started out well. Getting into Fred's Seliga and paddling with him was an honor. As we paddled out into the lake to await the rest of the crew, I was impressed with how quietly it moved on the water. Chuck reported all of our gear was accounted for as soon as he reached us. As we waited, I looked in every direction and could see that we would start with a clear day. I hoped it would stay cool as I knew we were in for a workout.

Fred headed for the southernmost part of the lake. I could see a small bay ahead, which would be about a mile from our campsite. We both had a map case and a trusty Pathfinder compass. Mine was on the floor between my boots.

We were out in front of the rest of the crew, and Fred did not seem in a hurry, so I took a moment to look at the Quetico Park stickers, which Joe had mentioned on the inside of the bow. Each one had a different design, and they fit neatly between the ribs of the Seliga.

When I'm 18, I intend to add a few more stickers to whichever canoe is assigned to me.

Joliat was a beautiful lake with several impressive bays. It looked like the kind of place where it would be fun to spend a layover day. I looked up and saw a bald eagle soaring majestically above the treeline ahead of us. It hardly moved its wings as it used thermals and light breezes to increase its altitude. I looked over my shoulder. Fred was smiling, and we both noticed the whole crew was gazing at this magnificent sight. We stopped paddling and let the canoes glide so we could witness this event.

Fred spoke softly, "The bald eagle is considered an endangered species. However, I am proud that the Base is cooperating with US and Canadian officials in researching the eagle's continued existence. Our crews travel and explore a great deal of the Quetico Provincial Park and the Superior National Forest each summer. When you get back to the lodge at the Base, I'll show you a map where we plot sightings of eagles and undiscovered nests. We should plot this sighting and alert the rest of the crew to be on the lookout for nests."

"Shall I announce that before we proceed from here?" I asked.

"Yes. Let's sit here until we see which direction our eagle is headed."

The eagle made a slow circle and moved on in the direction we would be traveling. As the eagle disappeared from view, I remembered a line Sig Olson had written in his book *Listening Point*, "Only when one comes to listen, only when one is aware and still, can things be seen and heard."[1]

The rest of the crew paddled close to us, and Gary said, "That was my favorite wildlife sighting of the trip! It was even better than the moose."

"I have been around for many years," said Mr. Greenlee, "and this is only the second eagle I have ever seen in the wild. I am grateful for this experience."

I told the crew about the ongoing eagle project at the Base and told them we should all look for additional eagles and nests.

"Where would we likely see nests?" Tom asked.

We all turned to Fred, who said, "They build nests near the tops of the tallest trees. A bald eagle's nest is called an aerie, and it can be six to ten feet in diameter and about six to ten feet high. The nest will increase in size each year as eagles reuse the nest and add sticks and other building materials. An old one can weigh several tons!"

"Wow," said Tom. "How does a nest which weighs so much stay up in a tree?"

Fred chuckled and said, "Just goes to show you how strong trees are and how good eagles are at selecting the best tree and building nests. It is also important to know that bald eagles are very territorial. Most breeding pairs return to the same nest site year after year. They may

---

1. Olson, *Listening Point*, 8.

use the same nest annually for twenty years or more. There is one in North Bay that looks very old."

"Let's keep our eyes peeled and help with the project to enhance their survival," said Henry.

I repeated the line I remembered from *Listening Point* out loud: "Only when one comes to listen, only when one is aware and still, can things be seen and heard."[2]

Fred smiled and said, "Guys, we are going to be spending the morning and part of the afternoon in an area through which few people travel. Perhaps we can spot the mate and even the nest belonging to the eagle we just saw."

We started paddling again, and as Fred and I pulled ahead, we discussed the small bay with an island in the middle. But, we agreed, staying to the left of the island would likely take us to what we hoped would be a stream that would lead us to the next lake.

As we passed to the left of the island, we found it hid a narrow inlet curving to the right. Fred paddled as far as we could, and then we came to a small stream. We had to get out and walk the canoe in the shallow water down the stream. Fred hoped we would get to a deeper portion that would be floatable, and we could get back into the canoes and paddle. I could tell the stream was swollen from the recent rains and hoped he was right.

Wading through cold water was not particularly fun. I slapped at a mosquito, which buzzed and landed on my ear. It was challenging but better than unloading and loading for several short portages all in a row. I could see a marsh ahead on the map which would require a long portage if we couldn't paddle through it.

Turning my head, I looked behind and saw the rest of the crew were right behind us. Fred told them to follow us for now, and as we moved further down the creek, it appeared we were in luck. The little

---

2. Olson, *Listening Point*, 8.

creek had enough water to float the canoes, but we would have to continue to walk the canoes since it wasn't deep enough to paddle.

The stream was blocked with downed trees every so often. We moved some of the trees and had to slide the canoes over some.

It was still cool, but we were already starting to sweat, and the pesky mosquito had called in some buddies, and they were trying to feast on my ears. Something bit me hard on the neck, and I slapped it. I looked at my fingers and found a dead deer fly and a spot of blood. Even though we had only just started, this portage had become more exhausting than any we had taken in the days before. The only thing good about it was I did not have the pain in my shoulders from the canoe's portage yoke.

At least I have a free hand to swat the bugs!

I was concerned about the Seliga, but Fred assured me we could slide it on the keel. He thanked me for being concerned and careful as we led the crew through the stream. As the stream curved south after 100 yards of a westerly track, we came upon a straighter creek. However, it still required us to walk the canoes through shallow water, which quickly became muddy. It was slow going. I found it difficult to slog through the swamp, tormented by what had now become a hoard of mosquitoes continually hovering over us. ·

I was concerned the guys might lose enthusiasm for this part of our day. I tried my best to encourage and compliment them on their toughness whenever we were close enough to talk. It was still early in the morning, and we were making steady but slow progress.

We continued this traveling pattern, pulling and pushing our canoes around downfalls, for nearly an hour. Fred stopped once and told us all to put on some more mosquito repellant as we were all sweating, and the sweat was washing off what we had used before starting.

At long last, I looked up after we struggled over a particularly difficult downfall and saw a hint of an opening up ahead of us. I shaded my eyes from the sun as it filtered through the trees, and it looked like the opening was a large meadow or an open marsh.

It took another 15 minutes, but we finally entered the clearing. There we found a small amount of open water.

"Mount up, Louis," said Fred. "Let's see how far we can paddle."

The other three canoes were close, and everyone broke into a smile when they saw the opening and saw us sitting in our canoe. Staying close to the marsh's right side, the narrow stream had enough water to float the canoes, although it required pushing off the muddy bottom at times.

We had to get out and walk twice, and I had to pull a leech from my left leg. I was surprised I could feel it and that it wasn't quick enough to connect firmly.

"Next time we have everyone close," advised Fred, "let's warn them to be as sensitive to the leeches as you are."

As we came to the end of the long marshy meadow, the stream took a turn to the right, and the tree-shaded shallow water required us to walk the canoes again. We let the other three canoes catch up, and I said, "Guys, I pulled a leech off of my left leg. It wasn't attached, and other than them being slimy critters, no harm was done."

I heard a couple of guys say, "Gross," and everyone gave themselves a quick inspection.

"I have had leeches on me while wading in Skunk Creek back home," said Dave. "I saved one in a jar and took it to biology class. Don't panic! They are just gross . . . and don't mention them to your mother."

It wasn't far to another but smaller marsh. We walked the canoes through the swampy marsh for about 600 yards to a navigable stream, which Fred said looked like it was about 1,500 yards long. It was good to be paddling, and soon we came to a small narrow lake. It was now late morning, and to say we were a muddy mess would be an understatement.

We stopped after we found a flat dry spot to have lunch. Since Fred and I had the canvas water bucket on the top of the Kettle Pack, we paddled out to deep water and brought in a bucket of clean water.

Gary cut up the bannock, and Chuck cut some thin slices of hard salami and cheese. Some peanut butter and jelly on our homemade bannock was delicious and a nice change from smashed bread. The Red-Eye was especially satisfying, and we all got a handful of raisins and dried apricots.

Everyone was exhausted and muddy up to their thighs, but at least our sweaty shirts had started to dry since we had gotten into the canoes and could paddle. The lunch break was a welcome rest.

"I'm pretty sure our football coach would be pleased with this demanding workout preparing me for football season," said Tom. "Slugging through mud and shallow water for much of the morning is a leg workout for sure!"

Tom also asked if the afternoon would be as hard.

"I don't know," Fred said. "I've never been this way. It looks like we may have a couple of pretty rough portages and some more of what we've had this morning."

I heard several guys groan at the mention of more rough portages and marsh, and then Smitty said, "But we can do it!"

"I thought this was supposed to be tough," said Tom. "But, hey Joliet, is this the best you've got?"

After lunch, we paddled down the unnamed half-mile lake, and at the southeast corner, there appeared to be a low spot in the shoreline between two heavy stands of timber.

"Louis, this is where a stream exits the lake and probably connects to another lake. It was in low spots like this where the Indians and the voyageurs would have made their portages. Would you scout around and see if you can find signs of a portage trail? It should be at the lowest appearing point. Do you see it?" asked Fred.

He put his paddle down and pointed.

"Got it," I said.

Fred paddled us over to the shore, and I got out of the canoe and walked into the woods. I walked east and west and only found a single game trail with deer and moose tracks. I followed it up a steady rise and finally could see water down the hill from where I stood.

I walked back and told Fred, "There is a game trail that heads in the direction we want to go. It will be hard to walk up and down a hill on rocky, uneven ground, requiring some clearing. I better go first with the axe and the saw to clear some low-hanging limbs."

Fred was all smiles at the news of water ahead connected by a game trail.

"Good job, Louis," he said.

He pulled the axe and the saw from the Kettle Pack and handed them to me.

"This is what is known as real bushwacking."

Fred told me to start, saying he would follow in 10 or 15 minutes after all of the crew had gotten to shore. He said he would ask them to wait until one of us came back and got them.

I started across. Moose and deer used this game trail heavily. It was about a 150 yards to where it ended at the next little lake.

I cut several limbs, pulled branches out of the trail, and walked to the other end of the trail, where it ended at the water's edge. I was happy to find a landing area, though it was a muddy one. I had to stop a few times to wonder how a bull moose navigated such a trail. I hurried back and met Fred carrying the Seliga, told him the axe and saw were leaning against a tree at the water's edge in plain sight, and that I would let the guys know what to expect.

I put the Kettle Pack on, and with the crew behind me, I hurried on across to meet Fred. We repacked the axe and the saw and loaded up.

We paddled to the right, and there, not far ahead, we could see by the map where our next adventure would begin. From the map, it looked like we would have a 500-yard portage to the next small lake.

While we waited for the rest of the crew to cross the lake and gather around, I asked Fred how we should handle this one. He suggested we do it like the last one. It looked like it might be more open, but I still pulled out the axe and saw and put the Kettle Pack on before starting across.

There was another game trail, more heavily used than the last, that headed west. I started down the more open path, but it still required a little trimming as I walked along. About halfway across, I noticed a small creek running to my left. There wasn't enough water to float a canoe, and it was dense and overgrown. However, I knew I was on the right track as the creek led to the lake ahead.

When I arrived at the lake, I found the landing solid, with lots of room for all our canoes. I set the pack, the axe, and saw down and walked back to Fred.

"This one is longer and required some trimming, but the little lake at the end sure looks inviting," I said. "It looks like there will probably be one more portage into Blackstone. I wonder if this lake wouldn't be an excellent place to wash the mud from our pants or legs and maybe take a little dip before proceeding."

"I like the way you think," Fred said. "I smell like I have been rolling in a feedlot."

I continued back to check on the crew. They looked pretty bedraggled but were happy to be nearing the end of a long and rugged day.

After an opportunity to clean up and swim a bit, everyone looked and felt better. No one complained when I told them that there was only one more portage. I could see where it started. It was not far from where we had taken our swim. I was hoping this final portage didn't turn out to be another muddy swamp.

Fred and I loaded up and headed for the last portage, It was unmarked, but it had to be in the corner of this small lake. From there, it should be a short distance through the woods to Blackstone, which would be our home for two days.

We left ahead of the crew so we could check out whatever awaited. This path was another game trail portage, and although it was a little muddy, it was only boot-sole deep. It was about 200 yards long.

As we waited for the crew to catch up with us, I thought back over the trails we had traveled this day. I realized I hadn't seen a single boot track or evidence of human travel. I looked across the small unnamed lake. Far to the west and above the horizon, I could see our eagle soaring to its immense nest at the top of the tallest tree in sight. It landed, and even a quarter mile or more away, I could see that there was a second white head in the nest.

The crew paddled their canoes in close. Without comment, I pointed to the nest. Everyone remained silent as we looked upon a sight I hoped would become common in the years ahead.

The day was arduous, and the experience of pulling canoes over downfalls, blazing unmarked trails, slogging through knee-deep sucking mud, fighting mosquitoes, climbing over rocks, and sweating like pack horses was an accomplishment I will never forget.

Fred and I quickly completed the day's last portage, and as we heard the first of the crew coming across, Fred handed me my paddle and said, "I think this day went very well. Everyone, including me, has had an adventure to remember. I am glad that I picked the right partner, Louis!"

He stepped to the bow of the Seliga. I felt a sense of pride when Fred said, "I think you've earned the right to paddle stern in this beautiful craft. Let's go find a campsite."

Chapter 30

BLACKSTONE

After the exhausting and muddy ordeal we had just experienced, I was relieved to be cleaned up and paddling the canoe across this clear and lovely lake.

As we approached the central part of the north arm of Blackstone Lake, it seemed as though we had the lake all to ourselves. Suddenly, I had the same feeling of being watched I had had at Kawa Bay. I looked around, and everyone but Fred was looking ahead, paddling. Then I saw Fred suddenly motion with a slight movement of his head to a location on the left near a small island up ahead. There was a green canoe sitting motionless in the shade of some trees along the shore, and two men were watching us as we crossed the lake.

When they realized we had seen them, they waved, and Fred and I waved back. The rest of the crew now saw the men, and several other Scouts signaled a greeting as well.

"Let's go over and check on fishing and which campsites are open," said Fred.

To the crew, he said, "While Louis and I are inquiring as to open campsites and the fishing prospects, you guys just lay back here and take a break."

So Fred and I dug in and moved smoothly in the direction of the lone canoe.

Two men sat motionless in a wood and canvas canoe, and as we pulled up near them, the taller man in the stern said, "Seliga, huh?"

"Yup," Fred replied. "What is yours? Is that a Chestnut?"

The man nodded and continued. "Joe Seliga builds the best wood and canvas canoe there is. Seventeen-footer?"

Fred nodded.

"I hope to get one someday," the man replied. "You guys from the Scout Base, eh?"

Fred nodded again.

It was a strange conversation with brief small talk. Both of these men appeared to be Indian. One spoke a little like Vic, the official at Canadian Customs, so I assumed he was Canadian.

Fred then asked about fishing and was told, "There is plenty for everyone, and they are biting on almost anything."

"Anyone else on Blackstone today?" Fred asked.

"Just us," the other man replied. "Not many folks come in here. Portages discourage most. How was Joliet?"

"Rough," Fred answered. "But these guys love it rough, and they did themselves proud today."

I had not said anything but noticed both men were really looking me over. One looked directly at me and said, "You a Scout?"

It didn't make me feel uncomfortable since it was a friendly look.

"Yes, sir, Troop 23," I said.

"Where are you and these Scouts from?"

"Sioux Falls, South Dakota," I replied.

The taller man smiled and nodded. "What's your name?"

"Louis Carter," I replied.

The man squinted and seemed surprised at the answer.

"We had best get on to our campsite and get set up," Fred said. "We plan to eat about seven-ish if y'all would like to join us. We may have some fish if these guys are as good at fishing as they are at portaging, and at least we will have some packsack stew to share. Coffee will be on as soon as we get a fire going."

"We'll be there, and the campsite on the island off the long point is the best on the lake. We will bring some fish," the shorter man said, adding, "I'm Eddie, and this is Bill."

"Fred."

Fred's reply was as abbreviated as the conversation.

A moment later, we were on our way to meet the crew.

After moving out of earshot, I asked Fred if he knew them since he seemed comfortable with the abbreviated conversation.

"I don't know them," he said, "but I've met a few Ojibwe and have learned friendly doesn't necessarily include talkative." He added that the conversation was typical of this part of the country.

I said I was looking forward to talking more with our guests that evening.

"Maybe they can tell us more about the Ojibwe who lived in this area."

We quickly caught up with the crew and led them to the campsite on the island at the end of the point. Fred and I arrived way ahead of the others and already had his canoe put up and had started the "look over" as the guys began to disembark.

It was an excellent campsite, as the men had said, and from the undisturbed area around the cooking area, it was clear it had not been used since at least the storm of three days ago. As soon as the crew arrived, Fred, Mr. Greenlee, and I conferred, and I told Mr. Greenlee about our expected guests.

Mr. Greenlee seemed pleased, saying, "I hope they come."

The crew set up the camp quickly. I was pleased they didn't need any direction or coaxing. I helped Tom and Mike collect firewood and assisted Mike with the latrine. Gary was doing fine and was working with Joe to get the food ready. He was protecting his finger but was more animated and involved than yesterday.

Several of the guys headed out to fish at Gary's urging in order to add a little protein to the meal. Everyone seemed busy and had something to do, so I looked for a quiet place to read with a bit of time before dinner.

The late afternoon sun was warm, and I found a place to sit, shaded by a large red pine. I rested my head against the rough overlapping bark and took in a deep breath. The pine resin scent filled my nose and mingled with the smell of the cooking fire Gary had started as a wisp of smoke drifted by me.

I looked out upon the beauty of Blackstone Lake. The water had a surface ripple from only a slight breeze. I watched the canoes as the rest of the crew went about their fishing. It was not long before I found myself imagining different lakes and portages as I picked up Sig Olsen's *Listening Point*. I opened the front cover and turned to the page I had marked with a piece of birchbark when I last read.

I started reading and felt a little sad being so close to the end. I wanted it to go on forever. As I slowly read each page, I frequently closed my eyes and tried to imagine a scene as he described it. It was not difficult. I had read just over two-thirds of *Listening Point*, and I found myself reading with a sadness that comes over me as I reach the end of an exceptionally good book.

Every page had surprising insights. The descriptions I read were much like the works of the master poets we studied in school except I could understand Sig Olson. It was like having a personal conversation with a trusted traveling companion. I found myself reading and then rereading passages to relish the thoughts and shared experiences. Sig Olson was already a good friend, and we hadn't met yet. However, I knew we would someday.

I found being seated in full view of a magnificent lake enhanced Sig's writing, and it had me imagining, even more, places in the wilderness. I knew I very much wanted to see more of what he wrote than this nine-day journey would permit. I was already dreaming of my next trip and the places it would take me.

A canoe came into my dream, and the paddlers were stroking in perfect unison. They were not my companions and seemed to be from a time in the past. They could have been voyageurs with their swarthy looks and stoic calm as they moved as one being made up of two bodies in one sleek green canoe.

I watched as they came closer. They had a particular look about them. I had seen it before, but where?

Grandpa! They remind me of Grandpa! But why?

I blinked and realized I was actually looking at our approaching guests from the other side of the lake, and they would soon be arriving for dinner. I leaped to my feet as Smitty joined me.

"I saw their paddle flash before I noticed the canoe," he said.

We watched the green craft as it became more detailed. The paddle flash caused by the low sun in the west was what first caught Smitty's attention. With steady strokes, the two men paddled in unison, matching stroke for stroke. Then they suddenly switched sides without missing a beat.

"Dip, dip, and swing and back, flashing like silver. Swift as the wild goose flys . . . dip, dip, and swing."[1]

They kept time to "The Paddle Song" . . . or was "The Paddle Song" written about a scene like this?

As they came closer, the wake of the canoe became apparent as it cut across the mirrored surface of Blackstone Lake. The bow bobbed slightly with each deliberate and forceful stroke. There was no sound as we had come to expect with our aluminum canoes.

As they paddled closer, Smitty murmured, "They look like Indians."

"Yup," I said.

Eddie, the sternman, called out, "Louis, how's the landing?"

I quickly stepped out on a rock and motioned a quartering angle that would provide the best place for a dry landing. I watched Eddie

---

1. "The Paddle Song."

expertly guide the fragile craft so Bill could get out on the small boulder. Bill turned and held the canoe and pulled it forward so Eddie could step out on the rock and join us onshore.

Bill then moved the canoe back so the yoke was next to him and then smoothly flipped the canoe onto his shoulders and looked to me for further instructions. I showed him a spot next to Fred's Seliga, and he gently flipped it down across his thighs and then placed it gunwales down next to the other green canoe.

He was looking admiringly at the Seliga. Fred, who had just arrived on the scene, asked Smitty to help him turn his Seliga over. Bill gently turned his Chestnut over as well in order to look at both wooden crafts side by side.

"Old Joe builds the best canoe there is," said Bill, the taller of the two.

Eddie nodded in agreement, and they both touched the gunwales, the ribs, and the caned seats. Then they moved from the bow to the stern, examining and feeling the deck, the triangular piece that holds the bow and the stern together. It was as though they were caressing someone they cared for.

"This piece holds it all together and is the most difficult to make," said Eddie. "I love to see how Joe shapes the deck so it slopes down on the sides and curves up at the point. Beautiful craftsmanship."

Bill looked up at Fred and said, "This one has been around for a while, judging from all the Quetico Provincial Park stickers. How many years have you had it?"

Fred smiled and said it had been assigned to him as a first-year guide three years before. "She's a good one and was well cared for by several guides before me."

Suddenly, Fred changed the course of the conversation.

"I just realized I don't know your full names, and you don't know ours. So my name is Fred Morton."

"My family name is Hotuya Kostache or Tall Bull in English," said Eddie. "I live on the Rosebud Reservation, where I work as a respiratory therapist at the hospital."

"Mine is Gekek or Hawk in English, and I am an emergency medical technician in Saint Paul," said Bill.

Fred then proceeded to introduce each of us with a brief comment on our best point. When he came to me at last, he just said, "Louis is our crew chief, storyteller, and our bear chaser."

Both men grinned, and then Fred asked me to introduce our Scoutmaster. I started talking before I could think and was pleased that the introduction seemed to flow. I told them he was the best Scoutmaster in Sioux Falls and probably the whole country. I included he was a master camper, teacher, and a proud Marine.

Every one of us had stepped forward and shaken hands with our guests as we were introduced.

After I introduced Mr. Greenlee, they both went to our Scoutmaster and presented themselves with their Army rank and outfit. They were about the same age as Mr. Greenlee, and both had served in Europe during the war, stating the particular actions in which they were involved. When Mr. Greenlee gave his rank of first lieutenant, Iwo Jima and Japan's occupation, they both shook his hand again.

"My uncle was a Marine and was killed in action on Okinawa," said Bill.

Neither Bill nor Eddie said anything else about the war. But their looks communicated respect, and it was evident that the admiration went both ways.

We all stood gawking, and I thought to myself, *Three warriors!*

Nothing else was said for what seemed a long time.

I finally broke the respectful silence and asked them if they were Ojibwe.

"I am indeed," said Bill, "but my friend, Eddie Tall Bull, is Lakota. Although our ancestors were enemies in the old days, we became friends while training for the war."

"Could you tell us the story of this area and your people's history here?" I asked.

He said they would be happy to.

"How's dinner coming along, Gary?" asked Mr. Greenlee.

"Fifteen to twenty minutes," replied Gary. "We have a sizable batch of fish, mostly northern and a few bass, and the cooks are ready to start frying them."

The crew, including Mr. Greenlee and Fred, moved away, leaving me alone with our guests.

"Louis," said Bill, "I would be willing to bet my last dollar you are part Ojibwe. You look like many of our mixed-blood young men. Do you have any Indian blood you know of?"

I told them about Grandpa and felt a sense of relief as I described him in detail. Bill asked how old he was, and I replied, "About one hundred and five, and he is actually my great-grandfather."

I also told them my dad had much lighter hair and different features.

"It is often said I favor Grandpa."

I told them of my concern for Grandfather's life and his physical condition when we left. I also shared my concern about his faith being respected.

"It may be even more complicated," said Eddie. "Many of our people of that age were raised in the Christian faith. Yet some still cherish their ancestorial beliefs. Does he speak any languages other than English?"

"He sometimes talks in a foreign language in his sleep," I said, "but it sounds more French."

"Are there any words you can remember, like when he greets you?" asked Bill.

"He sometimes says something that sounds like 'boohoo,'" I said, "but it is only when we wake him."

"I'll bet he says, 'Boozhoo,'" Bill said, "which means hello or greetings in Ojibwe."

"That's it!" I said.

I had tears in my eyes.

Oh God, I hope he is there when we get home! There is so much I want to learn.

Bill looked at me and said, "Aaniin, Louis!" I didn't know what it meant, but it felt like he was saying, "Welcome home!"

"Soup's on!" yelled Gary, and we moved to the fire.

Eddie put his hand on my shoulder as we walked, and he said, "Hau, Louis, tanyan yahi. That's, 'Hello, Louis, welcome home!' in Lakota.

"Lela ampaytu keen washtay! Today is a good day!"

We all gathered around the cooking area, and I immediately took charge and said, "Guys, you all know how I have been worried about my grandfather. I just learned more about him than you can imagine. My new friends have introduced me to a man I didn't know. A man I loved but didn't know."

I closed my eyes for a moment.

I opened my eyes, took a deep breath, and said, "Let's bow our heads for our Wilderness Grace."

Before I could speak, Eddie raised both hands and said, "Mitakuye Oyasin . . . May we live with all our relations . . . Mitakuye Oyasin!"

He nodded at me, and the rest of us said:

For food,
For raiment,
For life and opportunity,
For sun and rain,
For water and portage trails,
For friendship and fellowship,
We thank Thee, Oh Lord.[2]

"Good prayer, Louis!" It was Bill.

---

2. Traditional grace used by Sommers crews.

"Let's eat," said Mr. Greenlee.

So we all dug in and listened to the fish stories everyone had to tell as we ate.

As we concluded the dinner of northern pike and packsack stew, Gary said, "Save some room for dessert. We have a spice cake baked perfectly with a frosting made from Gary's special recipe."

Bill and Eddie seemed very impressed. We relaxed with either cocoa or tea.

Finally, Mr. Greenlee said, "We are delighted to have you as guests, and since we have planned a layover day for tomorrow, we hope you will come again. Now how about telling these Scouts about the folks who have known these same lakes and trails much longer than any of us could imagine."

"Eddie and I have made this fishing trip since a couple of years after we were discharged from the service, back in 1945," said Bill. "We got to be good friends in the service and talked a lot about the fact we both had this border country in common.

"The Forest Sioux occupied this area for centuries," he continued. "During the French and Indian Wars, my people, the Ojibwe, were steadily pushed west by several tribes pressed by other tribes moving from the east. This area of northern Minnesota and Southern Ontario was the site of great and bloody conflicts. This was a Sioux Nation. We Ojibwe drove the Forest Sioux from this area onto the plains of western Minnesota and the Dakotas in the early 1700s.

"There are unwritten records of this conflict between the Sioux and the Ojibwe, like the well-known warning left near 'Picture Rock' on Crooked Lake. It was described in a journal of explorer Alexander Mackenzie. He wrote of the arrow shafts he saw in the fissures in the rock face on a cliff overhanging the water not far from the last portage from the lake. It was believed the arrows were shot and left as a warning by the Sioux.

"There are paintings and pictographs on many rock faces throughout the Quetico and the Superior National Forest. They are ancient, and it isn't clear just who painted them. But they are to be respected and preserved for all who travel this country."

"Many of the Sioux arrived in the Northern Plains at about the same time horses started to populate the area," Eddie continued. "The Sioux bands adopted the lifestyle and horse culture of the tribes they drove from the immense territory. They became a dominant nation as they acquired vast land holdings extending from western Minnesota to Wyoming.

"When we found ourselves in the same military unit, we were at first hesitant to associate because there were still hard feelings between some of our people. But what we had in common was more important, and we soon became best friends. Like you guys, I was in Scouts as a boy and found the skills I learned to be very helpful."

Dave spoke up and asked if they knew about the voyageurs.

"Was it the Ojibwe who they traded with during the fur trade times?"

Eddie looked at Bill, who continued the story.

"The voyageurs were French Canadian canoemen who were the laborers of the North American fur trade. First, they paddled birchbark canoes over Montreal's rivers and lakes to the Pacific Ocean in the seventeenth, eighteenth, and nineteenth centuries. Then they traded with all Native people from Montreal to the Arctic and west to the Pacific.

"There were two classes of voyageurs: the *mangeurs de lard* or Porkeaters, a rather derogatory term, and the *Hivernants* or Winterers. The Porkeaters traveled from Montreal to the fur post at Grand Portage on the North Shore of Lake Superior in their thirty-five- to forty-foot *canot du maître* or Montreal canoes. They were paddled by nine to twelve men and carried eight thousand or more pounds of trade goods amounting to sixty ninety-pound bundles, called pieces, per voyageur.

"Arriving mid-summer at Grand Portage, the trade goods were transferred to the smaller *canot du nord* or north canoe. This smaller north canoe was about twenty feet in length and was paddled by six to eight men with their load of two to three thousand pounds. After loading the trade goods into the north canoes, the Winterers departed for the interior, hoping to travel as far as possible before winter."

Dave looked puzzled and said, "Mr. Hawk, you seem to know a lot about the fur trade and the voyageurs. How did you learn about this and especially the French words?"

"I identified myself as Ojibwe," Bill replied. "However, the designation is not entirely correct.

"You see, many of the traders, French, English, and even some Scotsmen, married into Indian families, and their children many times continued in the fur trade. I am what is referred to as 'Métis.' Métis in Canada are folks who can claim both Native and European ancestry. I am mostly Ojibwe. But our family story includes French voyageurs, and I am very proud of the distinction."

Bill Hawk was looking directly at me as he said those words with a smile. I felt warm and knew precisely what his story suggested.

God, I pray Grandfather is still with us when I return home.

"I hope we can talk some more tomorrow," said Mr. Greenlee. "I am sure these Scouts will have more questions then, so let's plan for another get-together.

"But I have a question," he continued. "My Scouts are familiar with Sitting Bull, Crazy Horse, Red Cloud, Spotted Tail, and other famous Sioux chiefs. Were there some Ojibwe leaders we should be aware of?"

"This very lake is named for one of our most famous chiefs, Chief Magatewasin, who eloquently argued for the rights of his people," replied Bill. "He argued so convincingly, he was compared to the well-known English lawyer, Sir William Blackstone. From then on, he was known as Chief Blackstone. His people appointed him to represent them at the negotiations for Treaty Three in 1873. He was chief at the Lac La Croix reserve from 1873 until he died in 1885.

"You guys mentioned Kawa Bay, and you might be interested to know his daughter, Shawbogeezigoh, married the son of Chief Kabaigon of the Kawa Bay Reserve. In the 1870s, there was a sizable band living around the mouth of the Wawiag river," he continued. "However, the population declined, and in 1915, the Kawa Bay Reserve was officially dissolved by the government, and only a few families remained. They were further affected by the devastating influenza outbreak of 1918, and most relocated to Lac La Croix."

Smitty was looking at me as if he was recalling my feelings of being watched at Kawa Bay's exact location that Bill mentioned. So I decided I would wait until tomorrow to talk with Bill and Eddie about the feelings I had at the mouth of the Wawiag.

"You mean we camped where Ojibwe lived back on Kawa Bay?" asked Tom.

"Tom, many, if not most of the campsites and portage trails we use, were in use long before the Europeans came to this area," said Bill. "The history of this land doesn't start with the explorers. In fact, the Europeans always used Native guides in their trips of exploration."

Henry told them of my story of the campsite we found and rebuilt on Joliat yesterday.

"We have never been to Joliat," said Eddie in response, "and we would like to discuss the route you guys took to get here. We may try on Tuesday as a side trip, and Louis, I agree with your thoughts on Joliat Lake being off the beaten track."

I now had several things to discuss with our new friends. I was feeling a real connection and wanted to continue the discussion tomorrow.

"Keep listening to the Spiritual Nation, Louis."

"Guys, we have had a very strenuous day ahead, and I think we may want to get a good night's sleep," said Mr. Greenlee. "Remember, we were on the water as the sun was coming up this morning.

"Bill and Eddie, we appreciate your sharing with us and hope you will come back tomorrow. When you see smoke, it means Gary has the coffee on. You are welcome to join us for pancakes with all the fixings, and tomorrow evening, Gary's pizza parlor will be open."

"We will be over. Migwech! Thank you for the invitation," said Bill.

The crew, including Fred and Mr. Greenlee, seemed to know I had more to discuss and held back as our guests began to leave.

I walked with Bill and Eddie down to our landing.

"I assume 'migwech' means thank you in Ojibwe," I said.

"That's correct, Louis, and I'll teach you some more words and phrases tomorrow. I would love to see your great-grandfather's face when you use a few Ojibwe words," Bill replied.

When we got to their canoe, we saw the full moon's reflection shimmering on Blackstone Lake. As my friends began their short trip to their camp, their canoe's wake was the only disturbance on the perfectly calm lake. Loons greeted their passing with one of their many calls.

After watching and listening for a while, I walked back up by the fire. I could sense everyone was watching me, as they were all waiting by the campfire when I returned. I turned and looked to see if I could still see Bill and Eddie, but they had disappeared into the shadows produced by the trees on the other side of the lake.

"Do you think they will be back tomorrow?" said Dave.

"I sure hope so," I said. "Actually, I am certain they will, and guys, I sincerely appreciate you allowing me to have some time alone with them."

"It looks like you may have found some family, Louis," said Smitty.

"Could be, and at least I feel like I understand my grandpa and a little about the 'Indian side' of our family. Now, guys, there is a beautiful moon tonight, and I know we are tired, but maybe we could just sleep a little later and spend some time enjoying a beautiful night," I said.

Everyone walked to the landing at the lake's edge, which was bathed in moonlight. Several loons could be seen as their swimming motion was the only disturbance on the smooth surface. Once again, and like the night before, the moonlight was so bright a campfire was not necessary for us to walk to the edge of the lake and gather together.

Mr. Greenlee spoke softly and commented on how proud he was of the way we handled a rough day. He said he was looking forward to our layover day and thought we might discuss the various options for spending this time.

"Fred," he said, "there are obviously northern and bass in this lake. Are we likely to catch some walleye and lake trout?"

"I can't guarantee I am correct," replied Fred, "but I have never heard about anyone catching walleye in Blackstone. We caught lake trout on a previous trip here, and I should tell you how they are usually caught.

"Lake trout like it cool and tend to be deep this time of the year, fifty or sixty feet or more," he continued. "I would suggest a big flashy spoon like a KB spoon. You will likely need some weight to get down where they are. Hooking a lake trout may cause you to think you have a snag. They usually don't fight until they are near the surface.

"Remember, northern are found at all levels, and you may catch some while fishing deep. Because not many folks come to Blackstone, you may catch some very large northern, and I recommend releasing the big ones. Since we haven't had lake trout yet, I would certainly encourage you to save some room. We don't want more than we can eat. You may also want to do some exploring in this lake with all its bays and islands.

"You may have noticed not far from the landing, it drops off rather quickly. If you want to fish from shore, this is an excellent place to do so. This island is pretty good sized, and you should find plenty of firewood back away from the campsite. Since we will be here for two days, gather an adequate supply."

Fred took a deep breath and said, "Louis, It looks like you have a lot to talk to Eddie and Bill about. I hope they come over for breakfast, and you can spend some time with them to find some aswers to your great-grandfather's background. I would like to request that we all pray for his health and that you will have lots to share and talk about when you get home."

I was moved by Fred's caring remarks and was even more touched by what came next. Henry immediately spoke up and said, "Let us pray."

> May the one who blessed our ancestors, Abraham, Isaac, and Jacob, bless and heal those who are ill and especially the one we all call Grandpa Carter. May the Blessed Holy One be filled with compassion for his health to be restored and for his strength to be revived. May God swiftly send Grandpa a complete renewal of body and spirit, and let us say, Amen.

With tears in my eyes, I began to recite the benediction from Numbers our MYF meetings close with:

The Lord bless you and keep you;
The Lord make his face to shine upon you
And be gracious to you;
The Lord lift up his countenance upon you
And give you peace (Num. 6:24–26 KJV).

After another look at Blackstone Lake, I turned and started walking back to our tent. Mr. Greenlee put his hand on my shoulder and walked next to me. The rest of the crew followed close behind us.

Chapter 31

LAYOVER ON BLACKSTONE

I must have slept soundly, for when I woke, Smitty, Fred, and Mr. Greenlee were not in the tent. I stretched, yawned, and then took a deep breath. I could smell fresh coffee, and I could hear the clatter of pots and the frying pan as they were set on the fire. I heard Gary tell Tom to blow on the fire in order to get it burning hotter so he could start the breakfast fish fry.

Wow! I have overslept. I've got to get up and dressed.

As I left the tent, I saw Bill and Eddie standing by the fire, just out of the smoke, having coffee. I waved and headed toward the latrine. The smell of coffee caused my first thoughts to be about Grandpa. As I walked through the dew-covered foliage along the path, I saw Henry coming toward me.

"Great minds, right?" he said and passed me the toilet-paper bag.

I told him I was still surprised and impressed with the prayer he offered last evening. He said it was a traditional Jewish prayer for healing.

"It was from memory," he added, "and I couldn't remember all the ancestors normally listed. I hope I got most of it right."

"Henry, it was perfect," I said. "Thank you!"

"And speaking of perfect," he said, "the benediction was one we Jews and Christians have in common."

"Hank, If I have learned one thing, it's we have a lot in common, and I like learning these things."

"I have a feeling you are going to learn a lot more after breakfast, Louis," said Henry. "Would you mind if Smitty and I sit in on your visit with Bill and Eddie? We talked earlier, and we would both like to visit your grandpa with you sometime after we return home."

"Please do," I said.

After returning to the campsite, I got a cup of tea from Gary and noted breakfast was well underway. I joined Mr. Greenlee, Fred, Bill, and Eddie.

"We just learned all about yesterday's trek and have almost decided to skip it," Bill said. "It sounds like an arduous trip. But hearing of it from Mr. Greenlee's perspective, we will probably give it a try, if not this trip, next year for sure."

Henry and Smitty joined us as we patiently awaited breakfast. We spread my Fisher map on the ground before us. Eddie asked if someone could show them our route thus far, and Henry traced it, including a description of each day's travel and the campsites. Fred smiled at me, and I commented on how proud I was that everyone engaged in the navigation process. Smitty pointed out the location of our best fishing results and proudly recalled the numbers and types.

"Let me recommend the lake trout found here in Blackstone," said Eddie, "and we suggest you keep only the medium-sized ones for eating. They are tasty any way you cook them."

Fred asked if they had ever caught walleye in Blackstone and that he had heard there were not any here. Eddie agreed with Fred.

Bill asked how we enjoyed Kawa Bay and Mack. Almost in unison, we all said the fishing was excellent.

I shared that the Wawiag is a must and then said, "I'm surprised you haven't made a trip to Kawa Bay."

"We started coming up here years ago and picked Blackstone because of its name," said Bill. "We enjoyed the solitude and the fishing here so much we just keep coming back. Of course, we have used all three routes into it, but not through Joliat. We like Knife Lake and love to visit with Knife Lake Dorothy. Ottertrack Lake is also a favorite. But we always come back to Blackstone for at least a few days."

"I think we may try some other routes," said Eddie, "and we appreciate your inspiration.

"Fred, can you show us where your travels have taken you over your years on staff?"

Fred pointed at the map, and as he did so, I noticed a slight smile at the corners of his eyes. He traced his routes, which were primarily in the Quetico. As Fred traced his routes, I looked at Eddie and Bill from time to time. At several points, I saw Eddie's eyes widen as he turned and nodded to Bill.

At one point, Eddie turned to Fred to ask, "Is there anywhere, or are there any portages you would recommend against traveling?"

"Hmm," Fred put one hand under his chin and made a few tracings on the map with the other and then said, "Here at the Base, we probably take more rough and unusual trips than most other groups. Scouts seem to like rugged. But I would say this Joliat portage ranks right up there with the roughest I have been on."

Gary walked over to us and announced, "Breakfast is ready."

Breakfast was delicious, consisting of pancakes, syrup, Plumrose bacon, fruit stew, and bulgur. I had never had bulgur, but Fred recommended it as an alternative to oatmeal, so we had brought a couple of meals worth.

The bulgur was great, and most of us put a little fruit stew on it rather than sugar. I made a mental note to ask Mom to buy some. Henry told us it was a Middle Eastern staple and that his mother used it in several recipes.

"This was a delicious breakfast," said Eddie. "If you want to add another word to your vocabulary, fruit stew in Lakota is 'wojapi,' a traditional berry stew or soup."

After breakfast, we cleaned up our cooking utensils and packed away our food so mice and chipmunks would not get into it. We also made sure the fireplace had a small fire for heating water for tea or coffee. Most of the crew, including Mr. Greenlee and Fred, were planning to fish and explore.

"Everyone come back to the campsite about noon and report on the fishing," I said with a chuckle. "You don't want to catch too many. Henry, Smitty, and I are going to stay in camp and talk to our guests."

I was happy Smitty and Henry were interested in what we would learn today. And about visiting Grandpa when we got back.

Gary's injury to his finger was healing, and I suggested he leave it uncovered to get some sun. Fred nodded. Mr. Greenlee grinned and said, "Just keep it clean and don't let a big fish bite it."

Gary smiled and said he left the teapot on for us.

After everyone decided who was fishing in which canoes, we found ourselves alone at the campsite. Bill and Eddie had refilled their cups with the black tea from the pot, which was still hot. I had become quite a fan of black tea since our first night on Lower Agnes.

We decided to go over to the sloping rock outcrop at the edge of the island. We had a beautiful view from the southeast to the large island to the west of our site. Before us, to the southeast, was an island similar to ours, which gave some perspective. A pleasant light breeze was coming from the northwest. The ever-present loons were fishing with and hooting to their growing young, who were quickly following their example.

We sat and sipped our tea as we enjoyed the scene before us. Nothing was said for several minutes when Bill said, "Boozhoo Niwiijiwaagan."

"'Boozhoo' is a word meaning greetings, and 'Niwiijiwaagan' means friends. If I were to greet just one of you, I would use 'Niijii' for a male or 'Niijikwe' for a female. Another word for greetings or hello is 'Aaniin.'

"Louis, last evening, we learned your 'Nimishoomis,' or grandfather, uses 'Boozhoo' frequently as his greeting to you. Let's pause and let this much sink in, and perhaps you should practice a bit."

After a break and some practice, Bill said, "Before you learn some more words, let's learn some terms, and I will write all these words down for you if you can find some paper. Ojibwe was anglicized as Chippewa, Ojibwa, or Ojibway. It is known to its speakers as 'Anishinaabe' or 'Anishinaabemowin,' an Algonquian language. It has five dialects spoken from Quebec, across Ontario and Manitoba to Saskatchewan in Canada, Michigan, Wisconsin, Minnesota, and North Dakota.

"Your great-grandfather likely speaks one of these since you said he sometimes speaks a foreign language in his sleep. Your comments regarding his using French words make me believe he has a similar background to mine."

"I'm the only person in my family who strongly resembles Grandpa," I said.

"I agree," said Smitty. "Louis doesn't resemble either his mother or father regarding hair color and skin tone. Louis isn't as dark as Grandpa, but he is several shades darker than his parents and tans very quickly."

Bill smiled and continued, suggesting I learn a few more words and phrases.

"We speak of the seven gifts of the grandfathers, and they may be words that would stir memories in your grandfather. The gifts are these we believe will help guide you to live a good life. We teach these gifts to our children, so they are never forgotten:

• Minwaadendamowin, which is respect

• Debwewin, which is truth

• Aakodewewin, which is bravery

- Nibwaakawin, which is wisdom

- Miigwe'aadiziwin, which is generosity

- Dibaadendiziwin, which is humility

- Zaagidiwin, which is love

"Gitchi Manitou is the creator god of the Anishinaabe. The name means 'Great Spirit' or 'Great Mystery,' common terms used to address God in many Native American cultures. Gitchi Manitou, or one of its many spellings, was used to translate for 'God' in the Bible's early translations into Ojibwe. Today, many Ojibwe people consider Gitchi Manitou and the Judeo-Christian God to be one and the same."

As soon as Bill mentioned Gitchi Manitou, a memory flashed before my eyes.

"There is an Iowa state park called Gitchi Manitou, southeast of where we live, and our troop once had a weekend campout there," I said. "I had no idea of the origin or meaning of the name back then. We did a service project and cleaned up the area where we camped, which was left a mess by previous campers. Mr. Greenlee had always told us, 'Scouts always leave their campsites cleaner than they find it.'"

I asked Eddie if there were any words from the Lakota we should know.

"I would be glad to share some with you," he said. "However, your grandpa uses Ojibwe words, and I think it's safe to assume Ojibwe is his background. Therefore, adding Lakota words, which is my language, might become confusing for you."

"I think you're right, Eddie, it would be very confusing, but you used a phrase last night before we said grace," said Henry. "Could you tell us what it meant?"

"I said, 'Mitakuye Oyasin,' and in English it means we are all related or all my relations. It is a phrase from the Lakota language. It refers to our being connected to everything. It's pronounced 'mee-tah-koo-ya oy-yah-seen.'"

"Eddie and I have discussed this concept many times," said Bill, "and he uses the expression as well. These words and phrases will get you started, and I would bet he will add more.

"But let's keep this simple because I think you and your grandpa will have a lot to discuss. I will give you our addresses and hope you will write with any questions and let us know how he is doing."

I had discussed my plan to help my mother be more respectful of Grandpa's faith with Smitty and Henry, and now I shared my concern and the plan with our new friends. They were both smiling and agreed with both the need and the solution.

Henry told them of the process by which his Jewish faith was not only recognized and respected but shared with our group.

"Just this past Friday evening, I led a Sabbath service back on Mack," he shared.

After additional discussion, our first fishermen arrived back at camp and reported they had two nice lake trout. They also said they knew one other canoe had a few as well. Bill suggested we get the fire going and prepare to have a shore lunch. He also said they would like to do a little fishing during the rest of the afternoon. I reminded them we were having pizza that evening and that they had been invited.

When Gary and his group arrived, they were happy to see the fire going, and with the morning's catch, it was clear we were going to have a wonderful shore lunch. The whole crew must have been thinking about a shore lunch because everyone kept the medium-sized fish, mostly trout.

When Mr. Greenlee and Fred arrived, everyone else was already there, busy cleaning fish and preparing lunch. Gary had already made the Red-Eye. He also laid out smashed bread and some peanut butter and jelly for those who wanted some. He had a pot of green beans and onions cooking as well.

When Gary called out lunch was ready, Henry volunteered to lead in the Wilderness Grace and began with Mitakuye Oyasin. Bill and Eddie grinned, and we all said the Wilderness Grace together.

The trout, breaded and fried in a mixture of lard and butter, was delicious. However, it tasted different from the other fish to which we had become accustomed. It had the skin left on the fillets. That was not the case with the northern, walleye, and bass.

Mr. Greenlee asked Bill and Eddie what they thought of our cooks. Eddie said he felt they were the best, and the trout was delicious. He looked at Gary and said the lake trout were also excellent when baked, and Gary said he would try it that evening. Bill asked if we would have time for the pizza we had planned.

"We will bake the fish first," said Gary, "and then the pizza will be baked after the fish is served. The pizza recipe involves a rather quick process of producing six or seven pizzas with a crispy crust.

"Don't worry," he added. "We have this all figured out."

"I wouldn't miss this meal for anything!" said Bill. "I've never had pizza on one of our trips."

"Bill and Eddie, what do you have planned for this afternoon?" asked Mr. Greenlee.

"Fishing and exploring Blackstone is what we love to do," said Eddie, "and spending time with your troop is a real treat."

"Guys, I think we need to do some planning before we head out for the afternoon, because I think everyone will be away from our campsite," I said. "Eddie and Bill, have you ever had bear problems on this lake?"

"We have never had bears in camp," Bill said. "They are very wild here and not snoopy at all. I think they tend to hang out where people camp more often.

"Blackstone is a destination lake, and few pass through on their way to somewhere else. There are some good trees for hanging your food packs if you choose. Then again, cooking pizza might attract some bear investigation tonight."

Fred said he was usually extra careful when cooking odorous meals.

"However," he continued, "Blackstone is remote. We should be fine, but I agree with the special care tonight after the pizza."

I asked Gary about the number of fish we needed for dinner and breakfast.

"A dozen medium-sized lake trout should be plenty," he said.

"So let's agree to keep no more than three per canoe," I reminded the crew, "and don't forget to wet your hands when handling your catch if you plan to release them."

I also reminded the guys to take their cameras to photograph any large trout or northern we would be releasing.

"After we do dishes and clean up," I continued, "let's make sure we have an ample supply of firewood for tonight and tomorrow morning. And, of course, for the next folks who use this campsite after we leave. I would also suggest a swim with a bar of soap. As my mom would say, some of you are getting a little ripe."

With laughter and smiles, everyone started to clean up lunch dishes.

Joe came over to me with another suggestion since someone in his tent had started to smell like dirty sweat socks.

"How about we all do a little laundry while we are at it?" he asked.

I spoke in a loud voice and said, "Joe has made an excellent suggestion for this layover day. How about everyone takes some time to wash their trail clothes and socks? Wear your spare clothes while you fish. Wading and sweating through all the mud yesterday likely produced some honest but foul aromas."

After everyone started on their respective projects, Bill, Eddie, Mr. Greenlee, and Fred came to me, and it looked like it was time for a staff meeting.

"Bill and Eddie just spoke to me and wanted to make sure they weren't imposing on our layover day," Fred said. "Louis, you're the crew chief. What do you think?"

I looked at Mr. Greenlee, hoping for some guidance. But instead, he just said, "You're the boss."

I thought for a minute to collect my thoughts.

"I think having Bill and Eddie sharing their knowledge and experience with us would be a highlight of this trip for all of us," I said. "I hope you both feel welcome and spend as much time with us as you wish. With all the fish we are catching on this trip, there is no problem with having enough food. So unless someone else has a problem, I declare you both honorary members of Troop 23!"

Nobody spoke, and then Mr. Greenlee, with a bit of a tear in his eyes, shook my hand and said in a soft voice, "Well done, Louis, well done."

Fred spoke up and said, "It looks like we have another canoe for fishing, and I would like to suggest Bill and Louis use my Seliga. I was hoping to talk to Bill alone and to do so in the Seliga was far more than I had ever expected. I would love to paddle your Chestnut, and Eddie, you and Mr. Greenlee probably have more to talk about, so let's you, me, and Mr. G. fish from this one."

"Where do you suggest we fish?" I asked Bill after he suggested I paddle stern as we headed out to fish on our beautiful Blackstone Lake.

"Louis, I would suggest we head over to the area where you entered this lake yesterday and look at the portage you will be using tomorrow."

So we began to paddle, and I immediately noticed the strength of Bill's stroke on the right side. I was glad I had started to paddle on my left, and after rounding our island, we followed the shore on the right.

We passed two small islands where Fred and I first met Eddie and Bill, and then we continued to the northeast, where the lake narrowed. Finally, we entered a small bay, and I spotted the portage landing directly ahead. Bill had me pull up to the shore, and we stopped and got out of the canoe. After we had placed the Seliga in a safe spot, we walked across the portage.

It was an easy walk, maybe 250 yards, ending at a long narrow lake. We stood at the end of the portage and looked out over the lake. We could see on the map that it had a stream exiting the other end.

"This will be a good first portage compared to yesterday's ordeal," I said. "I am anxious to reach Knife Lake and the border country."

"Lots of my people on both sides of my family traveled this border country just a few generations ago," Bill said. "It was heavily traveled and sometimes a bloody highway during the fur trade. You will have a full day tomorrow, but unless we have bad weather to contend with, it will be a breeze for your crew."

We returned to Blackstone and paddled to the place where we entered the lake from our Joliat adventure. Bill asked if we could walk the distance to the little lake one would take to get to Joliat, and I agreed to show him the portage.

It was interesting to backtrack. I was glad I had developed the habit of looking back on a recently covered territory to remember the next time I traveled the same trails.

"Eddie and I may take the route you guys took from Joliat while your portage tracks still show," said Bill.

Once back on Blackstone, we decided to start fishing. Bill suggested we troll down the large arm and stay to the center while fishing deep and then take the channel on the north side of the large island. Bill had his line on the right side, and mine was on the left as I kept us parallel to the shoreline. We moved along slowly, and Bill said we were staying well positioned for the lake's deep part.

In five minutes, I had a strike. Bill started bringing his line in as I said, "I've got a fight going on, and whatever this is, it's big."

"You probably have a big northern," said Bill, "because the trout usually don't begin their fight until they are closer to the surface."

I was glad Bill had retrieved his line because this guy was fighting for all he was worth. I couldn't see him yet, and Bill encouraged me to bring it in slowly so it would tire before I had to land it. I kept the line tight and enjoyed the battle when suddenly I saw he was indeed a giant fish.

I gave him a little line, and he broke the surface about 15 yards out from the canoe. He shook my large spoon, and I could see all the visible lure was outside his mouth, which meant it was likely hooked near the front and therefore easier to remove.

Bill had turned around on the bow seat to help keep the canoe positioned for me to land the very large northern. It was thrashing and leaping out of the water in its effort to get free of the lure. I played him in and then released a bit of line in hopes of tiring him. Finally, after several minutes of fighting, it looked like I might be able to bring him alongside the canoe for landing.

I brought it up on the left side and positioned it in front of my left hand. My northern was huge. I slipped my fingerstips inside the gill plate, being careful not to put them into the gills themselves. With my thumb forward, I could grab and lift the fish by the gill plate without fear of its teeth or touching the barbs of the treble hook.

Bill had slid his fishing pliers to me, and with a bit of a twist, the hook was free, and I was holding a giant northern. Bill and I had already discussed my camera, and he took two pictures of me holding it. We estimated the fish to be over 36 inches in length, and I now had a picture to show Dad and Grandpa. After the picture, I gently placed the northern back into the water and released him.

"That fish was big enough to feed the whole crew, Louis," said Bill. "Eddie and I catch a lot of large fish. We always release them and keep the medium-sized ones to eat."

"I'm sure glad I had a witness, because nobody will believe the size of this one," I said.

"There are lots of big ones in this lake," said Bill.

We continued to troll to the island, and Bill caught an excellent eating-sized lake trout. As we moved past the island, I caught a nice smallmouth bass that I released. Bill suggested we pull the lines in and paddle into the bay, back beyond the large island. I was captivated by the beauty of this part of Blackstone Lake. It had a beauty all its own.

The bay was calm, and we began to troll again. After circling the bay twice, we had caught another nice trout. We reentered the main southern arm of our lake, and as we approached the south side of the large island, we caught another trout.

"Louis, this makes three fish for us, and unless we find others didn't catch many, we better put the poles up for the day," said Bill.

"I agree with you, Bill," I said. "Perhaps we should head back to camp and see if we have a good count of fish. I would also like to talk with you about a few things I have found confusing on the trip."

"Good idea, Louis," Bill replied, adding, "And I thought we might be having more discussion about Grandpa. But it's more than about Grandpa, isn't it?"

I stopped paddling and said, "Let's just drift for a bit."

I took a deep breath before continuing.

"Bill, when we were up on Kawa Bay, we were camped on an island west of the mouth of the Wawiag. Each time I was near its mouth, I felt like someone was watching me. You told us about the Ojibwe who lived there. Any thoughts on that?"

"Louis, it sounds like you are experiencing many feelings because you are concerned for your grandfather. I think when one is open to such feelings, communications happen. Part of our need to pause and reflect on our faith and our loved ones, both living and deceased, is becoming open to feelings and the spirit world. Your thoughtfulness and mindfulness make you open to the people around you and the Spirits of Life. You seem to have an unusual and intense awareness of what you are feeling.

"Never stop listening," he counseled. "I can't interpret or judge those feelings. That's for you to figure out. Just be thankful this process seems natural for you."

"Does it happen for you as well?" I asked.

"Both Eddie and I have discussed this and agree it is important to remain quiet at times so that we won't miss such contacts," Bill replied. "When you are with another person, even those close to you, recognize their need to think and ponder. Sometimes we feel a need to fill all the space with talk and noise. Resist that urge and respect the quiet times and spaces."

I thought of Smitty and Joe, my best friends. I guess what I liked about both of them is that while we were always there for each other, we could spend time without talking and didn't feel a need to be together all the time.

"Bill, migwech! This has been very helpful, and I appreciate your advice and counsel."

We started to paddle back to our campsite. Bill must have recognized I had a lot to process because nothing was said until we approached the campsite's landing. He looked around and said, "Migwech, Louis."

We unloaded our fishing gear and our catch, and Bill turned to face the left side of the Seliga, reached under it, and flipped it smoothly onto his shoulders. He carried it back to the place where Fred had placed it and flipped it off his shoulders. Then he placed it gently onto the ground and said, "What a privilege to paddle such a craft."

Mr. Greenlee, Fred, and Eddie were sitting near the landing with their cups, and Gary was on his way with a cup of tea for Bill and me.

Bill held his cup up and said, "Aniibiishaaboo."

I replied, "Tea?"

Bill smiled and said, "Remember that one for Grandpa."

We sat near them, and Fred said, "We noticed your catch and can assure you we have plenty of fish for tonight and tomorrow morning."

Joe had grabbed our stringer and was with the crew cleaning them.

I looked at Fred, who said, "So . . . any fantastic fish stories?"

Bill spoke up and described my northern. Fred said, without a doubt, we had won the big fish contest.

"I'm pretty sure we got a good picture for proof of Louis's catch, but we won't know until he gets his film developed," said Bill. "Send me a picture, please! Too bad we don't have one of those new Polaroid cameras along."

After we finished enjoying our tea, I walked over to Gary and said, "How's the finger?" He held it up and showed me it was healing with a thin scar.

"How are the dinner plans?" I continued. "Would you mind letting me know when you are ready to make pizza? I want to make sure I am up to speed on the process."

Gary assured me dinner was well in hand, and he would let me and our guests know when he was about to start the pizza.

Mike and Chuck came up to the cooking area with one of our aluminum canoes and placed it over two logs to keep it level.

"This will be our table for rolling out the pizza dough," said Chuck.

Gary started to gather all the ingredients necessary for our dinner. I asked him about the flavoring for our pizza, and he showed me Fred's spice kit.

I had not noticed it before. It was a military-surplus mountain kit with a small stainless steel frying pan lid over two aluminum pots. I had noticed Fred used the pan for a plate most meals. The mountain kit had baking powder, cinnamon, Mapleine, chili powder, white pepper, cumin, curry powder, cayenne pepper, oregano, and regular black pepper neatly arranged in it. A small bottle of Tabasco® sauce placed on its side fit perfectly across the little pot, which held the spices.

Gary assigned Joe, Chuck, and Mike to start preparations to bake the fish. First, they were to set up and balance the reflector oven. They had estimated the firewood necessary for the fish and the pizza. It had already been split into thumb-sized sticks. Gary had them put the fillets in the two cake pans with a tablespoon of butter and lard in each pan. They then sprinkled cornmeal on the damp fillets. When the lard and butter became hot, they were to add all the fish carefully and bake uncovered for about 20 minutes or until one could flake the fish.

Mike was assigned to put the cocoa and coffeepots on the fire and start the dried carrots. Then he suggested frying up some dried potatoes after boiling and draining them.

"Great idea. Use the big frying pan to brown them, and we'll have hash browns."

As soon as the fish fillets were baking, Gary started on the ingredients for the pizza. In a medium-sized pot, he added two cans of tomato paste and two cans of water. Gary then added a handful of minced onions and a cup of thinly sliced and chopped salami. He added some spices from Fred's spice kit, including white pepper, cumin, cayenne pepper, and some oregano.

The pizza dough was a mix of four parts flour to one part lard, one-half teaspoon baking powder, and a pinch of salt. Fred suggested a little of the sourdough as well, and other than that addition, he remained one of the attentive crew.

Gary had made five fist-sized clumps of the pastry mix and kneaded each on the bottom of the canoe. He then instructed us to leave them to rise a bit until after we finished our fish dinner.

After Tom led us in the Wilderness Grace, we started eating our dinner of baked trout, cooked carrots, and hash browns, all cooked to perfection. Gary suggested we remember to save room for our pizza party. Fred, Mr. Greenlee, Bill, Eddie, and I sat close to the fireplace.

"It looks like you have become comfortable with this delegation thing, Louis," said Fred. "When you become a guide, you may find it challenging to let go and just observe as your trips progress. Remember, this whole thing is about developing leaders, and you do it by involving everyone and developing their skills. I think tonight's dinner is a perfect example of delegation."

Mr. Greenlee and our guests seemed to agree, judging by their smiles.

After the main course, Gary suggested we all relax while the cooking crew started the pizza. Joe moved to revive the reflector fire, and Gary asked Chuck to dice up some cheese and some more salami. While Chuck did that, Mike got Fred's driftwood rolling pin and a cup of flour as we gathered by the canoe.

After Gary had a brief conversation with his crew, they got to work. Mike dusted the canoe bottom with flour as Gary started to press the lumps of flour, which had risen slightly into flat oval shapes. After sprinkling flour on them, Mike rolled those shapes to about three-eighths inch thick pizza doughs, which filled the griddle, now hot from the reflector oven and carried by Joe. After placing the dough on the griddle, Joe put it into the oven until the dough started to bubble.

Gary then spooned the well-cooked sauce on the dough as Chuck placed the cheese squares and salami on top of the sauce. When the cheese melted, the griddle was taken to the canoe. The pizza was cut into slices for the waiting observers. This process was repeated five times. Dave and Smitty stepped in to complete the last three to give the cooks a chance to eat some pizza.

After our feast, Henry suggested we give our cooks a hand. Bill and Eddie nearly started to clap when they quickly recognized we were just holding a hand toward our cooks rather than clapping, the sound of which would scare the loons.

They both grinned, and Eddie said, "The more I see of you guys, the more I like Scouting!"

Nobody had to say anything to cause everyone to begin the chores we knew we always performed before we gathered for fellowship in the evening. With the nearly full moon starting to appear, it was unnecessary to have a fire. I suggested we have a little "campfire" by the water, without the fire.

After dinner, dishes, and chores, we gathered on the sloping rock near the shoreline.

"You guys sure make me proud to be your Scoutmaster," said Mr. Greenlee. "I don't know how this trip could get any better, but I suspect it will. It has been so fulfilling for me to see every one of you fellas grow before my eyes.

"Now, how about a little song?"

Mike said he would like to sing "The Far Northland," and we did, with Mike leading.

It's the far Northland that's a-callin' me away,
As take I with my packsack to the road.
It's the call on me of the forest in the north,
As step I with the sunlight for my load.

(Chorus)
From Lake Agnes, by Louisa, to Kawnipi I will go,
Where you see the loon and hear his plaintive wail,
If you're think'n in your inner heart, there's a swagger in my step,
Then you'll know I've been along the border trail.

It's the flash of paddle blades a gleamin' in the sun,
A canoe softly skimming by the shore,
It's the smell of pine and bracken comin' on the breeze
That calls me to the waterways once more.

(Chorus)
From Lake Agnes, by Louisa, to Kawnipi I will go,
Where you see the loon and hear his plaintive wail,
If you're think'n in your inner heart, there's a swagger in my step,
Then you'll know I've been along the border trail.[1]

Eddie asked about the origins of the song, and Fred told him many youth groups used it, and for the Sommer's crews, it was sort of our anthem. Since we were in the mood for some quiet music, I suggested another song.

"Eddie and Bill, when I saw you guys paddling over from your campsite yesterday, it made me think of 'The Paddle Song,'" I said. "We usually sing it three times, once softly as the paddlers are in the distance, again with more volume as they pass by, and then softly as they disappear in the distance. I imagine those voyageurs and Indians of this land as we sing this one."

Our paddles clean and bright, flashing like silver . . .
Swift as the wild goose flies . . . dip, dip, and swing

---

1. "The Far Northland."

Dip, dip, and swing them back, flashing like silver . . .
Swift as the wild goose flies . . . dip, dip, and swing.[2]

After we finished singing "The Paddle Song" three times, the loons began their serenade. We all sat quietly for several minutes.

Eddie and Bill stood and asked me to come forward.

"Louis, we are certain your grandpa will be happy to see you and to be greeted in his native tongue when you return," said Bill. "Traditionally, our young men are given names related to a story or an incident. We have discussed an Ojibwe name for you. Your mother will likely be somewhat horrified. However, your great-grandfather will be pleased to have a grandson named Makwa Zegi. An English translation would be 'One who frightens bears' or simply 'bear scare.'"

I was at a loss for words and couldn't think of what to say. Henry realized this and came to my rescue.

"Mr. Hawk and Mr. Tall Bull, all of us were worried that Louis was not going to come on this trip a few weeks ago," said Henry. "He, like many Scouts at our age, was beginning to lose interest. He was worried sick about leaving his ailing grandfather and has struggled with understanding his relationship with him.

"This trip was more than he expected, and you guys have helped him realize a big part of his family story. Finding you here on Blackstone Lake and spending time with willing teachers has been a blessing for us all.

"And I think I can speak for all of us by saying if either of you gets to Sioux Falls, you have a sincere invitation to visit Troop 23."

"I know you guys have been impressed with my service at Iwo Jima," said Mr. Greenlee. "While fishing with Eddie, I learned these guys were both in the Battle of the Bulge and later helped free thou-

---

2. "The Paddle Song."

sands of Jewish and other prisoners who were near death in some of the Nazi concentration camps.

"We seldom talk about our war experiences," he continued, "but all three of us encourage you to learn about the history and never let hatred and prejudice result in such things ever again."

Henry went to all three men with tears in his eyes and thanked them for their service with a hug. Then we all sat in silence and listened to the sound of lapping water and the loon songs.

I didn't want the day to end with everyone feeling sad, so I decided to speak.

"Mr. Greenlee, Mr. Tall Bull, and Mr. Hawk, we Scouts salute you and thank you for your service. All of us were born as the war was ending or shortly thereafter. Many of our parents, teachers, and neighbors are veterans. Many still struggle to live with the memories of those times. I hope you guys know the things you were fighting for are found in this program, one I hope all of us have come to understand better and appreciate. On this seventh evening of our canoe trip, I would like to invite any of you who wish to share a reflection at this time."

"Why don't you start, Louis?" said Smitty.

"Okay," I said.

I took a deep breath and began.

"It's probably no surprise I have learned my great-grandfather is Ojibwe and French Canadian, which means I am as well. I now believe if someone says I look like a half-breed, I shall consider it a high compliment."

Henry chimed in next.

"I have learned all this reverence and respect stuff really works when everybody works on it," he said. "Thank you for not only accepting me but also for showing respect for my faith. You guys are the best! Migwech."

"Bill and I are happy and proud you guys have allowed us to join you on your layover day," added Eddie. "You guys can be proud of the determination and toughness which brought you to this lake. But we both agree we like the young men we see before us. If you should come to the Rosebud, please call me. Louis and your Scoutmaster will have my number. Bill's too. There are some Scout troops out on the Rosebud that would love to meet you."

"You have a long day with lots of miles to paddle tomorrow," said Bill. "I am sure you want to get an early start, so Eddie and I will say goodnight, and we will bring some frybread for your lunch tomorrow before you leave."

"Before you leave," said Tom, "we would like to share another of our Troop 23 traditions with you. We end our meetings with 'Scout Vespers' followed by 'Taps,'" he continued, "and then I'll lead the benediction."

Tom led us in song:

Softly falls the light of day,
As our campfire fades away.
Silently each Scout should ask:
Have I done my daily task?
Have I kept my honor bright?
Can I guiltless sleep tonight?
Have I done and have I dared,
Everything to be prepared?
Day is done, gone the sun,
From the lake, from the hills, from the sky;
All is well, safely rest, God is nigh.[3]

Tom next led the benediction.

---

3. "Scout Vespers."

"And now may the Great Master of all Scouts be with us until we meet again."[4]

And we all replied, "Goodnight, Scouts."

Eddie and Bill went to their canoe without further comment, launched it, and paddled toward their camp.

We watched as the Chestnut's wake cut across the moonlit water of Blackstone Lake. After a period of silence, Mr. Greenlee spoke and said, "This was certainly a most memorable couple of days. I'm proud of you guys."

A loon began its call, and we all fell silent as if lost in our own thoughts. Everyone moved to their own tents, leaving the night to the loons.

---

4. Boy Scouts of America Troop Program Resources, "Closings."

Chapter 32

JOURNEY TO THE BORDER

Before anyone in our tent stirred, I dressed and exited as quietly as possible. There was a faint light on the eastern horizon, and it appeared we would have another clear day. Nobody was up except Henry, who had just lit the fire beneath the teapot. I quietly approached him and sat on one of the logs positioned near the fireplace. Henry turned and said, "I can't wait to meet your great-grandfather. I feel like I know him now, and I can see the pride you express whenever you speak of him. I am certain he is better and awaits your return."

"I sure hope you're right, Hank. I have the same feeling."

Dave was the next to join us, and the water was about to boil. I was just about to have him yell "Daylight in the swamp," but it was a beautiful morning, and I didn't want to disturb the sounds of nature, so I didn't.

I could hear other tent flaps stirring and a few muffled good mornings, but no one said much of anything as they stepped out of their tents. I watched as several of them stood a moment, stretched, and then looked at the eastern sky. I figured they were enjoying the quiet morning as much as I.

I thought Henry had already used the important papers since they were on top of a food pack. I grabbed them and headed for the latrine before the rush. As I walked back into the woods, I could smell the cedar and the pungent odor of a healthy boreal forest.

"Good morning, Grandpa," I said softly.

I was sure he was thinking of me. I remembered that when others spoke of the times before he moved to the nursing home, he was always described as an early riser.

I also said a short but sincere prayer of thanks for, well, just everything.

When I returned to the campsite, I noticed everyone was up and either assisting with breakfast or packing their gear. Smitty had already rolled my sleeping bag, and our tent was almost ready to take down. Joe said, "Next," and I tossed him the toilet-paper bag.

Gary and Mike were getting breakfast ready, including a good helping of trout to go with our farina. The cocoa, coffee, and tea were already being enjoyed, and fruit stew and raisins were set out to add to the cereal.

"Here come our new friends," said Mike.

Bill and Eddie were just pulling up to the landing. After putting the Chestnut up, both came up to the campfire for tea. They were bearing gifts. Each had a pie tin stacked with frybread!

"We made enough for your lunch plus a nice helping for this morning's breakfast," said Bill. "Frybread and trout go well together.

"Fred, I wrote the recipe down for you if you want to try it with future crews," he continued. "Louis, I added it to your notes as well. Your grandpa might like some next time you visit him."

Gary immediately reached out his hand and asked Fred, "May I see that? Wow, a new recipe! I'll write this one in the back of my trail cookbook. Joe's been heating the trout while everyone else has been packing. Breakfast is almost ready."

I thanked Bill and Eddie for helping me to understand my grandpa and myself better. Bill suggested I bring a tape recorder when we visit him.

Mom and Dad got a small Magnavox last Christmas to send record-ed messages to family members.

Then Bill said, "You may unlock lots of memories, and audio tapping will likely preserve an interesting part of your family's story."

"I'll be sure to do that," I replied. "I am pretty sure he has tried to tell me stories in the past, but I wasn't interested in stories of the olden days back then. During the past week, the olden days have become both important and real to me. Bill, thank you for introducing me to the Indian side of my family. I hope to be soon learning more about them."

Gary announced breakfast was about to be served, so we gathered around the fireplace where everything was ready. The frybread was transferred to a couple of our pans so our guests could use the pie tins for breakfast plates. As before, they brought their own utensils and cups.

Smitty led the Wilderness Grace, and we settled into another delicious meal. Everyone ate the frybread and asked for seconds. I even saw Smitty sneak a third helping.

The trout was cooked to perfection. Even the fruit stew tasted better. Because I had occupied so much of our guest's time, I was happy to see everyone sitting close to them and enjoying their fellowship.

I sat with Fred and Mr. Greenlee.

"We have a pretty long day today," Fred pointed out. "However, the portages won't slow this crew down.

"Now, there are two ways we could proceed south," he continued. "One would be a little quicker, and the other would take us across Cache Bay and provide us more time on the border route, the actual Voyageur's Highway. What are your thoughts?"

Mr. Greenlee just looked at me and said, "I would be willing to bet a small fortune on Louis's answer."

"Let's go with the voyageurs!" I replied.

"That's what I figured," said Fred. "Whom do you want to navigate today?"

"I need to sit and consider who has had the assignment. I'll talk with a few of the guys and announce it before we do dishes," I said.

I thought a moment and looked around. I saw Smitty stuffing his sleeping bag into the personal pack and went over to him and said, "Hey, Smitt, I want to delegate today's navigation to a couple of guys who haven't had the opportunity. What do you think? Dave and Mike did a great job bringing us down to Joliet from Mack. I think Gary would appreciate the opportunity. Who else do you think would like to guide?"

Smitty suggested Tom, and I agreed.

After breakfast, I told the crew of our plan to lengthen the trip and spend more time on the border. Everyone seemed pleased. I told everyone to keep their maps handy and follow along as we paddled through what promised to be an exciting day.

"This morning," I said, "I would like Tom to be the navigator, and this afternoon, Gary, would you do the honors?"

Tom grinned at me, and Gary said, "You betcha, Louis. I was hoping to get to do this."

"We have a long day ahead of us," I continued. "Let's do the dishes, get packed, and get this campsite cleaned up like nobody was here except for the ample wood supply for those who follow."

As everyone headed to their task, I went over to Bill and Eddie, who were talking with Mr. Greenlee. Fred joined us as well.

"I sure am glad you fellas could spend some time with us," Fred said.

"We thoroughly enjoyed it! I am thinking of volunteering with the troop at Saint Francis Mission School," said Eddie.

"I never expected this trip to be this educational," Mr. Greenlee said, "and I think you both have a lifelong friend in our crew chief. If either of you gets to Sioux Falls, we expect to hear from you. Remember, you are honorary members of Troop 23."

"Louis, please keep us informed on how your grandfather is doing," said Bill. We will say prayers and burn some sweetgrass for him. Both of our peoples use sweetgrass for such things."

He gave me a braid of sweetgrass and a slip of paper with instructions.

"When you get back, you might see if it would be possible to take your grandfather outside in a wheelchair and burn some sweetgrass as you pray with him."

"Migwech!" I said.

I had both their addresses and telephone numbers and promised to stay in touch.

"Guys, let's saddle up, say our goodbyes, and get this show on the road."

Everyone in the crew stepped up to shake hands with our new members, Chuck called off the gear, and we headed to our canoes.

Tom paddled stern, and Dave paddled bow as we headed for the first portage we would take to Blackstone Creek from Blackstone's northeast arm just over a mile from our campsite. Tom and I had walked over the portage before we began fishing yesterday. I pointed out to Dave and Tom that the light breeze was coming from the northwest. If it continued, it would mean it would be with us on Saganagons and Cache Bay, which were large enough for headwinds to be an issue.

About a half mile up the shore and on our right, I saw the place where Fred and I first met Eddie and Bill.

Did someone arrange that meeting? I'll remember this spot forever.

I was glad I had developed the habit of looking back as we left portages and campsites. Because as we passed the portage we took from our Joliet route, I quickly recognized it as the unmarked portage from which we entered Blackstone Lake. Tom was headed for the little bay from which we would portage into Blackstone Creek, which would take us to the northwest corner of Saganagons. On the map, it looked like the creek was about three miles as the crow flies and, adding in the curves and bends, it would likely be a four-mile trip.

Tom guided us to the portage, which was about an eighth of a mile long, and led us into a beautiful narrow lake. The lake was only a half mile long. When we got to the other side, we found a tiny stream and another short portage entrance. At its end, we found another stream that was deep enough to paddle.

After this last short portage, Tom, our navigator for the morning, had everyone gather so we could proceed together and not be strung out the length of the stream. Fred's advice to travel quietly was indeed paying off as we moved along Blackstone Creek.

Not far ahead, we came to where a smaller stream entered on our left, and we saw a cow moose and her calf standing in the shallow, slow-flowing water. They looked up but seemed unconcerned, and we slowly and silently paddled past them.

The creek was wide enough for two canoes to paddle abreast. However, we stayed in single file. We came to a bend in the stream, and in a marshy area on the left, we saw a bull moose that stood and watched us pass. At the end of the bend, we saw a doe feeding, and even with a fawn by her side, she just watched us glide past.

Another half mile brought us to yet another short portage. It looked like we could walk the canoes through the stream, as it wound through some very thick woods. It would be like walking through a tunnel, as the tree limbs formed a close canopy over the creek. Perhaps because we had washed our trail clothes on our layover day, we chose the portage instead.

We found our stream continued flowing through a more open and marshy area as we came out of the portage. Tom reminded us to be as silent as possible so we could add more wildlife to our count. The birdlife was both visible and noisy in this area.

We came to a medium-sized pothole about a quarter-mile wide. I made a note to try fishing here on a future trip. At the northeast corner was another small stream and a portage of about 300 yards. The portage took us to a narrow bay in the northwest corner of Saganagons.

I took over the bow position from Dave after the portage. Tom complimented Dave on a job well done since the bowman had to be very vigilant for rocks and deadheads during the twists and turns of Blackstone Creek. The narrow bay led to a larger bay we crossed before entering the central and more significant part of the lake Fred had nicknamed "Sag."

As Tom led us into the lake's central part, I realized we would have a quartering wind behind us. It was not tricky navigating this beautiful lake with its many bays, points, and peninsulas marked clearly on the map as landmarks. The tailwinds made our progress more rapid than usual. The wind was not producing whitecaps yet, but we would likely have them on Cache Bay, which was much larger and more open. I looked at the map and figured the wind would still be with us.

Tom led us to the left shore, and we followed it to a narrows. We hugged the left shoreline, and it did not take long before I heard the sound of a waterfall. I looked down at my map and found the falls marked. They were called Silver Falls, and the portage around them was on the left. It was marked as 700 yards or around a third of a mile.

As we gathered before starting the portage, Fred complimented Tom. He told us to paddle along the left shore for about 100 yards above the falls and then wait for everyone to arrive at that point before proceeding. Tom reminded everyone to keep a close watch on the gear if we encountered others. It is easy to pick up someone else's gear on a busy portage.

We had the portage all to ourselves, and we were now in a narrow arm which led into the central part of Cache Bay. It looked much like the narrows on the other side of the portage.

Fred asked Tom to pull into the second campsite, which we could see on our right about a mile beyond. I made a mental note of this stretch before the bay's central part as a spot I would like to visit again. The wind had reduced to a light breeze with the left shore's protection, and several loons were singing their greetings as we quietly passed. A loon chick must have strayed a bit because I heard a parent's hoot call to the youngster.

Tom and I paddled straight to the campsite as Fred directed. It was on a narrow point with a small bay on the south side. Fred suggested we take a short break and then waited to confer with Mr. Greenlee and me.

"So far, today has gone very well," said Fred, "and I wanted to offer y'all the opportunity for a new adventure.

"As you can see on the map, Cache Bay is almost as large as Bailey Bay, which we crossed on the first day. I have crossed it several times, going both ways. I have never had the wind at my back, and though there will be whitecaps, they will not likely build to a level of concern.

"How would you like to sail across Cache Bay?" he asked.

"I like the idea, but how would we do it? What would we use for sails?" I asked Fred.

"Some crews use the dining fly, but I suggest using a couple of the military-surplus ponchos some of you have. By attaching the ponchos to two long paddles, we can stretch them across two canoes. The advantage of using ponchos is they would be easy to drop down should the wind become so strong it's a danger."

"Sounds great," I said. "Do we tie the canoes together?"

"No, we just hold on to the gunwales of the canoe next to you. All four canoes will be held together in this manner, and the guys in the stern will rudder to keep us on course."

"Mr. Greenlee, is this all right with you?" I asked.

"You are the crew chief. It's your call."

"Should I review this with the rest of the crew?"

"As I said, Louis, you are the crew chief."

We gathered the crew, and I revealed the plan to lots of big smiles. I suggested we get the shovel and that everyone take care of any call-of-nature chores before we start.

Most of the crew headed off to find a place to take a leak.

As everyone came back, Joe said, "Hey, there are some nice poles by the tent sites. Could we use them for the masts for our sails? No, wait, we can't do that. They are for the tents and dining flies for the next group to use this campsite. Never mind."

"You guys are the best!" said Mr. Greenlee with a smile.

As we were about to leave the campsite, Tom asked if it was time for Gary to take over the navigation. I reminded him Gary would take over after lunch.

"Where should we plan to eat, Fred?" asked Gary.

"Tom, as we get underway, we will see two islands far to the southwest," replied Fred. "If we sail between them, you will see a point and an island to its left. Around the point is a nice campsite I would suggest as a lunch stop."

"Sounds like a plan," said Gary.

We paddled up the shore until we could see the vast expanse of water before us. We were on the left side of the four canoes with Tom in the stern and me in the bow. We had Dave's poncho secured to his paddle. Joe and Fred had Joe's paddle attached to the poncho sail.

We paddled away from the sheltered shore with everyone and all equipment ready until we had enough wind to fill our sails. Finally, we connected our canoes with our hands, and we were prepared to set sail. The wind was indeed with us, and although there were whitecaps, they were not very high yet.

"The wind normally comes up in the afternoon," said Fred. "It looks like our early start means we will probably cross the bay before it gets rough."

"Tom is still our navigator until our lunch stop," I said. "Tom, do you have a plan for the route across the bay and our destination?"

"I've got this under control," replied Tom.

"You did well this morning, Tom," Fred said. "Take us across the bay."

When the wind hit our sails, it became apparent our plan was going to work, and we would be moving faster than we could paddle.

The water moving between our canoes made a rushing sound, and the sensation of sailing was very invigorating. Tom had the map and his Pathfinder on the floor ahead of him, and he pointed out the two large islands far in the distance.

"I never expected to be sailing on this trip," said Joe.

"Not every crew gets to sail," said Fred. "Sometimes the wind is never right, and some crews aren't as well trained as this one."

Mr. Greenlee was smiling broadly. We were enjoying this adventure. Everyone was chatting with the person next to them or just looking at the beautiful bay we were crossing.

"I would estimate we are moving half again as fast as if we were paddling," said Chuck.

We were soon closer to the two islands, and as we passed a good-sized island on our left, Fred said there was a good campsite on the island. Fred told Tom to stay close to the one on the left when we got to the islands.

"I've been studying the map and have figured out the route to follow," said Tom. "By the way, there is a Canadian Customs Station on the island to the right. But since we checked in at Prairie Portage, there is no need to stop there, right?"

Fred smiled his agreement.

As we passed between the islands, Tom said, "Let's go back to paddling when we reach the island between the points up ahead."

Fred agreed.

The campsite around the point, after we entered Saganaga, was open. I was looking forward to a lunch break. Immediately after landing, Gary had several of his cooking crew start the lunch. He then moved to consult with Fred about the rest of the route, to which Gary would be given leadership after lunch. It was also evident he was willing and able to delegate and share the cooking responsibility.

We had the frybread that Eddie and Bill had given us, and the cooks were slicing salami and cheese for our sandwiches since it was to be unique with the frybread. There was butter, jelly, and peanut butter if anyone wanted it. And, since we had the frybread, we didn't put out the Hol-Ry crackers.

The frybread was delicious and a nice change of pace. I was thankful we had Bill and Eddie write down their recipe. I hoped I would be able to make some for Grandpa.

Sailing gave us a nice break, and everyone was upbeat and eager for some good paddling. I heard Gary ask Fred how much farther we might go on today's outing. By the map, it looked like we would be on Saganaga for a few hours, and then we would move into Ottertrack at Monument Portage.

"We can stay on Ottertrack or proceed to Knife Lake," said Fred. "Both are beautiful lakes. When we get to Knife Lake, we will want to spend an hour or more at Knife Lake Dorothy's so we can have some of her world-famous root beer."

While we ate our lunch, I sat with Smitty and Henry.

"I appreciate you two wishing to meet Grandpa," I said, "and I sincerely hope it will be possible. It is hard to believe we are nearing the end of our adventure, and I have so much I want to share with him. I hope I can keep it all straight. I wish I had brought a journal, and when I start guiding, I will carry a journal. We get back Friday night, and I am sure Mom, Dad, and I will go up to the home first thing in the morning. I'll let you guys know how he is, and we can visit soon after."

After lunch, we cleaned up the campsite and gathered some firewood for the next campers. Then Gary took charge after complimenting Tom's morning leadership.

"I am excited to be the navigator for the rest of the day," he said. "During lunch, Fred and I talked about the afternoon's journey."

"Although we won't have the wind helping us," Fred said, "it won't be a problem. We will just have a gentle breeze. The shore on our right will block the wind for most of the afternoon due to very high hillsides. We are now on the Voyageur's Highway and will be until we turn south on Sucker Lake after a brief visit at Prairie Portage, where we went through Customs on day one."

"We will continue on Saganaga Lake until we cross Monument Portage into Ottertrack," said Gary. "I have asked Fred to share the history of this route when we take a break."

I was beginning to understand more fully why Mr. Greenlee was so proud when we did an excellent job with a task or responsibility. I also realized that pride in others only occurs when one delegates and provides them with the opportunity to shine. The most challenging part of the process was in giving up things you love to others.

As I reflected on both Mr. Greenlee's and Fred's leadership, I saw this process playing out . . . and how effective it could be.

Chapter 33

MA HARRY

Gary was grinning as he led off with Mr. Greenlee sitting in the middle and Mike in the bow.

Today our route took us in a southwesterly direction on the border between Canada and the United States. This part of Saganaga, west of Cache Bay's entrance, had several smaller bays and a narrows. I saw several campsites as we paddled to our first portage, which would take us into Swamp Lake.

I'll need to remember these for when I'm a guide.

I made a mental note.

After the portage into Swamp Lake, we only had to paddle a half mile before reaching the next portage. I looked at the map. It was called Monument Portage, and the map indicated it was 80 rods long. By now, I found I could convert rods to yards in my head and figured this portage would be approximately 440 yards (or once around the high school track) long.

We pulled up to the landing area and unloaded our canoes.

"Why is it called Monument Portage?" I asked Fred.

"Look over there," he said, pointing. "Can you see the monument post? It marks the border and is an important landmark with a lot of history."

The portage started out muddy and slow going. Someone had put some logs into the swampy area, but Fred said to stay off the logs and just slug on through the mud because we might slip on a log and break an ankle or, worse yet, a leg. It was rugged going, and again we were wading knee- or thigh-deep in thick, smelly mud. Several of our guys were finding they had leeches on their ankles and legs. We made short work of the swamp, so it didn't take long to reach a nice dry path, which led to Ottertrack Lake.

Everyone who had leeches pulled them off in the clear water of Ottertrack Lake. Most of them turned loose with a pull. However, Fred had us pause and get the salt out of the food packs, and two stubborn ones quickly dropped off with the application of salt. He also had us wash any bleeding spots with the Phisohex soap. I heard the term "gross" used as we dealt with these interesting critters.

"Leeches are parasitic and predatory worms belonging to the phylum Annelida and comprise a subclass I can't remember," said Chuck. "Their soft, muscular, segmented bodies can lengthen and contract."

Chuck knew his physics. His knowledge of and quick recall of biological information was equally impressive. And Mike had the most of anyone on him and could readily attest to the leech's ability to expand and contract.

As we entered Ottertrack Lake, Gary and Mike took the lead, and Gary called to the rest of the crew, "Let's stay together on this lake."

As we paddled out toward the center of the lake, we followed Gary's instruction with a smooth and practiced ease. It was evident everyone had become quite proficient in this paddling business. I watched Smitty and noticed that after Mack Lake, he had started to paddle a lot like Fred. I imagined I had too. At least, I was trying to.

After Mack, I was starting to note how great it felt when bowman and sternman hit the combination of strokes that comes with miles of practice. I think we were beginning to paddle like the crew with Tom Clack we saw on their way back in on Agnes, our second day on the trail.

Smitty caught me looking at their teamwork and smiled. All our canoes were now moving in unison and stroke for stroke. It felt great, and I could easily imagine the voyageurs crossing this continent with the dazzling scenery, the camaraderie, the sense of mission, and the feeling that precision teamwork gives.

I began to imagine the voyageurs and Indians we had learned of as we listened to Bill and Eddie telling their people's history back on Blackstone. I again wondered if Grandpa and our family were descendants of those rugged people who had first traveled these same waterways.

As my daydream was ending, I looked over at the other canoes. We still matched stroke for stroke. Both Smitty and Mike were glistening with sweat. They might have passed as the Hivernants in their canot du nord we had learned about from Bill and Eddie.

I looked back at Fred and Mr. Greenlee's canoes and saw they were right behind us, and they were also in perfect unison with us. Wow! We were moving so well together, the paddling was effortless, and I had time to look around and not miss a stroke.

The northern shore of Ottertrack was magnificent with high cliffs. They must have reached close to 100 feet and continued almost the entire distance of the lake. It was gorgeous.

We kept our rhythm and speed for nearly an hour and made very good time. When I looked down at the map, I saw we were nearing the end of the lake. I knew I would miss the beauty of this section and vowed that I would return.

I could see that the next lake was named Knife Lake, and there were two ways to get there. One was through the narrows with a short portage, and the other was the one where we were heading, which involved a short portage with a slight climb and then a gentle slope down to the other side.

I was not disappointed after the portage when we entered Knife Lake. It was also a beautiful lake. As we paddled on, it was evident that we were moving faster than at any point on our trip. We were again paddling in unison. Fred must have noticed the same thing because he was beaming. Mr. Greenlee saw me looking at him and gave me one of his "way to go" looks. As we continued down the lake, it seemed everyone was digging deeper and pulling harder as I felt the mood that had fallen over us.

Suddenly we heard a loud "Hol-Ry," only it wasn't the deeper-sounding male voice of a Charlie Guide we had heard before. The voice was female, and it wasn't a voice. It was voices . . . lots of them.

"It's Ma Harry!" said Fred. "Head over to the campsite on the point on the left."

When we reached it, I could see it was a five-star campsite with a magnificent view of Knife Lake.

Ma Harry was a middle-aged woman, and she was standing on the shore with her hands on her hips surrounded by 15 or so girls and young women. The young women appeared to be in their twenties, and I figured they must be counselors. The rest of the girls looked like they were the same age as us guys.

Ma Harry said in a softer but still commanding voice as we pulled in closer, "Hol-Ry, Fred. I haven't seen you since last year. Where is this fine-looking group of Scouts from?"

Fred greeted her, introduced Mr. Greenlee and each of us, and included our job with the crew.

I was feeling kind of bummed at finding girls out in the wilderness. It seemed like it should be a guy thing, and I felt a sense of intrusion. I found myself looking them over with a rather critical eye when, suddenly, my eyes made contact with one of the girls who appeared to be about my age. I took in a deep breath. She was about the prettiest girl I had ever seen. She was wearing cut-off blue jeans and a white shirt tied at the waist over a white tee shirt. I felt a little ridiculous staring, but she met my stare and didn't look away.

As we gathered closer, my eyes followed the girl. I could not stop looking at her.

Smitty reached over with the tip of his paddle and poked me. It brought me back to the present conversation.

Ma Harry was telling us about her role as a Girl Scout leader from Hibbing, Minnesota, and that she brought her troop up to the "trails" every summer.

"The guides from the Base have been beneficial during these first years," she said. "In 1961, Butch Diesslin was the first Sommers guide to visit our campsite. He is a treasure trove of information on how to conduct a Scout trip. We always try to have a campfire together when we meet your groups on the trail."

As Ma Harry continued, my thoughts drifted, and a moment later, I again made eye contact with the girl. She smiled, and I felt my face flush. I knew I was blushing. The next thing I heard was Ma Harry inviting us to stop for lemonade.

Mr. Greenlee and Fred had one of their quick visual conferences and agreed a short visit would be okay.

As we positioned our canoes at the landing and started to get out, a thought crossed my mind. Mr. Greenlee and Fred had had a conference that did not include me as crew chief. I wondered why. Had they somehow noticed I was preoccupied? I felt my face flush again. Had they noticed I was looking at the girl? I looked over at each of them, but neither gave me a look that would indicate anything. Perhaps they hadn't noticed. I turned my thoughts to not slipping and falling into the water when I got out of the canoe. As I stepped into the cold water, I looked up, and there she was again. This time, she was smiling . . . at me!

We neatly stowed our equipment next to our canoes, and I turned my attention back to the crew and looked to make sure everything was in order. As the last few pieces of equipment were stowed, I could not help but notice something else. The crew had handled the task with much more skill and care than usual. Suddenly, we were standing there, and everyone had a "what do I do next?" look on their face.

I looked around at each of my friends, and my eyes came to rest on Mr. Greenlee. He was looking at me. I knew the look. It was incredible how he could communicate with me with just a look. I interpreted this particular look to mean "Be a gentleman, introduce yourself to Mrs. Harry, and show leadership to the rest of the group."

I stepped up to Ma Harry and shook hands with her. I referred to her as Mrs. Harry.

"Call me 'Ma,'" she said. Everyone else does."

Her voice was friendly, and she made me feel very welcomed and at ease. Then she said, "Why don't you and your crew introduce your-selves to my girls while we older folks make some lemonade?"

We began introducing ourselves to the girls. After shaking hands and quickly introducing myself to most of the girls, I came face to face with the girl I had shared eye contact with. She was right in front of me, and I could see her eyes up close. They were blue. I felt a now-fa-miliar flush in my face. She said her name was Betsy, and she had been watching us paddle down the last part of the lake and described the smooth way we approached. She said it made her think of the voya-geurs Ma was always describing.

Wow! We were thinking about the same thing at the same time.

I was trying to think of what to say, and since she knew of voya-geurs, I decided to tell her about my beads and the cross I intended to give to my mother. She seemed excited to hear of them and asked if she could see them.

"Sure, I'll be right back," I said.

I went to get them from our Duluth Pack and remembered I had put them in the little pouch at the pack's front. I looked to see what the rest of the guys were doing and saw they were all in groups, talking with the girls. Mr. Greenlee and Fred were near the fireplace with Ma. Nobody seemed interested in what I was doing except Betsy.

I was usually shy with girls, and I had never had a girlfriend, un-like many guys. My fingers fumbled a bit when I rummaged through the pack's front pouch, and I dropped a few of the beads when I got them out. I looked up and noticed Betsy standing where I had left her watching me. I picked up the beads and headed over to her. Suddenly, I did not feel shy at all. I felt like we were old friends.

I showed her my bead collection and my arrowheads. She was interested in how I had found them. Then I showed her the voyageur trade cross I had purchased at the Base trading post. I was amazed she was so interested. She held the cross and put the beads beside it in the palm of her hand.

It was then I noticed her bracelet. It was made with a light tan cord. It had lots of very intricate knots and tiny beads tied into it. I asked her if they were trade beads.

"Oh, these are from a craft shop," she said. "We all make these from hemp cord and sometimes from leather. We call them 'bear scares.' They are supposed to keep bears away."

"Do they work?" I asked.

"I guess they do. We haven't seen a bear so far. Have you?"

"Yeah, we have seen a few."

"Were they scary?"

"Nah, not really."

I was embarrassed to talk about myself, so I just left it at that.

"Lemonade is on!"

Ma was calling everyone together. Betsy and I reluctantly left our conversation and started over to join the group. On the way over, she said, "Are you guys coming back over this evening for hot chocolate, popcorn, and s'mores?"

"I don't know if we can. We are going to be going on a ways farther before we camp."

"Well, other Scouts we have met have come back after they set up camp. I hope you will as well."

I had never really paid much attention to girls at school, but this girl—Betsy—was different. She was beautiful and seemed to be interested in the same things I was. It made me kind of nervous, but I wanted to spend more time with her.

When we all got together, Ma said, "You fellas enjoy your lemonade break, but you will need your cups."

We all just stood there, not moving, when Mr. Greenlee said, "Go to your packs and get your cups. This isn't an A&W, ya know."

Everyone laughed as we ran to get our cups.

It was the best lemonade I had ever tasted, even though there wasn't any ice. After we all enjoyed a cup, Ma said, "You better get going so you can get to a camp and have your dinner. You don't want to be late for our party tonight. We will be serving hot chocolate, popcorn, and s'mores."

I couldn't believe it. I looked at Mr. Greenlee, and he smiled and nodded his approval. I looked at Betsy, and she just gave me an "I told you so" look. I walked over to her and wasn't sure what I was going to say or do. I didn't have to say anything because she said, "Louis, since you are coming back in a few hours, I would like to try something with your beads and the cross for your mother. If you don't like what I have planned, you can cut them apart, and I'll understand."

Without hesitation, I placed my beads and the cross along with the leather cord Fred had given me into her hand. I let my hand linger, touching hers for a moment, and then felt silly and pulled it away.

I stammered a little and said, "See ya," quickly joining my crew in loading our gear into our canoes.

Ma Harry came down to the landing and said, "Louis, hurry back. You can keep the bears away. Your crewmates have been telling of your adventures on lower Agnes."

I was embarrassed and proud at the same time that the guys thought the bear episode was such a big deal. We pushed out from shore, and as we straightened out to start paddling, I saw Betsy was standing near the landing. She was looking right at me and, for a moment, she was all I could see. Everything else was out of focus as she smiled.

I led off with the crew falling in behind. I suddenly realized I couldn't describe any of the other girls as I took one more look back. She was still there watching. As we paddled down the lake, I could tell the guys were trying to be as cool as possible, and I think we were pulling it off.

Once we were out of earshot, it started.

"Whoa! Did you see that girl, Linda?"

"How 'bout that Mary, with the black hair."

Mr. Greenlee broke in and said, "Okay, guys. Everyone settle down. Mrs. Harry has invited us back for a little party, and Fred and I have agreed to allow it. Let's remember we are all Scouts, and I will expect you to act accordingly. I expect any further conversation about your new friends to be gentlemanly. Understood?"

Everyone was quiet for a few minutes.

Chuck, Henry, and Smitty pulled up by us, and Henry said more quietly, "Louis, who was the cute blonde you were talking to?"

I didn't answer. He started to tease me about liking her. I gave him a look, one I guess he must have understood because he quit teasing and was quiet for the rest of the way to the campsite.

Smitty just smiled, and we matched strokes to the campsite. Smitty and I had lots of conversations about girls over the past year or so, and I knew we would be having another soon, but not now, and not in public.

"Fred and I looked at the map, and there are several sites about three miles down the lake from Ma's," Gary said.

The one Gary liked was open when we got there, and I said a silent prayer of thanks.

"Gary, you have done a great job navigating!" I said.

And thank you for finding a campsite so close.

"Thank you for the opportunity," he said.

Since we would be going back to Ma Harry's after supper, I suggested we may want to cook something easy without a strong odor that might attract bears. Gary agreed and said, "When my team paddled near the neighboring campsite, I told the people camping there we would be gone until after dark. We asked them about bears and were told there had been no sign during the two days they had camped at that site."

Gary, Fred, and I discussed the dinner plans. Fred also suggested something quick, easy, and as odorless as possible. We decided on macaroni and cheese with peas, and Gary diced up our last can of Spam® into the mix. He also made bannock, which was always a big hit. Since we would have s'mores back at Ma Harry's, he didn't make a dessert.

After supper, Mr. Greenlee came over when I was cleaning my plate and said, "Louis, Fred and I would have normally discussed the invitation with you. However, it appeared you were somewhat occupied at the time. I hope you are okay with our decision."

I laughed and said, "She sure was nice. I'm glad we are going back, and I promise we will be gentlemen."

Fred came down and joined us. He said part of the decision to allow the visit was the fact that we would have a mostly full moon to light the trip back to our campsite. He said he always enjoyed a few night paddles every season. I'm not sure, but I thought I saw him wink at me when he turned away.

Everyone washed up, and we were even able to come up with a few combs. We all took turns at Mr. Greenlee's metal shaving mirror. We hung the packs, which were much lighter now as we had used up most of the food, with some parachute cord so bears couldn't get to them.

It wasn't long before we were heading back up Knife Lake. When we got back to Ma Harry's, we noticed the girls had all neatly brushed their hair, and many were wearing different clothes. They probably noted we were all washed and combed as well.

I could tell Betsy was anxious to talk to me. As soon as we had put up our canoes, she met me by the cooking fire where she showed me what she had crafted for me.

The beads were arranged evenly on either side of the cross, with the larger ones to the center. The cross was attached so that it would always hang flat, and the braided cord and the black leather together were much nicer than the leather alone. The beads were still on the thin black rolled-leather cord, only now the hemp cord was braided and tied around them. The soft tan cord material separated all the beads. After the beads came to an end on the cord, the cord spiraled around the leather. She had added small metal clasps to join the ends of the necklace.

It was beautiful.

She waited as I looked at every twist and knot and then asked in a whisper, "Louis, do you like it?"

"It's beautiful. I love it. Thank you so much. I know my mom will like it. I don't know what to say."

I was at a loss for words.

She placed the extra beads that hadn't fit into the design into my hand. And again, we were touching for a moment.

"These didn't fit in with the others, so you have a few left over for yourself," she said.

I held them for a minute thinking and then said, "Thank you for what you did. I would like you to have these beads if you would like them."

She blushed and took them. I put the necklace in my pocket, and we looked up from our private little world. Thankfully, everyone else was talking and probably didn't notice our little exchange. I looked back at her and tried to think of something witty to say about how I felt.

Betsy spoke first and said, "By the way, I know you don't need a bear scare, Makwa Zegi'. But I would like you to have this one I have been wearing all summer. I am going to make a new one with your beads."

I can't even describe how I felt as she tied it on my wrist. I have heard people talk about love, and this might have been what they were speaking of, but whatever it was, I was sure I now had a special relationship, and I wanted to stay in contact with this girl.

I took out the little piece of birchbark I had been saving and asked Betsy if she had a pen. She left for a minute and came back with a ballpoint pen. We wrote our addresses on the bark and cut it in half.

"I promise to write as soon as I get back."

"I will too," she said.

Everyone was gathering around a little fire built near the shore. It was more beautiful than the cooking fire where we were standing. The mosquitoes were already becoming peskily active back at the campsite. However, neither of us had noticed them during the past few minutes. There would be more of a breeze by the lake.

One of the counselors came to check on the hot chocolate and asked us to join the others. We moved to the gathering of 25 or more people. The girls had planned a campfire program with songs and even a few skits.

Betsy and I stayed toward the back and enjoyed the singing. Even Mr. Greenlee got into the act and led "Good Ol' Mountain Dew." We had lots of popcorn and cocoa. The s'mores were great.

As the evening wore on, I noticed the moon provided enough light so you could see everything very clearly. I was looking up at it when Betsy took hold of my hand for a minute. We both knew Ma and Mr. Greenlee would disapprove, so we broke it off quickly. It was wonderful for a moment.

I looked at her and wanted to kiss her. I felt she wanted to as well. But we just smiled, and I think we both knew what the other was thinking.

Mr. Greenlee asked for quiet and said we would need to bring the party to a close since we had a three-mile paddle in the dark before returning to camp. Before we sang one last song, he said he would like to talk about this place where we were.

He told us we were right on the actual highway of the voyageurs. We were fortunate, he said, to belong to organizations that bring young folks to the border country where they can experience the exact sights, feelings, and even the smells of the past.

When he mentioned smells, I thought of my grandfather and quickly prayed he would be there when I got back. I had so much to tell him, and now I even wanted to tell him about Betsy.

As Mr. Greenlee finished, he began to sing "The Far Northland," and everyone joined in. Girl Scouts must sing the song, too, because they sang right along with us. Finally, we concluded with "Scout Vespers," and Mr. Greenlee led in the Scout Benediction.

"And now may the Great Scoutmaster of all good Scouts be with us until we meet again."

"Night, Scouts," we all said in unison.

Betsy was looking at me. And this time, I spoke first.

"We will meet again. I'm going to be a Charlie Guide in a few years, and you will be a counselor for Ma Harry. Okay?"

Betsy smiled, took my hand, and firmly squeezed it. "I sure hope you are right," she said.

I just hope this isn't the last time I would ever see her.

"Let's load up! Louis, gather the crew!" yelled Mr. Greenlee.

Ma Harry was down at the water's edge, saying goodbye to everyone in our crew like we were old friends. I felt it was going to be hard to get the crew going. So I called Tom and Dave to load up so we could pull out and lead by example. It had taken a few minutes before all the goodbyes concluded. We sat facing shore so I could see the campsite. I was looking intently. Suddenly, everything else faded, and all I saw was Betsy's face in the bright moonlight. She didn't move. Nothing was said.

I hoped I would see her again.

Once Fred was out on the water with us, he said, "Louis, do you think you can get us back to camp?"

"You betcha," I said, as I started paddling for our campsite.

I took one last look back at the camp before it faded from sight. Betsy was easy to spot with her white blouse and blonde hair, which seemed to glow in the moonlight. The moon was so bright it was like noon, only in black and white. She waved, and I waved with my right hand while pulling a hard stroke with my left. I took one of my memory photos and then returned to the business of leading.

After we were underway, Tom said, "It looks like we have a nearly full moon."

Chuck quickly said, "This is a waning gibbous moon and is close to ninety-five percent full."

Leave it to Chuck to know such things. I'm going to get one of those star charts before I start guiding.

The moon was bright enough to make paddling and navigating our way back to our campsite comfortable. Mr. Greenlee again complimented us on our gentlemanly behavior. He asked Fred if a visit with Ma was a frequent event with crews.

"I met her one other time on US Point in 1962," he answered. "She has become an institution with our staff, and much of her program skills were learned from several Charlie Guides who have visited and become friends."

We were about a third of the way to our camp when Dave suddenly said, "Holy mackerel, will you look at that?"

Everyone turned and saw Dave was looking up.

"There must be a gazillion stars out tonight."

Even with a nearly full moon, we could see stars clearly, and we all coasted to a standstill on the calm waters of Knife Lake.

"Gentlemen, enjoy the show!" said Fred.

"Can anyone name some stars or constellations?" Mr. Greenlee asked.

Chuck immediately pointed out the big dipper, also known as Ursa Major, and the North Star.

"And there is Saturn and Juniper, and over there to the west is Venus," he added.

Joe pointed out Ursa Minor and Cassiopeia. Scorpio was easy to identify, and I was impressed Joe and others were reasonably well versed on stars and constellations.

"I just started working on the astronomy merit badge," said Joe. "Perhaps I could ask the merit badge counselor to visit a troop meeting to create more interest."

"Count me in, Joe, and the sooner, the better," I said.

"I recognize many features of the night sky, but I need to get one of those sky maps and learn the names of more constellations," said Fred. "I just always enjoy the show and love the consistency of it all."

"Mr. Greenlee, are the stars the same on Iwo Jima?" asked Joe.

Mr. Greenlee paused, cleared his throat, and said, "Sometimes we felt like we were on another planet. On a clear night, you could see familiar stars of the Northern Hemisphere. We could even see most of the same stars and planets we are looking at tonight. We found it quite comforting to see, as Fred said, 'some consistency in the world.'

"The stars' positions are slightly different, depending on your latitude," he continued. "The night sky on Iwo Jima looked like it would appear to someone in South Texas or Florida.

"Scouts," he said, "becoming acquainted with the night sky is a good thing for many reasons. This wilderness is unique because there is a total lack of ambient light interfering with the brightness of the stars and planets. It's one of its most attractive benefits. May it always be so!"

We were moving slowly to the west and started to paddle while staying together. I was relieved mosquitos hadn't found us as we all enjoyed this magical evening. I had not noticed the loon calls with our low talk, as all my senses were focused on the sky.

And then it started. One long mournful cry. As if in unison, the bowmen raised their hands for quiet, and the serenade began. There was an echo effect on the water. We were treated to a chorus of calls. It seemed as though our friends were performing for the sheer joy of it. We coasted for five minutes or more, just listening. Not a word was said. It was amazing!

With the slow progress and several stops to admire other features of the night sky, I had lost any sense of our position. I had been concerned about finding our campsite in the dark but then recalled it was on a point where the shoreline cut 90 degrees to the south. The moon and stars' brightness made it easy to see the point, and we were soon stowing our canoes and paddles.

Nothing at our camp was disturbed when we returned. Gary had filled a pot full of water for our breakfast, so we all got a cup. Gary asked if anyone wanted a hot drink, and there was a consensus we were tired enough that a drink of water was all we cared for, and a fire wasn't necessary.

Smitty and I took our cups down by the water to talk as everyone else headed off to bed. "So . . .?" he said with a smile. "What do you think?"

"First of all, I must admit that I was disappointed to see girls in this man's wilderness a few hours ago," I said. "Meeting Ma Harry's girls convinced me that they not only love and respect the wilderness as we do, but they also belong here. I hope that someday we can enjoy trips together."

Smitty agreed with my thoughts, and then we sat and listened to the loons.

"I can't believe this trip is almost over," I said. "This will be our last night on the trail. Tomorrow we have a pretty good paddle to the Base, and then, that's it."

"Yeah, I was thinking the same thing," Smitty said.

"Remember when you weren't so sure you wanted to go? Again, Louis, now what do you think?"

I didn't know where to start except to say, "Smitty, this experience has been a life changer for me. I feel like I've learned and experienced things that will be a part of who I am forever! I'm not sure I can even list them all at this point. I appreciate knowing I have my best friend, who not only understands but also helps me sort things out."

Smitty smiled and said he had many of the same feelings.

"For me, it was education at its finest. Everything I learned was not only useful but taught by example. I'm glad I came, and maybe the best part of it all was getting to share it with you, my best friend."

Chapter 34

KNIFE LAKE DOROTHY

I woke just as the sun started to lighten the sky, and I spent a few minutes stretching and reminiscing.

Yesterday was a fantastic day and involved lots of paddling. Sailing on Cache Bay was a special treat. Meeting Ma Harry and Betsy was something I'll never forget.

Today was going to be an easier but still a relatively long day.

I crawled out of the tent carefully so as to not wake the others who were still snoring. I walked over to the fireplace and looked around. Everything seemed in place, and I breathed a sigh of relief that there had not been a bear visit. I looked at the bear-scare bracelet Betsy had given me and touched it with my fingers. Perhaps it did work after all.

Smitty heard me and was right behind me as I started a fire for some coffee or tea. I grabbed the essential papers and headed to the latrine.

"I'll watch the fire while you take care of business," said Smitty, "and I would implore you to move through this task as quickly as possible."

"Roger," I said as I looked for the trail to the latrine.

When I got back, Smitty and Henry were both anxious to be next. I tossed the bag between them and encouraged them to work it out.

Gary and Joe were restacking the firewood and looking through the food packs to find a tasty breakfast for us. We still had an adequate food supply to choose from because of our good fortune and fishing luck. I decided to get more firewood for breakfast, and Mike and Chuck soon joined me. There was a good deal of firewood around this site. However, the folks before us left a little garbage that we had bagged up during our setup yesterday. Fred told us to take it back with our trash as it was our duty to leave the wilderness clean, even to the point of cleaning up after others.

One of our food packs was empty since Gary's crew had combined the food into two: one for the food we had left and the reflector oven and one for the trash we were taking back to Base. The trash and smashed cans now had their own pack, and the cardboard liner kept the pack clean.

The whole crew was moving to various tasks along with packing so we could leave soon after breakfast. Mr. Greenlee and Fred were drinking coffee, and I chose tea as we met to discuss the day ahead. Fred reviewed the day's travel and told me he appreciated the early start. He said we needed to arrive back at the Base around 2:00 p.m. Mr. Greenlee again commented on how proud he was of our behavior with Ma Harry's girls.

I asked Fred about the name of this lake. He asked me to remind him during breakfast when everybody would be present. He said the day would likely be reasonably uneventful, with a visit to Knife Lake Dorothy being the highlight.

"She sells homemade root beer, and it's always a treat, plus she is a most interesting woman who lives on this lake the year-round."

Breakfast was fruit stew, bulgur, pancakes, syrup, bacon, and cocoa. I noticed Joe took a good helping of the fruit stew, and he grinned at me as he did.

As I finished my second helping of bulgur, I thought about how well Gary had done as our chief cook. I was going to tell him, but he was busy with the pots on the fire.

I then looked around at everyone. I wondered if our newfound skills and eating habits would continue when we got back home. I had already planned to introduce bulgur to my mom, as I loved its nutty flavor.

While we ate, I remembered to ask Fred about the name Knife Lake. He said that the names of this canoe country's lakes reflect this land's diversity, history, plants, and animals. The cultural legacy is found in the many French and Ojibwe words used and the names of soldiers, loggers, and park rangers, more recently. Some of the female names like Agnes and Sarah are likely some logger's sweetheart's name.

"Knife Lake was named for a unique rock formation the Ojibwe, French, and English all referred to. There are deposits and quarries of the blue-black, fine-grained stone that is nearly as hard as flint," said Fred. "I've heard it called 'siltstone.' It was used to make tools and weapons by the Indians."

I made a note to research further the unusual and interesting names found on our maps. Fred said several books in the library back at the Base provided more insights into the lake names. He especially recommended *The Voyageur's Highway* by Grace Lee Nute.

I drank the last of my tea and said, "We had better pack up and get moving down Knife Lake. It's another beautiful day, and Fred says it's a short paddle to Dorothy's."

Without hesitation, everyone in the crew moved to the various tasks, and in no time, we were ready to depart.

As we were preparing to enter our canoes, Joe spoke up and said, "Louis, I think it's your turn to navigate back to the Base."

There were comments of agreement, and with Dave in the bow, we began our journey.

As we paddled out from our campsite, we hadn't gotten too far when Fred said, "Louis, before we head south, I would like to show y'all Thunder Point, which is a high point back a little less than a mile from our campsite."

"Lead on, we follow!" I said.

As we backtracked, we noticed there were lots of campsites on both sides of the lake.

We quickly came to Thunder Point, and Fred suggested we climb to the top with our cameras for one of the prettiest views there is. As we got close to the shore, Fred pointed out where the path would lead us to the top, as it was not marked on the map. It was a short, steep climb and very much worth the effort. The view to the southwest was spectacular, with two islands visible in the distance. The sky was incredibly clear. The clouds contrasted against the blue and provided a scene that made me hope my little Brownie camera would capture this beautiful vista. After that brief stop, we resumed our journey to Knife Lake Dorothy's.

I moved out into the lead. Both Dave and Tom were strong paddlers. However, nobody in the crew was having any trouble staying with the group. We paddled out as one, and I chuckled and said, "I was just thinking of our first day leaving the Base."

"That was a noisy and humorous first few hours as we paddled like a bunch of tenderfoot Scouts," said Tom. "Now I think we could outrun the crew we were so impressed with back on Agnes."

Knife Lake was beautiful as we paddled our way along the US and Canadian border. We made steady progress toward our goal of Robbins Island and the legendary Knife Lake Dorothy's cabins.

As we paddled in perfect sync with each other, I looked ahead and could make out the shape I had memorized earlier in the morning on the map of Robbins Island. It was the larger island on the north side of an island called the Isle of Pines. I could see Robbins Island, a larger island on the north side of the Isle of Pines. I could see a small island on the south side of Robbins Island and a much wider channel on the north side. I chose the narrow channel to the south.

It was about a quarter mile to the Isle of Pines and an enthusiastic greeting from a welcoming committee made up of various ducks. Beautiful mallards and mergansers quacked and seemed comfortable being close to our little armada.

A white-haired middle-aged lady waved from the smaller of the two islands on the right, and Fred yelled, "Hello, Dorothy, may we join you?"

"You know you can, Fred," was her reply.

After we secured the canoes to her docks, we gathered around Dorothy, who said, "So where is this fine group of Scouts from? It looks like you are returning and not starting your trip, judging from the tan faces I see."

"Allow me to introduce Scouts from Troop 23 of Sioux Falls, South Dakota, and their Scoutmaster, Mr. Delbert O. Greenlee," said Fred. "Fellas, introduce yourselves to Miss Dorothy Molter, better known as Knife Lake Dorothy."

"I'd like to know your names and Scout rank," she said.

So we each stepped up and gave our name and rank as Dorothy enthusiastically shook hands with each of us.

I have never felt a handshake like hers. She had large hands. Her grip was firm, and her hands had the feel of soft leather. After greeting each of us, she repeated our names. I had the feeling if we ever met again, she would recall our names and ask about our rank.

"Is anyone interested in a root beer?" she asked.

Fred had suggested we all bring a couple of dollars for this famous North Country treat. She also had some candy bars. The root beer sounded great. However, I didn't want anything civilized like a candy bar, so I passed on the candy.

Mr. Greenlee said, "Let's all have a root beer. I'm buying!"

It was the best root beer I had ever tasted. Chuck asked her how she made it way out here in the wilderness.

"I have a recipe I have used for years," she said. "It's made with root beer syrup I get at the grocery store in Ely, or sometimes I order in bulk through the Boy Scout Base. Besides that, you need sugar and yeast. The carbonation comes from the yeast processing or fermenting the sugar, thus creating bubbles. After adding the mix and sealing the bottles, they have to 'sit' and ferment for three days up to two weeks, depending on the temperature."

Fred told us Dorothy lived there year-round and then asked her to tell us how she came to live there.

Dorothy said she was 23 when she first visited and fell in love with Knife Lake in 1930.

"I came to stay on a more regular basis in 1934 to help Bill Berglund, who owned and operated the Isle of Pines Resort," she continued. "I spent a lot of time here, returning to the Chicago area for as short a time as possible. I went to pick up some holiday hospital work shifts for extra income and to maintain my nursing certification."

She paused a moment, opened a bottle of root beer, and handed it to Fred.

"When Bill passed away in 1948," she said, "I became the resort owner, and I've operated the Isle of Pines Resort since then. I live in the winter cabin during the winter. It's located on the east end of the largest of the three islands. During the winter months, I make crafts, decorations, and gifts. Then, in spring, I move over to this summer island. I live in this tent cabin while renting out the Winter Cabin, along with the Trapper Cabin, the Point Cabin, and the Cady Cabin, located on the small island."

"How do you get supplies out here?" asked Mike. "Besides your root beer ingredients, it looks like you also require a great deal of food for yourself, your visitors, and to sell to folks like us."

"You are going to travel the same route I take to get to Moose Lake," she answered. "I arrange for friends to pick me up and take me to Ely from there. I use a motor canoe, which means that going in, I have to make a couple of trips across portages. Coming back, I make two or three times as many trips, as there is too much for one person to carry in one load. I can use my snowmobile and sled to move the bulk of supplies in the winter when the lakes are frozen. In the winter, friends come out to help me cut ice for the ice cellar. Friends are the greatest gift, and I am blessed with many."

I had noticed and admired her fences made from broken canoe paddles. A sign with KWITCHURBELIAKIN painted in neat letters was prominently displayed. I figured the sign was written in Ojibwe, but before I could ask, she said, "The fences are made up of paddles from visitors who have donated them. I'm sure many were broken on purpose or sawed in half to become a part of the fences. As more visitors donated broken paddles, it wasn't long before there were brightly painted paddle fences everywhere."

Tom asked about the sign and its meaning. Some of the crew started to laugh when Chuck said, "If you pronounce the parts of the word slowly, KWIT CHUR BELI AKIN, you will see what it means."

"Oh, yeah, my mom says that a lot," said Tom.

Everyone, including Dorothy, laughed.

This was one time I was glad I did not get the chance to ask my question about it being in Ojibwe. I am sure the exchange would have become one of our troop legends, like Mr. Greenlee's time gag.

I looked around a little longer, and then Fred approached me and suggested we might want to be on our way soon.

"We should be able to get to Prairie Portage where there is room to eat lunch without blocking other people from using the portage trail," he said.

I then told Gary of the lunch plan and started to pass the word to depart quickly.

On behalf of the crew, I told Dorothy how much we enjoyed meeting a true legend of the North Country, and she said, "You fellas are welcome anytime. Please come again!"

As I shook her hand, I quietly said, "I hope to swamp next year and become a Charlie Guide the following year."

With a big smile, she said, "I'll see you again, Louis Carter, I am sure of it."

We noticed some other visitors were arriving and quickly moved to our canoes. The guard ducks were greeting the new travelers, and several escorted us for 50 yards or so as we resumed our travel to the Base.

Chapter 35

THE END OF THE TRAIL

I looked at the map and saw several portages that provided a way to get around a stream and several sets of rapids. I wondered if the rapids might not be as difficult or dangerous as the ones we had portaged around before, and I had the thought we might run them rather than take the portage. It would be quicker and more fun than unloading, portaging, and then repeating the process over and over for such a short distance.

So I decided to ask Fred for his advice.

He answered without hesitation: "When headed out this way, I usually have the crew walk up the small rapids we will encounter. However, going down the rapids requires a little coaching, and with loaded canoes, the chance of wet gear is something we want to avoid. The portages will be very easy for this crew."

"Understood," I answered. "Safety should always come first."

So we headed to the end of Knife Lake. I looked back to remember this lake as we started across the portage, hoping visits to Knife Lake Dorothy would happen in my future.

As Fred had described it, the portage was easy. Although it was over 75 rods or about a quarter of a mile, it was a snap, and we crossed quickly.

First, it took us to Seed Lake, followed by a short portage to Melon Lake, and then another short portage took us to Carp Lake.

As we started to load our canoes after the portage to Carp Lake, Fred asked us to gather around so he could provide some information. Everyone sat near him, and he said, "I would like you all to become aware of how to apply to work up here, should you be interested. Many of you have asked me about the process, and I tell you, I would be proud to recommend any of you. When we get back to Base this afternoon, anyone who would like to apply to become a Swamper should stop at the office, which is in the lodge. A fellow named Mike Miler, our office manager, has applications and can answer any specific questions."

"Do Swampers get paid?" asked Tom.

"Tom, the Swamper program is an unpaid position and involves about four weeks. Two weeks are spent at the Base working on all kinds of projects with the guidance of Assistant Base Director Henry Bradlich. Two are then spent with an experienced guide as a guide in training on a trip like this. After that, the guide will recommend him for employment on the guide staff, a paid position if he does well. Guides must be at least eighteen years old since it requires a Canadian Guide License. So again, if you are interested in working up here, just let me know so we can discuss and answer any questions you might have."

As had become our custom after a portage, we inspected the area for any trash. We found none, loaded our gear into our canoes, and then headed out onto the southwest end of Carp Lake.

After a short paddle, we took the one-eighth of a mile portage to Birch Lake. It was the last portage before we reached the Base, and it then struck me that our trip was coming to an end. It made me a little sad. However, I looked back at the map and found that following our progress and location was becoming easy for me. There were plenty of campsites, and it was a pretty lake with lots of bays and excellent fishing spots. I was looking forward to a quick stop at Prairie Portage

Customs Station to check if anyone had claimed the gear we had found by Louisa Falls with Fred.

When we arrived at Prairie Portage, Fred had us stow our gear back out of the way, and Gary started on lunch. Fred and I left the crew and started walking over the portage.

"Louis, I am sure nobody claimed the gear we found," Fred said. "It's worth a try, and I want to report the bear activity on lower Agnes to Vic. I'll also pass the word with the other guides when we get back. We often report and consult on such things. I can also reintroduce you to Vic as a future Charlie Guide."

I'm sure I pulled a muscle in my jaw with my grinning.

"Who else do you think might be interested in swamping next season?"

"I'm sure Smitty would want to apply and perhaps Joe," I said. "However, Joe's mother would likely not be in favor of him being gone that long."

We discussed the rest of the crew members, and I indicated I would be surprised if several didn't apply.

Fred asked if the crew had decided on a skit to present at the campfire the following evening. I told him the guys had discussed several options and decided on one popular back in our council camps. I added that I had delegated the responsibility to Tom and Henry back on Kawa Bay.

Fred didn't say anything for a minute. Then, he did.

"Louis, you really got the message about delegation, which Mr. Greenlee and I had advised you about during the first few days. It is probably the hardest thing for a guide to learn."

"Why would that be?" I asked.

"Well, we Charlie Guides are blessed with a job for which we have both skill and love. Some guides are hired by outfitters to navigate, cook, set up camp, clean fish, and be good at everything. On the other hand, besides needing those skills and knowledge, we are hired to foster Scouting's leadership training.

"You guys are lucky to have a wonderful Scoutmaster who understands leadership," he continued. "Some guides have a hard time letting go of the things they love to do. After the instructions for each specific task are given, and you have confirmed the learner understands, has the willingness, and the skill, you need to step aside and just observe. You are never done observing, correcting, coaching when necessary, and making yourself available until your crew says goodbye and departs the parking lot.

"I have enjoyed watching this crew learn and grow," Fred said with pride. "Although y'all arrived with far better than average skills and knowledge, you have made your Scoutmaster and me proud of your growth and development."

Vic greeted us, and Fred reintroduced me, saying that I would be back next year as a Swamper and then a guide the next.

Vic looked pleased and then asked about our trip. Fred told him about the bear raid by Louisa Falls and the attempt at our campsite on the other side of the lake.

Vic said he had had several similar reports on lower Agnes, and that North Bay had had more bear trouble than usual. Fred told him of the gear and the abandoned pack we had found and asked if anyone had stopped to claim it.

"There was a group at about that time that stopped to report a bear invasion," Vic said. "They said they had to hurry away and left some gear. They also said they had no interest in trying to get their lost gear back. They bear really put a scare into them, and they said they were on their way in and only wanted the trip to be over."

Fred turned and said to me, "Looks like you can take home a pack, hatchet, and a Sven Saw."

"We shall add it to our troop gear," I said.

"Louis, I will look forward to seeing you when you take your Swamper trip, and I am sure we will see lots of each other during the years to follow."

"We'd best get back to the crew to see if there is anything left for lunch," said Fred with a grin.

It was a quick trip back to rejoin the crew. Gary and all the guys were relaxing, and there was plenty of food left for us. Fred told us the trip back to Base would be much quicker than our first day's travel.

As we left Prairie Portage, we did so with pride, knowing we would look a lot better going in than we did last Tuesday. We soon passed several groups who were beginning their adventure. They were paddling like we had when we started our trip, making noise and going off in all directions. As we passed each one, I could tell they were looking at us in awe.

We quickly crossed Sucker Lake and entered Newfound Lake. I was looking forward to passing Horseshoe Island, which looked like a neat area to explore. Then we saw another crew heading in, and they seemed as proud as we were. Their guide was Voldi, who had led singing at the opening campfire back at Base, and he and Fred greeted each other warmly with a Hol-Ry. They both replied with a Red-Eye! I am sure they were comparing their respective trips as they paddled next to each other.

Tom asked the guys in the closest canoe where they had been. They mentioned Kahshahpiwi Lake, another popular route like Agnes for going north. They also spoke of McKenzie Lake, where they had great fishing. They said they had heard wolves on the far end of McKenzie Lake. It was great to be able to compare adventures.

I will definitely visit McKenzie Lake when I am a Charlie Guide.

I looked at the map as we paddled. We were on Sucker Lake. We entered a narrow area, and if we were to take a sharp left, we would go to Ensign Lake. That route would provide access to many options and pathways to many places on the US side of the border if I decided to travel that way when I guided. I looked to our right and saw an island with a nice campsite before we got to Horseshoe Island. Following the left shore took us to the channel into Moose Lake.

The shore on the left would eventually take us to the large island across from the Base. I soon saw the twin islands we had passed when we left the Base on our first day in the distance.

Our crew was paddling together, and Voldi's crew was as well. I was tempted to challenge them to a race to the Base's landing but decided we needed to enjoy and savor this last mile or two. As we rounded the point, two loons were waiting to greet us with a serenade.

It was then we could see the landing at the Base. Nobody was there except for the staff awaiting our arrival. I asked Fred if we should wait and let Voldi's crew unload. He agreed, and I told our crew to hold up offshore for a few minutes while Voldi and his crew unloaded and moved their canoes.

While we waited, Fred said, "Louis, please assign everyone a job so we can get to the sauna as soon as possible. We need the canoes put up; the Kettle and food pack straps have to be oiled and then put in my locker. Any paddles not purchased can be turned in, and the personal packs go to your tents up in tent city. Be sure to unpack them, and don't forget to check the pockets in the front."

I had already been thinking about the process, and to the crew, I said, "Each canoe crew can decide who does what. Let's make sure we leave the next crew with clean packs, and as you bring the packs back down to Fred's locker, make sure the pack straps are oiled. That goes for the Kettle Pack and food packs as well. The tents, ground cloths, and tarp are dry and are ready to put in the locker.

"Fred, what do we do with what little bit of leftover food we have?"

"Leave it at my locker," Fred said. "You are welcome to take whatever you wish home with you. But, guys, try to put all of my canoes together. Normally we have the same canoes all summer, so leave the life preservers and bags just as they are."

After Voldi's crew was out of the way, we quickly began the tasks, with each canoe team taking care of their canoe and gear.

"When we complete all the necessary tasks," said Mr. Greenlee, "let's all meet near our tents before going to the sauna. Then, after we clean up, put on your uniforms.

"Put all your dirty gear in your duffel," he continued, "and then you can go to the trading post at the lodge. Listen for the dinner bell and then assemble by the lodge. We will walk up to the dining hall together."

After the sauna, we all tried to look our best, and then we went to the lodge. Smitty and I first went into the office to get a Swamper application from Mike Miler. I found him very friendly. He even seemed interested in our adventure and asked many questions about where we went and what we liked best about our trip.

Mr. Hanson was in his office, and Mike said we should meet with him. He took us in and introduced us. I was more than a little bit proud when he told Mr. Hanson we were the Scouts Fred had mentioned who would like to become guides.

Mr. Hanson was also interested in our trip and asked what we liked best about the experience. He asked us about our troop, what offices we had held, and what parts of Scouting were our favorites. Mr. Hanson explained the Swamper process Fred had described earlier in the day. I felt he was sincerely interested in both of us.

I'll have to thank Fred for the good word.

When we finished our meeting, we said goodbye, and Mike Miler wished us good luck. We walked across the porch and went into the lodge. The larger maps were in the back near the windows. I was anxious to look at our trip's route on one of the large maps. We noticed there were campsites marked on the charts, and I assumed guides added them so the rest of the staff could indicate them on their maps. There were several Scouts we didn't know sitting on the benches talking about their route. From overhearing their conversations, it appeared most of the crews made trips 80 to 150 miles in length.

I met a fellow from Houston, Texas, who had also applied to be a Swamper and had just come from Mr. Hanson's office. We compared trips and had a pleasant visit. His trip was to the west side of the Quetico, and we each shared information about our favorite campsites and good fishing spots.

A smaller map on the side wall showed plotted locations of bald eagle nests and sightings. It was a project to help with efforts to save the beautiful birds from extinction. They were on the endangered list. I hoped the efforts of both the Canadians and the US would bring them back from danger. This pristine wilderness was one of the areas where one could still see this magnificent bird. I made a mental note to ask Fred if we needed to mark the map with our sightings. I saw there was already a mark where we saw the first eagle, but not the one on Joliet Lake.

Mike, Henry, Dave, and Smitty were also looking at maps and chatting with the other Scouts. I motioned to them to join me, and we all sat on two benches so we could talk. I told them the guy from Houston had said their crew had chipped in to get their guide a gift, and one of their two advisors was on the way to Ely.

"I think it would be nice to do, but I'm concerned getting to town to buy gifts may be a problem," I said.

"Dad has been on a previous trip and knows about the custom of giving the guide a gift," Dave said. "He has a three-quarter Hudson Bay Axe in the station wagon with a sheath he made. He said to keep it quiet so it could be a surprise."

Just then, Mr. Greenlee entered the lodge with gifts he purchased in the trading post for his wife and other family members. When he saw us, he came over and said, "Is this a closed meeting?"

I told him we were discussing how to get a gift for Fred, and he said, "I have the solution in the back of our station wagon, and this would be an excellent time to plan its presentation. When I was here the last time, I noticed the practice, got a nice three-quarter Hudson Bay Axe, and made a sheath for our guide. What we need to discuss is where and when we present it.

"Louis, what do you think?"

I thought a bit and said, "We don't want to do it during the campfire since other crews may not have a gift for their guide. So, after supper, let's walk with Fred through the parking lot on the way to the lodge. That way, it is private, and he can put it in his locker in the guide's building called the Tepee before we walk to the lodge.

"Henry, will you make the rest of our guys aware of this?"

"Roger," Henry said. Mr. Greenlee took his bag and left us to say hello to Mr. Hanson.

"Guys," I said, "I also want to get something for Mr. Greenlee. I thought if we could get him to stop at Fisherman's Headquarters when we go through Ely, we could get him a Puukko knife like the one Fred has. I noticed them when we were there. What do you think?"

"Since my dad is the second driver tomorrow," Chuck said, "he will stay in Ely tonight and plans to be here right after breakfast. I'll have him remind me to get something for my mom and recommend we stop and get it at Fishermen's Headquarters."

"Perfect," I said.

Joe and Gary came in, followed by Chuck and Tom. Henry quickly told them of the plan, and soon we were all together reminiscing about the events of the past nine days. We had all taken our dirty clothes in our duffel bags to Mr. Greenlee's station wagon. We were ready to leave after breakfast without delay.

I asked the guys if they were ready for the skit. They said they were and to stop worrying. They were going to use the "Oh, What a Goose I Am" skit.

I grinned, recalling the first time I fell for it! It has never failed to be a hit at camporees back home.

Before supper, we spent time looking at displays in the lodge and visiting with Scouts from all over the country. Then, as the dinner bell began ringing, Tom and Mike, who had volunteered to be table waiters, quickly left to get ahead of the rush. The rest of our crew and Mr. Greenlee, who was with Fred, walked with us as we headed up the dining hall's steep trail. Everyone was assembling on the porch and awaiting directions from the dining hall steward.

When we entered the dining hall, Tom and Mike were standing at our table. We were amazed to see the bowls and platters filled with what looked like Thanksgiving dinner. Pitchers were filled with milk. All the fixings like mashed potatoes, gravy, dressing, corn, and lots of turkey were on the table. Before we sat down, everyone joined in, saying the Wilderness Grace. The dining hall steward and Sparky, the cook, stopped by each table to make sure everything was perfect.

After a dessert of cherry pie and ice cream, the dining hall steward told us the campfire would be in 20 minutes so the table waiters could clear everything and even wash the tables. Again, I was impressed with the operation of the dining hall.

As we gathered on the porch, I asked Fred if the Base's food was always this good.

"This is the standard dinner for returning crews," he said. "Sparky was a cook during World War One, serving troops on the front lines. He frequently says that this is much easier task, cooking without the shelling going on. He loves this peaceful place."

All the Scouts and leaders were talking as they waited for their servers to join them. Our guys were the first out, and we asked Fred to show us the progress on the workshop beneath the dining hall. After viewing the project, we walked around back to the road leading to the parking lot. Mr. Greenlee was talking with Fred, who didn't seem to mind the detour. Mr. Greenlee's car was near the road, and when we got there, Mr. Greenlee opened the rear door on the station wagon and said, "Louis, why don't you do the honors?"

I saw the axe and leather sheath. I picked it up and held it out to Fred, saying, "Fred, we all agree we had the best guide the Base has to offer. Thank you for making this trip one to remember."

Everyone in the crew shook Fred's hand and spoke to him about their feelings.

We walked to the cedar gateway from the parking lot and the road that led to the lodge. Fred had us stop as a middle-aged man with wire-rimmed glasses strode down the hill toward the parking lot as we walked up the rise.

"Hello, Henry," said Fred. "Are you checking to see if the Swampers completed their latest Henry project?"

Henry Bradlich grinned and looked us over as though it was a uniform inspection.

"Henry," continued Fred, "this is my latest and most outstanding crew of the summer, from Sioux Falls, South Dakota, and their Scoutmaster, Mr. Delbert Greenlee."

"Where did you take these fine-looking Scouts on their trip?" he said as he shook hands with Mr. Greenlee and each of us.

"We paddled up Agnes to Mack, down Kenny Creek to Joliet, and on to Blackstone for a layover day," said Fred. "Then we sailed Cache Bay and visited both Ma Harry and Knife Lake Dorothy on the way back in!"

Henry looked impressed and said, "Joliet, eh? That's impressive. Very few take that route."

Fred turned to us and said, "Y'all may recall I mentioned Henry Bradlich when we talked about the Swamper training program this morning. He is the person you will need to impress if you become a Swamper."

Then Fred smiled and continued, "He has been trying to teach me to say, 'you guys' instead of 'y'all' for three years. So if you become a Swamper, listen and learn from this good man."

After Fred put his gift in his locker in the Tepee building, we walked to the lodge. Fred joined the other Charlie Guides at the table by the front window, and we sat as close to the front as we could.

Jay, the Base's guide chief, made the Scout sign, and several Scouts said, "Sign's up." (The guide chief gives supervision to the 60-plus guides who work at Sommers.)

After he called us to order, he suggested all the Scouts give a big hand to our Scout leaders and added, "And I mean loud clapping and cheers."

It was *loud*!

Then he introduced each of the guides by name, and they received our sincere and enthusiastic thanks. Finally, he nodded to Voldi, who came up and led "Alouette" as he had on the first night.

After we sang, Jay called all the crew chiefs forward to receive a packet.

"We are proud to award the Charles L. Sommers Wilderness Canoe Base participant emblems to give to each member of your crew."

All the guides shouted in unison, "Nice patches, Jay!"

Jay replied in a loud voice, "As Clifford J. Hanson would say, 'Patches you wear on the seat of your pants, Emblems you earn!' Congratulations!"

These guys sure have fun!

Voldi yelled, "Let's see some skits!"

Each crew presented a skit or a song. They were predominantly the same skits we saw at Scout camps, but each routine was greeted with laughter and cheers.

One crew sang a song they wrote to the tune of Johnny Horton's "The Battle of New Orleans."

"In 1963, we took a little crew. . . ."

It was a joyful evening, and we ended with the singing of "The Far Northland" and "Scout Vespers." It was hard to say goodnight to all our new friends.

Back in our tents, I had difficulty getting comfortable on a mattress after eight nights on the hard ground with just a canvas tarp between my sleeping bag and the rocks and rocky soil. I was trying to imagine I was still out there when I heard "that plaintive wail." And soon, I was indeed back on the trail.

A loud tremolo awakened me. I think the loon must have been flying overhead from Flash Lake. The call was followed by "Daylight in the swamp!" Mr. Greenlee at his finest! It was still dark, but it was time to get ready for a continental breakfast. I just hoped they had hot tea, which was now my favorite beverage.

We all made our way to the sauna to brush our teeth. Joe was just leaving the sauna and said, "Don't forget to flush!" We had our trail clothes and gear packed in our duffel bags in preparation for an early start.

The dining hall staff provided a continental breakfast of cold cereal, sweet rolls, juice, milk, and coffee or tea so everyone could get on the road as early as they wished. I was happy to see Fred was already there. We talked about our trip as we ate together and then walked down to the parking lot to say goodbye.

Mr. Greenlee introduced Fred to Chuck's dad, Mr. Banwart, who had stayed overnight in Ely and came right out to the Base for an early start home. Fred spoke to every crew member and wished them well.

As he and I said our goodbyes, he said, "See ya next year."

We expected to be home by nightfall. Earlier, we thought we would do laundry in Ely but decided against it to get home by dark. Mr. Greenlee was okay with a quick stop at Fisherman's Headquarters as several of us had wanted to get gifts. We were on our way back home by 7:00 a.m.

When we got to Ely, Dave kept Mr. Greenlee occupied so I could purchase the knife we had discussed for a gift for him. Chuck and his dad helped me pick a nice one with a blue handle. I figured I could settle up with the rest of the guys when we got back.

I was sad as we left Ely. I rode in the Banwart station wagon. I thought a nap would feel good but didn't want to miss any beautiful scenery, so we answered all the questions asked by Mr. Banwart. He was interested in our fishing, both the catching and the cooking.

We made excellent time and had planned to stop in Forest Lake, a little town north of the Twin Cities, for lunch. From there to Sioux Falls would be an easy drive once we were past the Twin Cities.

We stopped every two hours. Again, both Mr. Greenlee and Mr. Banwart were in good shape and were also excellent drivers.

We talked about trying to stay in sight of each other going through the Twin Cities during stop for lunch. We were concerned that becoming separated could waste time.

After the Cities, it was primarily rural farmland, and staying together was effortless. With bathroom breaks and gas stops, we figured we would get in shortly after suppertime. We were planning to stop for burgers in Mountain Lake. Later, we would stop in Leverne to give some of the families a call with a reasonably accurate arrival time to pass on to all the other families.

It wasn't long before we could see familiar landmarks as we came to Sioux Falls. We exited Interstate 90 to I-229, took the Western Avenue exit, and proceeded north. We soon passed Parkridge Shopping Center on our right and the large vacant property in front of the Veterans Administration Hospital on our left. After we made a right turn on 22nd Street, we soon saw the tall white steeple of the First Baptist Church, where Troop 23 meets every Thursday night.

Chapter 36

THE RENDEZVOUS

We arrived at the church parking lot right on schedule. Mom and Dad were waiting for us with all the other parents. I was glad to see them and waved with excitement, but I was so worried about Grandpa that the first words out of my mouth were, "How's Grandpa?"

Mom's happy smile turned to a sad and worried look as she lowered her voice to a whisper and said, "Grandpa is doing very poorly. Dad and I don't expect him to last much longer. When we visited him last Sunday, I told him where you were, and you would be coming home soon. He did smile at me, and then he said in a whisper, 'Louis.'

"It was the last word he said. He closed his eyes and didn't open them again the whole time we were there."

I looked over at Dad, and he said, "We'll go up to the nursing home first thing in the morning."

I was about to ask Dad a question when Mr. Greenlee came over, shook my father's hand, and said, "You will be proud to know that Louis was appointed our crew chief. He did an outstanding job."

I watched as they talked. I noticed that Dad started to smile and had a proud look on his face, and then Mom reached over and held his arm as she whispered something into his ear. Dad looked at me, nodded, and then went back to talking with Mr. Greenlee. After that, they visited for a while as we began unpacking our gear.

The parking lot rapidly became a bustling place. All the parents were there to pick up their sons. The guys were all talking at once, telling their parents stories and sharing highlights of the trip. Whenever I heard one of the guys mention the bear, his mother would get a horrified look on her face and turn and stare at me. Thankfully, Mom didn't notice since she was so busy asking me questions.

Just as we were preparing to leave, I suddenly remembered we had gotten Mr. Greenlee a gift. So I stepped out in the middle of the parking lot and gave the Scout sign. Several of the Scouts yelled, "Sign's up!" Even the parents immediately became quiet.

"Scouts and parents," I said in a loud voice, "we have just one more thing we want to do before we officially end this trip. We Scouts all got together and decided to give Mr. Greenlee a couple of things to express our thanks for taking us on this trip. First, we all signed a crew picture. Then we marked a map with our route and all of our campsites and excellent fishing spots."

I stopped a moment and went over to Mr. Greenlee and shook his hand.

"Mr. Greenlee, thank you for taking the time to spend with us and helping us to appreciate an extraordinary place. None of us will ever be the same."

Mr. Greenlee shook my hand with a firm grip and nodded a thank you. I thought I saw tears in his eyes.

I turned to Mrs. Greenlee, who was standing next to him, and said, "Mrs. Greenlee, we also got a little something for you too. We want you to have a voyageur cross with our thanks for letting Mr. Greenlee be our Scoutmaster."

I stopped and reached down and into my pack. I pulled out a box and opened it, saying, "We all got together and got this Finnish Puukko knife for you. Thanks for telling us about your knife, and we hope you enjoy this one, just for fishing."

Mr. Greenlee shook my hand and stretched out his arm as Mrs. Greenlee cuddled close to him as they looked at the gifts. They both smiled as he said, "Folks, it's an honor to be your sons' Scoutmaster; thank you all for these reminders of a marvelous experience!

"Scouts, I'll see you at our regular meeting next Thursday at seven p.m."

When I went back over to the car, my mom looked like she was in shock.

"Louis, that was so well done!" she said. "Where did you learn to speak up like that?"

I felt a little flushed at the compliment and did not know how to answer.

I looked over at Dad to get a little help, and all he did was smile. He saved me when he quickly said, "Time to go," and then, "Louis, how was the fishing?"

He did not give me time to answer but quickly opened the door for Mom. I loaded my gear and climbed into the back seat as he got into the driver's seat and started the car so we could head for home.

On the way home, I gave them a fishing report and included the cooking for Mom's benefit. When we got home, we unloaded the car and then sat in the living room and talked. Dad was very interested in the trip, and I was enjoying the attention. Mom got a kick out of the loon calls I had learned and demonstrated for them. However, I only told them a little of the bear story for fear it would scare Mom. I was afraid she might not let me go on another trip.

When it was about time to go to bed, I remembered I had gotten Mom and Dad gifts. I gave Dad the coffee mug and Mom the cross. The cross hung from the leather string to which Betsy had added the hemp cord and the beads. Mom loved it and seemed genuinely touched by the story of the beads and the cross. She asked if I had done all the craftwork, and I told her I had a friend's help. I didn't figure Mom was ready to hear about Betsy just yet. She put it on and said she would be proud to wear it.

I had a lot on my mind but remembered something that Bill Gekek, one of the new friends we had met on Blackstone Lake, had suggested and said, "Mom, I'm sure Grandpa will be awake and may want to respond to some of what I tell him about the canoe trails. One of my new friends, Bill, suggested we bring a tape recorder to preserve anything Grandpa says. Would you and Dad please bring it tomorrow morning?"

Dad agreed and said he knew right where it was.

I then decided it would be a good time to bring up my feelings about respecting Grandpa's faith. I told them of my numerous conversations with Smitty and Henry and that I had prayed about it and developed a plan. I also told them what the Scout Law says about reverence.

"A Scout is reverent," I said. "He is faithful in his religious duties, and he respects the convictions of others in matters of custom and religion."[1]

I gulped, took a deep breath, and continued.

"I have always felt uncomfortable about the way some of my family often badgers Grandpa about his Catholic faith. So, instead, I think we should celebrate and support his religious convictions. I saw how doing that affected Henry when we observed his Sabbath with him."

Dad agreed, and Mom started to cry. I don't think she cried because she agreed but because my concern for Grandpa touched her. Then, at last, she finally conceded that we all needed to respect and support Grandpa and his faith.

I just hoped it wasn't too late.

Mom decided we needed to get up to Grandpa's as soon as possible, and we planned to leave early in the morning.

After saying goodnight, I went to my room and crawled into my bed. Mom had washed the sheets, and I took in a deep breath and stretched out, letting my feet feel the coolness.

---

1. Boy Scouts of America, "The Scout Law," in *Handbook for Boys*, 27.

Although I was happy to be back in my own bed and not have to avoid rocks and roots in picking a comfortable spot, I soon imagined I was next to a moonlit lake when I closed my eyes. The loon's tremolo, a long wavering call, announced its presence on the lake. I listened to the eerie and beautiful cries, and then I heard the softer hoot with which a parent calls to a chick as I fell asleep.

In the morning, I awoke to the smell of Mom's breakfast. Mom and Dad had already eaten, and as soon as I finished, Dad said, "Let's go."

As Dad drove and I sat in the back seat, it seemed to take longer than usual to drive to the nursing home. It was overcast and drizzling by the time we reached the nursing home's red granite buildings. We hadn't talked much as we drove. When we arrived at the gate, the meandering drive that led to the main building seemed to take forever. I wanted to get there, but I was afraid of what we might find.

The nurse must have been expecting us because she met us in the entryway. She spoke to Mom out of earshot and then came to Dad and me and said, "Mr. Carter, your grandfather is still alive but not responding to anything this morning. So you shouldn't expect any reactions from him, and Doctor Wessman is coming in earlier than usual to check on him."

When we walked down the hallway to his room, Mom stopped us and said, "Let's just talk to him and hope he realizes we are here. Louis, perhaps you could tell him about your trip?"

Yes, I'm thinking about doing just that. I only hope it is not too late.

As we entered Grandpa's room, I was shocked when I saw him. He was fragile when I left, but now I could tell he had lost even more weight. He hardly seemed to be breathing.

A young Catholic priest who introduced himself as Father Martin was seated next to Grandpa on the bed. I looked at Dad.

"After you had gone to bed, Mom suggested we call the home to see if they could arrange for a local priest to be here when we came," he said with a gentle smile.

Mom sniffed and tried to smile, but I could see it was an emotional smile. I thought I saw tears in her eyes as she reached for a facial tissue.

We sat down, and Mom reached over and put a hand on Grandpa's shoulder. Then she said in a soft voice, "Hello, Grandpa. Louis is here and wants to tell you about his canoe trip." She stopped and took my hand while she continued to rest her other hand on Grandpa's shoulder. Somehow, I felt a connection when she said, "Louis, tell Grandpa about the lakes and fishing."

I started to describe the lakes and the portages around rapids and loons. As soon as I said the words "portage" and "loon," he turned his head toward me. I knew he was listening, so I kept talking.

He started to move his lips, and I felt he was trying to open his eyes. I stopped talking for a moment and then said, "Grandpa, it's Louis, and I have dreamed about telling you about my canoe trip." I felt tears on my cheeks. "The loons were so beautiful. We heard them every morning, and we fell asleep to them at night. I wish you could hear them."

Mom broke in, saying, "Louis, make the call as you showed us last night. I am sure he is listening to you."

I cupped my hands and made the loon's tremolo call exactly as Fred had shown us.

Grandpa moaned a little and moved his head. Suddenly his eyes opened wide, and he moved his head back and forth as if he were excited and searching for something. I knew he had heard me!

I made the sound again, and Grandpa muttered something I did not understand, so I took a different tack: I stopped making the loon call, and remembering the words I had learned from Bill Hawk while on Blackstone Lake, I said, "Boozhoo, Nimishoomis."

He looked at me as though a fog had lifted. Grandpa leaned his head back on the pillow, closed his eyes, and as I watched, I saw the corners of his mouth turn up as if he were smiling.

I looked over at Mom, and she nodded her head, so I continued the loon calls, for I felt we were connecting. I stopped when the nurse came over to check on his pulse and breathing. She went back over to Mom, who came close. I think she feared Grandpa was dying.

When Mom got close to him, he opened his eyes and looked right at her. He looked at her face, and then his eyes lowered, and I could tell he was looking at the cross. When Grandpa saw the cross and beads I had given to her, I saw his eyes widen even more. He started to reach for it. He said something which sounded like he was speaking in French. I thought I could make out the word "cross," as he repeated it several times. But none of us understood exactly what he was saying as his speech was thick and slurred.

"He may be having a seizure," the nurse said.

She called for the doctor, who came right in.

As they were preparing to give him a shot to calm him, Grandpa frantically pointed toward his closet and said something we couldn't understand. The young priest held up his hand and stopped them, saying, "I don't think he is having a seizure. I believe he's trying to tell us something. He is pointing to that closet. Let's see what he wants first."

With a desperate look on his face, Grandpa looked right at the priest as he continued to point. I ran to the closet and started to look for what he might have wanted. I could hear Grandpa saying, "Baa ka . . . ma cassette."

What was he saying?

I dug through his things as he said, "Une boîte! Boîte en bois!"

Again, it made no sense to me.

"He's speaking French," the priest said, "and I think he said 'wooden box.' Look for a box or chest.

"I also think he is saying 'Croix de Lorraine,' which means Cross of Lorraine. I didn't recognize he was speaking French at first."

I saw an old wooden chest in the very back of the closet and realized what he had been trying to say. He calmed right down when I brought it over. Father Martin, the nurse, and even Dr. Wessman were interested in what was going on. The nurse said she had heard him speak French and something foreign she couldn't recognize in his sleep. Grandpa gripped the priest's arm and softly whispered, "Oui, ma vieille boîte."

Dad said he hadn't seen the box full of old stuff since he was a kid.

"Be careful with it," he said. "It's ancient.

"Grandpa used to try to teach us words in French and Indian when I was little," Dad continued. "There were also some songs, and at the time, we didn't think they were too cool. The only ones I can remember are 'Alouette' and 'À la claire fontaine,' but there were lots of others."

I opened the box, and right on top was a Cross of Lorraine similar to the one Mom was wearing. It looked more like tarnished silver, and it had a thin leather cord, which looked weathered and worn. It had beads similar to mine on it. The box also contained an old frayed red and white woven cloth sash, a clay pipe, and an assortment of arrowheads. There was much more, but it was enough for me to think, *Hey, this is real voyageur stuff! Was Grandpa a voyageur? Where did he get this stuff?*

Dad looked shocked.

"I saw this when I was a boy, and I remember Grandpa showed me this stuff and tried to talk about it then. I guess I wasn't listening. He always spoke of the olden days, but nobody in the family paid much attention. I barely recall what it was he talked about, except he went on and on about his grandparents and the others."

I remember Grandpa once talked to me about his grandfather and other people who must have been voyageurs. Some of Grandpa's family must have been made up of French voyageurs and Indians of the border country . . . and nobody was listening! Maybe Grandpa was a voyageur too. No, he isn't that old. I've got to know about this. What if it's too late?

Grandpa started making a terrible coughing sound, and it seemed like his insides were coming up."

"Let him cough it up and spit," said Dr. Wessman. "Get a bowl and some Kleenex."

The nurse did so, and after a lot of hacking and coughing, Grandpa finally got his throat clear.

It took him a while to catch his breath. He was exhausted and just sat for a few minutes, breathing deeply while he smiled at me.

After resting for what seemed like a long time, he started to speak in a low voice. His voice was still a little weak from coughing, but now we could understand him.

"Aaniin, Louis!" he said. "Please make the loon call. I want to hear it again."

So I made the call, and Grandpa's eyes seemed to sparkle and glisten.

"I want you to know my grandfather Louis Cartier and Little Elk, my grandmother," he said. "But first, I wish to rest a little, and then I would like some bread and tea."

I said, "Aniibiishaaboo?"

Grandfather smiled and continued, "Then I will tell you about our family. I think you are ready to meet them."

EPILOGUE

Grandpa lived for another full year. After his response to not getting a calming shot, I asked Mom to ask his doctor, Dr. Wessman, if the injections to calm him were necessary. He agreed they were not and put a stop to them.

From that time on, there was a significant change.

After years of finding it difficult to understand Grandpa's weak, slurred speech, I was fascinated that it rapidly became lower in tone and much clearer. I prayed that it would remain so. Grandpa enjoyed our regular visits plus new visits from all my Scouting friends and even our honorary Troop 23 members Eddie and Bill, who visited after their trip. Grandpa told us about many relatives and the traditions and stories of those family members we started to meet through his stories following my return from our canoe trip.

I'll never forget that first real conversation we had as the story unfolded. While the nurse went to get some bread and tea, Grandpa closed his eyes and spent a few minutes, breathing deeply and occasionally clearing his throat.

When the nurse returned with a tray, a cup, and a small pot of tea, Grandpa opened his eyes and looked around the room. Father Martin had moved to my chair, and I sat on the edge of the bed. I carefully poured the tea into his cup and said, "Grandfather, would you like some cream and sugar?" He smiled and spoke with a surprisingly clear and mellow tone in his voice.

"Louis, I like my aniibiishaaboo black."

He smiled broadly as he took a sip. Then, after a second sip, he continued, "Where did you learn those words you used?"

I told him of meeting Eddie Hotuya Kostache, a Lakota, and Bill Gekek, an Ojibwe, on Blackstone Lake.

"Grandpa, they gave me an Ojibwe name. I am called Makwa Zegi."

Grandpa smiled, looked at Mother and Father, and said, "One who frightens bears?"

Dad smiled, and Mom was about to say something when Grandpa continued, "Louis, I know how names are selected, and I am sure you will wear that name with pride. You must tell us the story sometime."

Another nurse arrived with a plate with several biscuits, and I said, "I learned to make frybread from my new friends, and I have the recipe. So we will bring some next time we come."

The wooden chest was still on the bed and open next to me. Before Grandpa even looked at the biscuits, he reached over and removed the sash, the cross, the pipe, and several arrowheads and placed them on the bed next to it.

The second nurse said, "We have a few more biscuits coming with more cups and tea."

Dr. Wessman and Father Martin said nothing, but it was clear they seemed interested and were hoping to stay. I looked at them and said, "You are welcome to stay."

The biscuits and tea arrived and were placed on the bedside table. I looked around the room and saw everyone was looking at me. So I stood and said, "Let's pray. Mitakuye Oyasin . . . May we live with all our relations . . .

For food,
For raiment,
For life and opportunity,
For sun and rain,
For water and portage trails,

For friendship and fellowship,
We thank Thee, Oh Lord."[1]

Grandfather, Father Martin, and one of the nurses crossed themselves. Grandfather grinned and said, "Good prayer, Louis! I like the part about water and portage trails."

"Except for 'For sun and rain, and for water and portage trails,'[2] that is the same as the Philmont Grace," said Father Martin, "which I learned back in my Scouting days. I am anxious to know more about your family!"

We all joined Grandfather with a biscuit and a cup of tea, and then he began to tell us the story.

"Louis, I'll start at the beginning. Our family name is actually Cartier. Remember your Grandpa Carter? My son, Benjamin, married Margaret Smith in England when he was serving in World War One. She was adamant that she would not marry him unless he changed his name. So it was agreed that Cartier would become Carter, a proper British name. She seemed to have a dislike for the French.

"Our oldest family legends are of rugged Frenchmen from Montreal who worked in the fur trade. Although there were others before him, Louis Cartier, who was born in 1798, worked as a mangeur de lard or Porkeater as a teenager. He traveled from Montreal to the fur trade post at Grand Portage on Lake Superior's North Shore. He and his fellow voyageurs would have paddled the forty-foot *canot du maître* or Montreal canoes.

"At Grand Portage, the trade goods were loaded from the Montreal canoes to the smaller *cannot du nord* or north canoe, which was about twenty feet in length and was paddled by six to eight men. These

---

1. Traditional grace used by Sommers crews.

2. Ibid.

most experienced voyageurs would spend their winters at a fort in the Interior.

"After several trips to Grand Portage, Louis dreamed of becoming a l'homme du nord or Hivernant. As he became more skilled, he was hired to be a Hivernant. His father and grandfather were employed in the fur trade as well.

"While at Grand Portage, Louis met a beautiful young Ojibwe woman named Mary Little Elk. They were married by a Jesuit priest. When he was about thirty, they had a son who they named Louis. Several other children were born to them, and all the boys who lived to adulthood worked in the fur trade. Louis also had a younger sister, but I believe she died young.

"Stories of Louis say he was a very strong and handsome voyageur and lived an exciting and long life of seventy years. However, after several trips to the Interior or Pays d'en Haut where he wintered, he injured his left hand, losing two fingers while fixing a bear trap. Upon his arrival back at Grand Portage, he was reassigned to apprentice with a numbers man since he could not continue the hard voyageur life."

I asked Grandpa if a numbers man was like an accountant.

"Yes," he said. "'*Comptable*' is the French word for accountant or bookkeeper. I will try to say all these things in English. I don't know the Ojibwe word for accountant."

He smiled at me and winked.

"Back at this time in our family's story, we learned that several of our line were good with numbers, and that skill served us well."

"Then I should thank all our ancestors," my dad said. "That ability has continued to be a business asset in my life as well."

"What was his wife, Mary Little Elk, like, Grandfather?" asked Mom.

"Both of my grandparents died when I was relatively young," Grandpa said, "but I remember she was an excellent cook and gave warm hugs. She spoke Ojibwe and French, as did all of the family. My mother, Marie Charbonnet, and my father both spoke Ojibwe and

French. My father learned English in midlife as his work required it. My mother learned it as well."

Mother looked impressed and said, "Your father and mother spoke three languages? I am so impressed! Please continue."

After a few sips of tea, my grandfather began anew.

"My father was born in 1828 and, like his father, worked as a voyageur in the fur trade until he was in his thirties. He married Marie Charbonnet, who was half French and half Ojibwe. Her mother was Lucile White Swan, and she and her husband, Jean-Pierre Charbonnet, knew my grandparents. They still lived at Grand Portage when I was born, and my father was working as an apprentice bookkeeper.

"My father loved the life of a voyageur," he continued. "Still, shortly after he married my mother, he realized that handling accounts and money was much more profitable than handling furs. I remember how he loved the wild country, and he instructed me in paddling the smaller birchbark canoes we had at the post.

"When I was ten years old, my grandfather died just after my father had taken me to a place called Height of Land, about a day's journey from our home. Voyageurs making their first trip into the Pays d'en Haut were always initiated after crossing that portage. And, like every newcomer, I was sprinkled with a cedar bough dipped in water.

"Father laughed as he had me solemnly swear that I would not allow another to pass that way without undergoing a similar baptism. And that I would never kiss another voyageur's wife without her consent."

Grandfather laughed, and his eyes brimmed with tears as he recalled the happy memory with his father at the portage called Height of Land. Then, he closed his eyes and was silent for a few moments.

Finally, my father, his grandson, said, "Grandpa, are you okay?"

He opened his eyes and reached out to my father, who moved close and took his hand. I took his other hand in mine as we sat surrounded by artifacts of our family's past. Then, at last, he looked at me and said, "Makwa Zegi', perhaps next summer you two could make a trip to

Height of Land as my father and I did. If you bring a cedar bough on your next visit, I will sprinkle you as my father sprinkled me."

Father looked at me, and his smile told me we had a date.

Glossary[1]

Bannock—Trail-made bread with no definite recipe, much like a coffee cake with flour, baking powder, or sourdough being the chief ingredients.

Bass—Two varieties of fish found in the boundary waters known for their fighting ability. Largemouth are native, and smallmouth were introduced in the 1930s.

Blackstone—A favorite lake named after Chief Blackstone, the eloquent Ojibwe Chief Magatewasin who argued so well for the rights of his people that he was compared to a famous English jurist, Sir William Blackstone (1723–80). The Ojibwe people appointed Blackstone at the height of land to represent them at the negotiations for Treaty 3 in 1873. He became the chief at the Lac la Croix reserve until he died in 1884. A daughter married the son of Chief Kabaigon of Kawa Bay Reserve.

BSA—Boy Scouts of America.

Bulgur—A cracked wheat cereal commonly used for a hot breakfast. It expands greatly, takes a long time to cook, and is filling.

Bushwhack—Making a portage through the woods without a definite trail using a compass and axe to clear a route to the next lake.

BWCA—Boundary Waters Canoe Area.

BWCAW—Boundary Waters Canoe Area Wilderness.

Camporee—A fun-filled weekend campout enjoyed by many Scout troops.

Canadian Customs—The border crossing entry point into Canada.

Charlie Guides—For many years, members of the trail staff were known as "Charlie Guides." This is a title worn proudly. Trail staff are well trained and highly motivated outdoor professionals, usually college-age men and women. In the mid-seventies, Charlie Guides were given a new title of "Interpreter." This was done as a practical measure and at the suggestion of officials of Quetico Provincial Park. The Canadian government had determined that professional fishing guides for Canadian fishing trips should be Canadian citizens or require a special Canadian work permit. Changing "Guides" to "Interpreters" was a way to avoid conflict with the new law. Canadian officials at the local and provincial levels have historically been very supportive of the canoe Base program. They recognized that it was not feasible to recruit an all-Canadian trail staff.

It should be noted that a top-flight all-Canadian trail staff staffs the Northern Tier's newer Canadian bases. The bases at Atikokan, Ontario, and Bissett, Manitoba, have provided a way to continue the program for as many Scouts as possible within the crew size and daily entry quotas used in the Quetico and the BWCAW.

Council—A small subdivision of one of the 12 and later 6 regions of the Boy Scouts of America.

Daredevil—An old standby spoon lure usually colored red and white but also in black and white.

Fisher Maps—An American company that provides canoeists with maps of the Boundary Waters area.

Grumman—A very sturdy brand of an aluminum canoe that the Scout Base has used for over 60 years.

Guide Trip—The boot camp-like canoe trip that the guides take in early June to get in shape for the summer canoeing season and to train in the new Swampers (guides in training).

Gunwales—The wood strips inside and outside the sides of a wood canoe, usually made of mahogany.

Hol-Ry—The hailing sign for voyageurs of the Northern Tier's Charles L. Sommers Wilderness Canoe Base. When a voyageur encounters another on the trail, it is customary for one to address the other with "Hol-Ry" and the other to respond with "Red-Eye." The origin of this greeting hearkened to the 1950s and '60s when Charlie crews carried a rye cracker with the tradename Hol-Ry. The Zinsmaster Bakery baked the cracker in Duluth, Minnesota. A Hol-Ry was a cracker that didn't break or spoil quickly, and for trail food, that is important. The taste of Hol-Ry was rather bland, but it made a perfect vehicle for delivering peanut butter and jelly at lunchtime.

Hunters Island—An area of land roughly tracing the perimeter of Quetico Provincial Park and the border lakes. This perimeter is over 250 miles.

Interpreters—Essentially the same as a Charlie Guide. This person's responsibility is to lead the Scout group into the wilderness, to teach them how to camp and canoe safely and adequately, and to teach the history and importance of this unique place of the world.

Kettle Pack—The packsack that contains all the cooking pots and pans, reflector oven, dining fly, axe, saw, shovel, and all kitchen gear. Usually, a Duluth A-2 pack was used.

Knife Lake Dorothy—A sweet lady who lived for many years on Knife Lake on the Canadian border. She was a registered nurse and sold homemade root beer and candy to passing campers from her cabin on Isle of the Pines in Knife Lake.

Largemouth Bass—A native species of bass. It can be identified by the size and position of the mouth.

Layover Day—A day of no traveling or moving of campsites. A time to rest, relax, fish and cook, and enjoy the woods.

Loon—The Minnesota state bird common in the Boundary Waters Area with a haunting, distinctive call. Loons are black and white with red eyes, weigh about nine pounds, and are very beautiful.

Lures—Inanimate artificial fishing bait that may be wood, metal, or plastic replicas of what fish like to eat.

MacKenzie Maps—A Canadian company that provides canoeists with maps of the Boundary Waters.

Moose—The largest creature in the north woods. An adult bull may weigh over 1,200 pounds and have an antler spread up to six feet across.

Moose Lake—The lake's name where the Boy Scout Base is located and the starting point for most Scout canoe trips. It is six miles from the Canadian border and is about three miles long.

Northern—A long, snaky, predatory fish commonly known as a northern pike. They have sharp teeth, do not school up, and can weigh up to 40 pounds and grow to five feet long. Probably the most commonly caught fish in the North Country.

Northern Tier High Adventure Base—The new name of the Charles L. Sommers Canoe Base when the responsibility for its operation passed from Region Ten of the BSA to the National High Adventure program of the BSA.

Old Town—A brand of canoe made by an old established company in Maine. It is one of the oldest and most reliable canoe companies around today.

Orient—The act of placing your compass on your map and turning your map so that north on the map points north like the compass so you can find your way in the wilderness.

Pack Sack Stew—A typical last meal on a canoe trip or whenever the cook tries to use up the leftover foodstuffs in one big pot of stew. The recipe color and flavor are different every time.

Pike—A category of fish most commonly applied to the northern pike but also the walleye pike.

Portage—The trail or path between bodies of water that allow you to travel through the Boundary Waters. Some are many hundreds of years old, having been used by Native Americans.

Prairie Portage—A heavily used trail linking the US and Canada at the end of the Moose Lake chain.

Quetico—The Quetico Provincial Park is a large wilderness park in Northwestern Ontario, Canada, known for its excellent canoeing and fishing. The 1,838 square-mile park shares its southern border with Minnesota's Boundary Waters Canoe Area Wilderness, which is part of the larger Superior National Forest. These large wilderness parks are often collectively referred to as the Boundary Waters or the Quetico-Superior Country.

Ranger Station—A staffed cabin where one can purchase Canadian fishing licenses and camping permits. They were located near the main entry points to The Quetico.

Red-Eye—The term Red-Eye comes from the noonday drink of the early loggers in the area. For decades, Charlie crews have used the same term for their lunch drink. The Scout Base used the presweetened beverage mix for years. If you hear another canoeist yell out Hol-Ry, you can bet it is a Scout or former Scout from Sommers Canoe Base. So by answering Red-Eye, you will identify yourself as one of Charlie's Boys or a Charlie Guide too.

Reflector Oven—A folded-up, flat, lightweight stainless steel or aluminum contraption that opens into a V-shaped oven with a shelf. The oven is used for baking by the reflected heat of a wood fire.

Region Ten—An old division of the BSA encompassing the Dakotas and Minnesota. The original 12 regions that the US was divided into have been condensed into 6 today to be more efficient.

Rod—A unit of measure commonly used on maps to designate the length of a portage. One rod equals 16-and-a-half feet, or about the length of an average canoe. One mile is 320 rods long.

Rollers—Tall waves that are tough to paddle through without shipping water.

Sauna—A steam bath originating in Finland, where the participants sit in a small enclosed building heated by a wood-fired stove. Atop the stove are rocks that are doused with water to create steam.

Seliga—A handmade wooden canoe of the highest quality crafted by the hands of Joe Seliga of Ely, Minnesota. Only 750 were made.

Sigurd F. Olson—A renowned naturalist, teacher, and author who made Ely his home. His great love for the wilderness helped preserve it for future generations. He was a regular visitor at the Base.

Soap the Pots—A procedure of coating the exterior of cooking pots (before they are placed over a wood fire) with soap to make the soot easy to wash off.

Sommers Canoe Base—Charles L. Sommers Wilderness Canoe Base was the original name for the present Northern Tier High Adventure Base created for the Boy Scouts of America. The name honors one of the founders of the Base.

Swampers—Former crew members who have returned to be trained to become guides at the Base.

Swamping—Tipping over your canoe in the water.

Thwarts—The wooden cross members of a canoe between the gunwales that help a canoe hold its shape.

Trout—Also known as lake trout. These are difficult to catch, deep-running fish species found only in the deepest lakes in the BWCA. The meat is pink, oily, and delicious. Trout are slow to reproduce.

Voyageur—Frenchmen employed in transporting goods and furs in trade with the Indians in the 1700s and 1800s. They were small and wiry and powerful but seldom lived beyond middle age due to hernias and injuries. They wore colorful sashes and hats and plied birchbark canoes through the great lakes and all over Canada and the northern United States.

Voyageur Tents—This tent style is much like a tall pup tent that could be set up without poles by tying to nearby trees. The Base used them for many years.

Wall Tents—A heavy canvas tent with short sidewalls use by the Base for over 40 years. They weighed nearly 25 pounds.

Yoke—The center thwart of a canoe that is usually curved and has shoulder pads mounted on it for comfort while carrying it on a portage.

---

1. My deepest thanks to Roy Cerny, author of *Keep on Paddling: True Adventures in the Boundary Waters Wilderness.* Roy was a Charlie Guide during my years and a good friend. His glossary helped me write mine with some of the same definitions and others related to this story. See Roy Cerny, *Keep on Paddling: True Adventures in the Boundary Waters Wilderness* (Bloomington, IN: Trafford, 2012), 210–226.